Deirdre Wilson was educated at Oxford and the Massachusetts Institute of Technology. She has been a lecturer in Philosophy at Somerville College, Oxford, a Harkness Fellow in America and a visiting professor at the Ecole Polytechnique in Paris. Now a Professor of Linguistics at University College, London and a Fellow of the British Academy, she is married to the historian Theodore Zeldin.

For Paula
From Kathy

Deirdre Wilson

SLAVE OF THE PASSIONS

PICADOR ORIGINAL
PUBLISHED BY PAN BOOKS

First published as a Picador hardback in 1991 by Pan Books Limited

This Picador paperback edition published 1992 by Pan Books Limited a division of
Pan Macmillan Publishers Limited
Cavaye Place London SW10 9PG
and Basingstoke

Associated companies throughout the world

ISBN 0–330–32577–9

9 8 7 6 5 4 3 2 1

A CIP catalogue record for this book is available from
the British Library

Typeset by Intype, London

Printed in England by Clays Ltd, St Ives plc

To
Theodore Zeldin

Chapter 1

Final exams were over. The sun shone into Oxford all day, making the walls white, casting short, squat shadows on to the flagstones, turning it into an Italian town. Music came spilling out of open windows; the trees dripped white petals into every breeze. Nights were for parties: couples walked the lawns, their shadows intermingling on the ground, their voices in the air. At one of these, Grace Ritchie, seeing a girl she knew, leaned quietly towards her and said, 'Oh God, isn't life grim?'

Somebody once described Grace Ritchie as a doll with teeth. Not an English doll: perhaps made in Korea for the English market, by an artist who couldn't get the English face quite right. Each of her features had an Eastern tinge. The eyes, particularly, were brown and faintly slit, two peepholes through which, from the outside, nothing could be seen. Her hair, doll straight, fell gleaming to her shoulders from a short, high fringe. Her skin was ochre and slightly shiny, as with a porcelain glaze. Her mouth was small and pale, and she never seemed to open it wide. She spoke in a swallowed voice, as if frightened to let the words escape. Occasionally, when she laughed, tiny sharp white puppy's teeth could be seen. Knowing her, it seemed not too fantastic to think of row upon row of these concealed inside, tiny, sharp, white and vicious.

Grace was someone you noticed in the street, though everything about her seemed designed to avoid the eye. Her clothes were elegant, dark and understated. She passed you by as if you weren't there. She never glanced at you or brushed your hand: she engaged with you no more than if she'd been a photograph. If you'd looked far enough ahead, you'd have seen her spot you, minutely change direction, fractionally lean away as you approached. Her face would be blank, storm windows hoisted. She was all defence. But you couldn't help noticing the way she walked. Each movement was beautiful and stayed in the mind, as if someone was pressing the freeze-frame button at every step. Click, she had turned her head and her hair flew out, the thin strands separating. Click, she had raised her arm to catch the flying strands.

Click, she was past, trailing an arm behind her. Her body was light and insubstantial, a dustsheet to cover her thoughts.

The description of Grace as a doll catches something of the impression she created: her lack of response, the feeling she aroused in people that she was not quite one of them. What it misses is the fact that she was undeniably alive. She might have been an animal of another species, say a woodland creature, alert and ready to run. Her appearance offended some people: they felt her almost as an insult. Like a creature, she seemed to them to call for the inanimate pronoun: 'Look at that,' they would nudge each other and say. Others were entranced, enticed. You could see them tiptoeing after her, a bunch of grass in their hand; then a twig would snap, her hair would fly, and she'd be off into the pine trees. They were all hunters to her.

Grace thought of herself as human: she'd been brought up that way. She was born of human parents; walked on two legs, not four; she didn't bark or browse the forest grass; was covered in skin, not fur. But the more she tried the human world on, the more she realized it didn't fit her. She kept catching herself thinking, 'Time to go home.' At parties, it was a thought that lapped around her mind. 'Hello, Grace. So glad you could come.' 'Hello. Well, time to go home.' It was a thought she'd had on first going to school, on first coming to Oxford; no doubt, on first being born.

People kept disappointing Grace. It seemed so obvious to her that we're all in this together: humans, plants, animals, tossed up by the four winds, dancing in the dark. The world seemed to her like an asylum for the dying: she wanted people to spare each other, treat each other with dignity. She wanted friends as guileless and innocent as rocks and trees. Each smirk or hostile look left her bewildered. Every time she saw someone cheat, or push, or jostle for position, she felt homesick for the way things should have been.

Grace kept being disappointed, but she kept on hoping. What seemed obvious to her must seem obvious to other people too. Perhaps not all of them. Perhaps it was a question of, as it were, emotional bloodgroup: simply a matter of finding a match. At Oxford, she'd thought, there'll be matches in plenty. And there were: but not for her. Wherever she looked, she saw sparks struck, hands held, eyes locked, foundations of a lifetime dug. Each failed encounter made her shiver. Could she be a sport, a freak? As the failures mounted she kept on hoping: a stepping stone longing for someone to love it; a sandcastle hoping the waves won't knock it down.

6

The girl Grace had spoken to had no time for chat; her partner stood, cigarette glowing, beneath the trees. She paused, head turned in his direction. 'Hellish,' she said politely, and walked on.

No matches here. Grace set off towards the house, eyes as blank as undraped windows. Someone smiled, but she didn't see him; she was gone before he'd finished clearing his throat. Grace was always doing this: he'd passed her in the street a hundred times, but she was as unrecognizing as a statue perched on a college wall. He told himself it was now or never, ran up behind and touched her shoulder. 'Hey,' he said. 'Would you like to dance?'

Grace turned, thinking of marauders. There he stood, puffing and grinning. He was ordinary, normal; he could have been any hitchhiker: a solid, squarish body, fair wavy hair, a lively, almost pugnacious look. To Grace, those cheerful, normal people were the worst. In the street, they'd snap their fingers in her face and call her 'Gloomyclogs'. 'Cheer up, darling, it may never happen.' Grace was flustered. She thought he was making fun of her: he'd go back to his friends saying, 'See what I just danced with?' and they'd nudge each other and grin. She wasn't going to let him make a fool of her. 'No thanks,' she said, and turned away.

She walked on towards the house, moving like a wading bird on her long, thin legs, hair flip-flopping against her shoulders. He was a hunter. He persisted. His feet came after her, whispering on the grass. She went inside, through the french windows. He padded behind, tongue lolling. 'What about a drink, then?' he said.

He was like a big, bouncy dog, that you meet out walking: you're never sure if it's romping or ravening. Grace ignored him and kept on moving, across the room and into the hallway. Nice boy, then. Now run along home.

As she crossed the hall, she could hear him following. Now she was starting to feel inhuman. She found the stairs, began to climb them. He lolloped behind, hot breath on her shoulder. She turned her face. 'Stop following me around.'

'All right.' He went away.

Grace felt unbalanced, as if she'd jumped an enemy who wasn't there. She went upstairs, hair flip-flopping, into the bathroom and locked the door. In a bathroom you're safe: no one to taunt you. Not a bad place to set up home. She didn't care if queues were forming. They'd have to saw through the floorboards to get her out. She'd install a phone; get milk delivered; never speak to a soul again.

7

Someone banged on the door. Surely not him again? She'd squeeze down the plughole rather than go out to him. Bang, bang, rattle. A woman's voice: 'Are you all right in there?' Grace came out, snooty faced, and went downstairs to join her friends. 'Where've you *been*, Grace?' 'Just looking around.' 'We've been waiting. It's time to eat.'

Grace's friends were people who fitted. They were party-goers and party-givers, enmeshed in a network of social bonds. Attractive, intelligent, successful, caring: the term 'civilized' was invented for them. Nothing ever jarred or jangled them. The world fitted them and they understood it. They knew when it was time to eat and when it was time to dance. They never thought 'Time to go home' unless it was time to go home.

Grace had grown up with these people; she could pass for one of them. Her clothes were right, her shoes were right, her voice was right, her walk was right: you could take her anywhere and she wouldn't disgrace you, like a discreet Cartier bracelet on the arm. She could swim in these waters, pressed into the shoal for camouflage; but they were not her waters, it was not her shoal. She ate with her friends like an actor on stage, miming enjoyment of cotton-wool cakes and a glass of cold tea; leaned back and laughed as they sharpened their tastes on their host's choice of food, furniture, bathroom fittings and friends. See, I eat, I laugh, I listen. I belong.

Grace was sure she was being watched. Wherever she went, she would see the boy who had asked her to dance, ignoring her. In the end, she almost bumped into him crossing the hall.

He stepped back at once. 'I didn't mean to upset you. I'll apologize if you like. If I've done anything to upset you, I'm very sorry. There.' He touched her shoulder, then took his hand away and smiled.

Grace looked at him, half turned away. Strictly speaking, an attempted introduction is not a criminal offence. Had she been a little harsh?

'I'm Andrew Lisle,' he said. 'And you're Grace Ritchie, aren't you? Now can I get you a drink?'

'All right,' she said, and if he hadn't blinked he might have seen her smile.

They took their drinks outside, away from the house. It was a lovely evening, warm. Around Grace, though, frost had gathered: you'd have needed a blowlamp to get through. He was from Wadham College; she looked as if she'd never heard of it. He'd just finished finals in engineering; she looked as if she'd never heard of that. He lived in the Iffley

Road. 'Oh yes?' she said, as if that explained it. They had no common friends, no common experiences. Their conversation couldn't get off the ground.

As they walked across the lawn in the twilight, heads down, silent, he said, 'I think there's a pond down here.' Beyond a low wall was a water garden: old stone and water lilies. They sat on the edge and looked for goldfish, watched the tracks of insects across the surface: the great wakes of the sea-going swimmers, the fairy trails of the surface skimmers. Grace dipped her fingers and shook off the drops. Whoosh, plop, something dive-bombed past them. 'Heavens,' said Grace, pulling back her hand.

'It's a bird,' said Andrew. 'Sshh. Don't frighten it.'

Whoosh, plop. Two rings in the water. Summer-time: the swallows had come.

Even a town dweller can't help feeling touched by magic when nature comes out to play so close at hand. Autobiography seemed pointless. Who cared what college she came from? As the swallows dipped and fluttered, he turned and said to her, 'Tell me what you think.'

Normally, Grace would have sent back a little flippant or mysterious remark. 'I do philosophy, politics and economics: I don't think.' 'I'm from Somerville: it's against the rules to think.' Now, perhaps touched by the same magic, she opened her mouth and emitted, like a single bubble in a fishpond, a single thought.

'The world is divided into two sorts of people: me and the rest.'

They sat in silence.

'What makes you think you're a person?' he said at last.

'What makes them think *they* are?'

There was no answer to this. Grace trailed her fingers in the water again.

'I don't want to disappoint you,' he said, 'but you look quite like a person to me.'

'It's not what you look like, it's what you feel like,' she said.

The swallows had gone. It was getting darker. 'I must get back to my friends,' she said.

Around the house, the lights had been switched on. Dancing couples had strayed on to the lawn, where, soothed by night breezes, their quick steps slowed. Voices grew softer, eyes more gentle. It was getting chilly. Time to go home.

Finals were over, but Grace was not happy. She cared enormously about her exams. Not the work: that mostly bored her. She'd spent three years sniffing at the footprints of great men. Here was one of Descartes'. Who had he been talking to when he made it? Where had he come from? Where did it lead to? Never mind, now here's one of Locke's. Grace had chosen a course that she'd hoped would initiate her, teach her how the world worked, how to be one of the boys. She'd hoped for a guide to life: now she needed a guide to the guidebook. She was more lost than when she'd arrived.

What she cared about was being graded. The thought of humans grading each other made Grace retch. Instead of holding hands in the void we treat each other like rotten apples. How could she have let herself in for this?

It was not just grading: the whole idea of being categorized repelled her. Tell her she was English, a woman, from Oxford, middle height, mousy hair, born under the sign of Scorpio, and she would scream in your face. Nothing *follows*, she would scream. It wasn't the facts that bothered her, but the belief that they were explanatory. She didn't want to be diagnosed, filed away as a statistic. She was not a coloured counter: her actions were *her* actions. She didn't want to march to music like a member of a military band.

Grace wanted to think for herself: she wanted to be responsible for her actions; but she also wanted to belong to the human race. She cared very much what others thought of her. What hurt so much about those smirks and nudges in the street was not just that someone could smirk at another human being, but that someone could smirk at *her*. She knew looks shouldn't matter: no human should have to suffer for a twisted smile, a ballooning forehead, a crumpled spine. But they do.

Grace didn't want to be hurt. She didn't want to be judged for the lustre of her eyes, dismissed for wearing last year's colour, yesterday's hem. She knew it shouldn't hurt her, she knew you shouldn't give in to it: and she didn't give in; she bent. Though her style was plain, it wasn't timeless. Her clothes evolved around her like slow branches on a tree. You wouldn't have called her fashionable: she was never frivolous or trendy; but if you opened this month's issue of Elle, you'd be sure to see something that reminded you of something Grace had been wearing last year.

To avoid hurt, you defend yourself. Grace defended herself with clothes. Those perfect dressers are often misdiagnosed: what drives them is generally not love but fear. Grace's clothes, her room were marvels of austere perfection, the best fortresses her limited money could buy. For her, the policy of perfection had a bonus: the winner wins the right to say that the race is unimportant, thus saving her principles too.

Grace's attitude to exams grew from the same rootstock as her attitude to clothes. For most of her time at Oxford, exams seemed to her as unimportant as hairstyles. Either a question was worth answering for its own sake, or it wasn't worth answering at all. Most of the questions her tutors asked seemed to her entirely pointless, and it never occurred to her to work on something that didn't interest her for the sake of an exam. Until exam fever swept the college and she realized that they were going to mark her for life. Then she began to work in a frenzy, not for the love of it but out of fear. As summer came on, she closed her curtains, superstitiously denying herself walks in the sun. Just a bit more work, just a few more hours; then surely everything would be all right.

Grace hated and despised herself during the exams. Not just the sneaky guilt that races up to all of us and rings the bell and runs away, but a steady, unblinking black hate. You have the ethics of a blancmange, she told herself. Who *cares* what people think of you? Write what interests you and let the exams go hang. You can't do it, can you? You and your principles. 'Hate the exams,' you say, then walk in backwards, pretending you're going the other way.

You might say this proves only that Grace was human. We muddle along; sometimes we're swept along; win some, lose some, maim some, bruise some: the great rich river of life. But if that's what being human means, Grace wanted none of it. She didn't want to be swept along, driven by her emotions like a child addicted to chocolate, tossed on the tide of history like a matchbox on a wave. When she did something, she wanted to approve of it. She'd rather do nothing than be ashamed of what she did.

The exams were a disaster for Grace. The questions she'd so carefully prepared did not come up, and she was too tired or disappointed to adapt herself to those that did. At first, she tightened her mouth and kept on writing, hoping next day her luck would change. Every day was a disaster, and she couldn't face the inquests after each exam. She walked blank faced through chattering crowds outside the exam hall. Snatches of conversation followed her down the street, voices rising now the pressure was off.

'God, wasn't it awful? Lucky two of my questions came up, otherwise I'd have been sunk . . .'

'What on earth was question three supposed to be about? I thought, there's been nothing on paradoxes, maybe it's that . . .'

'Couldn't believe it. I got everything I wanted. I kept thinking, this must be a trick . . .'

The voices rose and faded. Grace went back to her room and stared into space.

In Oxford after finals the parties never stop. Champagne, punts, picnic hampers, ballgowns, evening shadows on the lawn. Grace joined in like a corpse at a wedding, face turned towards the fun, eyes rolled up inside her head. She'd come to Oxford to get on terms with the world, master its unknown currents, stay afloat on its chugging tide. She'd stood on the shore while all about her threw off their clothes, plunged in and came up swimming; and decided that water was not her element after all. But she must have slipped or been sleepwalking, because here she was with her feet wet, ankle deep in muddy water. Just let me get out of this, she thought; just let me do well in my exams and I'll never so much as look at the sea again.

There never was an ideal time for calling on Grace. At her best she was a hopeless hostess: role-playing paralysed her; the thought of social chit-chat froze her tongue. Two human beings, hearts full of hopes and worries, heads full of thoughts and fancies, wondering if the Budget will mean another penny on the price of beer.

Making friends with Grace was like getting beyond the breakers in a rough, icy sea. Sooner or later, you'd start thinking longingly of Thermoses and rugs. Grace would sit behind her eyes watching you shiver, searching frantically for a warm lifebelt of words. She wanted to reach you, to feel the rub of soul on soul; but you can't just say cheerily, over the teacups, yes, it looks as if it'll keep fine for Wimbledon, and how do you feel about death?

One day, soon after the party, Andrew Lisle came to call. He found Grace in her big armchair by the window overlooking Walton Street, legs tucked to one side, eyes rolled up inside her head.

'Hello,' he said.

'Hello.'

'Round the corner. Thought I'd drop in.'

She looked at him politely, as if waiting for the password. His mind, normally so alert and frisky, fainted dead away. She seemed to be expecting some ritual phrase, some move from a tea-party manual. All he could think of was 'Anyone for tennis?' 'Um, any chance of a coffee?' he said.

She went to put on a kettle; at least he assumed that was where she'd gone. While she was out, he searched her room for inspiration. It had a bay window, white walls, deep red and purple cloths, a huge mirror propped against one wall, and on the bookshelf a large plain glass bubble with a few sticks of honesty in it. It suited her. It did nothing for him but make him feel clumsy. As he strolled around the room, his feet grew clumpier, his socks more ill-chosen. He sat in a chair that didn't fit him. By the time she came back, his limbs were dangling, his knees jerking, his ears misshapen. When she put the tray on the table in front of him, all he could do was grunt.

Grace picked up her coffee and returned to her chair. He extended a trotter towards the sugar bowl: not that he normally took any, but at least it was something to do with his hands. He bent over his coffee, stirred it slowly. There must be something to talk about. So far, all she'd said was 'Hello'.

He looked up. 'Did you enjoy the party?'

'Yes, thank you.'

Silence. He reached for the sugar bowl, added more sugar; lifted the mug to his lips; put it down again without tasting it. 'Good coffee,' he said.

Grace was as anxious for something to say as he was. I see from the weather forecast there's not much chance of snow this week. Only 150 shopping days to Christmas. Did you know that's the seventeenth spoonful of sugar you've put in your coffee? Why not just tip the coffee in the sugar bowl and drink out of that?

Andrew droned on. 'When do you expect your exam results?'

Her blank expression went even blanker. 'I'm not sure. A few weeks, I think.'

Silence. A bit too soon to ask for another coffee. He buried his snout in his mug.

He tried again. 'It's lovely out.' There was room for a 'Yes' there, but she didn't answer. 'Would you like to come for a walk?'

She picked up her coffee mug, sipped it thoughtfully. He stirred his coffee as the silence lengthened. He could feel his heart beat, see her breathing. The question lay there broken backed. She looked up: she was going to speak. No, too late; her interest had wandered. She returned her eyes to the street.

He put down his mug. 'Thanks for the coffee.' He stood up and went to the door.

Grace was galvanized. She couldn't let him leave like that: a human being, with human feelings. He was almost gone when she said in her swallowed voice, 'I'm a bit busy today. Perhaps I could manage something tomorrow.'

He looked round. Was she talking to him?

'Tomorrow?' he said, to check that he'd heard right.

'Unless you're busy.'

'No, no. How about dinner? We could drive out somewhere.'

'If you'd like to.'

'Fine. I'll pick you up at seven.'

As he left, he popped his head round the door. 'I tell you what. You've got a whole day to practise. "Knock, knock." "Who's there? Hello, Andrew, how nice to see you." You'll soon get the hang of it. It's easy. Try.'

He left before he could see her face. She cleared away the empty mugs and rolled her eyes back up inside her head.

Now you've done it, thought Andrew. A night alone in the tundra. The prospect of a whole evening with Grace made him stiff with fright. The only solution seemed to be to take a run at it, bounce and brazen, try to puff enough wind into her conversational sails to carry them through. He put on his brightest clothes: Madras seersucker jacket, orange shirt, turquoise trousers, tie with violent flowers, or weeds. He ran up the stairs two at a time and thumped on her door, shouting, 'Let me in. Let me in.'

She opened the door half-cross, half-laughing. 'Sshh,' she said. 'People will hear.'

'What makes you think they're people?' he said.

Grace, not knowing where he would take her, had decided to wear nothing: an elegant brown wool nothing that was so austere you could hardly see it. While she elegantly poured whisky, he swooped like a kingfisher around the room. 'I've brought you a present,' he said. 'A *Teach Yourself* book.'

She put his whisky on the bookshelf beside him. 'Oh yes? Teach Yourself what?'

'Conversation. Chapter 1: The word "Hello", its uses and functions. Chapter 2: Attempting full sentences. Chapter 3: Some simple replies. I think you'll find it jolly useful. We could practise tonight.'

She looked at him. 'I thought you did engineering. Did you get someone to read you the titles?'

'Next time I'll bring an etiquette book.'

Hey, it was working. That was definitely a conversation. And they'd only known each other a week.

Encouraged, he said, 'Of course, we don't have to talk if you don't want to. We could get quite a long way with mime. Look, this is me when you wouldn't dance with me.' He pulled his jacket over his head and hid his face, cringing against the wall. 'And this is me when you said you'd come out with me.' Actually, the same mime would have done for that, but it seemed more tactful to go for an expression of joy. He threw his arms out like a silent film hero. The back of his hand caught the glass bubble on her bookshelf, which was swept to the ground and shattered.

'Oh, *bugger*,' he said. The crude word lumbered out of his mouth and belly-flopped to the ground.

Grace told him not to worry, and went to fetch a dustpan. There was nothing to be done: the thing was broken beyond repair. He stood by as she dropped the bigger pieces in the bin – crash, grate, tinkle – then crawled over the carpet looking for shards. They'd got everywhere; wherever he looked he could see one winking. He had to pick them off the hem of her dress. Her stocking had laddered; he prayed she wouldn't notice. He swallowed his whisky. 'Let's go,' he said.

He'd booked at Percy's, ten miles out on the Swindon road, a boisterous place which was always crowded, where the food and wine were both good value; part of his plan to liven her up. Percy was an accredited character, a big squat man who insulted his customers, who charged them more or less what took his fancy – here's a free sweet for the little lady. Just the sort of place, he now saw clearly, that Grace would hate.

'My car's down here.'

'A car,' she said politely; though her voice tailed off in a question when she saw his van. It was a perfectly good van: a bit old and bumpy, but it took him where he wanted to go. She climbed in, noticing the laddered stocking. He would never ask anyone out again.

'I thought we'd go to Percy's,' he said, missing first gear, sending the van bucking and howling into reverse.

'How nice,' she said, chin jerking, shoulders leaping. 'It's a lovely evening for a drive.'

Percy was not in the restaurant that night; which was a pity because they could have done with the conversation. Andrew was feeling too wrung out to talk. Grace minded the loss of her bubble, and held it against him; but she didn't want to see him suffer. Like a proper hostess, tablecloth aswill with ruby wine, she tried to put him at his ease.

'This is a nice place. I haven't been here for ages.'

'What?'

Heavens, not deafness too.

'It's noisy, isn't it?' she said.

'I'm sorry. Maybe we should have gone somewhere else.'

Well, that was a good effort; now you've given him something else to feel guilty about.

She couldn't help it, she thought of him as clumsy, physically inept. In the van, as he went round a corner, her foot felt not quite imperceptibly for the brake. At the table, he saw her eyes on him as he poured the wine. It was unfair: he was not a clumsy man. He hated to be thought of as crude.

He lifted his fork before her eyes, searching for a witty but delicate remark. Plop. The load of spinach fell off the end of the fork. Her eyes followed it down. She tried again to put him at his ease.

'What are you planning to do this summer?'

'Assuming they don't get me for involuntary manslaughter, you mean?'

'Sorry?'

'I'm not *really* clumsy, you know. I don't normally go about breaking things.'

'Look, it's all right. It was an accident. It's not important.'

There you are: another conversation. And all he'd had to do was to wreck her room.

He tried hard to find a suitable topic. He ran through the list of people he knew at Somerville. She'd been there three years, but she didn't seem to know any of them. She thought she'd once sat opposite one of them at breakfast; even Einstein couldn't have made much of that. Grace tried, too. She'd once been to a lecture by a philosophy don at Wadham. What was his name? They managed to get through most of the pudding trying to think what it might be.

They gulped down their coffee and were ready to be off. On the way out, passing a particularly noisy table, they were stopped by a shout.

'Hi, Andy, how's it going?'

'Hello, Bob, OK,' said Andrew uneasily, like a dog about to be fed a pill.

'Aren't you going to introduce us to your lady friend?'

'This is Grace.'

'Hello, Grace,' said Bob, patting his knee. 'Come and sit here.'

'OK, Bob, we're busy. See you around,' said Andrew, hardly audible.

'Oh *I* see. Sorry to keep you then. Nudge nudge, wink wink,' said Bob.

Grace and Andrew hardly spoke on the way home. He drove very fast. As he parked in Walton Street she reached for the doorhandle, said 'Thank you' – whether for taking or leaving her was not specified – and 'Goodnight'.

'Goodnight,' he said, and drove off, straight to the nearest pub.

Things couldn't end there. Andrew's pride had been hurt: he wasn't going to be remembered for ever as the man who broke her vase. A few days later he called at Walton Street again. He'd spent hours going round the antique shops trying to find a glass bubble like the one he'd broken. At least, he was looking for a better one: the best glass bubble in the business. Seeing it, she would realize how wrong she'd been to think of him as an ignorant peasant. It would be the Ming masterpiece of all glass bubbles: it would speak to her soul. Unfortunately, the only one he could find was a bit squashed, with thick, greenish, cloudy glass, not clear and crystalline like the fragments of hers he'd touched. It cost a fortune, and as soon as he'd bought it he felt a fool: the bloody thing was probably made in Birmingham.

He drove it to Walton Street, shrouded in newspapers. He looked up at her window, but she wasn't there. He carried the bubble, hugging it, up the stairs and kicked (gently) at the bottom of her door. She was out, or not answering. He lowered the bubble carefully to the floor, found a piece of paper in his pocket, wrote, 'I did bring a present this time. Hope it's all right. Andrew,' folded it into the neck of the bubble, and ran for his van.

The next day there was a note addressed to him at Wadham. 'Dear Andrew, It's beautiful. Thank you. Grace.' Her handwriting was lovely.

A few days later, Grace went to a summer ball. This was a very un-Grace thing to do, but she was with a party of friends: those civilized friends who knew how the world worked, those dextrous friends with delicate senses, who'd coaxed and calmed and charmed her into their nets.

It's fair to ask oneself why they bothered. What did such people see in Grace? Someone of their own sort, of course: well-dressed, intelligent, observant, witty; but there was more to it than that. Grace's looks made her eminently collectable. Admiring her, you were proud of your discernment: like a gallery browser recognizing an unconsidered masterpiece, your immediate thought was to save her for the nation. The Friends of Grace Ritchie were like the Friends of St Pancras before the fashion for Victoriana came along.

Most of these friends had known Grace since schooldays. She had followed her elder sister to a slightly progressive mixed boarding school. At school, as at home, she was a younger sister, and that is how she was seen by most of her friends. Responsibility was not thrust on her; indeed, it was often snatched away. Grace turns up her nose at games? Fine, she can read a book. Grace a prefect? Little Grace? Even her classmates thought of her as younger than themselves.

Grace's friends at Oxford, then, were a sort of adoptive family: strong women inclined to mother her, gentle men like elder brothers. Grace was someone who was taken along. If you planned an outing, you'd go and pick her up. Now finals were over, one of them had suggested that it would be fun to go to a ball, properly, not climbing in. Get all dressed up, drive out to Woodstock for dinner. It seemed a good idea, and they of course took Grace along.

'Grace, we're going to a ball.'

'Don't be silly.'

'No, really,' said Fergus. 'We've decided. Dinner. Taxis. Champagne. A sitting-out room. Everything. How can we say we were at Oxford if we've never been to a ball?'

This had little force with Grace, who was not planning to say anything to anyone anyway; but she didn't really resist. How would she go anywhere if she wasn't taken along?

I'll go, thought Grace. I can't sit around and mope. If the ship's going down, I'll go down in evening dress. She thought quite hard about what to wear. She made a special trip to London, and found an amazing dark-red lace dress, with a low, square-cut neck and no sleeves, which just skimmed her body all the way down. She borrowed a long black velvet evening cloak. For the only time in her life she wore a flower in her hair, a creamy gardenia pinned behind her ear. By the time she was ready, she was quite looking forward to the ball.

'Grace, you look fantastic,' said Rowena, looking much as she always did. Rowena had been a slightly bohemian head girl: fingers weighed

18

down with silver rings, gypsy in her face. She was always one step back from life, a head girl with her tongue in her cheek, reporting the headmaster's wishes in an indulgent tone, like a mother humouring a five-year-old. You want to play head girls? Why not? Nothing disturbed her. She cared enough to play the game, but not enough to cheat.

Rowena always wore black or purple with silver rings and the sleeves rolled up. So here she was in purple silk, sleeves rolled up to the elbow. 'You look like the Archbishop of Canterbury,' said Grace.

'Oh, all that Latin,' said Rowena, happy to join in. You felt she might pop you in bed and sing you a lullaby.

Rowena's friends had all picked up this attitude from her. They would all go through life with their tongues in their cheeks, playing by the rules. These people help to keep England going. They are at the heart of village cricket, smiling indulgently, remembering how things ought to be done. They are there on ceremonial occasions, defusing the pomp with irony. They are there in the law courts, straight faced, laughing in private at their silly wigs and gowns. It's only a game, they imply, what possible harm? But they care enough to play.

They climbed into the taxis, smiling indulgently: Rowena, Fergus, Mark, Sebastian, Jenny and Grace. Rowena and Mark were childhood sweethearts. Sebastian was an outsider, brought in by Jenny; which left Fergus with Grace.

To an impartial observer watching Grace's friends that night, the word that occurred most often would perhaps have been 'style'. These people were stylish. They had mastered the conventions and added just that dash of cheek to them: in what they wore, in what they ate and drank, in what they spoke of, in how they lived. Their talk was full of ironical quotation marks: the expensive meal was a 'nosh-up', the aged waiter was '*le garçon*'. Their evening clothes flirted with parody: they weren't so much clothes as outfits; made to be not so much worn as carried off.

It seems mean-spirited to object to style, that marriage of wit and beauty. The trouble is that it tends to make you a snob. The stylist knows that looks matter; will even argue that looks *should* matter. The danger is that, having put all that effort into looking right, you'll end up despising those who look wrong. On a ball night in Oxford, the streets are athrong with stylistic failures: men with evening trousers tucked into bicycle clips; women in long chiffon ball gowns and short tweed coats. These people were, well, not quite people to Grace's friends. One would not, of course, dream of being rude to them, but well, really, oh dear.

Over dinner in Woodstock, they gossiped about the exams. They'd all cared enough to work quite hard – though not too hard; don't forget, it's only a game. They were full of jokey reminiscences: the questions they'd misread, the drab uniform decked out with posies, the howlers repeated by tutors from previous years.

Grace couldn't bear to think about the exams. She felt she'd been not only wrong but stupid: turning up at the last minute to join a race she couldn't win. If you're going to go in for worldliness, you should at least have mastered the conventions. But here she'd been caught, in the mental equivalent of tweed coat and chiffon, evening trousers and bicycle clips: aspiring but inadequate, willing but unprepared. She took no part in the jokes, and began to wish she hadn't come.

Fergus and Mark were at Corpus Christi, where the ball was held. Fergus, who knew how to organize these things, had a big room overlooking the gardens, which they used for sitting out. They had a table near the dance floor, champagne already chilling in silver.

'This is nice,' said Rowena, in that dry believe-me-don't-believe-me tone. 'Now what does one do first? Have a little dance, I think,' and she held out her hands to Mark.

Rowena, Mark, Fergus and Jenny had all learned to waltz, quickstep and foxtrot at school. Slightly progressive, yes. Socially unintegrated, no. They all knew the same steps in the same sequence, held their partners at the same angle, and kept their tongues in the same cheek. If you asked them what dancing was for, they would be in no doubt: it's a form of social interaction, like village cricket; it makes the wheels go round.

Ballroom dancing is based on the assumption that the man leads, the woman follows; the man goes forwards, the woman backwards; the man creates the pattern, the woman senses, anticipates his intention, trusts him to see the way ahead, ends up where he wants to go. That is the ideal; in practice, things fall a little short. The dance floor at Corpus Christi was full of uncreative men shuffling after their noses, one two, one two; of creative men who couldn't communicate their intentions, apologizing for their partners' dislocated shoulders; of blind men whose partners tumbled off the edge of the dance floor or stepped backwards on to silken trains. The big marquee was filled with whispered ooches, ows and sorries, as the ladies rubbed their elbows or went back for mislaid shoes. Rowena and her friends smiled indulgently through.

Fergus was a man who lived through his eyes. His room was a visual comfort and delight. He would sit in his leather armchair surrounded by art nouveau vases and drawings in just the right balance of array and disarray. What he lacked was a kinaesthetic sense, a sense of the disposition of his body in the world, of his limbs in relation to each other. As a result, perhaps, he lacked a partner in life. On the dance floor, he was one of the creative sort who have no idea how to communicate their intentions, launching on a whim into a fantastic knot-garden of skips and swoops, leaving his partner hopping brokenly backwards like a retreating army out of step. Grace had learned to look over her shoulder at all times, and remain cheerful while disentangling her legs.

Fergus, Mark and Rowena had a tame don. 'Look, there's James,' said Fergus, wrenching Grace's arm from its socket as he turned. James was on his own at a table, guarding handbags and champagne. 'Come and say hello to James.'

Grace had met James once or twice. He was a bachelor don, who lived in college and taught both Fergus and Mark.

'James,' said Fergus. 'Doing your duty.'

'I live in college, remember,' said James. 'It was this or Scotland for the weekend.'

'You must dance, though,' said Fergus. 'Grace, you'd like to dance with James, wouldn't you? I'll look after the bags.'

James had a kinaesthetic sense, all right. His foxtrot was smooth, no rise and fall of head, no twist or sway of shoulders, every step civilized and under control. His touch was firm, his leads decisive; he knew what Grace could do, and where the other couples would be. It was ballroom dancing at its best. There is no doubt that it was exhilarating. Then he thanked Grace politely and took her back to Fergus, his mind already elsewhere.

What's it all about? thought Grace. She looked around her at the silent couples in ballroom poses, bodies pressed together, heads turned away: no exchange of thought, or word, or glance. What's the point of dancing if it doesn't bring you closer? She cocooned herself with champagne, and began to wait for dawn.

At last the band took a rest, supper was announced, and Rowena thought it was time for a move. Fergus made them coffee in his room while they peered at the bicycle clips and bulging chiffon in the gardens below. 'Oh dear,' one of them would say, and the others would look and sigh.

'There must be another marquee somewhere,' said Rowena, as the saxophone struck up again. She knew how many marquees made a ball.

'There was something going on in the back quad this morning,' said Mark, and they went to have a look.

In a tent much smaller than the big marquee, there were four people on a makeshift platform. One of them was Andrew Lisle. He was at the front of the platform, singing. Behind him were two guitarists and a drummer, and Grace thought she recognized Bob, from Percy's restaurant. The music they were playing was far removed from the foxtrot. Grace thought it was rock and roll.

Rock and roll whooshed across the sky in the fifties like a bright new meteor shedding stars. In its wake came strange hybrids: white singers who sounded black, black singers who sounded white, wild men who dazzled onstage in lipstick, eye make-up and skyscraper curls. It landed in England, an exotic immigrant, and found no place in the social fabric. Headmasters banned it, newspapers were outraged by it, comedians made jokes about it, judges asked questions about it; the middle classes averted their eyes from it. It received the usual immigrant's welcome. Hop off, you Yanks.

Rock and roll burned out in a flurry of scandal, death and corruption. By 1960, the old stars had gone, but among the rebels and misfits of England their music had found a home. Disaffected schoolboys bought guitars, tuned their sets to Radio Luxembourg and taught themselves to play. They went to the docks and bought blues records from American sailors, spent their Saturdays in the listening booths at import record stores. Networks sprang up, with their own heroes: the boy who could howl like Howlin' Wolf, the one with his own amplifier, the one who could play 'Dust My Broom' on bottleneck guitar. Boys who had always thought they were freaks discovered kindred spirits. A new social category was born.

It was born in the grammar schools: seen by some as Jacob's ladders allowing bright young chaps to climb out of nowhere. To some bright chaps they were more like colonies, with their school caps, house teams, Latin mottoes, distant echoes of the Eton Boating Song. Irony seemed too weak a reaction. In the schools, rock and roll became the call-sign of something like a wartime resistance movement, whose members recognized each other by a word, a rhythm, who sang songs instead of throwing bombs.

Rock and roll was wild, but its world was recognizable: high school dances, sweet romances, race you to the junction in your daddy's car.

You could pass through it, though, to stranger country: a land of drifters, exiles, beer-drinking women, me-and-the-devil blues. A generation of English schoolboys grew up with their eyes fixed on this horizon, yearning to drag their weary feet down its distant, dusty roads. They were true lovers, filled with a vision. They created a curious, hybrid music, which caught the fancy of the listening public. Soon new home-grown stars were whooshing across the sky; they became rich and famous, bought mansions, manor houses, country estates. Then the English social fabric locked up its spoons, threw open the back door, and said 'Come in'.

The Corpus Christi ball took place just before that happened. The year was 1962. The old rock and roll stars had gone, the new ones had not yet arrived. The Beatles had not yet released their first record; rock music was not yet an English institution; it was still played for love, not money; it represented not a way up but a way out.

Rowena's group looked on for a while, with expressions that said 'Oh dear'. There were quite a few people dancing, some couples jiving, some doing the Twist, some doing the sort of social shrug that Rowena's friends used to domesticate the thing for polite consumption. Just one couple was really dancing: relaxed and smooth as a swan-glide, now responding to each other's movements, now off on sorties of their own. It was enchanting, inspiring to watch: how wonderful to dance like that.

'Hmm,' said Rowena as the song ended. 'Time to go, I think.'

They went. Grace didn't follow.

'Grace?' said Rowena, turning.

'You go,' said Grace. 'I'm staying here.'

She stayed for the whole of the performance. Andrew didn't seem to be disgracing himself. At the end of that first song, he smiled at the audience as if they were friends, then sat down at a piano on the right of the stage, and began to play and sing. Sometimes, he spoke a phrase or two between songs. She didn't think he'd seen her standing on the rim of grass at the edge of the dance floor, and was shaken when he said at the start of one song: 'This one's for Grace, dressed in red lace.' A few people turned to look at her, and she hardly heard any of the song; but she didn't leave.

What she stayed for was not really the music. She couldn't see what all the fuss was about; it didn't make her want to break up seats in cinemas, as the newspapers had said. But it was the dancing couple her eyes kept coming back to. These dancers wouldn't break up any seats. The music was a sunny wall around them; they leaned on it, relaxed against its mellow bricks, stepped slowly in and out of its scented arbours, meeting with gentle glances and parting once more. When the music ended they clapped, then strolled, side by side, never touching, into the dark.

In fact, the dance Grace was watching, like much of the music she was hearing, was not rock and roll but rock. Musically, the distinction is rather hazy. Some people ignore it; some use 'rock and roll' for the American original and 'rock' for its hybrid descendants; others see rock and roll as a sub-variety of rock. In dancing, things are clearer: rock and roll is the old world, rock is the new. Rock and roll dancing was not remotely revolutionary. Like the tango, it shocked people without really altering anything; it pushed back the frontiers, but left the heartland unchanged. In rock and roll dancing, the man still leads, the women still follows; the man moves forwards, the woman backwards; the man is the pivot around which the woman whirls. Rock dancing was a genuine revolution, brought about when the man and woman let go each other's hands.

Once ballroom dancing was revolutionary too. The earlier court and country dances were team dances. They had no place for couples: lovers lived on stolen handclasps within the pattern of the dance. Ballroom dancing broke up the pattern, set the couple free to wander as long as they kept to the steps of the dance. Rock dancing completed the process by setting the individual free. You don't need a partner in rock dancing. There are no set steps, no fixed direction. It's up to you to work out what to do. What Grace liked about the couple she had seen was that they'd kept clear of the old routines. They weren't chasing each other, or taunting each other, or threatening each other, or bargaining with each other. They weren't warder and prisoner, or sun and satellite, or victor and vanquished, or treaty partners: just two people, going their own ways, with minds turned towards each other, senses tuned to each other. However far they went, they remained together; however close they came, they remained apart.

She followed the dancing couple into the quad, round the corner into the main gardens where the saxophone still played. She didn't want to go back to Fergus yet and, avoiding the lawns beneath his window, flitted up the shaded path beside the garden wall. Andrew, cross-eyed from bowing while watching her go, dropped microphone and dignity and rushed after her into the dark.

She was gone. No red lace and gardenia among the penguins on the lawn. They turned to look at him in his seersucker jacket and purple shirt. Where's Grace? What have you done with Grace? He parted the bushes, and there she was, turning towards him at the end of the path. He approached her decorously, from the front.

'Hello, Grace.'

'Hello, Andrew.' She smiled at him. It was the first time she'd used his name. 'Surprise, surprise.'

He'd never seen her so warm or so relaxed. He, on the contrary, was very subdued.

'I was wondering . . . ,' he said, 'what you thought of er . . .' He gave up, and his voice faded off.

'It was lovely.'

'You mean you liked it?' he asked eagerly. 'You're not just saying that?'

Of course she was just saying it: what did he expect? A detailed critical analysis? She searched her memory.

'I particularly liked the one about the car.'

'What?'

God, surely there'd been one about a car? Anyway, what was all this? Why should it matter to him what she thought about his music? 'Did you write it yourself?'

'What are you talking about? I was asking you how you liked the vase I bought you.'

Oh. How awful. She'd completely forgotten. 'Oh, Andrew, I'm sorry. It *was* lovely, of course. It was sweet of you to bother.'

'That's all right,' he said, stiffly. Then he threw himself off a high cliff. Why could he never get anything *right*? 'Um, you wouldn't like to come and dance?'

She had to, of course. They turned back towards the music tent, where a gramophone filled the gap between the acts. There were only a few couples dancing. On the empty floor, Grace did her social shrug, while Andrew performed the most extraordinary jumping writhe. They were both too embarrassed to speak. As they danced, like two people determinedly ignoring their own convulsions in public, Rowena and Fergus appeared in the entrance to the tent, come to return her to the social fold. They looked at Andrew, looked at each other, and went out. As the record ended, Andrew said, 'Well, I've got to go. Have to pack up the equipment. I must rush.'

'Do you do a lot of this?'

'At dances? Quite a lot.'

'It must be fun.'

25

'Yes. It is. Well, must be off. See you, maybe. I might come round.'

'Why not?'

And off they rushed, propelled by centrifugal forces.

Grace found Fergus, Rowena and Mark at their table by the dance floor. She approached a bit guiltily, like a child caught playing truant.

'Secrets,' said Rowena in that humouring, let's-pretend tone. 'Grace is having a flirtation, imagine.'

'Aren't you going to introduce us to your boyfriend?' said Fergus.

'Do,' said Rowena. 'Such a *nice* little man.'

'Such a stylish dresser,' said Fergus.

'Come and dance, Grace,' said Mark.

For the rest of the evening, Grace danced to the George Delavine Band. The George Delavine Band was an abstract object, like a Beethoven symphony, simultaneously realizable in many different physical forms. While George Delavine was playing a foxtrot at Corpus Christi, he could also be playing a samba in Mayfair, a waltz in Harrogate, a quickstep in Buxton. The musicians were interchangeable, the sound remained the same. The whole world danced to a George Delavine tune.

Andrew helped pack up the equipment, then went away and thought. He had no idea why this particular girl should attract him so much. Right from the beginning, he'd noticed her in the street; it always pleased him to see her walking along next to the wall, with her delicate strides, her body slightly stiff, her face blank and unnoticing. There was just something about her for him. He wanted to know her. When he talked to her and their eyes met, he had the impression of someone waving from a window. He wanted to break the glass and touch the person inside.

Grace could have this effect on people. It had as much to do with what she wasn't as what she was: that quality of being simultaneously present and absent, within grasp and out of reach. She didn't just appeal to the aesthetic sense, she touched the emotions. She was someone you could hang your fantasies on. She was a beautiful outline on an unfinished canvas. You could fill in the gaps from your imagination and, having coloured her in just the way you wanted her, you couldn't help falling a bit in love.

In fact, Andrew's heart was already taken. Music, for him, was not a diversion but a passion; it had captured him mind and body in his teenage years. He loved it in the way one loves a human. To him, the physical substance was only an outer covering, a clue. Behind the music lay the great legendary heroes, reconstructed from the sound of their voices, from third-hand anecdotes, from fleeting glimpses on record covers, in films. Andrew yearned to know them, to be them. Grace, with her rare descents from aloofness, lent herself to similar yearnings. In Andrew's mind, she didn't occupy a separate place; she had somehow slipped into his pantheon of gods.

He began to make enquiries. The first thing he discovered was that everyone in Oxford had noticed her in the street. Most of them had found out her name and college; beyond that, there was little reliable information. No one he knew actually knew her. Although she'd occasionally been seen at parties, she moved in circles that his acquaintances had little access to. All his friends *did* something: they sang, they played music, they produced newspapers, they acted. In her circles, it appeared that nothing got done. In fact, if he hadn't seized that moment at the party, he would probably never have spoken to her at all.

Ideally, though, if you speak to someone they should speak back. Her silence made him tongue-tied; her cool look made him conscious of his walk, his hair, his clothes. He'd caught the silent oh dear that passed between Fergus and Rowena as they saw and heard him. He was not used to being swept under the carpet like an inconvenient mouse-dropping. Was Grace worth persevering with, or was he just wasting his time?

What Andrew did, or thought he did, was make a rough calculation of the odds. Here he was being handed, for a fee in small instalments, a ticket to the Loterie Nationale. He might win, he might lose, but in the meantime he would have his dream. A small fee for a large dream. If the dream fades, if the price becomes too high, you can always stop.

Chapter 2

'Hello, I'm Grace Ritchie. I have an appointment with Dr Sullivan.'

'Oh yes. Hang on a minute and I'll see if he's free.' The secretary put down her cigarette and picked up the phone. 'Kip? Your next interviewee is here. Shall I send her up?' A pause, a smile, a chuckle, almost a snigger. 'Sshh. Wait and see.'

She turned back to her cigarette, still smiling, and then to Grace, who had gone rigid at the sound of the chuckle. 'He won't be a minute.' Puff. 'Would you like to sit down?'

Grace peered through the cigarette smoke and found a chair. 'Thanks.' And puff to you.

'Sorry, things are a bit chaotic today,' said the secretary. It wasn't her fault: she'd stayed late every night that week retyping a paper for a certain member of the department who couldn't make up his mind; every morning he would come in and start scribbling again. Grace, outraged by the chuckle, made no reply. The secretary, good natured, tried to put her at her ease. 'Did you have any trouble getting here?'

As Grace was running through in her mind the conceivable hazards attached to getting from Oxford to London on a clear June day, there was a clattering in the corridor and a young man rushed in. His thoughts were quick; his body was quicker. He was already turning to leave as he looked at Grace with narrowed eyes. 'Hi. I'm Kip Sullivan. Let's go.'

Dr Sullivan, of the London Institute of Behavioural Science, was small, thin, young, intense and American – young, intense and American enough not to wait to be introduced. What you sensed about him was a huge impatience. He set off up the stairs, two at a time; at this rate, the interview would be over before she found his room. At the top of the stairs, there was no sign of him. When she stood in his doorway, he was reading her application form and didn't look up. Grace felt slighted. When Grace felt slighted, you soon felt her teeth in your leg.

'So,' he said, still reading. 'You're Grace Ritchie from Oxford. What makes you want to do an MA in Human Behaviour?'

'My total inability to answer questions like that.'

That got his attention. A narrowing of the eyes. 'OK, let's try it another way. What did they teach you about human behaviour at Oxford?'

'Do you mean what they tried to teach me, or what they succeeded in teaching me?'

He smiled, briefly. 'Succeeded.'

She didn't pause: one pause and he'd be taking out his sandwiches. 'Reason is, and ought only to be, the slave of the passions. Hume.'

He looked at her: legs primly together, hands clasped in her lap, back straight in his upright chair, like a schoolroom photograph come alive to advocate anarchy. 'I'm sorry. You lost me. Why?'

It was sad for Grace that the one thing she'd managed to learn at Oxford was something she'd rather not know. It's not reason that gets you out of bed in the morning, it's not reason that stops you eating the bathmat or trying to vacuum clean the postman. You can't do anything unless you want to, and reason alone can't create a want. 'Reason is like a map,' she said. 'If you know where you want to go, it can tell you how to get there, but it can't tell you where you want to go. It can't stop you wanting something either. What people want has nothing to do with reason. You can't reason your way out of a passion: all you can do is oppose it with a stronger passion. That seems quite interesting to me.'

It didn't seem terribly interesting to Kip Sullivan, clearly a man at one with his passions. The world is divided into two sorts of people, thought Grace.

'Well, I have to say if that's the sort of question you're interested in, this may not be the right place for you. We like to think of ourselves as scientists, and science hasn't got around to the passions yet.'

Grace wanted to know what Kip Sullivan did, that filled him with such huge impatience. 'What do you work on, yourself?'

Kip Sullivan's passion was language. What excited him was not thought or feeling but the ability to talk. Once started, he hadn't been able to stop himself: she'd sat like a buyer in a Persian market while he spread his treasures at her feet. 'I work on language. It's always seemed to me the most important thing. The only thing, really, that distinguishes us from animals. Imagine where we'd be if we didn't have language: we couldn't tell each other what we think, what we want, how we feel. If you're going to understand human beings, you have to know how language works. Who was it said that language is a mirror of the mind?'

Not someone on the philosophy syllabus at Oxford. At that time, you could study philosophy virtually anywhere in the English-speaking world without even realizing that humans *had* minds. Grace had been taught that language was a mirror of society, a stock of habits, customs and conventions embodying the accumulated wisdom of the community: you say what society has trained you to say. She found the whole idea repugnant. To her, it made the very act of speaking seem like capitulation to an occupying force.

'At Oxford they tell us that learning a language is just a matter of habit and training.'

'What do they tell you about spiders? Do spiders train each other to build webs? Do beavers train each other to build dams? Why should humans need any training to speak?'

Grace found her interview with Kip Sullivan both intriguing and depressing. Intriguing because it seemed to hold out some hope. Society might not, through language, be able to infiltrate each human head, crouch behind each tongue. Grace hated to think of herself as a prey to external forces, an empty stage on which the great social drama would act itself out. Kip Sullivan seemed to be offering some alternative. His words rang out like the hooves of cavalry coming over the hill.

All that talk of bees and spiders was depressing, though. Grace had no objection to animals, but that didn't mean she actually wanted to *be* one. One wouldn't, of course, dream of being rude to them, but well, really, oh dear. Language seemed such a small thing to hold humans apart from animals: a gingerbread rampart, an icing-sugar wall.

Grace spent the night at her sister's in Chalk Farm. Joanna was four years older. She was quite like Grace to look at, but a bit tamer, more normal: a cross between Grace and an English lady. She could play the lady, too. At five, she understood the social function of birthday parties: could hand over the present without snatching it back, refrain from cramming her pockets full of jelly, and make a pretty thank-you speech as she left. At school she was a popular prefect, much copied by the younger girls, who performed her duties with cool charm, neither seeking nor repelling admiration. Grace had always thought that no one could be better than Joanna, allowing the world to come up to her fingertips – so close, and no closer. Recently, though, she'd begun to dread seeing her sister.

Something was wrong between Joanna and the world. You could see it in the Chalk Farm flat, which she'd furnished with such care and flair on leaving Oxford. Joanna had what they call an eye: 'Let's go and buy an object' had been her remedy for depression, as others would say 'Let's go and buy a dress'. But in the last year or so nothing really had been bought or looked for. The invitations had gone from the big French mirror on the mantelpiece; the walls were just beginning to need repainting; Grace noticed a trailing cobweb in the hall. There was nothing disastrous in the flat, no disastrous change in Joanna. If the term didn't sound so inappropriate applied to someone so civilized, you would have said she was pining.

A key in the door: Joanna. 'Hello, Grace, you got here. How was the interview? I'm dying for a drink.'

'Fine,' said Grace. 'Well, I haven't a clue, actually. I may have failed a crucial test when I refused to race him upstairs.' Joanna poured whisky. 'What about you? Ready for holidays?'

But Joanna was having trouble with holidays too. She'd booked a villa in Spain, with friends: the depressing remnants of her Oxford circle that she seemed to spend all her time with now. There were John and Tess, and Peter and Millicent, and Cara, who'd recently taken up knitting. Nice, staid, sociable people with something frantic about the eyes. It had all been fixed: Joanna was to share a room with Cara, they were travelling out on the same plane. Now Cara had met a new man, and with wistful looks and brave renunciations – No, Joanna, we must make the best of it – had made it quite plain where her preferences lay. Grace couldn't believe this was happening to her cool, competent sister. At Oxford, everyone had wanted to know Joanna: on Sundays her room was like a salon. She'd been the leader, Cara the scuttling follower. Now even Cara was squeezing her out.

'Come to Greece. We could travel together.' Their parents had been lent a house there, and Grace was spending August with them.

Joanna thought. 'I could, I suppose.'

'Please come. I'd like it,' said Grace.

Grace cared for Joanna, and worried about her. The worry she felt was partly for herself. She'd heard herself compared to Joanna so often, longed to be like her so much, that she'd come to see Joanna as a picture of her own future. The question was: had something happened to Joanna – some event that Grace could watch out for and avoid? or was it there in the genes, gradually creeping up on her, like madness or middle age? Would she too wake up one day to find herself a guest at a table set on quicksand, chattering the louder as shoes, ankles, table legs vanished into the sand?

It was clear, at least, that Joanna was suffering from disappointment. Enough like Grace to feel uncomfortable in the world, she had so far been more willing to accommodate herself to it. Her adult life had been an extension of those early children's parties, her good behaviour a sort of bargain with the world: I observe the rules, you give me my slice of cake and leaving present at the end. But whatever it was that Joanna wanted, the world was failing to provide it, and she was beginning to give up hope.

For some time, now, Grace had suspected that what was wrong with Joanna must have something to do with men. At Oxford, there had been a string of distinguished, eligible admirers, among whom Joanna distributed smiles, light chat and cups of tea. There was usually a slightly more favoured one, with, as it were, a silver-gilt medal; but no one, so far as Grace could see, had come near to winning the gold.

'So Cara's met someone new,' said Grace, close as she dared to a direct question. 'Is he nice?'

'Perfectly nice. They're all perfectly nice. They're all so nice it's hard to tell them apart.'

'No one new on your horizon, then?'

'You don't meet anyone new after the age of twenty-five. Someone once told me, and it's true.'

'Don't be silly. Honestly. That's ridiculous.'

'I used to dream of falling in love. Everyone falls in love, I thought. Every man I met, I thought this might be the one. But if it hasn't happened by now, it's never going to happen.'

'Oh, Joanna. How could there be an age limit?'

It didn't seem an appropriate time for a diatribe on love.

Back in Walton Street, notes had gathered under her door, like footprints in the snow showing who had passed by. 'Came to see you. Where are you? Andrew,' was one.

Grace had lunch in college, and in the queue for food stood next to Anne-Marie Archer. Anne-Marie was a comedy actress and a member of a quite popular revue group; Andrew had mentioned her as someone at Somerville he knew. She was a loud girl, who liked not only to know people but to be seen and heard to know them. Grace used to lower her eyes in shame when Anne-Marie would shriek into a café with her becloaked, beposturing friends. You would never have known to look at her that she knew she was unattractive. She took the world by the throat and said, 'Patronize me if you dare.'

Grace now, uncharacteristically, said 'Hello'; and was immediately knocked off her feet by a bucketful of love. Anne-Marie had love to spare: give her an inch and she'd give you a mile. Grace was sucked along to lunch in her slipstream. She heard (as did their neighbours, Rowena and Jenny across the room, the dons at high table, the Principal in her study, and probably Fergus and Mark at Corpus Christi) how awful the exams had been, don't talk to me about exams (Grace couldn't, she didn't get a chance), an anecdote, with funny voices, about buying a ball-dress, and selected extracts from the forthcoming revue.

'I'm flaked,' said Anne-Marie at last, pushing back her plate and pantomiming a yawn. Over coffee, Grace asked if she knew Andrew Lisle.

'Andy, of course, super guy. Going places. Lots of big people are on to our Andy.' She looked at Grace. 'Why? Do you know him, or what?'

'Well, I've met him.'

'Super girlfriend too, comes down from London at weekends. Still, that leaves all week, doesn't it? Oh Lord, is that the time? Must rush. Bye.'

There is no doubt that this conversation altered Grace's attitude to Andrew Lisle. It's hard to be totally dismissive of someone who has lots of big people on to him and a super girlfriend who comes down from London at weekends.

He called round that afternoon. This time, he was neither brash nor subdued. He looked her glass bubble in the face without flinching and asked her out for a walk. 'Come on. You look like a little pale ghost. Put on your sheet and we'll get you some fresh air.'

They went into Parks, past the cricketers and along by the river. The good weather had set in, and the sun was so warm they had to idle along. Andrew was pursuing his fantasy. 'You know,' he said, 'if you're a ghost, it would explain an awful lot. Ghosts don't speak, do they? Speak to a ghost and it looks straight through you.'

'*Anyone* can see straight through you, Andrew, it doesn't need a ghost.'

'If you're not a ghost, why are you haunting me? Hey. That sounds like a song.'

Grace wanted to talk about Andrew's music, but didn't know how. 'Do you write songs?' Not the right question; he was suddenly shy.

'We engineers, you know. If you can't read, you have to pass the time somehow. Look, cricket. Did they have cricket when you were alive?'

He was a curious mixture of advance and retreat. Strange, to catch a glimpse of someone's soul.

What do new acquaintances talk about on a sunny afternoon in Oxford? Rowena would have known, but for her the trick would be never to set off with Andrew Lisle. Stick to your own. Grace didn't have an own to stick to: to her, everyone was as strange as Andrew Lisle. She seized on the one person they had in common. 'I was talking to Anne-Marie Archer at lunch.'

'Oh yes?'

Well, that's exhausted that. What shall we talk about next? 'Er, what do you think of her?'

'She's very nice.'

Very nice? Very nice? Come on, I gave you a sitting target: surely you can do better than that? But Andrew was someone who took people as they were. Some people were Anne-Marie Archer, some weren't: what more was there to say?

Go on, Grace, tell him what you think, what you want, what you feel; remember, that's what language is for, what distinguishes us from beasts.

Woof woof.

Their talk was a grasping at flotsam, a snatching at straws. 'What's that?' said Grace from the bottom of the conversational barrel, pointing to a willow.

'Let me see. Wait a minute. Yes, it's a tree.'

'Fantastic. Do you think it's any particular type of tree, or just a tree?'

'Well, at first sight I'd say it was just a tree, but appearances can be deceptive. If we look a little more closely . . . Yes, you're right, there's no doubt about it, it's definitely a type of tree. Look, you can see quite clearly, it's got leaves and branches. It's what we botanists call a leafy, branchy tree.'

'Thanks very much, I'll try and remember that.' And along these lines, they papered over the void.

They stopped for tea in the shabby upstairs room where Oxford's starlets used to meet: where Rowena and Mark would join Fergus for coffee, and Anne-Marie Archer would stamp and shout to let the world know she had friends. The place was almost empty: the weather was

34

really too nice to be inside. They sat at a big table by the window. Grace was just working up a comment on the sugar bowl when in came Andrew's friends.

Andrew's friends all looked the same. They were all tall and dressed in jeans, and were all too big for their bodies. They were quite unable to keep still; the pressure would build up inside and erupt in a short burst of foot-tapping, head-shaking, finger-clicking. It was like sitting down to tea with a range of active volcanoes.

There was Bob, and Davy, and Rick, and as long as they didn't change places Grace thought she could tell them apart. They turned out to be Andrew's group: the two guitarists and a drummer who'd been playing with him at the ball. They tried to be friendly to Grace. 'Hello, Grace', 'Hi, Grace', they said, and Bob (if it was Bob) repeated the invitation he'd issued at Percy's to sit on his lap. Grace, intimidated by all this naked energy, focused her eyes on the middle distance. 'Don't worry about Grace,' said Andrew. 'She can't see you. She's a ghost.'

'Really. What did you die of?'

'Boredom, mainly. I've spent the afternoon with Andrew,' said Grace.

'Hah! Got you there.'

'I thought of a song,' said Andrew. ' "If you're not a ghost, why are you haunting me?" '

There was a pause. 'We couldn't do that, it's a ballad,' said Rick, and they drew in their breaths as if hearing about a nasty accident down the road. Grace would have liked to know why it was so awful to be a ballad, but to do that she would have had to speak.

Having addressed a few remarks to Grace, and received little more than 'Yes' or 'No' for an answer, Andrew's friends simply ignored her. Even Andrew ignored her, and began talking about some party they were playing at later that week. Grace felt superfluous. She stood up coldly and said to Andrew, 'I'm afraid I have to go.' She'd expected him to jump up and follow her, but he just smiled and raised his hand. 'OK. See you, then.'

Grace went home quite cross. Much though she regretted her frosty manner, much though she besought it to dissolve and leave her normal, she did expect it to have some effect. In her kind circles new acquaintances would try quite hard to draw her out, offering choice morsels of conversation like relatives round a sickbed offering grapes. The only response this solicitude brought was a slight increase in frostiness; but it was a bit much if some people were too thick even to try.

Catching herself out in this train of thought, Grace couldn't help but giggle. To give her credit, when she sometimes surprised herself behaving particularly outrageously, she had the grace to smile.

End of term had come and gone. College lawns were emptying. Grace was longing to get away, but couldn't escape yet. In those days, before announcing the results, examiners had the right to call in borderline cases and question them further to establish their true grade. They call it a viva, a term related to vivisection.

On thinking things over, Grace began to suspect that she might have done well enough to be a borderline case. Again, she tried to ignore the temptation to work; again, she found it impossible to resist.

Mulling over her books one evening, she heard a car door slam in the street and Andrew rushed upstairs. 'Come on,' he said. 'We're going to a party.'

'What, now? Just like that?'

'Yes. Quick. The others are waiting.'

'Don't be silly. I can't.'

'Why not?'

'I'm exhausted. I've been working all day.'

'It'll do you good. Put the roses in your cheeks. Make your hair curl.'

'I'm not dressed.'

'Those look like clothes to me.'

Grace was dressed as casually as she ever was: beatnik black from head to toe.

'It doesn't matter what you wear,' said Andrew. 'Come on. Come with us. Please.'

Going downstairs, Grace felt quite giggly. She usually spent hours getting ready for a party, having a bath, washing her hair, trying on all her clothes to see which of them would make her look least awful. Imagine: going to a party, just like that.

In the van were Davy, Bob and Rick, not necessarily in that order. As she climbed into the back, they all said 'Hi!'. They were in high spirits, rapping on the windows and talking nonsense. The van set off up the Woodstock Road. 'Right, would someone tell me where we're going?' said the driver, who might have been Bob.

'The instructions leave a certain amount to the imagination,' said Andrew. 'Well, it's not so much a set of instructions, more the ramblings of a mentally handicapped sheep. We're heading for a place called Little Nethercote Manor, and I'm acting on the hunch that that involves a Little Nethercote rather than a little manor. Of course, it could be both.'

'Or neither,' said the driver, staring gloomily through the windscreen.

'Don't mind Bob,' said Andrew. 'He failed his Geography O-level. He has trouble finding his way upstairs.'

'With your directions, that's no surprise,' said Bob.

As they headed for Woodstock, Grace, aware that the intellectual level of the conversation could hardly be lowered, felt brave enough to ask a question. 'Whose house are we going to?' What shoals lie ahead?

'Some chap,' said Andrew. 'His sister's having a twenty-first birthday party. She's called Daphne, that'll give you some idea.'

'Andrew, really.'

'Yeah, watch it, Andrew,' said Bob. 'Old Grace here has probably got a sister called Daphne. Or a horse,' he added under his breath.

There was a pause. Grace looked out of the window. Someone sniggered. Time to go home.

They went through Woodstock and on into the Cotswolds. The van rattled through the clear, sunny evening, bouncing them in their seats, throwing Grace and Andrew against each other as Bob took a corner too fast. 'Help me read the instructions, Grace,' said Andrew.

'Go on, help him, Grace,' said Bob. 'Last week it took us so long to find the place, when we got there they were all in bed.'

When you saw Little Nethercote Manor, your first thought was 'hunting lodge'. If it had been better looking, it would have been handsome rather than pretty. As things stood, it was a jolly good chap. The proportion of dogs to humans was roughly three to one. The furniture, hardly sophisticated enough to be called rustic, was one stage along from the tree. Your feet struck damp against the flagstones; in the dim light, you expected to stumble on scattered rushes and bones.

The inhabitants of the house were a breed apart, for Grace, as well as for Andrew and his friends. She'd always held herself aloof from the sporty crowd at school; actually, it was easy to do this at Grace's school, which regarded academic achievement as something over and above the ability to decipher a Cordon Bleu cookbook. Grace was a town girl, and had never really been into a house like this.

Bob, in some lunatic misperception of a county accent, kept calling Daphne 'Dauphne'.

'Hello, Dauphne,' he shouted, beaming, as he bowed over her hand when they were introduced.

'Hullo, er,' she replied, smiling gamely, and he was convulsed.

'Look, chaps, there's Dauphne,' he would bellow in his husky voice at intervals during the evening. 'Hullo, Dauphne.' And Dauphne would gather her skirts and wag her head almost in time to the music and smile her jolly, good-humoured smile, and bravely ignore the thought that he might be making fun of her.

Daphne's friends danced for sport. Their dancing was rough, a pursuit of the fox by other means. They were the Morris men, the chieftains. They jumped and stamped and clapped their hands above their heads. They threw their hearts over the fences. They jostled and hallooed and chased and chortled, forming and dispersing, advancing and retreating. If you asked them why they danced, they would look straight back and say, 'What?'

Their women had a choice of roles. They could hunt with the chaps, take the part of fox, or roast a nice haunch of venison for when the men came home. Grace's eyes went to the aliens, uncomfortable in their clothes and their companions, who could find no place in the dance. If she'd been an invited guest, she would have suffered with the aliens: liked none of the roles on offer; felt hurt at being passed over by people as barely evolved as their furniture. From the edge of the platform, things looked different. These people posed no threat to her: she was with the band.

At ten, the group took a break. They sat on the terrace and watched the garden get dimmer and the lights brighter as they ate. Bouncy before, they were bubbling now: Bob would drum on the table top; Davy would pirouette. Daphne came to shout hullo and ask if there was any chance of fitting in an eightsome reel. 'For you,' said Bob, 'anything.' When she'd gone, he said, 'What *is* an eightsome reel?'

As Grace walked back towards the marquee, Andrew came up beside her. 'All right? Not too bored?'

'Just so long as you play the eightsome reel.'

'For you,' he said, 'anything,' and ran off to join the band.

Grace followed him inside and sat on the edge of the platform, chin on hand. The dancers were getting boisterous now, forming private armies, looting and pillaging: it hardly mattered what music was played. At the start of one song, Bob left his drums and leaped at her across the platform: 'Come on,' he said. 'Let's dance.'

Why not? thought Grace. There's no one here to see.

Now rock dancing, like brain surgery, is not really something you can just get up and do. Nor are there any institutions that will teach you: there's no Royal Academy of Rock Dancing, no grade structure, no bronze-medal routine. So how does anyone learn to dance like Bob? Grace had never seen anything like it. He might have been just messing about, imitating a giant monkey; looking at him, you'd have thought he was simply having fun. But every movement seemed newly created; each step blended into the next with an effortless exuberance that made the foot-stomping highlanders look very silly. Grace didn't know she was dancing with an expert, but she was captivated when he turned his big, beaming face towards her, and circled around her, prancing.

Grace couldn't dance, and didn't try, just smiled at Bob and raised her arms and moved her weight from foot to foot. It might have been different if she'd been short and stubby, but Grace was lucky in looks. However you viewed her, from whatever angle, she was like a snapshot that just happened to turn out right. So Bob was pleased as he danced with her, and she felt as proud as if some strange animal had curled up and gone to sleep at her feet.

Later, she danced with Davy. He was a charmer, a young bohemian prince with a shy smile and knowing eyes. He was the old Etonian jazz musician brought up to date, the rebel who never steps beyond the bounds and is always invited back. Rick was less fathomable: smaller than the other two, and silent; he didn't ask her to dance. By the end of the evening, each was a separate character for her, and she didn't see how she could ever have confused them. She sat in the back of the van with Andrew and Davy, inserting the odd remark into their chat. They dropped her off at Walton Street, and Andrew patted her on the shoulder as they said goodnight.

For Grace, that evening was full of promise. For an hour, she'd been a part of something, and felt the difference in her dealings with the world. Maybe she could take sides, she thought. Wear a badge, stick up a poster. Here was a world all newly minted, with no frontier posts, no police force: just walk in and pick up your passport. With a passport, you can go anywhere safely. People might laugh, but they wouldn't hurt her. She'd be with the band.

There was a slight embarrassment one evening that weekend. Fergus, Mark and Rowena had had their (expected) results and were leaving next day. They took Grace out for a curry, apparently the correct meal to have on one's last night at Oxford. Grace looked across a mountain of rice to see Andrew Lisle come in. He was with a lovely, bubbly girl, unquestionably the super girlfriend from London, with a Brigitte Bardot face, pouty lips, huge eyes, little straight nose and blonde hair all piled up and falling down. The waiters elbowed each other aside in the rush to reach her first. One pulled out her chair with a flourish and said 'Madame,' and she put her soft arms on the table, wriggled in her seat and laughed up at him. Super indeed. For Fergus and Rowena, though, she was another oh dear. Catch Rowena flirting with waiters.

The next time Grace looked over, the blonde girl had stopped bubbling and started to cry. She was sitting very straight, head up, eyes wide open, tears running down her cheeks, making no sound at all. Andrew immediately called for the bill. As he left he gave Grace a distant smile.

Grace's suspicions had been right: she was a borderline case. Again the curtains were drawn; again she worked all night. On the day before her viva, she was frantic: even if you'd known her you'd have said, 'Grace is a little cool today.' Andrew came to the library to ask her out to tea. He was afraid of upsetting her, and they both spent some time staring into their teacups as if expecting a message. At last he said, tentatively, 'Don't worry about the viva. I'm sure you'll be fine.'

Grace showed her teeth. 'It's not much help to be told "Don't worry". You'd be worrying if it happened to you.'

'You'll be all right. Really.'

'I just can't stand this stupid pretence: all your mistakes were slips of the pen, all the answers were in your head, and the only reason you didn't produce them was that time ran out. When they all know perfectly well that you've been slaving your guts out for weeks trying to find out what you should have said.'

'It doesn't have to be like that. That's not at all how my viva went.'

'What do you mean: you've had a viva?'

'I had one last week.'

It had never occurred to her to wonder about his results.

'Oh, what happened?' she said. 'You never told me.'

'It was a bit unexpected, really. They called me in and said that some of my papers were incomplete and they wanted to know how I would have completed them. "Well," I said, "how I would have completed them then and how I would complete them now are two quite different things. I knew a lot more about engineering when I wrote those papers than I do now." So they gave me back one of my scripts and said, "Look, you only wrote half a page on your last question. Would you care to elaborate on it?" "Now this is a case where I couldn't even have elaborated on it then," I said, "and I was very relieved when time ran

40

out. Every scrap of knowledge I had on that topic you'll find written down somewhere in my script." "Let's see if we understand you," they said. "There's nothing you'd like to add to any of your papers." "Exactly," I said. "Well, in that case, we won't take up any more of your time. Thank you and goodbye." '

'I don't believe you. Have you had your results yet?'

'Yes, the next day. I got a second.'

'You mean you almost got a first?' Grace was aghast.

'Not really. I worked hard enough to get a second, and that's what I got.'

'But if you'd only done a little work before your viva you might have got a first.'

'So what? I'm still the same person. An exam result won't change the way I am.'

Grace, of course, had said exactly the same thing many times; but she would have been no more capable of acting on it than of sailing singlehanded round the world. He wished her good luck at the library door, but she felt as if she'd been caught sneaking into chapel.

At the viva, Grace did everything she could short of throwing herself at their feet. She answered every question. She didn't crack jokes. She tried to look as if the geometric propensities of demand curves kept her awake at night. They looked at each other afterwards. 'Didn't seem to care much.' 'Rather unforthcoming.' 'Just misses, I think.'

When the results went up, Grace looked at the second-class list, and the line 'Ritchie, Grace, Som.' leaped out like fire. She looked at the first-class list: maybe there were two Grace Ritchies doing PPE at Somerville. But there weren't. She'd got a second. A very good second; she would still get her grant; she could still go on. But a second.

Grace discovered that the heart has room for contradictory expectations. Hiding away under the feeling that she was, of course, a fraud, second rate, a confidence trickster soon to be unmasked, had been a deeper feeling: it's all right, they'll never find me out; and even deeper: I *am* good, I know it, surely they must see.

The results were a serious shock. It was like being told during a routine medical that you should go to hospital, fairly quickly, for investigation. Her mind lapped round the terrible fact, trying to smooth it into an acceptable shape. To have done brilliantly on some papers, appallingly on others, would have been tolerable. Being brilliant but erratic is something most of us would accept. This was the gloss she

41

put on it to herself. Some things I really worked on, others I didn't, because they didn't interest me.

The truth, if she'd known it, was sadder: it was the things she really worked on, that she tried to tell the truth about, that had dragged her down. The neat, indifferent packages were considered jolly good; the heartfelt bits were considered jolly naïve. Don't tell Grace; it would break her heart to know.

If a tomato had a soul, it would feel like Grace when she saw her results. Here I am, a wonderful, unclassifiable being, both fruit and vegetable, a unique combination of properties, red and round and soft and friendly, and along comes a botanist and says, one or the other, you know you can't be both.

But beneath the disappointment was a deeper feeling of shame. Grace was not just an innocent tomato fallen into the hands of botanists; she was a tomato who had seized the arm of a passing botanist and *asked* to be classified. No one makes you go to university. No one makes you take university exams. If you choose to play with a loaded gun, you can't complain if you're shot.

Andrew went down to the exam halls that afternoon to look at the lists. He found Grace in Walton Street, eyes rolled up inside her head.

'I saw the results,' he said. 'What did you do to them? Throw rocks?'

'I wish I had.'

'I expect they noticed. Never mind. I've booked a table at the Elizabeth. Let's go and celebrate. It's over at last.'

Just missing a first that you've tried very hard for is not something that can be officially grieved. So Grace accepted Andrew's invitation. He arrived in a suit which instantly put him into the category of people who shouldn't wear suits. Generally, his clothes fell wide of any criteria known to Grace: checked seersucker jackets, plum flannel shirts, and trousers which were, well, just trousers, with no other properties at all. You couldn't have called him indifferent to clothes: some positive principle must have gone into choosing just those shades of plum. Indifferent to suits, though, he must have been. His suit was shabby and too thick for summer. His hair was newly washed and brushed.

Grace drank and drank. The frostiness diminished; so did the polite passivity. She herself raised the topic of the girl she'd seen in the restaurant with Andrew.

'Was that your girlfriend with you the other night?'

'She was my girlfriend. We've broken up.'

Grace was human enough to think, 'Aha!' And drunk enough to probe for compliments. 'She's very pretty': a statement which expects the answer 'Not as pretty as you.'

'Yes.'

Grace drank. 'She seemed very upset.'

Andrew wasn't prepared to discuss it. 'Not really,' he said. 'She just cries a lot. She would have been just as upset if one of her ear-rings had got lost.'

This achieved the intended effect of shutting Grace up. She was a specialist herself in cynical remarks, and indeed cynical remarks about love; but it's not for the one who's caused the grief to make the jokes. Grace, shocked, returned her attention to her plate.

In fact, though he immediately felt guilty, Andrew was not exaggerating much. In the end, he'd just lost heart with Susie. All that unquenchable emotion bubbling out. He was marvellous, and so was the salad, and that cloud up there, and the belt she'd just bought. He was a monster, and so was her landlord, and the bus-conductor on the way to work. He needed a rest. Not that it was any of Grace's business.

He filled her glass. 'So what are you doing this summer?'

Grace told him of her plans.

'I was thinking of hitching round Greece myself. Tell me how to find you, and I'll drop in if I'm passing by.'

'We're on an island, actually, rather off the beaten track.'

'You never know.'

She told him how to find her.

But on the way home, his cheerfulness disappeared. In the middle of a sentence he tripped over a crack in the pavement and swore. She no longer seemed at all drunk, and was discoursing gently on the bothers of packing one's bags. He was running over in his head, trying to recapture the tone he'd practised for the words, 'Aren't you going to invite me up for a drink?' which he'd decided to use. True, she ought to invite him up spontaneously, but he was a practical man and a realist. Or, as she would have put it, an engineer. The last time he'd practised it, he thought he'd got it almost right, but then Bob had shouted through the keyhole, 'Hey, chaps, come and listen to Andy talking to himself.'

One problem was that even if he got upstairs, he had not the remotest idea what to do next. The mind just stopped short with squealing brakes. If you laid a hand on her, you felt she might crumble into dust, or bite your arm off. It wasn't so clear that she even *had* sexual organs,

43

let alone knew what they were for. The whole idea of laying hands on Grace seemed sacrilege.

On they walked, on she discoursed. He couldn't even reach out and take her arm. The door of Walton Street arrived.

'Well,' she said, 'thank you for a lovely evening.'

'Thank *you*,' he said. 'And goodnight.'

All the long walk back to the Iffley Road he called himself a cretin, a coward, a cabbage, a cockroach and a cringing creep.

Grace hardly slept. She replayed every minute of the viva: if only I, if only he, if only they. All night the thoughts tripped and tumbled in her brain. I needn't have tried. I could have been out in the sunshine. I could have got a second in my sleep. I could have been rude to them in the viva, I could have made them remember me. I *tried*. I played their game and they still didn't want me. Never again. They'll never get me again.

She was still dozing next morning when Andrew came round. No one was going to see that Grace felt rotten: she straightened the bedspread, combed her hair, and opened the door clear-eyed.

'Hello, Grace. Can I come in? I'm doing a tour of the boudoirs of the stars.'

'You mean there are other stars than me?'

'All right. I'm doing a tour of the boudoir of the star.'

As she brought coffee, he said, 'How are you, Grace? Did you sleep well?'

'Fine, after all that lovely food.'

'Not too upset about the results?'

He'd thought of her waking, alone and unhappy.

'Of course not. It's only an exam.'

'Well, the reason I'm here so early is, you know you were talking about packing?' What she'd been saying on the walk back to Walton Street had only really registered with him in the middle of the night. 'Where are you taking your things? I might be able to help you move them with the van.'

'I'm going to leave them at my sister's in London.'

'A sister. Is she like you?'

'No.'

'Well, it's no trouble to drive to London. What do you say?'

So later that week, they loaded the van with books and cases and chairs, and Andrew's glass bubble wrapped in blankets. As they drove over Magdalen Bridge, he said, 'Goodbye, Oxford. Are you sorry to leave?'

'Heavens, no. All those uniforms, end of term reports, drinks with the dons. It's just a glorified boarding school.'

'We clearly went to different schools.'

'You mean you liked it?'

'To me,' he said, 'it was an education.'

She couldn't tell whether he was being serious or not.

Andrew still knew virtually nothing about Grace. That's not a bar to loving, but it does limit the possibilities of talk. For all he knew, Grace might be longing to tell him about her family, childhood, hobbies, hopes and dreams. She might be a passionate football fan, play first violin in the Hallé Orchestra. Somehow, when it came to personal questions, he lost the nerve to ask.

'What's your sister's name?' he tried; that could hardly be thought intrusive.

'Joanna.'

'Oh. I've got a sister called Jan.'

'Oh, really.'

They tried to look as if it formed a bond to have a sister whose name began with a J.

'Jan's younger than me,' said Andrew.

'Joanna's older.'

'Ah.' And, shortly afterwards, 'Do you mind if we have the radio on?'

Andrew listened to the Top Twenty every Sunday afternoon. He hadn't been going to inflict it on Grace, but he needed the relief. 'Top Twenty. It's my homework,' he said.

Grace didn't mind. She mightn't know anything about rock music, but she'd soon pick it up.

One song she thought was rather nice. 'What's that?' she asked, tapping her feet.

'It's what you'd call grim and I'd call a load of old rope.'

Grace stopped tapping her feet. 'I thought it was rather nice.'

'Yes, well.'

'What's wrong with it?'

'It's what we call a Happy Song. Just right for Daphne and her friends to dance to. A great beat for jumping up in the air and landing on the ground.'

It was true that on closer listening not all the songs sounded the same. Here was a whole new dimension of social assessment to master. It would be no joke to be caught tapping one's foot to the wrong record.

The van clattered towards London in the late afternoon. Grace directed Andrew through the silent, leafy streets to Chalk Farm, where Joanna waited like a spider in her sunny room.

'This is Andrew Lisle. Joanna.'

'Hello, Andrew.'

'Hello.'

Joanna turned to Grace. 'Is there much to carry up?'

'The usual debris.'

'I've cleared out the little room. Let's see how much of it will go there.'

They all carried things up. Cardboard boxes full of books, cups, knives. 'What's this?' asked Joanna, as Andrew's glass bubble emerged from its nest of blankets.

'Andrew gave it to me,' said Grace. Warningly?

'Really? How sweet.' She put it behind a door.

They sat round and sipped Joanna's whisky. Joanna and her room had sent Andrew's throat into spasm. Every sip came out as a hollow gulp that echoed round the room reverberating off each dainty object, bouncing against the ceiling and diffusing across it, like the smoke from a thousand cigarettes.

'So it's all over,' said Joanna. 'Isn't it awful to be leaving Oxford?' Gulp.

'Oh, I don't know,' said Grace. Andrew was sitting with rigid throat, holding the whisky in his mouth, waiting for the conversation to get under way again so that he could surreptitiously slip it down his throat.

'Are you sorry to be leaving Oxford, Andrew?' said Joanna.

GULP. 'Well, yes I am,' said Andrew, fearing an outbreak of hiccups.

'I was absolutely heart-broken,' said Joanna. 'I really think those are the best days of your life.'

'Good God, I hope not,' said Grace. 'I'd commit suicide straightaway if I thought that was true.'

(Gulp.)

It was not enough to swear off alcohol, liquids, any item with the smallest percentage of moisture content.

'Well,' said Andrew, putting down his unfinished glass. 'I've got to be going.'

No one tried to stop him. Joanna twittered him out of the room, arms clamped to his side to avoid the further disaster of a disarranged Chippendale curtain or an overturned Ming ashtray.

'Thank you for the lift,' said Grace.

'Sweet,' said Joanna as he hanged himself from her front porch.

Early next evening the phone went. It was Andrew. 'Are you doing anything this evening?'

'Why?'

'I thought we could have a meal, see a film, that sort of thing. I'm at Davy's place in Highgate. You could come and have a drink here first.'

Joanna was also planning to have a meal, see a film, that sort of thing, with some of her depressing friends, and had invited Grace to join them if she had nothing better to do.

'All right,' said Grace. 'I'll come.'

Davy's place in Highgate was rather grand, and although his parents were away on holiday you could see just what they were like. 'Come in,' he said with a smile, and you could see just how his mother welcomed guests. He flopped gracefully back on to a sofa and splayed one leg across the other, ankle resting on knee, miming 'Don't mind all this. I don't'. His mother would probably have tossed her fur wrap on the floor.

Andrew must have been used to the place, because he showed no tendency to gulp. He was full of suggestions about where they should eat. Grace didn't mind where they went, and Davy maintained a discreet silence, no doubt practising for the Diplomatic Corps. In fact, he seemed to be waiting for something. Soon the doorbell gently cleared its throat. 'That'll be Lindsey,' he said, springing up as if shot through the thigh.

Lindsey was a sharp-faced girl with a pointed nose and cheeks like a chipmunk, which bulged on either side of her mouth, giving it a faintly complacent look. Her hair was fairish and unevenly cut, straggling to her shoulders before giving up. She showed no interest in Grace or Andrew, and indeed little in Davy, as she rearranged an armchair, grabbed an extra cushion and sat down.

'OK,' she said. 'Where's the action?'

'We thought we might try the Javanese restaurant down the road,' said Andrew.

'Forget it,' she said. 'The nearest that cook has been to Java is the far end of the Balls Pond Road.

'What about Rumanian, then?'

'No thanks. The waiters are all from Cyprus.'

'Basque?'

'Don't make me laugh.'

'We've tried most of the places round here,' said Davy apologetically. A singularly disastrous courtship they must have had of it, trailing from restaurant to restaurant in a wake of untouched dishes and seething waiters.

On the question of restaurants, Lindsey certainly knew her own mind. They were going, it turned out, to the Light of Delhi, and when they got there they were told to keep off the prawns. Grace's reaction to Lindsey was one of fear and loathing expressed by a slight increase in the frostiness of her stare. It was lucky for Andrew that none of his choices of restaurant had prevailed, because with Lindsey vomiting over the food and throwing plates on one side, and Grace in a catatonic coma on the other, it would have taken considerably more than Davy's powers of diplomacy to make the evening go with a swing.

Lindsey was not really a shrew. Her relationship to Davy was more that of a snapping poodle to a large, good-natured golden retriever. The retriever steps along, tail waving, head up, turning occasionally to look at the little snapping monster at its ankles with a puzzled but hopeful face, thinking to itself reassuringly, 'I expect it's only trying to be friendly.' Sometimes the poodle manages to sink its teeth into the retriever's leg, and then the large dog turns on the small one and drives it away, shrieking hysterically, to its owner's skirts.

Lindsey, it seemed, was doing a secretarial course, though to hear her talk you would have thought she was working down a mine.

'I was had up today for slouching,' she said. 'There I was, typing "The quick brown pox jumped over the lady don", or whatever daft thing they get you to do, and up pops this maniac old bag screaming, "GET YOUR SHOULDERS OFF THE TYPEWRITER, LINDA." Then she thumps me one between the shoulder blades and I nearly choke on my gum. I almost thumped her back. "KEEP YOUR HANDS OFF ME, MISS BLOGGS, OR I'LL CALL THE VICE SQUAD." That's what I'll say next time.' She speared a bit of mutton off Davy's plate and forked it into her mouth.

'How long have you got to go?' asked Andrew in the deferential tone one would use to a long-term prisoner.

'Three months. I'm counting the days. We've still got what they call the theoretical bits to do. You know, 2,000 years of filing systems; what to do when you see a footnote; how to empty the boss's flower vase when he isn't looking. God help me, it's driving me up the wall.'

So why do it? thought Grace.

'Don't ever do a secretarial course,' said Lindsey to Grace. 'Not if you want to stay sane.'

'I suppose it could lead to something interesting,' said Grace, carefully not maintaining the pretence of conviction till the end of the sentence.

'Don't make me laugh. The most interesting thing those girls will get will be a trip to Selfridges to buy the boss's wife a birthday present. Anyway they don't give a stuff. They're just waiting to get pregnant so the boyfriend will have to marry them,' said Lindsey, forking another piece of mutton off Davy's plate.

If she puts her fork near my plate I'll have her hand off, thought Grace.

'Who wants coffee?' asked Andrew.

They all wanted coffee except Lindsey, who said, 'You must be joking.'

Grace and Davy sat back and sipped their coffee while Lindsey and Andrew bickered about whether there was a film worth seeing within a fifty-mile radius of central London. Davy was sent out to buy the evening papers. By the time they'd made a tentative choice, the film had already started and the project had to be abandoned.

'Actually,' said Grace, 'I think I ought to be getting back.' Lindsey didn't raise her eyes from her purse, where she was ferreting for money.

'I'll drive you,' said Andrew.

'It's not necessary,' said Grace.

'Yes it is. The streets of London are paved with wolves. I'm not letting you go home alone.'

'Christ almighty,' said Lindsey under her breath.

On the way home, Andrew offered to drive Grace to the airport when she left for Greece, and wouldn't take 'No' for an answer.

'Joanna's coming with me,' said Grace.

'Fine. I'll take you both.'

It really would save them quite a lot of bother, and she eventually agreed.

'I suppose people are always telling you how alike you are,' said Andrew. 'I bet the teachers were always getting your names mixed up at school.'

'I don't think we're very much alike,' said Grace in her swallowed voice.

'Well, you know, she's a sort of tamer version of you. If you were a swallow, she'd be a budgie.'

'People pay good money for budgies,' said Grace.

Joanna had been shopping; her hair was newly cut. The night before they left, she was full of excitement, and kept popping in and out of Grace's room.

'Isn't it nice to be driven to the airport? It's useful to have someone like that.'

Someone like what?

They were up early next morning, wandering around in their long smocks and woolly slippers. The bell rang at exactly nine o'clock and they were off.

'Here comes summer, Oh it's summer-time at last,' sang Andrew. Grace waited for Joanna to respond with a suitable stretch of *Aida*, but she merely said, 'What's that?'

'Some people would call it a song,' said Andrew, and Grace was able to tell that he was being sarcastic.

'What would you call it?'

'A piece of Wrigley's Spearmint set to music. I'm sorry I brought it up.'

Grace giggled. Joanna looked at her watch.

'Andrew may be coming to visit us,' said Grace, 'later in the month.'

'How nice,' said Joanna. 'Will you be bringing your van?'

Andrew swallowed, very quietly. 'Nearly there,' he said.

When they reached the airport, Joanna said goodbye to Andrew and moved discreetly away.

'Grace,' said Andrew. 'You wouldn't *mind* me dropping in to see you if I happened to be passing?'

'With or without your van?'

'No. I mean it.'

'Of course I wouldn't mind. I don't know what the house is like, but I expect we could even find you a bed.'

'No, no, I wouldn't need that. I've got a sleeping bag. You sleep on the beach.'

'Well, do come. There's sure to be someone who can tell you how to find us.'

'We'll see,' he said. 'I'll send you a postcard if I get down that way.'

'All right. Goodbye. And thank you for all these lifts.'

'It's been a pleasure. Have a good summer. Goodbye.'

He drove on to Oxford, musing over Grace as over a tricky engineering problem. His position on engineering problems was that they all had solutions. The first thing you thought of mightn't work, but if you went on long enough, one of them would.

For the moment, his approach to Grace was that of the warrior horde. Thousands of men advance, hundreds are mortally wounded, but still they come. Grace sat on her battlements with her bow and arrow trying to stem the advancing tide. 'Whing,' went the arrows, and a general would be knocked off his perch and fall head over breeches into the dust; his troops would simply pause momentarily, regroup, and continue to advance. As has already been noted, many of them were distinctly unclear about what would happen when they finally stormed the battlements, but they were under orders and they advanced. Andrew's return to Oxford was simply a rest and rehabilitation operation, not a retreat.

Chapter 3

As Grace and Joanna walked down the aisle of the plane, heads turned. Grace retreated behind her eyes; Joanna looked carefully up at the seat numbers, as if to check that they were all in the right order. Sometimes, Grace wondered what it would be like to see free and friendly faces instead of these surreptitious, often hostile, stares. Suppose she smiled first, bought different clothes, wore her hair all piled up and tumbling down? As well change her feet for flippers.

They caught the ferry for Kalauria in the heat of the afternoon. Grace sat with a book and their baggage in a shady place on deck. She'd thought it would be a pleasure to read a book that didn't have to be analysed, criticized, committed to memory. Before, the sun in blue skies had been an enemy, engendering all sorts of celebrations that she'd been debarred from and longed to observe. She would hear a little shriek, a snatch of music, the sound of a tennis ball being hit, and she would make another note, turn another page, put another question mark in the margin, thinking, one day, I'll sit in the sun. But now, as the boat rustled along, dipping and rising more powerfully as it left the sheltered water, her mind opened and the misery rushed in.

The thoughts weren't new. She heard them constantly as an undertone in her mind. I tried when I needn't have. I could have been out in the sunshine. I could have kept my distance, the result would have been the same. I *tried*. I tried to join their club and they still didn't want me. Never again. They'll never get me again.

The exam results were Grace's first big disappointment: the first time she'd consciously, publicly, aimed for something and missed. It wouldn't have been so bad if she'd been aiming for something worthy; but she felt like a fallen woman betrayed by passion: compromised, sullied, stained. The world had seduced her, offered its protection. Come along, says life, here's a lovely path through the sand dunes. Landmines? Pooh. The war was over years ago, we've been over every inch with metal detectors. Come on. It's a lovely path, you'll enjoy the view. Off we go, tiptoeing at first, now picking up our skirts to skip and run. Then boom; and out comes the refuse squad, whistling, to pick up the pieces. Never again, thought Grace.

Joanna couldn't sit still. Away she went like a puppy off the lead, up ladders and down hatchways, in and out of corridors, touching ropes, peering through thick window glass, standing at the very front of the deck with the breeze flapping her hair. The boat was quite full, almost all young people, many of them English. Everyone wanted to meet everyone else; it was a whole kennelful of puppies. People talked to Joanna and Joanna talked back. Sometimes she would trot up to Grace, wagging an enquiring tail, but would totter off happily when Grace said she was fine.

They came into Kalauria in the cool of the evening, the time of the promenade. Everyone was out, dressed up for the evening, walking along the quayside, watching the boat come in. The tables were ready, menus chalked up on blackboards, water carafes warming on plastic tablecloths. Normally Grace would have wondered aloud why everyone didn't just stay at home in Blackpool, but it's hard not to be a little excited in a boat approaching a harbour in the evening sun.

The ropes were thrown out, the boat just touched the quayside, and everyone trooped off. They were to spend the night in Kalauria and catch the morning ferry for Teusia. Grace lay on her bed and shut her eyes. Joanna began pulling clothes out of her bag and holding them against her.

'Grace?'

'Yes.'

'I met this rather nice group of English people on the boat, and I sort of said we'd have dinner with them.'

'Oh God.'

'We don't have to stay long if you don't want to. After all, we've got to be up early tomorrow.'

'You go by yourself.'

'You have to eat, Grace,' said Joanna, pulling rank. 'We won't stay long.'

'Oh hell. Well, I'm certainly not going to change.'

'No, no, absolutely not necessary,' said Joanna, putting on a gold lamé dress and spats.

With dragging feet and clanking chains, Grace followed Joanna to a terrace where her new friends were sitting at a table with two spare chairs. 'Shall I sit here? Or here? Grace, where would you like to sit?'

53

chattered Joanna. Grace slumped into the nearest chair and began to study the menu.

'A rather nice group of English people' turned out to mean 'at least one of them did modern languages at Oxford'. Grace sat next to one of these, a young woman called Penny whose most salient feature (indeed, her only salient feature) was a nose with flattened tip and flaring nostrils, as if permanently pressed up against glass. 'Pig-like' was the word for this girl. There is a strong association between such features and British embassies in hot countries. These noses go hacking through the desert, yearning for hot muffins and Marmite. Grace added a helping of frostbite to the tip of this one.

On her other side was a Guardsman, left over from the Charge of the Light Brigade. He was very gallant, and kept saying solicitously, 'Grace'. It is clearly part of officer-training to remember the names of one's mess-companions. Unfortunately, the manuals offer little guidance on the conduct of conversation. 'Do much hunting?' seemed out of place in a taverna in Kalauria; perhaps later on they could talk about beach warfare. For the moment, though, their conversation was a thing of stops and starts, hers and his respectively. Whatever she said was greeted with a little snort of indrawn breath, cut off in mid-stream, a cross between a hiccup and a retch. She politely ignored this for some time, before realizing that it was a conventional sign of merriment.

She left while they were sitting over their coffee. 'I'll be along later,' said Joanna. 'I'll try not to wake you.' She came home in the middle of the night, tripped over every available shoe and suitcase, and had to be dragged out of bed in the morning. They only just caught the Teusia ferry.

'I hope I didn't wake you,' said Joanna when they'd got their breath back.

'Only when you came in.'

'I had a lovely evening. We went dancing. You should have come.'

'I wasn't sure I could take any more of Porky and Algy.'

'They were really very nice,' said Joanna.

'Yes, well,' said Grace.

Teusia is a curious island, with a horned head of granite cliffs surrounding a deepwater harbour at one end, and a pleasant spit of sandy beaches at the other. The main town, Troulos, is on the cliffs above the harbour, connected with the water by a series of huge steps carved out of the rock, climbed by convoys of donkeys. The view on the way up is spectacular if you're not the sort who thinks about death.

Grace and Joanna were met at the deepwater quay, not yet shadowed and sinister. 'Grace, Joanna,' said their mother. 'Joanna, Grace,' said their father, evening things up.

The road runs along a high plateau from the cliffs at one end to the tapering foothills and sand-dunes of Kiafa at the other. The Ritchies' house was on the upper edge of Kiafa, a village of perhaps forty or fifty houses, which straggled down to the water and up into the hills. The house was new, with small shuttered windows and cool rooms. There were benches and arbours on the land around, on which one could sit and stare at the sea.

Geoffrey Ritchie was a foreign correspondent for a newspaper, and Grace and Joanna had been sent to boarding school from the age of twelve, flying to and fro on British planes loaded down with migrating children. Grace's attitude to her parents was one of inarticulate yearning (as for hot muffins and Marmite), far removed from the experience of her friends. While all around her screamed and rocked the boat, spewing out hyperbole about the pathetic clothes Mummy forced them to wear, and the frantic boredom of Daddy's conversation, Grace sat yearning meekly. While elopements were planned to the sound of Daddy's foot going down, Grace sat with hands folded neatly in her lap, obedient to the echo. The cockney filmstar whose only remaining ambition is to build his mum a mansion was no stranger to Grace. She wanted to build a palace, a folly, with all the furniture made of gold. In the meantime, she wrote dutiful letters. Dear Mummy and Daddy, Hope all is well with you. Everything is going well here. Hope to see you soon.

In the evening, Grace and Joanna went to look at the village. Quiet and closed in on itself, it exactly suited Grace. There were one or two shops with their doors open, flies flitting in and out, no hotel, and few people in the dusty cart-tracks that ran between the houses down to the sea. There was not really a harbour, just a few hitching posts on a wooden dock. The beach started at the end of the village, and they walked towards it.

'Look,' said Joanna, 'a nightclub.' And there was. A string of fairy lights festooned the entrance to a tiled terrace built above the beach. A sign decorated with wreaths and eddies of vine-leaves read 'The Grape'. Tables were scattered on the terrace, and there was a space in the centre for dancing.

'It doesn't take much to put up a few fairy lights,' said Grace. 'But who do they expect to come?'

'Maybe there is a hotel after all,' said Joanna, as one would say 'Maybe there is a Santa Claus.'

And indeed, Joanna's wishes were to come true. The Grape was quite a decent restaurant, said Mr Ritchie. People came in taxis from Troulos to eat and dance.

'I think there'll be lots for you to do,' said Mrs Ritchie, 'won't there?'

'Oh yes,' said Joanna happily.

'Oh yes,' said Grace.

Grace spent her days like a fly in a cobweb. The eyes were free, she could see the world going on; but the wings and feet were caught in a sticky bandage from which, with just a little more effort, she could surely get free. With laborious thought she would disengage one foot and wave it hopefully in the air. But as a foot came free, a wing would catch. She would stand all summer, pulling and buzzing, thinking just one more pull and I'll be free.

Everyone could see that Grace was moping, but no one dared to ask why. What could she have told them, anyway? Officially, her second class was jolly well done, and she could hardly explain that she was ashamed of herself for trying to get a first.

The holiday was sweet and sour. What better place to be miserable than an island in the sun? The days were filled with sensual pleasure: the warmth of sun on skin, of sand on toes; the cool of waves so calm they seemed almost sunbathing too. They ate outside in shaded arbours, hired a boat and toured the ruins on a neighbouring island. One evening, they went to the Grape. The music started loud and ended louder; Grace could hear it if she went outside before going to bed. As they finished their meal, the dancing was just beginning. 'We're going to dodder off home,' said Mrs Ritchie. 'Why don't you two stay on and enjoy yourselves?'

The place was almost full: most of the guests in shorts and shirts, a few more formally dressed. There was one group, soigné enough to be called a party, that Grace had been conscious of Joanna being conscious of all evening. They were well past student days. The men were groomed, the women were gowned; at the heart of them was a vivid, dark-haired young man who narrowly missed being coiffed. As the music started, he approached Joanna with a smile. 'You wouldn't take pity on a poor lonely bachelor, I suppose?' Joanna was out of her chair and on to the dance floor like a rocketing pheasant.

The music was provided by an accordion band, four men in frilly tutus and cummerbunds with expressions ranging from the world-weary to the persecuted. Not everyone in Kiafa had approved of Mr Diomas's new nightclub. There were already too many ill-kempt couples sleeping in the sand-dunes, stealing tomatoes from the vegetable plots, breaking branches for their bonfires. Mr Diomas talked of business opportunities, bringing new life to the village. Let's welcome these guests, he said, show them our heritage. If there had been room for a motorway, he'd have been in favour of that.

Kiafa indeed had a musical heritage, based on the old Kiafa handkerchief dance. With its huge cast of characters passed down from father to son, its two days of circling and bowing, this had a deep significance for the villagers, only no one could remember quite what. Each year the rich shirts and handkerchiefs were brought out, the dead dancers replaced, the first-time dancers shy in their hand-me-down clothes. Everyone knew the first few figures, handkerchiefs crisp in the clear dawn air. Children clapped and looked forward to the day when it would be their turn. But the dance was long; no one was really sure how it was supposed to go.

The guardians of the dance were the players in the lute, violin and clarinet band. This changed in political temper over the years. Until recently, it had been controlled by pragmatists, who dealt with crises in a spirit of compromise, prepared to accommodate to the ways of the world. During their reign, there had been a change in timetable so that the main delivery boat from Troulos no longer arrived during a rest period in the dance. The pragmatists had no difficulty remembering that in the *old* old days the rest period had been much later, coinciding exactly with the new delivery hour. Now a schoolteacher sent from the mainland had taken over the clarinet. A serious ideologue, committed to maintaining all the old customs set up in their wisdom by ancients in touch with the spirit of the island (and the timetable of delivery boats from Troulos), he swore an oath that no clarinet of his should pass the threshold of the Grape, no rich shirt or handkerchief prostitute itself for the entertainment of the incomers.

Mr Diomas didn't mind. He wanted a heritage, he didn't care whose. Mrs Diomas ran up the frilly tutus and cummerbunds. Their youngest son was conscripted, hating himself for his weakness, knowing his father despised him for being unable to say 'No'. Mr Diomas had three cousins, men of the world (i.e. smugglers), who could let you have a beautiful heritage, cheap. They played on their accordions a medley of the ancient songs, including 'Hava Nagila' and 'It's a Long Way to Tipperary', followed by a limited repertoire of 1940's hits.

There is no reason why, from such inauthentic beginnings, something of value should not emerge. The present generation of accordionists seems hopeless, but who knows? In fifty years, the guidebooks may give special mention to the Kiafa accordion band.

Joanna and her partner came from different dancing traditions. She danced with the minimal head-tossing and shoulder-shrugging endemic in her group. He had clearly been exposed to the Twist, and adopted those instructions to pretend to be drying your bottom with a bathtowel while stubbing out a cigarette with your toe: an odd thing to do while emerging from the bath, no doubt accounting for the ghastly grin and rabid stare, as if confronted with a materializing troll. Both sides, though, were willing to compromise. Joanna did some tentative cigarette stubbing and smiled at her partner. He shrugged his shoulders, tossed his head and smiled back. A couple was emerging before Grace's eyes.

At the end of the dance, they stood talking for a moment, and then came over to Grace.

'Grace, this is Stefan Coulter,' said Joanna. 'Stefan, my little sister Grace.'

'Hello, Grace,' said Stefan Coulter. 'Come and have a drink.' He jerked his head towards the table where the rest of his party were regrouping.

'That would be lovely, wouldn't it, Grace?' said Joanna, setting off.

Grace followed her over, like a child being dragged to the piano to play its party piece. Whatever Andrew might say, people preferred budgies to swallows. A budgie will sit and twitter on your finger. Swallows probably have fleas. Hell, she thought as she sat down, and her neighbour who had been about to speak to her swallowed his tongue.

He was a nice man, though. She could feel him taking pity on her. 'Isn't this charming?' he eventually said. 'Did you come by taxi?'

'No, by plane.'

He laughed, nicely. 'No, I meant how did you get here from Troulos, ha ha?'

'Oh, sorry. Actually, we've got a house here in the village.'

'Oh, *I* see, that explains it then, ha ha.' He paused for a response, an answering smile. In vain.

'We've been cruising round the islands,' he said.

Silence.

'We came down from Troulos by taxi,' he added.

'Really.'

He waited hopefully; she ignored his outstretched ears.

He soldiered on. 'Er. Have you been here long?'

'About an hour, I suppose.'

'NO. In the VILLAGE, I meant.'

'Oh, sorry. Just a few days.'

'I hear they have some lovely sandy beaches down here. We're thinking of coming over for a day or two. Bring the boat, you know. You're free that way. When you've had enough of a place, you just up anchor and move on.'

'How wonderful,' said Grace.

'Yes. Excuse me. I must dance.'

He upped anchor and foxtrotted off. 'Grace,' said Joanna firmly. 'Come and sit here.'

Stefan Coulter was undeniably charming; especially when not doing the Twist. He was the sort you dream about after reading too many Georgette Heyer novels. The eyes were quizzical and grey, the hair dark and unruly, the mouth humorous but wry. It was the sort of face that makes you think, 'At last I know what "saturnine" means.' He had a lovely soft, apologetic way of talking, and he looked at you when he spoke, very gently, like a doctor testing your wrist for broken bones. He didn't say much, but he listened beautifully. You felt he might hand you a prescription when you left.

'Would you like to dance, Grace?' asked Stefan, flashing a little apologetic look at Joanna.

'Later, perhaps. Why don't you two go ahead and show me how?'

'Would you like to, Joanna?' asked Stefan. Yes, she would.

Grace, looking at her watch, realized that her parents would be in bed by now, and that she could legitimately go home. Spraying goodbyes around like machine-gun bullets, she edged round the dance floor, signalling to Joanna as she went, and escaped into the night.

In the morning, she was sitting outside with her coffee and a book when Joanna came up.

'Grace, I'm going in to Troulos later to have lunch with Stefan. Would you like a lift?'

'No, thanks. I'm just going to flop around here.'

'What did you think of him?'

'Very charming.'

59

'Isn't he? Whee. Well, I must get ready. Bye.'

'I gather,' said Mrs Ritchie when Joanna had left, 'that Joanna's gone off to meet a starving young artist.'

'I don't know about starving. What's a starving young artist doing on a yacht? Retouching the cabins?'

'I gather he's painting a portrait of the owner.'

'Oh, you mean a starving young parasite,' said Grace.

Mrs Ritchie giggled. 'Joanna said he was *very* charming.'

'Oh, he is, he is. He could charm the money right out of your pockets.'

'You don't mean there's anything *wrong* with him?'

'No. Of course not. No.'

Joanna came home late; Grace was reading in bed when she heard a knock on her door.

'Did you have a good time?'

'Oh, Grace, he's marvellous. I've never met anyone so nice.'

'What did you do?'

'We had lunch, then we looked round the town. We went down to the harbour and *walked* up. All those steps! It took hours! Well, we didn't do much, really, but I had a *marvellous* time.'

It was as if Joanna had just been reconnected to the mains after operating on emergency generators all these years. All her circuits had been slightly sluggish. Now her voice was transmitting on the correct frequency, her brain cells were firing vigorously, even her blinks were over more quickly. Normal service had been resumed.

Grace responded with secret despair, filled with the certainty that this was only remission, not cure. To her, happiness was organic. It had to grow from a tiny seed, watered each day, vulnerable to frost, animals and disease. If you pulled up its roots to look at it, it would die. Someone could step on it and it would die. One seed in a million might produce a plant. You couldn't get happiness just by pulling a switch. 'Doomed, doomed,' she croaked.

'Did you see the yacht?' she added aloud.

'No, but guess what? They're bringing it here. We're meeting again tomorrow.'

'Oh, that *is* nice,' said Grace. 'Good for you.'

She was sitting up in the foothills the following day when the boat came into sight, pure white against the deep blue sea, a tiny V shape in the water. From where she sat, you could hardly see that it was moving, except for the two white lines of foam trailing out behind it like smoke. Then it swept round the end of the island, churning up its wake, and came to a halt in the middle of the bay with a rattling of anchor chains.

Later, a dinghy was put down, a baby jet plane being let out to play. It zipped round the side of the boat to the bottom of a ladder, which a group of people casually descended; it headed for the beach, arousing all the sunbathers, then shed its load and sped back to its mother. The newcomers wandered this way and that, deciding where to establish base camp. A suitable spot was found; the sunbathers, reassured, settled down. When all was peaceful again, a friendly native girl could be seen slipping along the beach to fraternize. Joanna, dressed in her best.

When the sun shines, the world expects you to take off your clothes. Joanna was friendly enough, or trusting enough, to oblige. Sundresses with bootlace straps became her: her fair skin turned to honey in the sun. Grace saw no reason to give in to expectations. She had a supply of long-sleeved shirts, whose sleeves she would roll up if the temperature went above ninety; faded cotton trousers, whose legs she could hitch up to the knee; and a straw hat big enough to shelter both her face and her book. When you saw her walking through the streets of the village, you looked around for paddy fields.

She had a plain black swimsuit she was rarely seen in. The sea was in any case a hostile element, but it was the walk to the water, between the clothes and the waves, that sent the blood to her ears. She didn't go strolling through the streets in her underwear: why should she behave differently just because there was sand beneath her feet? She was private property, keep off.

So when Joanna tracked her down in her arbour and asked her to join the new arrivals on the beach, Grace said quite forcefully, 'No.'

'We're going to have tea on the boat. Come on. I'm dying to see what it's like.'

'I'm not sitting round on a yacht in my underwear.'

'No, we can go as we are. They're sending the dinghy. Look.'

Someone had indeed untethered the boat and was setting off for shore.

'Come on, they're waiting. Quick.'

Grace got her trousers wet climbing aboard, but it was a lovely feeling cruising across the water, dipping smack smack against the waves as the dinghy gathered speed.

The side of the boat looked enormous when they reached it. Stefan held the dinghy against the bottom of the ladder, and told Joanna, 'Climb.' She went up the ladder like a circus seal.

'OK, Grace, now you.'

'Come on, Grace, it's easy,' said Joanna. Climbing Everest is easy once you've done it.

'I'm coming,' said Grace. And I hope your noses drop off.

It was cooler now, and they had their tea on deck, sitting in padded chairs while the boat swung slowly round to show them the whole shore. The owner of the yacht, having learned from Stefan that Mr Ritchie was a foreign correspondent, was anxious to meet him.

'We'll be eating ashore this evening,' he said. 'Perhaps you and your parents would be free to join us?'

'Oh, that would be lovely,' said Joanna. 'I know they'd be delighted.'

That was true. Mrs Ritchie's only comment when Joanna announced the impending arrival of the fleet had been brief. 'I'm not cooking dinner for any yachting party,' she said. But to have dinner cooked for her, and with no doubt a chance to have a little look round the yacht, would be different. Mr Ritchie lived by the ear, and was already showing withdrawal symptoms after a few days in a village where he didn't speak the language. Dinner out would be a treat for him.

While they were talking, one of the crew had gone off in the dinghy, leaving Grace and Joanna stranded.

'Let's swim back,' said Stefan. Grace smiled, thinking it was a joke. Joanna, who would have followed him into the path of the Calgary Stampede, said only, 'Can we? Super.'

'There's nothing to it,' said Stefan. 'Got your swimsuits on? We'll send your clothes back later in the dinghy.'

Grace couldn't believe this was happening. 'That water's *deep*,' she said. You should *never* go out of your depth.

'Oh, it's much easier swimming in deep water,' said Stefan, looking reassuringly at Joanna, who stood up and began to take off her dress.

The two of them walked to the railings, and he put his arm around her as they looked down. She turned her face towards him and he kissed her forehead. Then he went over the side.

'Come on, Grace,' she said, excited. 'We'll race you to the shore.'

Grace left her clothes next to Joanna's. She walked to the railings and looked over. Stefan was at the bottom of the ladder, beside Joanna, who was just dipping her foot into the water, shrieking, 'It's cold.' The steps carried her down further, and she let go of the ladder and began to float, with Stefan's hands on her waist. 'It's all right, Grace,' she shouted; then they set off side by side for the shore.

Grace walked to the ladder, turned her back to the sea, and began to climb carefully down. As she climbed, the boat continued to swing. By the time she reached the bottom, she could no longer see the shore; there was open water all round. The side of the boat was in shadow, and the water at her feet was dank dark green, as if filled with nameless seaweed. When her legs went beneath the surface, she felt freezing cold. She hung there, half in, half out of the water, wanting to whimper. Then she let go of the ladder and began to swim, very slowly, round the side of the boat.

Suppose it suddenly started up? She would be ground up by the propeller. Suppose it kept on swinging, barring her for ever from the shore? But she came slowly round it, and could see the shore, and Stefan and Joanna already half-way there. She concentrated on breathing regularly, in, out, in, out, moving her arms and legs in a steady rhythm though her heart was beating at twice the normal rate. Now Stefan and Joanna had reached the shore, and were gambolling on dry land, waving to her. One, two. The boat receded into the distance and the water began to feel a little warmer. She wasn't tired at all. Perhaps she would swim on like this for ever, across the Mediterranean, down the Suez Canal, into the Indian Ocean where she would be eaten by sharks. Maybe she could put her feet down now. No, keep on swimming. There. Her knees had touched the bottom, and she could stand up and splash out into the sunshine. Stefan and Joanna, far away on the beach, looked back and waved.

Grace walked across the sand to the cart-track home, picking her way along it barefoot, elbows raised as she almost stumbled. The little boys looked, but she didn't notice. She was white with fear and rage. For one kiss, Joanna had left her: joined the world and left her floundering. Come back, thought Grace. Come back.

Luckily the Ritchies were out, and Grace was able to dress and wash her hair and drink some tea before they arrived home.

'Did you have a good afternoon, dear?' asked Mrs Ritchie.

'Yes, fine.'

At dinner, Stefan and Joanna were unspeakable. Stefan, like most Georgette Heyer heroes, was over thirty. But Joanna had determined that they were two crazy young lovebirds, mad with joy, who get up to all sorts of escapades while the older generation look indulgently on; for example, like leaving your younger sister to drown. Stefan, anxious not to betray her trust, lumbered after her like an ageing Peaseblossom, breathing heavily.

'Mummy,' said Joanna. 'We swam all the way back from the yacht this afternoon, didn't we, Stefan?'

'Yes. Wasn't it *super*?'

Anyone for a midnight feast in the dorm?

'Grace thought we were *mad*, didn't you?' said Joanna.

'Yes,' said Grace, wishing she could get hold of the wine.

'More wine, Joanna,' fawned Stefan. 'Must keep your strength up, you know.'

'Oh no, no thanks. I don't seem to need any wine this evening.'

'Could you pass the wine, please,' said Grace.

The adults were chatting happily, Stefan and his budgie were gazing into each other's beaks, and Grace was looking at her wineglass, when Joanna was hit by a sudden thought. When you're in love, there is room in your heart for everyone. You cast sunshine instead of shadows wherever you walk, noticing the meanest and lowest, bestowing happiness wherever you go.

'Oh Stefan,' she cried, raising her beak. 'We're being selfish. We mustn't talk to each other *all* the time. Why don't you go and dance with Grace?'

'I'm not a bathtowel,' said Grace.

'What?'

'I said I'm too tired to dance.'

At this Mrs Ritchie looked up. 'Are you ready to go back, dear? Because I want to finish a letter this evening, and if I leave it any later, I'll drop.'

'No, you go. I'm fine.'

She was dying to go, but she wasn't having anyone saying her nose was out of joint. She would sit and suffer till the end.

The next day they all had dinner on the yacht. The following day, it left. Joanna kept the song in her heart, because Stefan would be back in London soon after she was. Her last few days went quickly; when the taxi came to collect her, you would have thought she was off on holiday, she was so excited.

One day Mrs Ritchie came back from the village with a postcard for Grace. 'I'll be in Teusia on the 25th. Hope to see you then. Andrew.'

'Is that someone from Oxford?' asked Mrs Ritchie, curiosity overriding her basic desire not to get her head bitten off. But Grace was relatively friendly.

'Yes. They're all swarming round like flies when they hear you've got a house in Greece.'

'Shall I get Joanna's room ready?' Another hand into the lion's mouth.

'No. He's just a passing acquaintance. I gather one sleeps on the beach, along with the driftwood.'

'I shouldn't think they'd sleep much with all the bouzouki music.'

'Well, that's their problem.' Grace retired to the foothills with her book.

Andrew reached the village towards evening. Grace had assumed he would come by taxi, but he came on a motor scooter, buzzing along the plateau like a motorized bee. She rushed down the cart-track to meet him. 'Andrew. Andrew.'

'Hello, Grace. How are you?'

'You got here.'

'Just happened to be passing.'

'Where did you get the scooter?'

'I hired it in Troulos. Great, isn't it? Want to come for a ride?'

'There's no room for me with all that luggage.' Strapped to the passenger seat was his rucksack and guitar.

'I tell you what we'll do,' he said. 'Are you busy? Not revising for exams or anything?'

'No.'

'Let's find a patch of beach for me to set up home on, then you can introduce me to your parents, and we'll have something to eat. There must *be* somewhere to eat? I won't have to catch fish with my teeth?'

'There's a nightclub, called the Grape.'

'Just the one grape? Like the boudoir of the star?'

'Something like that. You'll love it.'

The sand-dunes behind the beach looked deserted as you approached; once among them it was like walking through an ant hill. Every hollow held a tent or sleeping bag; every bush held washing spread out to dry. Andrew went off to explore.

'OK,' he said, coming back. 'There's a vacant lot up the far end.' He dumped his bag and propped his bike against a bush. 'Let's go and meet your parents.'

'You don't have to,' said Grace, cringing.

'I want to. Besides, they'll have to offer me a drink.'

65

Grace's parents were already sitting outside with their evening drinks. 'What'll you have?' asked Mr Ritchie.

'Anything,' said Andrew, 'so long as it's in a pint glass.' Cringe. 'This is an amazing island, isn't it?' he added when he'd been given his beer to swill. 'Like the Himalayas at one end and Brighton Beach at the other. I'd love to be there when that incredible staircase down to the harbour collapses.'

'Andrew's an engineer,' said Grace.

'Really, what sort?' asked Mr Ritchie, interested in anything that spoke English.

'Oh, a bit of everything,' said Andrew. 'I'll mend your washing machine if you've got one.'

Oh, great. Joanna could conjure starving young artists out of yachts, and all Grace could produce was a repairman who would drink anything as long as it was in a pint glass.

Grace had never had to introduce a young man to her parents before, and was desperately embarrassed. Was he going to gulp? I am *not* responsible for my friends, thought Grace, I can *not* be judged by what they do. But she did *not* believe it.

Andrew didn't gulp. He chatted for a while, and then stood up. 'I'm taking Grace down to the Grape for dinner,' he said. 'That's not easy to say, but I might say it's even harder to do. We may dance a little if I can keep her sober enough. I'll deliver her back well before the neighbours start talking. Goodnight.'

'*An*drew,' said Grace as soon as they were out of the house. 'How *could* you?' As a parent might say, 'How *could* you pour ink over the teacher?'

'How could I what?'

'Talk like that to my parents.'

'Like what?'

'The way you did.'

'That's the way I talk, Grace. What do you want me to do? I talk that way to everyone.'

It was true that this was one of the peculiar things about Andrew. His intonation, vocabulary and style of delivery hardly varied from person to person. You might have thought Grace was the same, since she never spoke much anyway. From the inside, though, the minute variations she could ring in her manner felt enormous. From the outside, all Japanese flower arrangements may look the same; yet to those who speak the language, the minutest displacement of a dead fern may have a profound significance.

They went straight to the Grape. 'Not bad,' said Andrew, tasting the food. 'I think it would be safe to bring Lindsey here.'

'You haven't heard the music yet.'

'Oh, I can guess. I've been in and out of these places all week. Have you been in here much?'

Grace gave him detached and witty excerpts from her week as a wallflower.

'Ah,' he said at the end. 'Feeling a bit hard done by. But Cinderella, you *shall* go to the ball. See, your E-type pumpkin awaits.'

'I am *not* feeling hard done by.'

'No.'

The musicians had assembled, and began to play their introductory selection of the ancient songs. 'Good God,' said Andrew in the tone of a surgeon confronted with a bright green liver. 'You were right. This is really something special.' Grace, pleased with her powers of diagnosis, stopped sulking and began to cheer up.

'Does it go on like this all evening?' asked Andrew, as the musicians ended their first song and began to play it backwards.

'No, this is the good bit,' said Grace.

The dancing was as strange as the music. The parties from Troulos who came down by taxi favoured the foxtrot, quickstep and waltz; none of which looks entirely right to the tune of 'Ten Green Bottles'. The scruff from the beach had evolved a sort of bouzouki boogie requiring a desperate flapping of the whole body; the dance floor looked like a deckload of dying fish. Andrew averted his eyes. 'We're not dancing to this. It's against union rules. Wait till tomorrow. I'll have something organized by then.'

'What do you mean?'

'There's always someone in the sand-dunes who can play a guitar. We'll bring our own music tomorrow. Now let's go for a walk.'

Grace knew all the right places to go: where you could sit in the foothills and see the whole beach and the bay; where you could climb up and see both sides of the island at once.

'This is a great place,' said Andrew. 'I want to go over the whole island. Come with me tomorrow and we'll explore.'

'All right,' said Grace.

'You know what I dream of? That one day you'll show a little enthusiasm about something I suggest. "All right." "That would be very nice."

"Thank you for a lovely evening." You're a clever girl. You can do better than that. You must have said more in your essays than, "Mr Rousseau was a rather interesting man." '

'I'm sorry.'

'Yes,' he said. 'You probably are.'

Her only further remark to him that evening was addressed to his left shoulder. 'Good night,' she said, as he dropped her at the door. It bored a hole right through.

'Hell's bells,' he thought as he went back to his sand-dune. All the long way through Europe he'd been telling himself, 'Relax.' 'One step at a time.' 'Everything comes to him who waits.' Like a long-distance runner biding his time. All that way, all those miles. Ruined half an hour after he got off the boat.

Next morning at eleven he rode up to the house, chatted for a few minutes to Mrs Ritchie, and waited for Grace to appear. In she came, as warm and cuddly as a penguin. He'd actually been worried that she might produce some awful forced friendly greeting, but no. He installed her on the back of his bike. She placed two fingers on his shoulder, and nearly fell off when the scooter started with a jerk. She chose survival, and threw her arms around his waist; he nearly fell off too.

For the first few miles, the road went steadily up, then it levelled off as they reached the plateau, and Andrew signalled that he was stopping. She let go of him as soon as his foot touched the ground. 'All right?' he asked.

'Yes, fine.'

'I thought we'd investigate some of these side roads and end up in Troulos. There should be a road off to the left along here, with a fishing village at the end.'

'OK. I mean, what a marvellous suggestion. I've never heard anything so wonderful. How on earth did you manage to think of it?'

'Get lost.' They allowed each other a cautious smile.

The road down was steep and full of hairpin bends. 'If I'd designed this, they'd have thrown me off the course,' he shouted.

At the bottom was a fishing village, with a café overlooking the harbour and a sign saying MPAR. 'Let's go in the MPAR and have an MPEER,' he said.

'Do you know what I dream of?' she said. 'That one day I'll meet someone who doesn't think that's a funny thing to say.'

'You know what?' he said. 'I think you're very sweet.'

It was impossible to tell whether he was serious or not. Poor Grace. She never dared say 'Thank you' to compliments in case they replied 'April Fool'.

A few miles before Troulos, the road becomes rather spectacular; flanked on both sides by steep cliffs as it passes over a narrow neck of land, before opening out into the horns on which Troulos is built. Andrew, craning this way and that to see the view, kept swerving the bike to the edge of the cliff and cheerfully shouting 'Whoops!' Grace, who hated heights, kept remembering her broken bubble. She tried it with her eyes open, she tried it with her eyes shut. Neither was much fun.

'OK?' he asked, full of high spirits, as they parked in Troulos.

'Fine.'

He looked again, the exuberance gone. 'Grace. Your legs are shaking.'

'Nonsense.' She took a step and her knees chattered. 'Well, I'm not too wild about cliffs.'

'Why didn't you *tell* me?'

'It's all right. Everyone's frightened of something. I bet you're scared of spiders.'

'No,' he said. 'The only thing that scares me is you. When I get home after seeing you, my legs shake.'

'Don't be silly.'

'It's true.'

Grace talked quite freely over lunch. The release which in anyone else would cause babbling enabled her to engage in almost normal conversation. Andrew told her about his journey through Europe; she released more edited extracts from the Romance of Joanna and Stefan. Then they looked at the shops, bought postcards, saw the sights, and no doubt followed in the footsteps of Joanna and Stefan in every respect except where these led down the winding staircase to the harbour.

Going back was much easier; it always is. When they were past the neck of land, Grace relaxed and felt the wind on her face, and wanted to sing. Andrew did sing. She could see his head jerking in time to the music, and feel the sound vibrating through her hands; but the words came past her too fast and plunged over the side of the plateau and were lost.

He dropped her at her parents' house. 'I'm off to fix up the music. Why don't you come to the beach tomorrow? Then we could eat at the Grape.'

'All right,' she said. She'd *meant* to say more, she really had.

That evening, Grace went up into the foothills, to the place where you could look down over the beach. The island had changed for her. She knew the road, all the way to the other end, as if she'd walked it. She knew what happened beyond the bit she could see. The beach had changed too: a part of the sand dunes belonged to her. Andrew was there; she thought she could trace his movements by the sound of guitars. She felt left out: she wanted to be down there with him. Be on the scooter again, her arms around his waist. Perhaps when they stopped, he would help her off, and be filled with a sudden passion. She might fall off when he took a corner too fast, and he would run back, desperate with fear, and cradle her in his arms, and whisper heartbroken words of tenderness in her ear.

Poor Grace.

When she went to the beach next day, he was stretched out, sunbathing. She stood over him in her straw hat, shirt and trousers.

'You've forgotten your fur coat,' he said.

'I don't like sunbathing.'

'I can see that. I thought you were going to lie beside me in a bikini.'

'Two minds with entirely different thoughts.'

'Well, what would you like to do?'

'I don't know. Go for a walk, go somewhere on the bike.'

'You don't mind the bike, then?'

'No. I liked it.'

'Let's go.'

A few miles along the road, they branched off on a cart-track that turned this way and that, through a riddle of tributaries, down to the sea. Something was being harvested, perhaps the legendary Grape, and occasionally they would have to pull off the track to let a cart go past. 'I see they get their hats in the same place as you,' said Andrew.

At the bottom, there was no beach, only rocks and goat-paths. When they stopped, Grace didn't instantly remove her arms from Andrew's waist, and they sat there for a moment, thought and motion suspended; then the film started rolling again and they got off the bike.

They walked along one of the paths beside the sea, single file, or climbed over the rocks with little oohs and ouches as they slipped or jumped. They hardly spoke. They were both occupied internally with the feeling of her arms round his waist: two minds with but a million thoughts.

'Come on, your turn to drive,' he said, back at the bike. They started with great jerks and leaps, but were soon buzzing up the cart-track, gathering speed as Grace gathered confidence, in a trail of rising dust and falling stones. Grace never hesitated among all the network of cart-tracks. When they were back on the road, she accelerated like a cat in a comic strip, and they steamed along, her hair whipping into his face so that he had to keep shaking his head.

He hadn't dared put his arms round her waist. He rested his hands on her shoulders, and there was no flesh on them, just bones. Every time she moved her wrists on the handlebars, he could feel the movement being transmitted through her shoulder bones. Susie had been all pouts and curves, like a grown-up cherub. Grace made him think of starving kittens buried in shoeboxes.

He put his lips close to her ear, and began to sing:

> *'Here she comes in her old grey bonnet*
> *In her beat-up roadster with the drag tyres on it.*
> *You'll be cruising at thirty like they told you and then*
> *She'll buzz you at the lights and you'll be racing again.'*

She turned her head and he could see her smile, not her normal polite flash which you could miss if you blinked. She drove him straight through the village, along the beach without stopping, and back to his home in the sand-dunes. Then she tipped him off. She smiled again. 'That was nice,' she said.

'There's more fun planned for this evening. Will you come?'

'What exactly is going to happen?'

'Well, first the home team plays in their frillies, and then we show them what's what.'

'Do they know about this, or will you just stand up and start playing?'

'Oh, it's all arranged. I got the boys together and made sure some of us could play the same tune, then we went along to Mr Diomas. "Look here, old chap," I said, "your music is, how shall I say it, filth." "FEELTH?" he says. "Feelth," say the boys. "It's in all the guidebooks: worth the detour," he said. "Worth the detour to avoid, they mean." "AVOID?" "Avoid," say the boys. Anyway, we told him that if he'd only let us play for a bit this evening, we'd get everyone from the beach to come in to dinner. "And PAY?" he said. "And pay," said the boys. "Now you're speaking my language," he said. So we're playing tonight. Didn't you hear us practising this morning?'

'No. I thought someone was out strangling the goats.'

'So beautiful, but so cruel.'

Back at the house, Grace found her parents getting ready to go out. 'We're popping down to the Grape, dear. Would you like to come?'

'I'm meeting Andrew there later. He's doing the floor show, it appears.'

'The floor show?'

'Yes. He sings. At least, he calls it singing.'

'Oh. Well, see you later, then.'

Grace prepared for the evening as if about to go on stage. She washed her hair, put on the pale foundation and thin black eye-line that protected her from the world. She was all shades of brown: hair, skin, lips, eyes; and she wore a plain shift the colour of café-au-lait, with a round neck and half sleeves. You're always safer in sleeves.

The restaurant was much fuller than Grace had seen it, and there was a pre-festival air about. People were talking or strolling from table to table, but in a slightly muted way, as if waiting for the bunny to pop out of the cake or the spider to fall on the teacher's head. 'Come on, Grace,' said Andrew. 'If we don't eat now, there'll be nothing left.'

The smugglers picked up their accordions, and the yachting parties from Troulos stood up to dance. Shuffle, shuffle, quick quick shuffle. The beach boys stayed in their seats. The accordion players were not happy, and they knew who to blame. Andrew, with a forkful of tarama half-way to his mouth, was blasted out of his seat by an almighty crash of cymbals overhead. The next song was a stamping one, and stamping Diomases clustered round.

'HOOTS,' screamed one cousin, directly into Andrew's tarama.

'Soddy, soddy, SODDY,' replied another.

Andrew levelled his fork at the nearest smuggler's groin. 'Shall we dance, or do you think they'd follow us?'

'For heaven's sake don't move. We'd be stamped to death.'

When the song ended, it was like the peace after a bombardment. Andrew and Grace raced for the shelter of the Ritchies' table, where they waited until the accordions returned to base.

'OK, here we go. Over the top, chaps,' said Andrew when the session was over. 'Grace, come and give us moral support.'

'Watch out for booby traps,' she said as Andrew and his party headed for the stage.

As the first sounds of the drum vibrated over the beaches, the crowd from the sand-dunes arose and advanced on the floor. There were no shorts in sight. Everyone had dressed up to the limits of their rucksacks;

hair was combed and washed, beards had vanished. You could almost see them spitting on their hands.

The yachting parties from Troulos never had a chance. Before the 'Might' of 'Might I have the pleasure of this shuffle' had fully formed, the floor was engulfed with a wave of writhing, twitching shapes. The words died on their lips, as if they had all simultaneously come face to face with the materializing troll.

'Well the joint started jumping,' sang Andrew, and everyone jumped. 'Reeling and rocking,' sang Andrew; the beach boys rocked and the yachting parties reeled. It was stupendous.

'Come on,' said someone to Grace, and she joined the writhing masses.

After the first few songs, Andrew left the stage to someone else. 'How's it going?' he asked.

'Fantastic. Look at them all.'

It was true. The bunny had popped out of the cake; the spider had descended on the teacher's head, and the class was out of control.

'We shall fight them on the beaches,' said Andrew, but the fight was over. The yachting parties had joined in. The carnival had come.

Andrew's group held the floor for a full hour. At the end, everyone clapped and stamped and cheered. Then the restaurant began to empty, as people finished their drinks and wandered out on to the beach.

Grace and Andrew wandered too, but away from the beach, up to the foothills where you could look down over the sea. They were still excited, and he took her hand and began swinging it as they walked. When he stopped swinging it, he didn't let it go. On they walked, two nervous systems joined by a handclasp.

As they reached the place where you could look down, he said to himself 'Over the top, chaps,' and put his arms round her and kissed her.

She didn't throw back her head and howl, or pull a knife from her sleeve and stab him. She stood there, frozen. Andrew couldn't contemplate the look she would give him when he let her go. He would have to remain here, clamped to her lips like a Siamese twin, perhaps for ever. It might take an operation to separate them. He pulled her closer and could feel her heart beat. At least she was still alive. Then she put a hand, tentatively, on his arm, and he felt a slight returning pressure of her lips. It was as if a coma victim had fluttered her lashes. He was seized with wild joy, and let her go. Then he clasped her to

73

him and hid his face on her shoulder so that he wouldn't have to look into her eyes. 'We'll have to sit down,' he said. 'My legs are shaking.'

They sat down, then lay down side by side on the sloping ground, his arm under her back, the blood supply gradually draining out of it. Anyway, who needs a left arm. He pulled her slightly towards him and she put her head on his shoulder and lay there looking at the stars.

He felt as if he'd just won the Alpine segment of the Tour de France: exhaustion and elation so intermingled that he couldn't tell them apart. He tightened his arms around her and hid his face in her hair. 'Oh Grace,' he said. 'Oh Grace.'

An American weather satellite on its way to photograph the weather around the Soviet rocket stations in Murmansk took a shot of Andrew and Grace, motionless in the foothills overlooking the sea. Her legs and arms were bent at odd angles; her hair was spread out, her face turned to one side. She looked like a body fallen from a high building. Andrew lay beside her, his fair hair catching the light. His body looked quite solid and unbroken. He could have been a police inspector come to investigate the accident, who had lain down beside the victim, crying.

At last Grace moved. She sat up. 'I must get back,' she said. 'My parents went home hours ago.' They stood up and brushed themselves down, Andrew nominally, Grace passionately. 'My back,' she said. 'Can you brush my back?' Andrew brushed her back, producing a shower of grasses, sand and dead ants. 'Oh God, my hair,' she said. 'I've got grass in my hair. What on earth will my parents think?' Andrew hadn't heard anyone talk that way since he was fifteen.

'Tell them you've been practising headstands,' he said.

Grace fussed and fretted her way back to the house as if she'd spent the evening at an orgy. She went in, very cool and collected, to find her parents having a goodnight drink.

'Would you like one, dear?' asked Mrs Ritchie.

'No thanks,' said Grace, shedding grass. 'I think I'll just go on up.'

'Well, that was a very entertaining evening,' said Mr Ritchie. 'Quite an organizer, your chap.'

'It was fun, wasn't it?'

'She's got grass in her hair,' said Mrs Ritchie when she had gone.

'I expect she's been practising headstands,' said Mr Ritchie.

Andrew stayed for a week. Mr Diomas allowed his band to play in the restaurant, and gave them free meals. In the mornings, he would plan the evening's programme with the boys. In the afternoon he and Grace would go off somewhere on the bike. One day, they and another couple went by boat to a neighbouring island. In the evening, the two couples came back, one behind the other in the moonlight, hands interlaced, like teenagers at a drive-in.

Another day, another yacht came into the bay, shedding its baby jet plane, and Grace and Andrew raised their heads lazily to watch. Grace had by now compromised with the sun, leaving her fur coat in the cupboard, and merely putting on a towelling wrap when she came out of the water. They would lie side by side on the beach, and sometimes he would put out a hand and touch her arm.

Conversation was becoming easier. They could reminisce now; they had a history. He never ventured on anything personal: Grace kept her soul as secret as her body. One day he asked her idly, 'What are you going to be when you grow up?'

'I don't know. What are you?'

'I'll tell you what I'd really like: to be an inventor.'

'Inventing what?'

'Oh, things.'

Grace was not terribly interested in things. 'I thought you were going to be a rock star.' She turned her head away.

Tread softly when you tread on his dreams. Andrew rarely spoke of his desire to smooth and shape, amend, alter, invent, improve. Wherever he went, as he drove along, he would be moving houses, cutting a tree here, planting a coppice there; straightening a curve in this road, putting a bend in that one; redesigning the petrol stations, burying the telegraph wires underground. Whenever he cooked a meal, he would be thinking of square saucepans, built-in kettles, cupboards under the floor. These secret visions of changing the world he'd been going to offer to Grace. But Grace was not terribly interested in things.

As for being a rock star, that was something he wasn't prepared to talk about even to Grace. Of course he'd dreamed of it: of being on stage, exchanging secret signals with the rest of his group, winking at them when he turned his back to the cheering crowd before plunging into the music once more. Leaving a concert, he would feel shut out. He wanted to be backstage, drinking, celebrating, clowning around. It was only a fantasy; he didn't admit it as a possibility even to himself. And now she'd clomped all over it in hobnail boots.

'Grace,' he said, 'if you weren't so perfect and desirable in every way, I would feel impelled to point out that you often don't know which way is up.'

His tone was not entirely friendly, and she turned her head again to look at him, puzzled. 'What's the matter?' she asked, and he lost his nerve. She was not a dream that he was yet prepared to give up.

'Nothing,' he said, and smiled.

On the day before Andrew left, Mrs Ritchie asked him to lunch at the house. 'What will you do when you get back to England?' said Mr Ritchie. 'You've finished at Oxford, haven't you?'

'Yes, I'm out on parole. I'm going to do a computer course in London.'

'That should be jolly useful.'

'Yes, he'll be able to mend your telephone, too,' said Grace.

'How interesting,' said Mrs Ritchie, wondering if she should nip down to the shop and buy some more olives.

'Where are you going to do this course?' asked Mr Ritchie.

'King's Cross Polytechnic.'

'Where?' said Grace.

'You know what we used to call Grace in Oxford?' said Andrew. 'We used to call her the Little Sister of Charity. She would always have a word or a smile as she walked through the Bodleian distributing soup. "There goes the Little Sister of Charity," we would say. "Keep your head down or she'll strike you dead." '

'Andrew's just showing off,' said Grace. 'He'd never even heard of the Bodleian until after his finals. He still hasn't learned to spell it.'

'Are there any more olives?' said Andrew.

Grace never meant these remarks to be taken seriously. 'It's a joke; can't you take a joke?' she would have said. She had not yet taken the Introduction to Jokes at the London Institute of Behavioural Science. In any case, with most people she had only two basic modes of operation: she could make either ice cubes or acid drops, freeze you or etch you. She much preferred the second mode, which at least enabled her to participate in a conversation at a level distinguishable from the wallpaper. She would be so thrilled when the switch flipped into this second mode, that she had no eyes for the destruction it caused.

Andrew, his skin lightly scarred, said nothing and held on to his dream.

Grace had been thinking of a last ride on the scooter, but Andrew needed time to convalesce. That afternoon he packed up, had a swim, and wandered up into the foothills, to where he could look over the beach. Even the winner of the Alpine stages sometimes wonders whether he can bear to go on. Then he saw Grace walking down the cart-track towards the village, and his feet jerked back automatically on to the pedals. He thought she might turn towards the sand-dunes, and he was ready to rush down the hill after her; but she walked on towards the village without turning her head, going to buy more olives. Andrew felt for Grace as he felt for the rock group after a concert. He wanted to be backstage, behind the footlights, with her.

He suddenly thought that perhaps she mightn't come to the Grape that evening, and he leaped to his feet and ran down the hill to the village, after her.

'Grace,' he said as he caught up with her outside the shop. 'You are coming this evening, aren't you?'

'Of course,' she said, and he went off thinking how you could design a machine which would read people's thoughts from their voices.

That evening was a farewell party for the musicians at the Grape; it was not only Andrew who was leaving the next day. Everyone from the beach came in. The band had collected a lot of requests, and the festival air of the first evening was back as people clapped and shouted when their request was played.

Andrew had spent much time in his sleeping bag thinking of how he would communicate his feelings to Grace by means of a song played for her on their last evening. It would be a public declaration and a secret memory that they would always share. When the song finished, Grace would run to throw her arms about him, and they would walk out into the moonlight together.

Then he replayed the scene more realistically. The tolerable romantic songs he could think of were not particularly easy to sing or play, and Grace would almost certainly not know the original: it would be like giving a knitted copy of the Mona Lisa to someone who had never seen the painting. Andrew could hear his voice bogging down half-way through the first verse, the accompaniment leaden, people beginning to leave the dance floor, Grace, embarrassed, walking out.

Towards the end of his performance, Andrew picked up the microphone and walked to the front of the stage. 'I'd like to dedicate this next song to a very lovely lady who's here tonight. She'll know who I mean. Sometimes it's a little hard to explain to someone how you feel, but I hope this song will do it for me.' Then he began to sing:

'She sits all day in her pretty room
Where poppies nod and roses bloom

But when the sun goes down at the end of the day
The sweet old lady goes out to play.

Here she comes in her old grey bonnet
In her beat-up roadster with the drag tyres on it
You'll be cruising at thirty like they told you and then
She'll buzz you at the lights and you'll be racing again.

Hot rod granny, oh she's really canny
She can get you busted and be home by ten.'

As she recognized the song, Grace smiled at him, a little, secret smile
that was here and gone, and he nearly swallowed the microphone.

At the end of the session everyone clapped and stamped, and clustered round Andrew and the others to say goodbye. At last, Andrew
and Grace escaped into the moonlight and set off for their usual place
in the foothills. They would now walk hand in hand, and when he
kissed her she would put her arms round him, not quite automatically,
so that he had to wait for it each time. They would lie together, pretty
much in silence, as the weather satellite flew by. She wouldn't look at
him after they'd kissed; God only knew what she was thinking. But he
was relatively content with his placing at this stage, and he had no
intention of making further demands.

'When will you be back in England?' he asked as they walked up the
hill.

'In about ten days.'

'Have you decided what you're going to do?'

'Oh, the London Institute of Behavioural Science.'

'Where will you live? At Joanna's?'

'Heavens, no. Well, only while I'm looking for somewhere else.'

'I'll give you a ring when you get back. If you like.'

'Yes, fine.'

Trudge, trudge, trudge.

But as they reached their usual place in the foothills, she looked
quickly at him, put her hand out to touch his arm, and said, 'I liked
the song.'

'Oh Grace,' he said, devastated. 'I love you.'

Where that remark slipped out from is not clear. Love had not been
in his thoughts. He was horrified. She'd have him out buying the ring
in no time. No, no, of course he didn't mean that, he didn't mean
anything. It was all ruined. He didn't want to behave like someone in

love, to be a recognized suitor, to make little measured declarations as part of the price. It had just come welling out, like a sigh.

Luckily, she treated it as if it had just come welling out like a burp. She ignored it; in his gratitude, he nearly said it again. Instead, he stroked her back, feeling the bones breathe in and out, and they lay down together in silence.

In the morning, she came to see him off, and he rode away on his scooter, waving.

Chapter 4

The London Institute of Behavioural Science was set up after the war by a rich American, John Bradley Farrell, who had lost a son. Fighting hurt with hope, he spent the long hours planning a gift to the people of London that would advance the cause of human understanding and help to prevent future wars. He bought, with love and hope, six ethereal Georgian houses off Regent's Park, abandoned during the war. His wife, with love, walked through the rooms, oversaw with him the plastering and wiring, the curtaining and carpeting, the shelving and cupboarding, the repaving and replanting, each concealing the blackness, each spying out the blackness in the other's off-guard looks. The American Ambassador opened the building; Winston Churchill was there. Above the main door was written, '*Humani nihil a me alienum puto*': nothing human is foreign to me.

The administration of the huge endowment was left to a board of trustees. While of course respecting Mr Farrell's wishes, they felt that what was needed, in these vital early stages, was a sound administrator who could forge links with existing bodies, set up the necessary machinery, get the whole thing on a solid footing. Jack Cadwallader, a down-to-earth committee man, the author of a well-organized textbook on local government, had been the perfect choice. For the Farrells, he had set up a two-year MA course in human behaviour, the only one of its kind in the country. On a more practical level, the Institute had affiliated itself to London University, and offered regular graduate degrees in politics, economics, international relations and social sciences; it had become, to all intents and purposes, a graduate college of London University. Every year a report went off to the Farrells, describing the Institute's contribution to the cause of human understanding, local government and peace.

On the first day of the academic year, Grace was summoned to a meeting of the new students and staff. You could tell the students by the inquiring tentacles sticking out of their heads. Kip Sullivan stood up. 'OK,' he said, and all the inquiring tentacles turned to him. 'Welcome to the London Institute of Behavioural Science. I guess some of you already know me from the interviews, but in case you've repressed the memory, I'm Kip Sullivan.' There was an answering shuffle, a few polite chuckles. 'Now let me introduce the faculty.' He recited a string of names, each of which provoked a response in some member of the row of staff sitting round the room: an embarrassed nod and smile from the more socially adept, a convulsive knee jerk and grovel from the less advantaged. The probing tentacles quivered slightly; the students looked on in disbelief.

'Each of you will be allocated to an adviser who will organize your tutorials and deal with any problems that arise. The MA students will be assigned to me and to Jerry Bastable there, and we'd like you to come with us after this meeting so we can get started. The research students have already been given the names of their advisers; if you have not been assigned an adviser, please put up your hand.' Everyone looked round, but no hand was raised.

'There's one other thing I'd like to say before handing over to our Director, Dr Cadwallader. The people you will learn most from in your time here are not the faculty but your fellow students. We want you to get together, in the pub, in the common room, after class, and discuss things. Work on problems, hold informal seminars. You are the guts of this institution, and what you can give each other is much more important than what we can give you. We can provide the food, but it's up to you to digest it and make something of it. Thank you.'

As Kip Sullivan ended his speech, there was silence. Grace looked up; every student head was bowed, every probing tentacle limp. Some people had their heads in their hands, others were staring fixedly at their notebooks. You would have thought a flying bomb had just cut out directly above them.

Shuffling towards the front of the room came a smiling, white-haired, grey-moustached, red-faced man with glasses. 'And now I'll hand you over to Dr Cadwallader.'

'Thank you, Kip,' said Dr Cadwallader in his down-to-earth north country voice. He smiled like Santa Claus in a TV advertisement, and you expected him to continue, 'And now a word about Aramis aftershave.'

'I think Kip here has covered most of what you need to know. I just want to say something about the purpose of this institution. I've been Director since the Institute was founded, many years ago.' A tiny, visible but inaudible sigh ran along the row of staff and was registered on the quivering tentacles of the students. 'Mr Farrell, our founder, was, and still is, a man of vision. He wanted this Institute to play a small part in helping to solve the problems of the world, to prevent fighting, to enable people of different cultures to understand each other.' The students stirred as another flying bomb came over the horizon.

'Now I'm a practical man, and I don't pretend that this Institute has helped to prevent any wars or anything like that. But by taking young people like yourselves, and giving you the privilege of two or three years of uninterrupted study in the company of some of the finest minds of our generation, we hope we can send you out into the world to become trade union leaders, administrators and teachers in your turn, and that you will help to spread that vision a little further.'

He looked down at a three-by-five-inch file card concealed in his hand. None of the students noticed, since they all had their heads under the tables. 'Now about your research.' The change in his tone was so startling that forty heads were instantly raised: Santa Claus replaced by Santa Claws. 'I always say that research is a long, lonely road.' Another tiny heave ran along the row of staff. 'But let me give you a little bit of advice. What I did when I first started my own research, many years ago, chuckle, was to go out and buy myself some three-by-five-inch file cards, and whenever I came across something I wanted to record, I wrote it down. It's quite important to make your writing legible, or if you have a typewriter, that would be even better, because it may be months, or years, before you need to look at those cards again.' Some of the students were now tunnelling out of the room. 'Well, that's all, so don't forget, legibility, correct spelling and three-by-five-inch file cards.'

As they filed out, Grace's nose hurt from being looked down.

The MA students followed Kip Sullivan up the stairs to his room. Here, he divided them into two further groups, one to have tutorials with him, the other to go along the corridor to Dr Bastable. Grace was in Dr Bastable's group.

Dr Bastable peeped round his door like an old woman expecting the bailiffs. 'Oh, er, come in,' he said, stepping back and pulling the door open welcomingly wide. It hit a filing cabinet and bounced back, catching him on the toe. 'Would you, er, like to sit down?' This was said in a slightly puzzled, self-questioning tone, as if the correct answer might emerge from the intuition of pure forms. In fact, it emerged on a more empirical level, when the five students sat down on a row of waiting chairs.

'Er, I'm Jeremy Bastable.' Five pairs of inquiring tentacles swivelled in his direction. Silence. Perhaps the interview was already over? 'I believe I'm to be your tutor.' Silent, quivering tentacles. 'Er, would you like some coffee?' The students wriggled in their chairs. 'Oh no, her her, I think we finished it last term.' He looked at the shelf on the bookcase where a few mugs and a little heap of sugar stood beside a congealed and rotting milk bottle. The tentacles pulled out their handkerchiefs. 'Still, we could go over to the refectory. Unless it's not open yet.' He looked efficiently at his watch. 'I'm afraid it probably doesn't open till tomorrow.'

He was now in full flood. One of the students appeared to be taking notes. The possibility arose that Dr Bastable would set about chartering a coach to take them in search of a cup of coffee. It was hard to break into this monologue, since it was still being conducted in a spirit of self-examination, on which one felt it would be impolite to intrude.

A student with some potential as a national leader seized the sheep by the horns. 'I think we can do without coffee,' he said. 'Perhaps we could just fix the times of our tutorials and go over the lecture list?'

'Oh, OK,' said Dr Bastable, surprised but willing: we cater to every whim. 'Well, when would you like to meet?'

'Maybe we should look at the lecture timetable first.'

'Oh, OK. What lectures would you like to go to?'

Grace put her notebook away.

'Do you think you could give us some idea of what's on offer, as it were?' asked the future ambassador to the United Nations.

'Oh, OK. Well, wait a minute, I don't think I've *got* a timetable.' Her her. Caught you there.

'Perhaps you know where we might be able to find one.'

'Well, I tell you what, why don't you go and ask Val, she's our secretary. She could probably let you have one. Then you can see what lectures you want to go to, and so on. And we can fix up a time for tutorials after that. Well, then, er.'

A beady tentacle reached out and gripped him round the throat. '*When* shall we come and see you to fix a time?'

'Oh, er, when would you like?'

Her her.

Jeremy Bastable had been the pioneering knee-jerker in the chorus line of staff presented to the students. He liked to be called Jerry, but Jerky would have been more appropriate. He was a good sort. He tripped over the carpet on his way to the door.

'Right,' said the student leader as the door closed on Dr Bastable's fingers. 'Let's go and see Val.'

'Are there any timetables for the MA course?' they asked her.

'Oh, it's absolute chaos at the moment,' said Val. 'First week of term is a real madhouse. Well, look, I've done you some timetables, you can have one each. Who's your tutor?'

'Dr Bastable.'

'Oh. Well, I'll just tick the lectures you really ought to go to this term, and put a question mark against some you might find interesting. Dr Bastable likes to have his tutorials on Tuesday mornings or Thursday afternoons.' She gave them a well-organized lecture on the workings of the tutorial system and the various courses at the London Institute, and sent them back upstairs.

'I think I'd rather have tutorials with Val,' said a drowsy voice in Grace's ear. She smiled and walked on into Dr Bastable's room.

'We thought that Tuesdays at twelve might be a good time for tutorials,' said their leader. 'Would that suit you?'

'Oh. Er, yes, I don't think I do anything then, do I? Yes, why not? Well, then, er.'

'What would you like us to do for the first tutorial?'

'Molluscs.'

'I'm sorry?'

'Molluscs. I think that would be a good place to start. Do something on Problematic Aspects of Mollusc Behaviour. Unless there's something else you'd rather do?' A pause for intuition of pure forms. 'OK? Good. Well, then, er.'

'Is there a reading list?' asked the student leader. 'You see, most of us are new to this field, and we don't really know where to start.'

'Oh, *I* see. Reading lists. Reading lists.' He looked at the rotting milk bottle, then at his watch. 'Well, I tell you what, why not go and ask Val if she can give you a reading list on molluscs. Just follow up anything that seems interesting. Well, er, then.'

'See you next Tuesday at twelve.'

'Oh, OK.'

'Come and have some coffee,' said the sleepy voice in Grace's ear, after they'd collected their reading lists from Val. The owner of this voice, though maybe not a potential prime minister, was certainly the potential winner of any beauty contest held among the students of the London Institute. He was tall and fair, and could perhaps be best described as an effete, or drawing room, cowboy. There is a class of people whose eyes have to be propped open with gold toothpicks, whose lids seem to operate on sticky rollers, going up and down slowly and with effort. He was one of these. Below, all was elegance: the flowing cowboy walk, the well-cut jacket and trousers.

'How are you finding the course so far?' he said as they walked along, in a weary voice that couldn't be bothered to rise at the end of the question.

'Pretty inspiring. I want to rush straight out and buy my supply of three-by-five-inch file cards.'

'They stopped making them in 1952. Shows how long it is since he had an idea worth writing down.'

You would have thought he was on drugs, his voice was so slow and slurred. Grace found it enormously appealing: it made her feel more lively. They sat by the window in the refectory. The coffee, like everything material in the place, was good.

'What's your name?' he said.

'Grace Ritchie. What's yours?'

'Horace Wotherspoon.' His tone demanded disbelief.

'It isn't.'

'Why not?'

'It can't be.' She laughed, worried.

'Well, there's someone called Horace Wotherspoon on the course. I've seen the list. Three women, seven men. Ten people who saved the world.'

'What is your name, really?'

'You can call me Hor for short. Or Wothers. No, actually, it's Patrick Slade.'

They smiled at each other with the secret superiority of knowing that he was not called Horace Wotherspoon.

When she got home, Grace felt toyed with. She thought she might have behaved badly, and felt she'd been led into it. She wished she could wipe that afternoon out and start again.

She rang Andrew. They hadn't planned to meet that day, but she was a bit unsettled.

'Hello, Grace,' he said. It was the first time she'd rung him. 'How did it go?'

'Oh, fine.'

'Good. How are you?'

'OK.'

'Good. No news?'

'No.'

'What are you doing now?'

'I'm at a bit of a loose end. I was thinking of going to the pictures or something.'

'Good idea. Why don't you? I wish I could come too, but I'm doing my homework.'

Andrew's course had already started: he'd only just got back from Greece in time. He'd found a flat to share with Davy and Bob, driven Grace round while she looked for hers, helped her move in, all during his first two weeks of term. Now he was doing his homework.

'Oh. Well, if you're too busy.' The frost came down like thunder, but he resisted.

'See you on Friday, then. I'll ring you.'

She hung up without saying goodbye.

She'd found a big room at the top of a house in Camden Town, with a bathroom on the same floor that she didn't have to share; put up her old curtains, draped the furniture with cloths, moved the armchair next to the window. You could hardly tell it from Walton Street once the mirror, rug and glass bubble were in place. Andrew was in King's Cross. Grace could have walked there in fifteen minutes, but she hadn't yet been inside the flat.

These days, her attitude to Andrew was changeable as April weather. One minute he'd be stretching his limbs in wintry sunlight; the next, the sea-mist would have come down. The thought behind these sudden cut-outs was, 'Don't encourage him.' Don't encourage him to think he's your boyfriend: your social partner, Grace-and-Andrew, linked by a flow of goods and services; I'll cook the supper if you'll bring the wine. Don't encourage him to think you like him. Grace took pleasure in Andrew's devotion, but the fact that it was unsolicited was quite important to her. Unsolicited devotion creates no responsibility, arouses no guilt; like a box of chocolates with no calories attached.

She didn't want to commit herself to Andrew. No bell had rung to say he was the one. The only bells she'd heard were alarm bells. 'Such a stylish dresser.' 'Such a nice little man.' And the alarm bell that rang the loudest was her own. Grace came back battered just from walking down the street. She would no more have thought of entering into close relations with an untried, untested human than of stretching out her throat to the butcher's knife.

She rang Joanna. They'd hardly seen each other since the holidays, partly because Grace had found her own place very quickly, partly because Joanna had been out every evening with Stefan Coulter. It was not just a holiday romance. Joanna was still lit by a thousand-watt bulb. Grace would have quite liked to know what was going on, but Joanna was never there. 'Must have lunch soon,' she'd said when Grace moved out, and that was the last Grace had heard.

Joanna's phone didn't answer.

Then Grace's own phone rang.

'Hello, Grace, it's Davy.'

'Hello, Davy.'

'Want to see a film?'

Sorry, wrong number; afraid I seem to be out; preparing for exams; dinner party in progress; fell and broke my ankle; police on the premises; phone unaccountably gone dead.

'That would be lovely.'

'I'll come and pick you up.'

Davy was as charming a guest as he was a host. That shy twinkle as she opened the door. He was prepared to work for his whisky, had found just the right film, at just the right time and place. On the bus to Baker Street, he showed just the proper interest in Grace, revealed just the proper amount about himself. He'd read Italian at Oxford: his name was Santini, remember; his grandfather had come from Genoa. Like Grace, he'd done well enough to qualify for a grant.

'Are you all doing graduate work?' asked Grace.

'Hardly Rick. He was lucky to get a degree. And Bob has his job.'

'What job?'

'He's a hairdresser, didn't you know?'

'A *hair*dresser? That's a strange job for an Oxford graduate.'

'Bob's not an Oxford graduate. He was a hairdresser in Oxford, too.'

That big, beaming, prancing, husky voiced man was not Grace's idea of a hairdresser. 'Oh, I didn't know.'

After the film, they decided to walk back to King's Cross. Grace, having been denied Andrew, wanted to see him.

'How's Lindsey?' she asked when they'd discussed the film for just the proper amount of time.

'Still looking for jobs, poor lamb.'

Lamb? Lindsey? This man needs his head examined.

'I didn't know it was so hard to become a secretary.'

'Lindsey wouldn't become a secretary to save your life. She wants to be a journalist, and she got fed up trailing round the newspapers being told they wouldn't even look at her because she can't do shorthand typing. But she'll find something: she's a very determined girl, is Lindsey.'

'Yes.'

When they reached King's Cross, Davy led the way into what Grace thought might be a slum. There were no trees. The buildings looked like station depots and factory blocks. Some places were simply empty lots where a bomb had once dropped. Every so often, like the remaining teeth in a badly dentured jaw, two or three old terraced houses stood, in grimy yellow brick. It was gaslight and Jack the Ripper country to Grace.

'Here we are,' said Davy, stopping in front of one of the remaining teeth. She followed him down some dark stone steps. 'Come in,' he said, in the tone of the Highgate hostess. She stepped in, to the smell of rotting floorboards. 'Can I take your coat?'

They walked into a room with the high, uncurtained, barred windows that one imagines in Victorian prison cells, badly lit by a bare bulb. There was a sort of thick sacking on the floor, with an electric fire in the middle of it, which had possibly warmed the layer of air immediately below the ceiling. All the furniture was low: a tin trunk with white lettering, covered with records in their jackets, two broken divans with rugs over them and records spilling off; a blue painted table with a full ashtray and some papers; cushions and newspapers on the floor.

'I am a mole and I live in a hole,' sang Andrew as he came through a dark, doorless hole in the wall. 'Welcome to our humble home.'

Humble, thought Grace. It's positively obsequious.

'Just turning over the record.' There was a great crackling sound as he bent over the record player. 'Doobedoo Owwwwww.' The voices moved from double bass to screaming falsetto in the space of four syllables, at a volume which would have got them banned from American airspace if they'd been planes. Andrew sprang for the volume control. 'Sorry, a bit loud.'

'WHAT?'

'There, that's better.'

Grace was too busy that evening on the purely perceptual level, analysing all the new information that was cascading in, to come to any conclusions. Afterwards, the thought came to her: the music furnished the room. It spread a tapestry around them, a carpet under their feet, put pictures on the walls. She lounged over the broken divan, cushions at her back, drinking the dregs of the whisky, while Davy twitched to the music and Andrew read the papers. You didn't have to talk here; indeed you were positively encouraged not to, the music was so loud. Here they were, like a clutch of rabbits in their little dank womb.

As the record finished, Bob came monkey-stepping into the room, chin jerking in time to the last song. He stopped in mid-jerk when he saw Grace. 'Hey, there's Grace. Hello, Grace.' She smiled. 'Hello, Grace with the pretty face. Hey, has anyone ever written a song called Grace? There's lots of rhymes. Grace. Face. Lace.'

'Embrace,' said Davy.

'Chase,' said Andrew.

'Suitcase,' said Bob:

> *Hello Grace*
> *With your pretty face*
> *Won't you help me carry*
> *This heavy suitcase.'*

'I like it,' said Davy. 'It'll sell a million.'

'Thrace,' said Andrew.

'Who?' said Bob.

'Carapace.'

'It's time I was going,' said Grace.

'I'll drive you.'

Grace didn't disagree. She was not going out in the gaslight alone.

'Bye then,' said Bob. 'See you.'

'See you,' said Grace. 'Goodbye, Davy.'

'Goodbye. Drop in any time you're passing.'

'You can't help it with our stairs,' said Bob.

Grace shook her coat slightly before putting it on.

'The van's just round the corner,' said Andrew. 'Did you have a good evening?'

'Yes. Did you suggest it to Davy?'

'You might say so. There I was trying to do my homework, and there was Davy bleating away about going out. Bleat bleat. Shut up, Davy, I'm working. Bleat bleat bleat. Look, I said, I've just had Grace bleating down the phone at me. Why don't you two get together and go and bleat somewhere else?'

'Andrew, I don't bleat.'

'Yes you do. You were bleating.'

'I was not.'

89

'Hello, Andrew, bleat bleat bleat.'

No one had ever spoken like that to Grace before. She was secretly pleased.

He parked the van in front of her house, and said, 'I'm coming up.'

'It's quite late.'

'Bleat bleat bleat.'

He'd been in her room two or three times while helping her move her things, but she'd never invited him up when she had the option. Having established base camp in Greece, he was not anxious to get out his Alpenstock and crampons and go charging onwards, but he did want to hold the ground he had gained. So when he went inside her room, he put his arms around her and kissed her, and made her sit on the bed beside him while he stroked her bones.

'You had a rough day, then,' he said.

'Don't remind me. It was awful.'

'What went wrong?'

'I don't know. They have these little pep talks about how you can learn from one another and write down your research on three-by-five-inch file cards.'

'That's not so bad, now, is it? Nothing to bleat about.'

'I *don't* bleat.'

'Anyway, look. If ever you get really low, you just come round to King's Cross. Walk out of your lectures and come round. There's almost always one of us there.'

'All right, thanks.'

Grace tidied her room after he left, dusting the surfaces, straightening the cushions, tidying the papers. Then she hung up her clothes and went to bed.

In the morning, she dressed carefully and went to the Institute to see about molluscs. The library was in one of the large Georgian houses, beautifully shelved, with good tables and comfortable chairs. Because it was the beginning of term, each table was packed with students who, though they might appear to be reading busily, were in fact waving their tentacles like periscopes. You couldn't walk into a room without attracting a forest of seaweed-like inquiry.

In Oxford, Grace had mastered the library in the end, by wearing rubber-soled shoes and going in to the same seat at the same time each morning, so that people saw her appearance as, if not normal, at least natural. She'd forgotten what it was like to be a new girl in a strange library. When she opened the door marked *Animal Behaviour* a mass of furry heads went up, like a flock of grazing rabbits arrested by a snapping twig. She hesitated, went in and shut the door. It was a good room in the sense that there was a carpet on the floor, and you could get across it without your feet making great sucking noises as if wading through a bog. She put down her file on an empty chair, and took her list to the shelves.

The first two books were out, their absence marked by a slip of paper that said Trent-Horsley, seat 13. The next three were also out to Trent-Horsley. In fact, every book in the room that had the slightest reference to mollusc behaviour had been tracked down, clubbed over the head and hauled off to Trent-Horsley's lair. She could see him working away, surrounded by books. He felt her eyes on his neck, and looked up as a dog does when you go too near its food dish. The gaze fixed and hypnotic, the head lowered, the back stiff, the faint rumble in the throat.

Grace advanced with her fowling piece. 'Have you finished with any of these?'

'Sorry,' he said, receding chin at the ready. 'I've only just started.' All the furry ears went up. 'And I'm afraid there's someone waiting for them when I've finished.' He nodded at someone watching them aggressively from the other side of the room. 'Awful bore, isn't it?'

Grace picked up her file without speaking and walked out of the room. She went straight to Val. 'How does one get hold of books in this place?'

'It's ghastly, isn't it? But you'll soon find your way around. If it's for an essay, your best bet is to nip straight down to the university library and take them out. You can pass them on to one of the others when you've finished. Actually, I've just sent that tall fair chap, Patrick I think he is, down there a few minutes ago. I expect you'll catch him if you hurry.'

It was now Thursday, and Grace was afraid that if she let Patrick Slade make off with the whole reading list, she wouldn't even see any of the books until after the weekend. She set off for the university library. By the time she found the molluscs section, the books had gone.

Two of the references, though, were to journals. She went into the periodicals room, found the right shelf, and saw the two gaps for the missing volumes. As she turned away, flicking her hair, she saw Patrick Slade, chin on hand, staring drowsily towards her. He activated his facial muscles, which transmitted the signals slowly along to arouse a smile.

She smiled faintly back, and squelched towards him. 'Have you got *Animal Behaviour Studies* 1959?'

'Yes. You can have it, though. It's not really my cup of tea.' The words pushed their way up his windpipe and out of his mouth, like a sluggish stream of bubbles. 'Talking of that, let's go and have a drink.'

'I must read these articles. It's taken me the whole morning to find them.'

'I tell you what. You have a look at *Animal Behaviour Studies* while I finish this. Then I think you'll need a drink.'

Grace carried the journal to the next table, and began to read about molluscs.

The news was not good. Grace, applying to the London Institute, hadn't read the label on the bottle with any care. It was a famous place, quite hard to get into, and full of prestige. The MA in human behaviour sounded interesting. Here she was, a rank amateur at life: she wanted classes, training, a professional qualification. Besides, what else was there to do?

Expecting a course on humans, she'd been puzzled by the title of her first essay and the fact that her reading list seemed to contain only references to animals on the intellectual level of the protozoa. Perhaps, she thought, the behaviour of the protozoa has implications for mankind. Perhaps molluscs are eating away at the foundations of Venice, and we are asked to predict the consequences of this activity. It was with some intrigue that she began to read *Animal Behaviour Studies*. But the news was not good.

The article was on the avoidance of predation in molluscs. Molluscs are the natural prey of birds, fish, humans and other molluscs; but they are not defenceless. They take flight, propelling themselves away with great jets of water; leaping for yards on their single monstrous foot. They surround themselves with vile secretions, or sting. To delay pursuers, they change both colour and shape; spread an inky cloud to cover their tracks; as an added distraction, they leave their foot behind.

This information aroused some sisterly feeling in Grace, who had her own techniques for avoiding predation; but it seemed to have as little bearing on the general conduct of her life as a recipe for soused herring or an article on how to plant snowdrops. She regarded it as unsolicited. From the footprints of great men to the slime trails of the lower animals. Out of the frying pan into the lobster pot, thought Grace.

As she was wondering whether to take a note or two, Patrick Slade stood up, stretched slowly, yawned loudly, and came over. 'Need a drink?'

'Yes.'

In the lift, he said across the intervening heads, not bothering to lower his voice, 'There's a sort of bar thing in the Students' Union, or the Lamb and Flag round the corner.' All the heads turned to look. Grace, unable to speak, stared at the floor indicator until they were down.

It was early; the Lamb and Flag was still empty. When they were settled, he took a large bite of his sandwich and said, slowly chewing, 'What do you think about molluscs, then?'

'Basically, I would say they were irrelevant.'

'Ah, to you and me. It takes a mollusc to appreciate another mollusc.'

'Dr Bastable seems to like them.'

'There you are, then.'

'Yes, but what are we supposed to *write*? I thought this was a course on human behaviour.'

'Well, it's all the same, isn't it? Molluscs, squids, people.'

She didn't know what to make of this, and took a small, neat bite of her sandwich.

They exchanged academic histories. He'd left Cambridge a couple of years ago. What had he been doing since?

'Oh, this and that. Going up and down. In and out. You know how it is.'

If there was one thing Grace didn't know, it was how it is. She picked up her drink, holding her hair back as her face sloped forward.

He chewed away, unembarrassed as a horse by the shreds of lettuce and ham that fell out of the sides of his sandwich as he bit. He surveyed the room, arm along the back of the banquette. He couldn't have been more at ease if he'd had both feet on the table.

Patrick Slade had a strange effect on Grace. He made her feel both threatened and protected. Protected against nudges and smirks by his obvious acceptability. She could walk into a pub with him and know she was all right. When he spoke to her, though, she felt uneasy. Every utterance seemed like a dare: there was a hint of roister-doister about him; a whiff of the gentleman wolf.

'I don't know how I'm going to write this essay without any of the books,' she said.

Chomp. Chew. But perhaps she had misjudged him. 'I expect I could pass them on to you when I've finished.'

'Oh, could you? That *would* be nice.'

They exchanged addresses and phone numbers. Back in the library, he let her have the second periodical and what he judged to be the least useful of his other books, and went away.

Joanna rang that evening. She was having a few people round on Saturday, to meet Stefan. Could Grace come? Would she like to bring Andrew?

Andrew who? No Andrews here. I don't know any Andrews. 'I'm not sure what Andrew's doing on Saturday.'

'Well, let me know.'

'Who else is coming?'

'Cara and James – that's her new boyfriend. Peter and Millicent. Do you think that's enough, or shall I ask Tess and John?'

Grace thought it was too much. Not Cara and James, not Peter and Millicent, not if Joanna wanted to hang on to Stefan.

'That sounds lovely. What time shall we come?'

On Friday, Grace was outside the Institute when the library doors opened, and worked her way through every item on that week's reading list. She was still there when the doors closed. On Saturday, she rang Patrick to tell him she wouldn't need his books. When she went to return the one she'd borrowed, he gave her coffee in his top-floor flat. They were both rather cagey about the progress they'd made on molluscs, but agreed in future to share the books. Then she went home to prepare for Joanna's party.

Andrew's winter outfit was a red checked Canadian lumberjacket, black sweater and baggy black corduroy trousers. 'Come IN,' said Joanna, thrilled. 'Grace, you and Stefan already know each other. Stefan, this is Andrew, er.'

'Lisle.'

'Stefan Coulter,' said Stefan, holding out a black velvet arm.

Andrew, though in gulp country, sat urbanely on a French gilt chair. Grace joined Joanna on the sofa. Stefan stood with his elbow on the mantelpiece. Except for Andrew, who should have been tidied away, Joanna's room looked like the opening scene of an Edwardian play. Perhaps Andrew could be the undergardener, come to announce the discovery of a mangled sola topee in the shrubbery.

'How's the course going, Grace?' asked Joanna.

'I'm waiting to see.'

'What about you, Andrew?' Have you finished replanting the asparagus beds?

'I'm studying to become a computer,' said Andrew. 'I'm thinking of moving out to Surbiton, then I can be a commuter computer.'

'Computing,' said Stefan from the mantelpiece. 'I believe there's good money in that.'

'Well, I won about £5 in the class poker game this week, but I gather the real money doesn't come till you know how to get at the Salaries and Wages computer.'

None of them had the correct response to this. Joanna went downstairs to answer the doorbell, whispering to Grace to get the peanuts out of the kitchen. Cara, James, Peter and Millicent had arrived.

It was Stefan's evening, and he handled it perfectly. He stood against the mantelpiece so that everyone could inspect him. He smiled his humorous smile and let them discuss art. Andrew wasn't interested in art; you could tell by his jacket. James smoked his pipe and swapped exhibitions with Stefan. Stefan and Millicent swapped people. Cara looked for someone to swap knitting patterns with.

Joanna had set the table with candles and flowers. 'Super,' said Millicent. 'Joanna, you do things so well.' Joanna did. She would be in no doubt about what to do with a mollusc: poach it in white wine. The only problematic aspect would be for how long.

Half-way through the evening, Grace realized that Stefan was going to fit in with Joanna's friends. At first, they'd been wary of his velvet suit, but he turned out to be just a more elegant version of themselves. All the pulling out of chairs, the settling of the women in place, the solicitous passings of the vegetables. He behaved as James and Peter tried to behave, talked as they hoped they were talking. He was the model, they were the faint copies.

Millicent was breathless. She used his name whenever she could. 'Peter, I think Stefan would like some wine.' 'Stefan, thank you.' 'Oh Stefan, I know Sally Entwistle too.' No one bothered to remember Andrew's name, though the red jacket glowed luminous in the candlelight.

Once, Grace eliminated Andrew from his seat and put Patrick Slade in his place. He would outshine even Stefan Coulter. On the other hand, he would probably fall asleep with his head in the plate. Andrew, trying to do Grace credit, was sitting straight and keeping his hands off the table, and there was a little, eager look on his face, eyebrows alert, as if waiting for someone to throw him the ball. But the ball soared by above his head, in an atmosphere of exhibitions one had been to and people one knew. Grace was sitting diagonally opposite Andrew, as far from him as she could be, and it cost her some effort to say eventually, at the end of a guided tour of the Prado that Millicent had just completed, 'Andrew, how is your group getting on? Andrew has a rock music group.'

'Baroque music,' said Cara, raising her head. 'What instrument do you play?'

'Rock music, not baroque,' said Andrew.

'Oh.'

'Stefan,' said Millicent, 'what sort of music do you like?'

'There's room for all sorts.' He smiled good-humouredly. They could probably squeeze Andrew's sort in alongside the dogs who barked the national anthem and the men who played 'My darling Clementine' by dropping prawns on their toenails.

After coffee, when the conversation seemed set for the evening, Grace said to Andrew, 'I'm afraid we ought to be going. I have to finish my essay.'

He looked at his watch. 'Gosh, it's ten o'clock.' Gosh, it's only ten o'clock. 'Yes, we certainly ought to be going.'

'I'm afraid we must,' said Grace.

'Sorry,' she added outside. 'Not a very inspiring evening.'

'That's all right. Do you really have to work?'

'Not immediately.'

'Let's go to your place. Bob's invited some of his mates round at ours, and things might turn out a little rough.'

'What did you think of Stefan?' she asked in the van. Andrew and Stefan hadn't got on, in a much more positive way than Andrew and James or Andrew and Peter hadn't got on. You could see their backs bristle as they avoided each other's eye. More seemed to be involved than a natural feeling of inferiority on Andrew's part.

'He's a creep.'

'Is he?' said Grace, delighted. 'How do you know?'

'I'll give you an example. You know when Joanna went downstairs and you went out for the peanuts or something? He sort of nudged me man-to-man and said, "Nice work if you can get it." '

'What?' Pause. 'Oh gloom. Joanna's crazy about him.'

'I expect she'll cope. Anyway, that's her problem. Your problem is finding some decent records for us to listen to.'

'I like my records.'

'Yes, well.'

Grace had never thought much about music. Left to herself, she chose the harpsichord: every note neat, nothing wild or stray. Rowena's group chose, and gave her for Christmas, songs that they thought cool and sophisticated, by performers whose natural home was the cabaret. When Grace said she liked these records, she didn't mean she actually played them: not to wake up to, tidy her room to, dress up for a party to. To her they meant late nights after essays with Rowena and Jenny, whisky with Fergus, Sunday before the cinema with Rowena, Jenny, Sebastian, Fergus and Mark. Grim, of course; but waking up in Camden Town she sometimes felt a rush of longing for her Walton Street home.

'I can't listen to these. I really can't,' said Andrew, sorting through the pile.

'What's wrong with them?'

He looked at her. 'Oh. I don't know.'

'Go on. Please tell me. Try.'

For Grace he would try. He picked up a record sleeve and put it down. 'See? Even the covers make me uncomfortable. This music stands for things I just don't like. Fur coats and diamonds. Candles and flowers. Rich people in restaurants, men who walk on the outside of pavements and hold open car doors. It's like listening to the national anthem of a country I don't approve of. Who in their right mind dreams about things like that?'

'A friend of mine gave me that record.'

'Sorry. You did ask.'

Grace would have liked to pursue the topic. Too late: he'd tuned the radio to something loud and fast. He danced towards her, holding out his hand, but she wouldn't join in, wouldn't display herself in front of him. 'No,' she said. 'I can't.'

He moved away and picked up a book. He closed his ears against the music, but it seeped through his skin and into the bloodstream. Like an addict resolved to master temptation, he didn't even tap his feet or nod his head. Well done, thought Grace: he's freezing to death. She was trying to wrestle herself out of her chair when the music changed and Andrew sprang to life. 'Rock and roll,' he said, bursting out of his chair. 'Can you do rock and roll?'

Grace said miserably, 'I can't do anything.'

'Come on. Please. Let's try.'

For two shy people, rock and roll, like ballroom dancing, is a good place to start. There are definite steps to do, routines to master. You can practise them together and see yourselves improve: it's like setting up house. Rock dancing is more like being stranded with a stranger on a desert island: no common round, no daily task, just you and him and the void.

Rock and roll is perhaps the only dance that is centred on the wrist. When the bodies come towards each other, it pushes them apart; when they separate, it pulls them back again. It's a dance of countervailing forces. Step close, but not too close; run away, but not too far. The very dance for teenagers: paradox personified, flirtation on legs.

Andrew took Grace's hand. Used to dancing with Susie, he set off on their routine. Susie had been a delight to dance with: she seemed so happy to be looked at, so ready to smile, at him, at their missed steps, at anyone she bumped into. But behind the smiles was a Pandora's box of misery. Here was this lovely, efficient girl, who would cry for hours before a party, outsparkle the cider when they were there, and then come home and lie rigid and gaping beside him. What Grace would reveal behind her scowls, who knew?

What did become immediately apparent was that she had the principles of rock and roll dancing backwards. Her wrist was all compliance. When he pressed, it gave way; when he pulled, it didn't resist. The body, by contrast, was in permanent retreat. When he pulled her wrist, her arm and shoulder went out towards him, but her body stayed where it was. When he pushed, expecting an answering pressure, she gave way, stepping back. By the end of the first chorus, they were up against the wall.

'Look,' he said, and switched off the radio. 'Let's practise the basic steps.'

Once she understood the principles, Grace learned the dance quite quickly. In half an hour, they had the beginnings of a routine: a rock or two, a twirl or two, a walk, a twist, a turn. Grace was thrilled. She wanted to go on.

Andrew felt a rush of fondness for her. She'd stood up for him at Joanna's party in her own way, and he thought one thread had grown between them of what might one day be a cat's cradle. Next time he pulled her towards him, and she came trustingly, sure of an answering pressure, he dropped his hands and took her in his arms.

When he kissed her, she kept her eyes tight shut. 'Grace,' he said, his face close to hers. 'Open your eyes.' The eyelids tightened a little, the small child refusing medicine. 'Come on, Grace. Look at me.' The eyelids quivered. Then she opened her eyes and looked at him.

It was like parting the grasses casually and finding the brown, shiny eyes of a small rodent looking back. The eyes don't move; you can see the fur jerking as the heart thumps. He looked back with love and relief. Another thread grew in the cat's cradle.

When he left, he went a few steps down the stairs, then came up again, two at a time. When he opened the door, she was sitting on the bed, legs crossed, leaning back on her elbows, face turned towards him: a vignette of Grace alone. He put his head round the door, said, 'Nice work if you can get it,' and went off downstairs. She could hear him all the way down to the street and out into the van.

Next day was essay-writing time. Grace assembled her notes on molluscs, wrote, 'Problematic aspects of mollusc behaviour,' and put down her pen. There was no shortage of information. She now knew, for example, that some molluscs have a homing instinct, returning to the exact spot on a rock from which they set off; that some are tool-users, propping open with stones the shells of other molluscs they wish to eat; that some can distinguish objects by shape, texture, colour or weight, can tell squares from circles, horizontal from vertical rectangles. No doubt each discovered fact opened up new avenues of research, was rich in problems for the practising mollusc-fancier. For Grace, to whom sky and earth and ocean were a mystery, these gaps in human knowledge left no wrinkle on the brow.

Wrinkles there were, but it was the behaviour of the humans, not the molluscs, that had caused them. Embedded in the dispassionate prose, in tones so measured that she almost missed them, were phrases that made her look back in disbelief. 'With one eye removed, the animal circles toward the eyeless side when light is directed from above.' Human beings were amputating the eyes of snails to see how it made them walk; destroying the nerve centres of octopuses to see if they could still wave their arms; starving them, applying electric shocks to them, to see if they could tell blue from green.

Grace's reaction to this discovery had much in common with the snail's. Unpleasantness simply made her draw in her horns. If Lindsey had been in the same position, everyone would have known of it; but Lindsey was manifestly engaged with the world, a social agent among social agents. For Grace, it was just another reason for keeping herself to herself. Passive resistance was her métier. She'd decided on a sort of boycott. Her reading took on a curious focus as she picked through her notes for innocent facts, like a vegetarian searching for carrots in a steak and kidney pie.

So. Problematic aspects of mollusc behaviour. 'Molluscs,' wrote Grace, 'constitute a highly diversified group descended from the worm. Their study raises a variety of problems, evolutionary, physical and psychological.' Not to mention the problem of remaining awake. 'Mollusc behaviour is affected by a wide range of exogenous factors, including tides, temperature, humidity, season, time of day and phase of the moon.' For example, an oyster placed in the centre of the Sahara desert has rarely been known to swim. By lunchtime she was making progress; by suppertime she was almost there. She could leave the molluscs to simmer overnight. There were a few points to follow up tomorrow, but for now, she could relax.

She ought to ring Joanna. She must ring Joanna. With luck, Joanna would be out.

Ring ring, ring ring, ring ring, ring ring. Grace was just about to put down the phone, duty done, when Joanna picked it up, breathless. 'Hello?'

'Hello, it's me. Have you run upstairs?'

'Well, er.'

Oh God. She'd horned in on a moment of passion. Unless Joanna had been practising headstands.

'I just wanted to thank you for the lovely meal. I'm sorry we had to leave so soon, but I've been writing my essay all day.'

'I thought it went rather well, didn't you? Everyone seemed to like Stefan.' She could feel the air waves caused by Joanna and Stefan's fond exchange of smiles.

'Yes.' Almost everyone. 'Well, I'm just on my way out, but I thought I'd give you a quick ring. Maybe we could have lunch sometime when I've got my lectures sorted out.'

'Lovely.'

'OK, goodbye.'

'Bye.'

Grim.

She rang Andrew. 'Hello? Davy?'

'Hello, Grace.'

'Is Andrew there?'

'Yes, hang on a minute. Andrew, it's Grace.'

'Hello, Grace, how's the essay?'

'Not too bad. I'm fed up with it. Can I come round?'

'Fine. We're just sitting around in the wreckage.'

'The what?'

'Bob had a bit of a rave-up last night. A few things seem to have got damaged.'

'Oh yes? How could you tell?'

The place wasn't hard to find: you just had to steer by the drumbeats pouring out of the ground. 'I don't need to borrow your records,' she said as she went in. 'I'll just open my windows and listen from there.'

'Turn the music down a bit,' shouted Andrew. 'Grace has weak ears.'

'Christ,' said Lindsey into her *News of the World*.

The room seemed no more wrecked than last time, unless you counted the people. There was the usual debris of a Sunday: papers everywhere, full ashtrays, empty mugs. And sprawled in armchairs, on the divan, on cushions on the floor, were Bob, Davy, Lindsey, Andrew, Rick, and what Grace took to be Rick's girlfriend, by his side. Everyone but Rick and his girlfriend moved when Grace and Andrew went in. Lindsey looked up from her paper and said, 'Hi,' Bob and Davy said, 'Hello, Grace.'

'Have you met Heather?' said Davy. 'Heather, this is Grace.'

Heather didn't make the normal nod or shuffle one makes on introduction. She just looked at Grace and said 'Hi,' her lips opening and closing like a fish. A quick-thinking mollusc could have propped them open with a stone. She was big, with black hair half-way down her back, red cheeks, and a mouth that if she had let it would have looked sweet. A milkmaid in motorcycle gear.

Everyone settled back, leaving Grace and Andrew to get on with it. The place seemed to function like a makeshift common room, perhaps dug out by the officers in a prisoner-of-war camp, using whatever came to hand to create the illusion of home. You didn't engage in conversation with the other inmates. There was little exhibition-swapping. You just read your paper, brewed yourself some coffee, listened to your music, made the odd remark, and shoved off when you felt like it, to add another few inches to the tunnel out. Nothing seemed to be expected of you except that you refrain from asking for the music to be turned down.

Andrew and Grace went into the kitchen. Perhaps it would be better to call it a cooking hole. There was a small, bare, barred window that gave on to nothing, a marble sink that seemed to have been fixed crooked, with no draining board on either side. The floor covering might have been lino, overlaid with the heavy sacking material used in the big room, which was here damp, rucked and stained. There was a white painted table, with a few dirty plates, knives and mugs; Andrew washed two of them while the kettle boiled on the gas stove not recent enough to be called a cooker. Again, the music made this all right.

They took their coffee into the big room, where Lindsey had finished the *News of the World* and thrown it aside with some force. 'What's all this about Tuesday nights?' she said, not bothering to establish who her question was directed to.

'We're fixed up to play in the George and Dragon,' said Andrew. 'You start on Tuesdays, and if no one throws beer-mugs at you, you move up to Wednesdays and Thursdays. If you're really great, you get Fridays or Saturdays, and then you're a star.'

'That's fantastic.'

'It was Bob who fixed it up.'

'No sweat,' said Bob.

'I'm glad all that banging about's getting you somewhere,' said Lindsey.

'Banging about?' said Bob. 'Banging about? Are you talking about my drums?'

'It's all right for you. You haven't got neighbours like mine. If they so much as see Davy just walking up my stairs with his guitar they're on the phone to the police. He looks pretty silly, I can tell you, coming in with his guitar stuffed up his jumper. When he gets in, they sit round with their ears to the floor waiting for the catch on the guitar case to move. Thump thump. "Good evening, *Miss* Brooks. I hope your *friend* isn't thinking of playing any music tonight. We don't want any trouble with the landlords now, *do* we?" Silly old bats.'

'No one minds the noise round here,' said Bob. 'Frightens the cockroaches away.'

Grace looked down, but nothing moved: the cockroaches were all sitting in their holes with their hands over their ears. Lindsey reached for another newspaper. You certainly knew where you were with her. None of this time-wasting on closing down a conversation politely, just fold up your ears and hop off.

Grace drank her coffee, listened to the music and read the *Observer*. Eventually Rick and Heather, who had sat staring at nothing the whole time she'd been there, stood up together without any apparent communication between them. 'Got to go,' said Rick, and they went out.

'Christ, those two get on my wick,' said Lindsey, not waiting for the front door to close. Grace began to think how she could escape without leaving Lindsey behind her to comment.

'I'm going to lend Grace a few records,' said Andrew. He began picking through the piles. 'Here,' he said, handing her a sample. 'Your homework for this week.'

'Thank you. I'll play them while I read about molluscs.'

'About what?' said Bob.

'Molluscs. It's a sort of shellfish.'

'Grace is learning how to communicate with the lower species,' said Andrew.

'I'll see myself out,' said Grace.

On Tuesday, Grace put on her new clothes and left for the Institute in plenty of time. In the common room, she thought she recognized three other members of her tutorial group. She didn't join them. She couldn't walk up to them and say, 'Hello, are you waiting for Dr Bastable's tutorial?' Suppose they weren't, or were but didn't want her to join them, or didn't hear what she said and asked her to repeat it, or were the morning cleaners just going off duty. She gave them a faint, superior smile and walked to the far side of the room.

At two minutes to twelve, she followed them up the stairs to Dr Bastable's room, where the one who had negotiated tutorial times with Dr Bastable knocked on the door. No answer. They looked at each other. 'Maybe he's forgotten,' whispered someone. Been knocked down, lying dead in the road.

'Our essays have gone,' said their spokesman. 'I checked.'

He knocked again. No answer. The leaping promise of a cancelled tutorial lurked behind every eye.

Just then a voice perked up behind them. 'Waiting for me?' They lifted their ears off the door and looked round to see Dr Bastable. 'Come in,' he said. 'Come in.'

In they came, on their best behaviour. 'Now,' he said. 'What can I do for you?'

'Perhaps we'd better introduce ourselves,' said their spokesman. 'I'm Jim Wotherspoon.'

'Let me just get hold of my list.' He rummaged through the papers on his desk, occasionally pausing to read a letter. 'Ah yes. Is that Horace J. Wotherspoon?'

'Yes, but I'm called Jim.'

'Oh, OK.'

'I'm Jackie Parker,' said a young woman who had obviously had a rather tragic experience at the hairdresser's. She was wearing a grey suit which did nothing to conceal the girth of her legs. Grace automatically thought, 'Oh dear.'

'Short for Jacqueline?'

'That's right.' Dr Bastable nodded modestly; such insights into human nature were everyday occurrences to him.

'Trent-Horsley,' said the third member of the group. 'Christopher. Usually called Chris.'

'And I'm Grace Ritchie.'

Just then, there were two slow bangs on the door. They were on the margin of being insolent. Without waiting for an answer, Patrick Slade came in. Everything he did was on the margin of being insolent, but just enough on this side of the margin for him to be able to prop open his eyes with innocent, or insolent, surprise if anyone accused him of anything. He walked slowly across the room, lassoed a chair and sat down. 'Sorry I'm late,' he said as an afterthought, in the voice that was only half awake.

'That's all right,' said Dr Bastable. 'We were just getting to know each other. You must be Patrick Slade. What do they call you?'

Patrick said, with courteous puzzlement, 'They call me Patrick Slade.'

'Well,' said Dr Bastable. 'What about some coffee? It won't take long to boil a kettle. Oh no, I've forgotten to bring some in. But we could go over to the refectory if you like.'

'We left some essays for you,' said Jim Wotherspoon. 'Did you have a chance to look at them?'

'Oh. Yes,' said Dr Bastable. 'I've got them here somewhere. Ah, yes. Now let's see if I can remember your names. Jim, Jackie, Chris, Grace, and Patrick. There you are. They were all jolly good.'

Grace looked at her essay. It had 'B+ Good' written on the bottom. There were no further comments at all. The other four put theirs aside quickly, as if there was nothing to read on them, either.

'Were there any questions?' said Dr Bastable. 'Anything you didn't understand or would like to follow up?'

Jackie Parker turned out to be rather impressive. She had a degree in physiology and a lively mind. She also had to face the fact that most of those present were sitting there thinking, 'Yes, but she's got fat legs.'

Chris Trent-Horsley, though he seemed to know a lot, was beaten by his personality. In earlier life he would have been the class sneak. His face was bright, his eye twinkled with enthusiasm. He scattered names and facts at Dr Bastable's feet like a dog retrieving twigs, giving a snortle of pleasure when Dr Bastable said, 'Quite right.'

These two and Dr Bastable soon left the others behind. Jim Wotherspoon listened without talking. Patrick Slade stretched his legs in front of him, leaned back in his chair and closed his eyes. Grace, who couldn't have told you the difference between an oyster and a species crocus, was anxious to understand. 'What's an aplacophoran?' she asked, interrupting a vigorous exchange. A shell-less marine mollusc, they told her; as its name implies. 'Aplacophorans *are* molluscs,' she noted, 'as evidenced by their reduced radula. NB look up "radula" later.' Then she gave up.

'Now,' said Dr Bastable after forty minutes. 'Is there anything else you'd like to bring up? OK, what shall we do next week?'

'What topics are you covering in your lectures?' asked Trent-Horsley, not only an enthusiast but a bootlicker.

'Well, this afternoon I'm doing molluscs, so you'll be well prepared for that. Next week I'll be doing the arthropod, and the following week we may get on to the fish.'

'Could we do the arthropod?' asked Trent-Horsley. Oh Mummy, could we do the arthropod?

'All right,' said Dr Bastable. 'Problematic aspects of arthropod behaviour. OK. See you next week.'

Patrick Slade filled the room with a death-defying yawn and pulled himself upright in his chair.

'I was just wondering,' he said, and they all sat down again, 'whether all our tutorials are going to be like this.'

'Like what?'

'Are we going to do anything other than the topics covered in your lectures?' He yawned again. 'Interesting though those no doubt are.'

Dr Bastable paused for thought. 'What sort of thing?'

'The human being, perhaps.'

'Ah, well, that's not really my province. That's a bit outside my field. I think we'd best stick to my area, really.'

'Perhaps you could tell us,' said Patrick Slade, 'how your area fits in, as it were, to a degree in human behaviour.'

'It's on the syllabus,' said Dr Bastable. Can't quarrel with the laws of nature. He looked less democratic now.

'Well, that's it then,' said Patrick, and stood up to go. They walked out after him, Jim Wotherspoon, Chris Trent-Horsley and Jackie Parker stopping to say goodbye at the door.

Outside, Chris and Jackie nodded to the others and went off still talking.

'Let's have some coffee,' said Patrick. 'Unless the refectory serves beer.'

Patrick, Jim and Grace had lunch in the refectory, with beer. 'To the squid,' said Patrick, picking up his drink. 'May its reflexes get knotted.'

'Look,' said Grace. 'I didn't come here to do a course on marine biology. I came to do a course on human behaviour.'

'Ah,' said Patrick. 'Look at the syllabus. Can't quarrel with the syllabus. The syllabus says do the squid, we do the squid.'

'But what's it *doing* on the syllabus?'

'I wouldn't look too closely at what it's doing on the syllabus,' said Jim.

'Got to get a good grounding,' said Patrick. 'Can't run before you can walk, can't walk before you can swim, can't swim unless you've got gills, and there you are.'

'You were expecting this, weren't you?' she said to Jim.

'If you look at the MA exams, one of the sections is on animal behaviour.' Grace hadn't dreamed of looking at the MA exams.

'But *why?*'

'You could say it lays a good foundation for the study of humans. A look at our origins, a basis for comparison. It's a point of view.'

'I wish I'd stayed in Oxford,' said Grace.

As they finished their lunch, Patrick stood up. 'I'm off to Senate House to pick up the books. Coming?' he said to Grace.

'It'll be a bit of a rush to get back by three o'clock.'

'Who's getting back by three o'clock?'

'For the lecture on molluscs.'

'I'm not going to a lecture on molluscs. I've done my essay on molluscs. He'll only go over the literature for those who're lucky enough not to be in our group.'

'I think I'd better have a look, all the same,' said Grace. She still felt there was some secret, some key to why this topic was on the syllabus, that Dr Bastable would surely reveal in his first lecture. 'Aren't you coming?' she said to Jim.

'Yes, I'll give it a try.'

In fact, Patrick turned out to be right. In the lecture were nine of the ten MA students and a scattering of others, perhaps from other colleges, perhaps simply sheltering from the rain.

'Ah,' said Dr Bastable, coming in. 'Now I wonder if there's any chalk. Oh dear. Perhaps I'd better get some,' going out. He was gone for a long time, but Grace knew better than to hope that he'd fallen downstairs. 'Ah,' he said, coming back. 'Now I wonder where the board rubber is.' He looked around and went out.

When he eventually got started, he was very cheerful and democratic and kept dropping the chalk. 'This is an Introduction to Animal Behaviour. Today we're going to talk about molluscs,' he said, and wrote MO on the board before the chalk snapped, one piece hitting him on the forehead. 'Oh dear.' He gave up. Gradually, the board became covered with the first syllables of words, which were all he could manage before the chalk broke, and the floor became covered with stepped-on pieces. If this was the Institute blackboard technique, no wonder they had to keep going off to look for more.

Grace had decided that Dr Bastable was not the incompetent twit that he appeared to be. No one could be the incompetent twit that Jeremy Bastable appeared to be. She began to wonder about the problems, evolutionary, physiological or psychological, which had led to this strange behaviour.

By the end of the lecture, she had produced a first draft of her theory. Dr Bastable didn't care. He didn't care what he taught them, he didn't care what they thought of him, he didn't care what they thought. The hesitations, waits for answers, offers of coffee, hunts for chalk and board rubber were simply nature's way of wasting time. Dr Bastable knew his priorities, and helping students wasn't one of them. In the classroom, he was the very opposite of a demagogue. He had negative magnetism.

The hesitations, though, had definite limits. 'Isn't there a homologue in the behaviour of oligochaetes?' asked Trent-Horsley, seeing a chance for a quick bootlick in an utterance that Grace hadn't even bothered to work out the syntax of.

'No. There isn't,' said Dr Bastable with authority and without explanation. He knew his own mind. He just wasn't letting them see any of it. Underneath that waffling exterior, there might well be a potential for discourtesy that would make Lindsey look like a geisha girl.

Andrew rang later. 'How was the tutorial?'

'Fine. Next week we do the acoustics of rabbit hutches.'

'Have you been playing the records?'

'Yes. Maybe they'd sound better in a rabbit hutch.'

'Just keep on listening. You'll soon get the idea.'

'Are you doing anything this evening? Oh hell, you're playing at the George and Dragon.'

'That's right. When you can tell the Everly Brothers from the Beverley Sisters, I'll take you along.'

'When you can tell Monet from Manet, I'll come. Oh well, I'll just have to go out with someone else.'

'You do that. Bye.'

Grace thought for a while, but there was no one she wanted to ring. Neither Fergus nor Rowena had been in touch since the beginning of term. Grace wasn't one for weaving networks: she would be the one who waited for the phone to ring. The pieces of her life from Oxford had been thrown up into the air and hadn't yet fallen into a pattern. The pattern, when it happened, would not be of Grace's making: you wouldn't be able to accuse her of setting it up wrong.

Chapter 5

Andrew's life had always been filled with music. His mother was a great singer from her days in the church choir; Andrew and his sister Jan learned to harmonize at their mother's shoulder as she played the old songs. It was Jan who took to piano lessons, Andrew who, when sent to practise, would look at her sideways and say, 'Oh, Mum.' At thirteen, at a birthday party, he heard a new sort of music; since then, his fingers had scarcely been still.

Before the party, he'd been no more than a classroom acquaintance of the sinister, solitary Rick Hayes. 'Why don't we see any of your friends?' asked Rick's mother. 'Why don't you bring any of them home?' There was a simple answer: Rick didn't have any friends. If he had, he would have wanted to keep them secret. As it was, what he wanted to keep secret was the fact that he didn't have any. 'OK,' he said, 'I'll get a few of them round.'

Six invitations went out, almost at random. Rick couldn't face speaking to those he had chosen, and left notes on their desks. Five boys turned up to nursery tea and Mississippi blues. Rick was not just an enthusiast but a fanatic: he needed those records playing to see him through. Four boys enjoyed the jelly and sausages; and Andrew fell in love. He was not content just to listen to the music. He took it apart and reassembled it. Saturdays, Sundays, evenings, holidays. He wanted to feel the music in his flesh and sinews, to make it part of his soul.

Rick and Andrew became inseparable, swapping names, opinions, records, tapes. Rick's mother had her wish: they were always in each other's houses, annoying the neighbours with piano and guitar. They played at a school dance, which brought them another guitarist and a boy with his own drum kit. All over England, similar groups pecked through the shell, shook wet wings and began to chirp.

Rick was not just a listener but a reader, in the same fanatical mould. Most books he spurned; he read only the literature of the sad, the mad and the bad, the outcasts and sufferers, the exiles and aliens, the youths who snuffed themselves out. He had a whole vision of life. 'Try for

Oxford,' said his form master. Rick, uncompromising, unfolded his vision on the entrance paper. 'Interesting,' said the dons, and let him in.

At Oxford, he began to live out his vision. Missed tutorials, skimped essays, drunken night-scalings of the drainpipe outside his room. 'Quite a character,' said the dons, scenting another Shelley. The more he rattled the bars, the more they said proudly 'Hush!'

This tolerance was more than Rick could bear. His interest in literature began to shrivel; in his need for rejection, music became his refuge: no benevolent don would surely follow him there. He was driven, moreover, to the wilder shores of music, where no blonde, blue-eyed teenager had been before him in her Daddy's borrowed car. His tastes became narrower, his aesthetic merged with an ethic. Many of the songs he had so lovingly mastered he no longer wanted to play.

Rick went to the blues for a sort of comradeship. He wanted songs that echoed back to him the way he felt. He wanted the company of midnight exiles in smoky rooms, spilt whisky on rough-grained tables, bottle blondes in tight red satin lounging at the bar. For him, authenticity was important. He didn't think it was possible to fake the blues.

Andrew was not a purist. He liked invention, imagination: the varieties of rock music filled him with delight. He loved blues; he loved gospel: a gospel song was no good to Rick because of the note of hope. But authenticity wasn't everything to Andrew. He also loved rock and roll. A rock and roll song is unashamedly a performance, directed at an audience: there's not the feeling you get with blues, that the song would have gone on just the same if the audience weren't there. Andrew didn't appreciate the music less because the man who wrote the high-school songs was no longer a teenager, wouldn't even have been admitted to the same school as the sweet little rock and rollers he helped to create. Not every blues singer has to walk the country roads.

Andrew relished idiosyncrasy; he had a parodist's eye for oddities of performances or genres. Each new girl group, each stylistic innovation was to him a source of pleasure. The sophisticate faking innocence, the innocent faking sophistication, the shallow faking deep emotion: he was brimful of affection for them all. As Rick's tastes narrowed, Andrew's expanded. By the end of their time in Oxford, every tide was carrying them further apart. Rick didn't argue; just grew increasingly taciturn. He was becoming an outcast within the group.

The records Andrew had lent Grace were like a diary of his life. Here were the Mississippi shouters and boogie-woogie pianists of his thirteen-year-old days, the sweet little rock and rollers whose rhythm fitted so well to his own heartbeat, the car racers, the riders on trains and buses, the young men who fell for the toss of a head, the blink of an eye, who sang to cheer themselves up when their girls walked out. Grace played them, replayed them, did her best to come to terms with them. She was prepared to try.

The music became part of Grace's day. She would stack the records on the turntable when she got home; she and Andrew would see a film, or eat round the corner in Camden Town, then sit and listen with the lights down low. The songs were like a family to Andrew: he was anxious for Grace to love them. 'See?' he'd say, jumping the needle from track to track. 'Listen to this one. See?'

What struck Grace first about Andrew's records was that all of them were songs: sung by people whose voices had clearly not been trained, whose quirks and idiosyncrasies had not been ironed out. She was attracted by the attitude of the singers. The songs were knockdown, self-mocking, unpretentious: the singers sang the way they spoke. She had liked the image, in Greece, of the sweet old lady in racing sneakers, though there was no one to match her on Andrew's records; perhaps he had made her up? But the attitude she reflected, the feeling she brought to mind, were everywhere in the songs. Every stereotype was subverted, every pose was mocked. The love songs were funny; the patriotic songs were funny; even the sad songs were funny. I hope your teeth fall out, your pet dog dies, your car gets wrecked, your records break, your dress gets torn, but I'm not angry, just forlorn.

Wit was important to Grace. She saw it as a form of gallantry: it put grief in its place. What she thought of as the height of courage was the joke cracked on the steps of the guillotine. To master fear and anger and hopelessness and dread, trump them with laughter, would always seem to her the bravest thing.

Trying to dance to Andrew's records, she noticed something else that pleased her. These songs were the very antithesis of a military march. They didn't encourage the measured step: ONE two, ONE two. If you tried to do a military march, the beat would land between your steps and you'd end up hopping and skipping. In martial music, the rhythm is like a straitjacket, holding the group together. In a rock song, the beats are beacons, enabling wandering humans to keep each other in sight. In fact, in a rock song even the beacons are rebellious: every other beat is light or missing; every other beacon is absent without leave.

111

Grace played the records in the morning as she dressed: they sent her off to the Institute in just the wrong frame of mind. Dr Bastable's classes got on, as threatened, to the arthropod. It's perhaps not generally known that arthropods can be trained. Put an ant or crayfish in a maze; give it an electric shock when it takes a wrong turning; and after a few hundred volts it'll be coming round to your point of view. In fact, it'll be coming round to your point of view even if you've taken the precaution of removing its brain. It's amazing what an insect can do with half its nervous system on the cutting room floor. An ant will go on sucking honey with its whole abdomen removed. A bee will continue to search for food when half its head's gone missing. Removal of the entire head prevents certain females from mating; but they'll go on laying eggs if you cut off their thorax and legs, though the textbook notes that these are no longer deposited in neat rows.

'It's a bit revolting. Don't you think?' said Grace one evening to Andrew. But he couldn't see any harm in treating insects as animated circuit diagrams. 'They don't feel pain, do they?' he said.

There wasn't much mention of pain on Grace's reading list. At that time, it was considered unscientific to attribute feelings to animals: just because an animal's writhing and screaming, it doesn't *prove* it's in pain. Most insects don't writhe and scream in any case, the textbooks added reassuringly: as witness the ant that goes on eating honey while its body is cut to pieces around it. Just because you're not writhing and screaming, it doesn't prove you're *not* in pain, thought Grace.

At the Institute, the new students were beginning to find their feet; unlike those insects that had passed through the experimenters' hands. Grace's days began to fall into a pattern; her room in Camden Town began to seem like home. Rowena rang, and they had supper one evening. Rowena had been offered a traineeship at the BBC; Fergus was taking a course in art history; Mark was frightfully busy in the diplomatic service: all flexing their fingers to pick up the reins. They had done with academic life, they had left their natal waters and were heading for the sea.

Grace began to look forward to late Sundays with Andrew, when the first draft of her essay was finished and she could join the bodies in the King's Cross basement lounging around. There was something relaxing about the basement. It didn't aspire to be civilized; it was the very opposite of a salon. No one seemed to have any expectations of anyone. If someone spoke, you didn't have to listen; if you wanted coffee, you went off and made it; even Davy became less solicitous as he passed through the door.

'What are you doing on Wednesday evening?' Andrew asked one day as he walked her home.

'Wednesday?' They often met on Wednesdays. 'Nothing that I know of.'

'Come to the Newt and hear us play.'

The Newt was the George and Dragon. The pub sign showed a large St George and a rather puny dragon. 'Oh look, a newt,' said Bob when he first saw it; so they called it the George and Newt.

'You've been promoted,' said Grace.

'Well, the previous incumbents got sacked for fighting. One of them tried to stuff the piano up the lead singer's nose.'

'Is that the sort of place I want to go to?'

'You have to enjoy yourself sometimes, you know.'

The George and Dragon was a high street pub in Crouch End. Grace went with Lindsey, who had been there before. 'How's the secretarial course?' asked Grace on top of the bus.

'I finish at Christmas. Graduation they call it, can you imagine? First-class honours in envelope addressing with a distinction in business envelopes. Then they turf you out with a year's supply of Tippex and you're on your own. We're doing practice interviews now. "What are your hobbies, Miss er?" "What's that to do with you?" "No, Linda, they often ask you that. Haven't you got a nice hobby you could mention?" "Bat breeding." "That's not very nice, Linda, we're only trying to help." "I'm not *applying* for a job as a secretary, you silly old ratbag. What do you think they're going to say on the *Daily Mirror* when I tell them I spend my evenings crocheting doilies?" "There's no call to be unpleasant, Linda, even the editor of the *Daily Mirror* might like a doily to put under his flower vase." God help me, I can't wait to get out.'

Upstairs at the George and Dragon, Andrew's group were already playing. As Grace came in, Andrew gave her a little smile. The place was more informal than she'd expected: just a bare room with a platform at one end and tables round the edge. 'I'll get drinks,' said Lindsey, and went to the bar.

Grace sat down at an empty table away from the band, frosty faced to ward off nudges and smirks. They were playing a song she recognized, the one about the boy who used to sit on the river bank making the fishes jump and the river captains honk in rhythm to the sound of

113

his guitar. Andrew played well, now reproducing the wonderful floating piano that went off on its own devices, leaving the voice behind. He was not what you'd call a performer: his concern was not with how he looked to an audience, but with something more intangible. As he sang, his gaze seemed to be turned inward. If he was courting anything, it was the music in his head.

The song ended, and a couple near the stage began to talk to him. Bob climbed out from behind his drums. Lindsey came back with the drinks. 'Bit far away, aren't we? Can't see anything from here.'

'Hey,' said Bob, like a mother cat dropping a kitten. 'This is Sherry. Look after her, will you?' and was gone.

Sherry, thought Grace. How can anyone be called Sherry? These are my three children, Sherry, Rum and Vodka Martini. There was no denying, though, that Sherry was lovely: her arrival had reoriented the room. Chairs and glasses repositioned themselves, backs of heads turned into profiles, profiles into faces, as if the room were full of flowers and the sun had just been moved. Sherry had fair hair, brown eyes, and a low-necked sleeveless knitted top. Naturally fair hair; she was not heavily made up. When she stood, she didn't pose; when she looked, she didn't pout. You couldn't accuse her of anything, except perhaps the sleeveless knitted top. Try as hard as you might.

'Whoo, I'm knackered,' she said sitting down, reorienting all the faces again. Grace waited for Lindsey, who was technically the hostess, to reply. Lindsey gulped some beer and began to count her change. Sherry didn't mind. 'It's all that dancing on top of standing up all day.'

'Might as well be in the next room,' said Lindsey, ferreting in her handbag.

'What do you do?' asked Grace.

'Hairdressing. That's how I met Bob.'

They looked at Bob behind the drums. The song was one of the old Mississippi shouters. Rick, who had previously looked sour, was singing and playing with ferocious intensity; Bob was beaming around. Joy, pain, Memphis, Chicago, all filled Bob with boundless, bouncing goodwill.

'You work at Goldilocks?' said Lindsey, cuffing her purse into place and shutting her handbag. 'Must be some good stories there.'

Goldilocks was one of the four or five best-known hairdressers in London. 'Hair by Kevin at Goldilocks,' you would see if you bothered to read the details under the photographs in the fashion magazines. To go to Goldilocks was a guarantee of quality, like having a Chelsea address. Grace hated the hairdresser's. She thought she looked awful with wet hair, and shrank from having to look at herself in the mirror while the assistants tittered behind her. But you had to respect someone who had tittering rights at Goldilocks.

'Well, I've only just started. It's murder on the legs. Most evenings, I just want to go home and put my feet up.' She put her feet on a vacant chair and began to rub her legs. There was no calculation behind it. Her legs were tired: she rubbed; smiling at Grace as if it went without saying that Grace would have done the same. This was too much for one of the nudgers who, propelled by a waft of giggles, came over with a strut and a shamble to ask her to dance.

Sherry was glad to accept. She smiled and stood up, making the fishes jump and the chairs squeak in rhythm. She didn't really dance, just became a sort of distillate of herself. She breathed in and straightened her spine, as if her lungs were full of a precious liquid. She raised her arms and began to do a kind of shimmy, hips and shoulders rotating around the axis of her spine, while her partner, torn between embarrassment and wonder, looked round to grin at his friends. Watching, Grace and Lindsey caught sight of each other's expressions and exchanged a guilty smile.

Sherry came back at the end of each dance, but was always snapped up again. 'I wouldn't mind a bit of a stomp myself,' said Lindsey. 'At least I might get close enough to hear the band.' Her wish was granted as someone hopeful of another shimmy took her away. It's pretty grim to be left a wallflower, publicly labelled the least attractive of the bunch. They prefer Lindsey to me? thought Grace. Ridiculous. 'Would you care to dance?' said someone eventually, and Grace stood up, relieved.

You feel on these occasions like a bar of chocolate in a bran tub, wondering who's going to pull you out. Blind hands reach down, feel, fail to fancy and move on. Then someone decides to take a gamble, and out you come to discover your fate. Grace's was a courteous man with greasy hair and the physique and flexibility of a stick. 'Do you come here often?' he asked.

'This is my first time.'

'I don't get out much either.' When he danced, she began to understand why.

He didn't have a style of dancing, just hopped occasionally from foot to foot. Though the hops were separated by random intervals, they never coincided with a beat. Why did he dance? His face was closed, his hops were earnest; you couldn't imagine he was enjoying himself. He was like those male spiders who attract a mate by waving their legs.

There seem to be no innate aesthetics of leg-waving: one waving leg is as good as another to the female spider. The same is not true of humans, as Grace's companion was about to discover. The song ended, shortly followed by his penultimate hop. 'Would you like to come to the pictures tomorrow?' he added. And that, of course, was why he danced.

'I'm afraid I'm rather busy,' said Grace, outraged that he should consider her a possible life partner.

'Next week, then.' It hadn't occurred to him that she might want to refuse.

There was a roll on the drums, a crash on the guitars, and Andrew announced, 'That's it for now, folks. We'll take a break.'

'I'm sorry,' said Grace. 'I must get back to my friends.'

Andrew caught up with her as she reached her seat. 'Hello, Grace. Haven't seen you dancing much.'

'I was waiting for the music to start.'

'How would you know if it did? I'm dying for a drink.' He went off downstairs.

'Where's Davy?' asked Lindsey, having eaten her partner.

'In the bar, I think.'

'Look, I've got a splitting headache. Can you tell him I've gone home?'

'Will you be all right? Shall I come with you?'

'You stay where you are. It would break old Andrew's heart if you walked out on your first evening.'

'He's hardly noticed I'm even here.'

'Oh, he's just showing you how famous he is. They all come running back when the last fan's gone home.'

Fans. Andrew couldn't have fans. Could he? As Lindsey left, Sherry returned, still full of the precious liquid. 'I'm boiled.' She fanned herself, pulling the knitted top away from her skin. 'Gone quiet all of a sudden, hasn't it?'

'If I'd known it would be this quiet I'd have brought some knitting,' said Grace.

'Oh, do you knit? I knitted this top. Didn't take long. Well, there's not much of it, is there?' There's more of you than there is of it, thought Grace. 'My mum says there's more of me than there is of it. I tell her she's jealous.'

'Where *is* everyone?' said Grace.

Bob bounced up and patted Sherry's shoulder. 'Isn't she wonderful?

I nearly fell off my perch when she walked in. There I was, doing some old dowager's hair. Snip, I went, and half the old dear's hair fell off. "Short cuts are all the rage this year," I bellowed in her good ear, and snipped off the other side. "I'll just put your curlers in and you'll look a treat." Then I went and forgot her in the dryer, and she came out looking like a golliwog. "I don't know what to think. I'm going to the Palace tomorrow," she said. "You'll be a knockout," I said. "Stick your hat on over it and they'll never know the difference." "Well, if it's the fashion," she said, and tottered off quite happy.'

'I'm not letting you do my hair,' said Sherry.

'Your hair doesn't need doing,' said Bob. 'Hey. What's happened to Lindsey?'

'Gone home,' said Grace. 'She's got a headache.'

'Davy, you've been jilted,' shouted Bob, and every female ear in the room pricked up. Davy was the young master of the group, the one the village girls dream of as they haul in the coal. He kept his dignity by holding himself a little distant from the fun, smiling his handsome smile, a few locks of fringe falling gracefully over his forehead as he strolled around the stage, bending the occasional knee, leaning the occasional lean to one side or another as the beat went on. While Rick frowned and threatened and wrestled his guitar, Davy did nothing that would disarrange his face. In the songs of sadness or frustrated passion, he twinkled his eyes to show that he was only pretending, really. He was the rock musician you could take home to mother knowing she'd love him too.

Davy elbowed the fans aside: 'What's happened to Lindsey?' he said to Grace.

'She asked me to tell you she was tired and going home.'

'She's not ill is she? How was she looking?'

About as awful as she usually does. 'I think she had a bit of a headache.'

'Oh dear.' He really looked worried. 'Poor lamb. I'll pop round afterwards and see how she is.'

At odd moments in the remainder of the evening, Grace found herself pondering an intractable problem: what on earth was a monster like Lindsey doing with a monster like Davy?

Andrew came back at last. He put down his beer mug and smiled at Sherry. 'You're not drinking. Can I get you something?'

'Yes, would you like some sherry, Sherry?' said Bob.

She laughed good-naturedly, though the joke could not have been

117

new. She was an awfully nice girl. The world smiled at her and she smiled right back. 'I don't drink, thanks. I don't like the taste.'

Grace wasn't feeling good-natured. Vanity hurt by her lucky-dip partner, she'd thought when the interval was announced that Andrew would come running to claim her, proving she was no wallflower but an incognito princess. Instead he'd run straight to the bar. Now he seemed more interested in Sherry. Grace began to feel she might have a headache coming on.

'Rick,' shouted Andrew. Rick looked round, cigarette dangling. 'Must talk to Rick,' and left.

After the interval, Andrew made an announcement, speaking to the audience, as always, as if they were friends. 'We've got some new songs tonight. Well, we've had them for a few months, but Rick wouldn't let us play them before. Davy brought them back from California.' Davy looked modestly down – it was nothing, really, just a few screen tests. 'I think this music's really great; let's see if you agree.'

None of Andrew's records had been like this. The songs were unusual in subject matter: the object of the passions was less likely to be a girl than a beach, a breaker or a car. The music was crisp, clean-cut; no darkness lurked beneath the surface. The songs were sung in college-boy harmonies with a falsetto wail, as by an American football squad just over the edge of madness. The first, 'Little Board of Mine', appeared to be a close-harmony hymn to a surfboard ('I get up in the morning and you're waiting for me; when we're riding on the breakers you're so wild and free.') The second, Grace recognized immediately: it was the sweet old lady in racing sneakers. 'That,' said Andrew, 'is a whole new genre of song. I'm writing one myself at the moment, called "Put on Your Old Grey Bonnet (and Let's Stomp)".'

There was no doubt about the audience's reaction. By now nearly everyone was dancing; Sherry got even more knackered; Grace's partner came back for another try. 'Sorry, I don't feel like dancing,' she said, condemning herself to sit still for the rest of the evening: you can't hurt someone's feelings just because he hops.

Later, the band played some blues. Rick stopped staring at the ceiling, and bent with love and fury over his guitar. Grace, who now knew the originals, felt sorry for Andrew. Those deep, dark songs didn't really suit him. He tried hard, but he sounded like a little girl in lipstick and her mother's high heels.

The evening ended with a return to rock and roll. Rick left, guitar strings still vibrating, for a club that played his sort of music. Davy left for Lindsey's as soon as the last fan had gone home. Grace, Sherry, Andrew and Bob loaded the equipment into the van and drove back to King's Cross.

Sherry took the basement rather well. She pulled a sweater over the knitted top, shook out her hair, curled her feet up on the divan and said 'Well.' Well, where's the apron and I'll run you up a nice little soufflé. Well, where's the paint stripper and we'll soon have this place looking shipshape.

'Well, what did you think of it?' asked Bob, hurdling a tin trunk in his exuberance. 'Aren't we a knockout?' Andrew, who was pouring whisky, looked round.

'It was most enjoyable,' said Grace.

'Mimsy mimsy, it was most enjoyahable,' said Bob. 'We don't often hear such music back at the Palace.'

'Shut up, Bob,' said Andrew. 'She's doing her best with the limited powers of expression God gave her. We mustn't mock those who are less fortunate than ourselves.'

'Everyone's less fortunate than yourselves,' said Grace. 'You don't have to listen to yourselves playing.'

'It was great,' said Sherry. 'You've got the makings of a really nice little act.'

'See,' said Andrew.

'Except for the clothes.'

'Pardon?'

'Well, what are you trying to look like?'

'You mean they wear those clothes voluntarily?' said Grace.

'You're a bit of a mish-mash, aren't you? There's Davy in his cravat and denims, Rick in his leather jacket, Andrew in his fancy colours and Bob in his suit and tie. Whatever you sing, one of you's going to end up looking wrong. You can't sing surfing songs in drainpipe trousers and a bootlace tie, now can you? It'd look silly.'

'It'd look pretty silly even if they weren't singing,' said Grace.

'Shut up a minute, Grace, we're trying to think.'

No one understands me, thought Grace.

'So I'd put in a bit of work on that if I were you.'

'Isn't she wonderful?' said Bob.

Grace kicked a flea out of the way and stood up.

'You're not going, Grace,' said Andrew. 'Please don't go. We'll be finished in a minute.' Grace hesitated, then sat down.

119

Sherry didn't stay long. 'I must get back. My mum's probably lying awake listening for the door.'

'What's the matter?' said Andrew when Sherry and Bob had gone. 'What's wrong?'

'Nothing. I'm just a bit tired. I think I'd better go home.'

'You know what I've been thinking about all week? You know what I thought might happen this evening? That you'd really enjoy yourself. You'd tell me how much you liked the music. You'd come back here feeling all affectionate. And you'd stay with me tonight.'

Grace hadn't been expecting this. It was out of the question; the problem was to know why. Forgotten my pyjamas? No toothbrush? Allergic to fleas? Close relative gravely ill? Not allowed out after midnight?

'I can't.'

'Why not?'

'I just can't.'

'You're going to have to make up your mind, you know. We can't go on like this for ever.'

'Oh well, that's it then.'

'Grace.'

'Look. I never asked you to follow me around. If you'd just go away and leave me in peace we'd all be very happy.'

'It's just an accident that you've been seeing me all these months.'

'I'm quite happy to see you.'

'Well, if we go on like this we're never going to get to know each other at all. You never tell me anything unless I ask. You never do anything unless I suggest it first. I never know what you're thinking. I never know what you're feeling. It's a struggle every step of the way.'

'I don't see why you bother, then,' said Grace in her swallowed voice.

'Because I thought it was worth it. I was sure you were struggling to get out just as hard as I was struggling to get in. I don't want to force you into things against your will. I mean, if you really are hating this, perhaps we'd better call it a day.'

Never to sit around on Sundays reading the papers. Left to the company of the stickleback and the squid. Never to have somewhere she almost belonged. 'I have been trying.'

'Try some more.'

The victim stands on the roof of the burning house, surrounded by smoke, not exactly happy, but fairly sure that he can make it through. Down below stands someone with a safety net. 'Come on. I'll catch you. Jump.' Back comes the strangled cry. 'I'm all right up here.' 'You'll be better off down here. Come on. Trust me. Jump.' The victim's mutilated body is buried next week.

Grace edged cautiously towards the parapet to have a closer look. 'What exactly do you want me to do?'

'You could stop asking me what exactly I want you to do. Why not develop a want or two of your own? Suppose you'd actually asked to come and hear me play one night, instead of having to be dragged along. Suppose you'd said one evening, "Andrew, I don't want to go home." '

'You ought to know by now that's not the sort of thing I do.'

'You could change.'

'If you want a different person, why not go out and find a different person?'

'I don't want a different person. I just want a bit more of you.'

'You can't just decide to fall in love,' said Grace. 'It has to happen naturally.'

'I know. All I'm saying is, don't run away. Look at me. I'm your friend. I care for you.'

There seemed to be a safety net down there, thought Grace, peering over the edge.

'I don't want to rush into anything.'

'I don't think your worst enemy would accuse you of that.'

Grace took a deep breath and moved an inch forward. A small step for a human being, a giant leap for Grace. 'Well, it's getting late. It's a bore to have to walk home. Could I sleep on your couch?'

'Good try, but think of my reputation. What's Bob going to say when he comes in? Look, I tell you what. You come and sleep in my room, and I'll pretend to be a perfect gentleman. You'll hardly even know I'm there.'

Grace hesitated. 'Well, all right.'

Grace had never been in Andrew's room. It contained a piano, a gas fire, a chair, a mattress, a table and a bookcase. He must have tidied it, because all the papers were in piles. The floor was lino; the curtain was a piece of sacking pinned to a rail. Grace borrowed a shirt and changed in a bathroom which Andrew hadn't thought to tidy. When she came back, he was already in bed.

'You know what this reminds me of?' he said. 'One of those 1930's comedies where the hero and heroine are trapped in the same hotel room for the night and he ends up sleeping in the bath.'

'If you slept in that bath you'd get typhoid,' said Grace.

'Now you just lie there and relax, and I'll tell you a bedtime story. Once there was a beautiful girl called Grace, who was so poor she couldn't afford any clothes. But all the townsfolk loved her because she sang as she went about her chores. One day a handsome prince came riding by and said, "Do not despair. For if you come with me, I will lend you a shirt of the finest lawn, and you will never need to go naked again." And all the townsfolk said, "This man must be out of his mind," and stoned him to death.'

'What is this, the Arabian nights?'

'Only a thousand more stories and we'll be able to get some sleep.'

He kissed her, noted the surfboard-like quality of her response, sighed, and turned his back.

It was a long night. At first Grace lay huddled, sidearms at the ready, ears flapping at every move. Occasionally he would give a plaintive sigh, which as time went by turned into a plaintive snore. He was asleep. This was outrageous. The host had fallen asleep.

Later, someone came creaking into the flat. She could see the light under the door, hear the occasional swallowed curse as he tripped over an ashtray. Then the light went out and the night returned.

Andrew was not a peaceful sleeper. There seemed to be a method in his movements: each turn brought him fresh territory. He approached Grace like the tide moving across the sand: first a knee lapped against her leg, then a hand washed over her back, then he was up against her, snuggling his head against her neck. She retreated; he followed. She spent some time hanging over the edge of the bed. Passive resistance exhausted, she tried to divert him into other channels with furtive prods. At the third prod, he was awake.

'Grace,' he whispered, engulfing her completely.

'Go to sleep,' she said, but gently. Etiquette forbade her to mention that she was about to fall out of bed. Gradually his breathing became slower, his grip on her shoulder loosened and the tide began to go out. Sighing (or snoring) gently, he turned away. Grace dozed off again, listening to the lorries squeal up and down above her head, unloading their stolen goods.

In the morning, she woke to find him crawling out of bed. He tiptoed out of the room with big, echoing steps. She opened her eyes to see the pattern of sun against bars on the sacking hung over the window. When he came back, he brought two mugs of coffee, great rough beakers giving off steam. He unhooked the sacking from the window so that the pattern of the window-bars was transferred to the floor.

'I was going to wake you with a kiss,' he said. 'But at least I've brought you breakfast in bed. Now I come to think of it, if I'd woken you with a kiss you'd probably have screamed the place down.'

'Thank you for the coffee.'

'Can I come in beside you? My toes are dropping off.'

They propped themselves against the wall, and warmed their hands on the coffee. Outside, the first record of the morning plopped on to the turntable; music came filtering through the cracks in the door.

'Would you like something to eat?' said Andrew. 'There's some bread. I could scrape the fur off for you. Or boil it.'

'Perhaps I'll wait,' said Grace.

The dust drifted around in the shaft of sun, stirred up by their breaths. Grace began to think about how to get out without being seen. Disguise herself with mop and brush? Wait till nightfall and fuse the lights? Saw through the window-bars and chin herself up to the street? There was a loud throat-clearing outside and a gentle tap-tap-tap at the door. 'Come in,' said Andrew. The door creaked open; Bob and the music rushed in.

'Look,' said Bob. 'Hello, Grace. Andrew, can you lend me five quid till Friday? I thought I was going to have to push the van home last night. Sherry lives half-way to Scotland.'

Andrew climbed out of bed. Grace snatched the blankets back. 'Here, my man,' said Andrew. 'Don't spend it all at once.'

'At least I earn mine. Late for work. See you. Bye.'

'I'd better get up,' said Grace. 'Unless you're planning to invite any more friends and neighbours in. Have you got a dressing gown?'

'There's no one here except you and me.'

'I'm cold.'

'No comment.' He wrapped his dressing gown round her shoulders. 'That's how I'll always remember you. Beautiful but cold.'

Grace dressed in the freezing bathroom, and came back to find Andrew sitting at the piano.

'There goes Grace setting off to town
In her fur-lined boots and her dressing gown
Mittens, scarf and a little frown
All topped off with an eiderdown.'

'That's me trying to keep warm in your bathroom,' said Grace.

'Oh, we only use that in summer.'

'See you next June, then.'

'Do you really have to go?'

'I've got an essay to write.'

'But I'll see you on Sunday?'

Pause.

'Yes.'

Grace walked home (in her fur-lined boots and dressing gown). She ran a bath, changed her clothes, put on a record and made some more coffee. The window looked bare without bars.

She worked on her essay until Sunday. She had to redeem herself: the last one had come back marked 'C+ Bad'. It was all Kip Sullivan's fault. 'This is a course on language,' he'd announced in his first lecture. 'Now I don't suppose many of you have studied language before, and you're probably wondering why you have to start now. My job is to convince you that the study of language is worthwhile.' You could see that doing something worthwhile was important to him. He was not one of those patient teachers who start from basics and inch their way forward; he set off from the basics in racing sneakers, and was not too happy when asked to slow down. 'I already explained that,' 'We did that last week,' he would say, tossing the chalk in his hand.

'The reason I'm interested in language,' he told them, 'is because I'm interested in the mind. That, I might say, is an unfashionable position. Most psychologists these days will tell you that minds can't be studied scientifically. You can't measure them; all you can see is behaviour. So why not forget about minds and just study behaviour instead?

'I'd answer that question with another. What makes you think that *behaviour* can be studied scientifically? Behaviour is complicated; too many things affect it. Trying to produce a theory of behaviour is like trying to produce a theory of my grandma's rummage bag. You can't have a theory of mess.

'So when someone tells me he's studying human behaviour, I become suspicious. The first thing I ask myself is what he's leaving out. One thing most psychologists leave out is the humans. It's easier to study animals; so they study animals instead. Another thing they leave out is the mind. You may be under the impression that your thoughts and feelings affect the way you behave. Not so, these people will tell you.

Your behaviour is shaped by external events: rewards and punishments, food and electric shocks; like a rat learning to run a maze. You're just a bunch of senses, glands and electrical circuits waiting for someone to drive you. You only *think* you have a mind.

'And the third thing they leave out is the environment. They breed their animals in the laboratory, teach them a bunch of tricks, and then come out and tell the world that animal behaviour is just a bunch of tricks. If they looked at animals in their natural habitats, they might get a rather different picture. That's what ethologists do. What ethologists have shown us is that animals live largely by instinct. If you read most current textbooks on psychology, you'd hardly know that instincts exist.

'Which brings me back to language. Most psychologists will tell you that learning a language is a matter of training. On the other hand, most psychologists have never really looked at language at all. Now the fact is that that the more you look at language, the more you realize that training hardly comes into it. Speaking seems to be more like an instinct; only this time we're talking about a *mental* instinct. If that's true, then the whole of current psychology needs rethinking. And that's why I think the study of language is worthwhile.'

Grace liked listening to Kip Sullivan. The world as he saw it was somehow exciting, full of hope. Grace lived on hope: sometimes on hope against hope; but it's hard to keep your spirits up when people tell you cheerfully that you're just another ant or crayfish setting off on the maze of life. Grace was weary of being told that language was a social phenomenon, shaped by the group. She *hated* the thought of being shaped by the group. Kip Sullivan was saying she needn't worry: the group can affect the hairstyle of language, but it can't affect the bones.

That, it seemed to her, was what Kip Sullivan wanted to get at: the bones of language, the bones of the mind. It offended him to think of humans as dumb animals – it offended him even to think of animals as dumb animals – driven by prods and goads, by hand-me-down habits that could vary without limit. For him, the bones of language were not unlike the rhythm in rock music: they imposed a basic structure, resistant to whim or outside influence, and set you free to wander. These ideas struck a chord in Grace.

They struck no chord in Patrick. Though he went on attending Kip Sullivan's lectures, he sat through them with his eyebrows raised, as if he knew exactly where they were heading and why you couldn't get there from here. Not that he ever said so outright: he had probably never said anything outright in his life; but you could tell it from the way he smiled. One day when Kip was lecturing, a bird flew against the window. 'It instinctively wants to learn a language,' said Patrick. Kip laughed with the rest, but he tossed the chalk in his hand.

Grace went away and read some ethology. Here she met animals who were recognizably human, who chirped and courted, chased and quarrelled, raised children, sickened and died. Animals, she saw, were slaves of passion, though not in a way she'd quite expected: fear is a passion too. Fear increases with the distance from home. Approach a stickleback on its doorstep and you'll be ripped to shreds by a ravening monster; approach it when it's far from home and it'll slink off belly down in the mud. Courtship can be a desperate business, two frightened souls stepping forwards and backwards, swept by contradictory emotions, unable to advance or retreat.

When conflicting emotions are equally balanced, an animal often behaves quite strangely: a bird torn between fight and flight will give up and start grooming itself; a turkey cock will break off a quarrel to scratch for food in the sand. Ethologists call this displacement behaviour. It's very widely found in courtship. It's even been claimed to exist in humans: scratching the ear, smoothing the skirt, stroking the beard or moustache in situations of embarrassment or conflict. Nonsense, thought Grace, flicking back her hair.

She enjoyed her essay on the fish. Abandoning Dr Bastable's reading list, she wrote on displacement behaviour in the stickleback. It seemed to her an acceptable way forward: even the ethologists seemed more human; she found no phrases such as 'with the head removed'. She handed the essay in well pleased, feeling she'd exercised both her mind and her independence. It came back with the mark C+ and the comment, 'I think you got blown a bit off course!'

Grace took no part in that day's tutorial. She sat blank-faced beside Patrick, who chose a moment when Dr Bastable was comparing the respiratory systems of dogfish and trout to yawn, stretch out his legs, clasp his hands over his stomach and close his eyes. After tutorials, there was now an established routine: Jackie Parker and Chris Trent-Horsley would nod and leave Patrick, Jim and Grace to go off to lunch. 'Goodbye,' they said to Dr Bastable. 'Most stimulating,' said Patrick as he shut the door.

Jim dropped his briefcase on the stairs; as they bent for the scattered papers, Patrick became quite lively. He snatched Jim's essay and backed away. 'What did you get, then, Wothers? B+ Good?' He turned it over. 'A— Very Good. Aah.'

Jim took the essay back smiling. Horseplay held no fears for the man who had organized tutorials with Dr Bastable.

'Who's a good boy, then?' said Patrick. 'Been fraternizing with teacher?'

'No, I just read some papers he's written. He's interested in mazes; so last week I gave him maze-learning in ants, this week I gave him maze-learning in fish.'

'Maze-learning,' said Grace. 'What's that got to do with human behaviour?'

'Not a lot, unless you happen to have been born in Hampton Court.'

'Then why on earth is he teaching us?'

'That's the wrong question,' said Patrick. 'All you really need to know is whether he's got gills.'

They were now researching the frog. Plenty on Dr Bastable's reading list to avert the eyes from. One group of experimenters impaled a fly in the centre of a ring of needles and allowed a frog to tear its jaw to pieces by helplessly lunging and snapping at it. This tells us that fly-catching in frogs is a reflex. It tells us a certain amount about humans, too.

Grace put the reading list aside and wrote her essay on communication in the frog. Frogs communicate by singing. They have a huge range of calls: mating calls, warning calls, distress calls, territorial calls, 'release me' calls and calls conveying comments on the weather. Enough to get one through the average day. Singing plays a vital role in courtship. Frogs congregate to breed, brought together by the song of the males. The different species recognize each other by differences in their song: in some species, the males simply grab at anything that moves and might be female; others have more sophisticated courtship aids. In tree frogs, for example, the ears of male and female are differently tuned. When a male sings, other males hear only the aggressive, keep-your-distance notes; females hear only the seductive, come-and-get-me part, and approach the males without waiting to be asked. The more fool they, thought Grace.

Grace couldn't bear the mindlessness of courtship. Blind nature, latching on to anything that moves; blind memory, latching on to accidents of looks. She hated men who said they liked redheads, brunettes, long-limbed beauties, women with a bit of flesh on them. If you're going to love someone for belonging to a certain category, you might as well be a frog.

On Sunday she was deep in tadpole biology when Andrew rang. 'It's a beautiful day. Let's go for a walk. I'll come and pick you up. Don't forget your mittens.'

He arrived full of affection. Grace, having made a concession, was on her dignity, like a soldier covering up a misstep in the march.

'Hello, beloved, how's the essay?'

'Fine.' Ignoring his movement towards her, she retreated to her desk.

'It's beautiful outside. Let's go and feed the ducks.'

No smile, no lightening of the face as she marked the place in her book and picked up her coat. She really knew how to kill a mood.

They went into Regent's Park, along the river, under the bare trees and the yellow sky. What had she done since Wednesday? he asked.

Grace had had supper with Fergus, lunch with Jim and Patrick, and coffee with Patrick on Saturday when they met to exchange books. She had listened to Andrew's records, read a novel, bought a fashion magazine; and worked as hard as she always did, to hold the world in place. 'Not much.'

Affection ebbing, he shored himself up with music. 'Surf surf surf,' he sang under his breath as the river rippled brown beside them. 'I think I'll go to California this summer. Learn how to surf. How would you be able to resist me then?'

Grace hadn't thought of herself as resisting him. She was a scarlet woman who'd spent all night with him. How much more did he want? 'Well, I suppose there's just something resistible about you.'

'Oh, Grace.' He slowed, then stopped. 'Nothing really changes, does it?'

Not if I can help it. 'Look, I have been trying.'

'Well, you have and you haven't. You've done just enough to keep things going, but never enough for me to be sure you really meant to. If anyone asked, you could always have said, "Oh, he's the one who wants it, not me."'

This was quite accurate. Grace, unused to being fathomed, stared at a passing duck.

'Please don't let's quarrel,' she said. 'I was going to tell you how much I liked the music on Wednesday. I did enjoy it, you know.'

'If you did, why didn't you say so?' They were standing still, looking ahead along the way they were to go.

'I don't know. It never seemed the right moment. I didn't want to say it with all those people around.'

From Grace, this seemed plausible enough, though he didn't understand it. 'Why couldn't you say it? Even out of politeness?'

Her reaction had been based on feeling, not thought. 'I did start to say I liked it, and Bob laughed his head off.'

'That's true.'

The storm seemed to have passed. He took her arm and they walked on, the ducks grunting beside them.

'Why doesn't Rick like surfing music?' she asked, when they'd gone some way in silence.

'Too frivolous. He thinks we should only sing about the fundamentals, and however you look at it, those don't include surfing and cars.'

'But there's not much to *say* about the fundamentals. Who needs reminding that life is grim?'

'You think life is grim?'

'If it's not, I can't think what is.'

'I'll never understand you.'

No.

'You know what I like most about the music?' she said, the pale sun lighting their eyelashes and the tips of their hair. 'It's funny. I wouldn't like it half so much if it didn't have words.'

It moved him to think of Grace, crouched in her shell, listening to the lines he loved so much. 'We used to listen for hours,' he said, 'trying to get the words down, playing the same bit over and over again.' In the good old days. He pushed the thoughts away. 'So you don't object to funny songs. Why? Maybe I can explain to Rick.'

She looked at him, her face alight. 'If it's dark, whistle.'

They walked on in silence, occupied by their thoughts. The sky turned orange and the birds went home to bed. As they came to the gates, he stopped again. 'Well, what now?'

Remembering her assurances, she summoned up a want. 'Let's have tea at your place,' she said.

'There, that wasn't so hard,' he said, and she swallowed a snarl.

In the basement were Davy and Lindsey, Rick and Heather, Sherry and Bob. The place looked cleaner than normal: either Bob had cleared up in honour of Sherry or Sherry was already at work remodelling things. Grace missed the old mess. These intruders, they come in without a word, and before you know it the old slum has gone and you're into a high-rise.

Grace no longer bothered what sort of welcome she got. She sat on a cushion while Andrew headed for the cooking hole.

'There's fresh tea in the pot,' said Sherry.

'Good-oh.'

I bet she's baked some scones, thought Grace.

Had they interrupted a quarrel? Everyone seemed to have become caricatures of themselves. Rick was dangling off the divan; Heather sulked beside him. Davy was offering the sugar to Sherry with charming deprecation; Sherry was lifting her shoulders as if she'd been offered a bowl of diamonds. Bob was beating time with his whole body, though the record had finished and was circling in whispers on the turntable. Lindsey looked as if she was about to park her chewing gum under Sherry's chin.

Andrew came back with tea. 'What's new?' he said.

'Nothing,' said Davy, in the tone of a schoolboy caught with his hand in his neighbour's tuckbox.

'Sherry's been handing out a few fashion tips,' said Lindsey. Sherry picked up a newspaper and began to fold it. 'I was trying to read that,' said Lindsey. Sherry put the newspaper down and went back to the couch. 'Uniforms,' said Lindsey. 'She wants you to wear uniforms.'

'I'll get some more tea,' said Sherry, and went out.

Bob followed Sherry to the kitchen. Lindsey blew her breath out at the ceiling and said, 'Strewth.' Davy looked at her, looked at the kitchen and gave up. 'Did you have a good walk?' he asked Grace.

'Very nice. It's a beautiful day.'

'Lin, do you feel like a walk?'

'Walk? It's pitch dark out there,' said Lindsey. It was true that the light had begun to go.

'Let's go to a film, then. Where's the paper?' And he herded Lindsey out of the flat.

Rick and Heather stood up like Siamese twins. This time, Grace saw how it was done. Rick tensed his elbows and began to uncross his legs. All Heather's senses must have been turned towards him, because her body moved as if by reflex, and she was on her feet. 'Davy,' shouted Rick as they shut the door.

Silence returned and Bob poked his head in. 'They gone?'

He disappeared and came back with Sherry, who looked as if she might have been crying. She sat on the couch, drained of the precious liquid. Bob put his arm round her. 'What's got into Lindsey?' he asked. 'She's been at Sherry all afternoon.'

'I expect she's shy,' said Sherry. 'Doesn't like strangers around the place.'

'It's not even her place,' said Bob.

'I expect she feels as if it is.' Sherry stood up and tidied Lindsey's cup away. 'She'll soon get used to me.'

'What was that about uniforms?' asked Andrew.

'Sherry and Davy were just talking about clothes, and Lindsey went ape.'

'Have you had any ideas?' Andrew asked her.

'I just thought maybe you could all wear the same suit, or the same jacket or something.'

'You won't get Rick to wear a suit.'

'All right,' said Bob. 'I'll wear my leather jacket. Then I'll match him. Look.' He came back wearing the jacket, and Sherry stepped back and forwards, pulling it down, turning up the collar, patting out a wrinkle. Getting ready to build a nest.

'There, that's lovely,' she said, and he put his hands on her shoulder. Turning her head, Grace caught a look of longing on Andrew's face.

What can you do, these sparks and flashes all around you as the other fireflies meet and greet and fall in love? At a distance. In the darkness. Fall in love with a flash of light.

Grace did her best. She asked if she could listen to some of the surfing tapes that Davy had brought back from California. Bob shuffled round trying to work out how to dance to them; Grace and Andrew read the newspapers; and Sherry washed up. Later, they had a Chinese meal. This time, when Bob left with Sherry, Grace didn't suggest going home. In the morning she had to leave early. She hadn't slept much and it had started to rain. Andrew was late for a class and had no time to bring her coffee. Moral: unexpected pleasures never come twice.

Chapter 6

Towards Christmas, Grace became depressed. It crept up gradually, like a squid, stirring its tentacles below the surface of her awareness. Little phrases would occasionally pop up. 'That it should come to this.' Suddenly, you look down and your nest has gone. Your claws are clinging to a damp, lichen-caked branch, and this is all there is between now and death. Hop, hop, a change or two of branch, a change or two of fungus and ker-splat, you're dead.

Grace had always thought of life as something that would happen in the future. School was a waiting period, a dummy run. The missed tee-shot didn't count; the bombs weren't real. Oxford was just a natural extension of school: if you forget the exams, that is, and she was doing her best to forget the exams. Grace had made an illicit inference from the past to the future. It's only been a game so far, so it won't get serious yet. She'd gone to the Institute thinking she was in for just another stroll through the antechamber to life. Suddenly she happened to look down and bingo, no nest.

The thought that came to her more and more clearly through that first term was, 'I don't need to be here.' The London Institute of Behavioural Science was not at all part of the natural progression through life. It was just one slimy, fungus-caked branch among others. Grace was outraged and terrified. Surely some mention should have been made of this in the prospectus?

She clung to her branch, twittering. All the other branches were equally uninviting. Maybe there were whole other trees with eiderdown branches, empty nests, bird-tables full of worms and saucers of water. Or maybe this was the last tree in the world, surrounded by flood water, and if she left her mouldy branch the flying fish would get her. If everyone were like Grace, there would be no migratory birds.

Meanwhile, there was Andrew yelling at her to come in, the water's quite warm. Put away childish things. Come and shelter in my fungus-caked basement. This is not, repeat not, a dummy run.

132

Andrew and Grace, Rick and Heather, Bob and Sherry, Davy and Lindsey. That it should come to this.

Grace had her dreams. She would meet a man with wit and charm and crinkles around the eyes. The understanding between them would be so deep that they'd never need to touch or talk in public. Everyone would think, 'How cold those two are,' but at home, in their own little mansion, all would be dignified warmth. She'd sit on an Isfahan rug, resting her head on his knees, as he sat in his armchair, eyes crinkling in the firelit dusk. Occasionally, they'd exchange a glance and a fleeting, secret smile.

Or something like that. She didn't know all the details. You don't look too closely at the ideal man or you'd find yourself starting to giggle.

Grace was a romantic, at heart if not in mind; and the more alien she felt from other humans, the more romantic she became. At first, she'd dreamed a world of soulmates, then a handful of kindred spirits, then a single lifetime's love. For her it was going to be that or nothing. This was her final offer; she wouldn't settle for less.

The problem with dreams like Grace's is that there's nothing you can do to make them come true. She was dreaming of a genuine romance. You can't go out *looking* for the man of your life, like a predator out for a quick meal. Some day he'll come along, eyes a-crinkle. All you have to do is stay awake. To *work* for any of this would instantly turn it into a cheap imitation, a desperate makeshift, a Stefan-and-Joanna affair.

Now Andrew was simply not on as the man of one's life. The ideal man surely never makes one cringe. Though it's not, of course, the reason one loves him, he surely just happens to be so austerely handsome, so elegantly dressed, that people turn their heads and smile when he comes into the room. Grace knew she shouldn't want such things, and she didn't, she really didn't. But what's the point of the ideal man if he can't slip you some of the things you want and shouldn't, along with the things you should?

Andrew's failure to live up to expectations she didn't have made Grace understandably sharp with him. The more he reminded her that this was real life, the sharper she was likely to become. As term wore on, and the suspicion grew stronger that real life was indeed under way, she became more depressed and muddled. Obviously, you can't *say*, even to yourself, 'I believe in the ideal man.' Grace would have denied, with retching and vomiting, the existence of any such thing. So

133

why did she feel like shouting at Andrew, with retching and vomiting, 'You're not my ideal man'?

Perhaps the best analogy is with thoughts of death. Ask me whether I'm going to die and I will say, 'Of course.' Show me a man who believes in immortality, and I will point out crisply that he is a fool. But though I believe that everyone has to die, I have a sneaking suspicion that there may be an exception in my case. That was the way of Grace with love. Stefan and Joanna in love? Phooey. Davy and Lindsey in love? Piffle. There's no such thing as love; at least, not for anyone else.

At the end of term, the Director had his annual Christmas party in the Director's mansion. Grace went alone. You never know where the ideal man might turn up. He wasn't there, however, unless he was crouching. The Director welcomed Grace. He had the house, he had the rug, but he was not the one.

'Hello,' he said. 'Come in. You'll be?'

I'll be going now. No. 'I'm Grace Ritchie. MA in Human Behaviour.'

'Ah yes. Come in, come in.' He turned to a Toby jug dressed in a green chiffon boiler suit. 'Jennifer, this is one of our women students. We never seem to have many.'

'Hyuf hyuf,' said the jug.

'My wife, Jennifer.'

'Hello.'

'So glad you could come,' said Mrs Director. She gave Grace a thump on the shoulder blades. 'The food's through there.'

Grace slunk through the archway, eyes fixed, and helped herself to wine. Turning, she saw Chris Trent-Horsley, Jackie Parker and Dr Bastable getting in a quick tutorial under the chandelier. Normally she would have done no more than smile, but democratic Dr Bastable was paid to fraternize. 'Oh, there's Grace,' he said. 'Come and join us.'

He was holding a glass of wine in one hand and a plate of mince pies in the other. 'Have a mince pie.' Flakes of pastry clung to his chin, then launched themselves on to his tie, like sycamore seeds leaving the mother tree.

Grace shook her head. And I'll thank you to keep yours to yourself.

He balanced his wine glass on the edge of the plate; it resettled itself, slopping liquid over the neighbouring mince pies. 'Whoops.' In setting things to rights, he severely injured Jackie Parker's toe.

They were discussing something indescribably weary, like how to get from Wapping to Palmer's Green without changing buses more than twice. Jackie, bulging out of plum-coloured satin, had given the hairdresser another chance, put on a touch of lipstick and was all aglow. Smiles came tumbling from her lips as fast as pastry flakes fell from Dr Bastable's. She was feeling pretty tonight; or had been till she saw Grace look at her and quickly look away.

Grace watched Jackie losing her nerve. Who knows, this might have been Jackie's evening: when eyes would meet across a crowded room, and all her past humiliations be forgotten. But no, she had seen Grace's look, and was stranded, a pumpkin in shiny satin. There'd be no Prince Charming tonight.

Grace wanted to go, but didn't know how. If the group didn't spontaneously disintegrate, she'd be there all night, lashed to the mast, a sycamore seed unable to leave the mother tree. If everyone were like Grace, there would be no sycamore forests.

She was quite aware of this inability. She would expend much energy and adrenalin waiting for a natural break in the conversation into which she could inject her excuse. 'Ah, I think that phone call's for me.' 'I'm just popping out to get some bread before the shops shut.' 'Bother, I've just remembered that my house is on fire.' Somehow, the right pause and the right excuse never came. Why not simply 'I must get another drink' or 'There's someone over there I want to talk to'? It would hurt them; Grace was hurt when it happened to her. As well say, 'You bore me. I'm off.'

Grace was therefore listening with fixed attention to the words that flew past, hoping to hijack one and ride it off to freedom, when a voice droned in her ear, 'Come and have a drink.'

'Ah, there's Patrick. Have a mince pie,' said Dr Bastable.

'No thanks. They cause flatulence,' said Patrick. 'I just came to ask Grace for a dance.' Dr Bastable was left holding the mince pies.

'You looked as if you needed rescuing,' said Patrick.

'I did.'

'Have a drink. I've got a few bottles stashed away over here.' He pulled aside a curtain, to reveal a row of opened wine bottles. Grace giggled.

'Where on earth did those come from?'

'Oh, a bottle here, a bottle there. It soon adds up.'

It was hard to tell whether he was drunk, because his normal voice was so slurred, his normal eyes so drooping. There was just the slightest impression that he was more out of hand than usual, more on the verge of going too far. It made Grace feel both giggly and relaxed. Power without responsibility, the life of the gangster's moll.

She helped herself to some more wine. A glass here, a glass there, it soon adds up.

Patrick was a bit of a dandy: his dark suit had a cut to it, his shirt had a frill to it. Grace, as for all parties, had defended herself with clothes. This was just a little black dress with sleeves, very straight and plain. All the women in party dresses were thinking, 'She hasn't even bothered to dress up.' But Grace knew, and Patrick knew. You couldn't beat Grace on clothes.

'There's Jim,' said Patrick. 'Here, Jim. Have a mince pie.'

Jim seemed to know how Patrick worked. He couldn't possibly have recognized this as the idle allusion to Dr Bastable that it was. However, he didn't hesitate: no looking round for a plate, no glance of puzzlement at Patrick's face, just a slight amusement in the expression as he went ahead and said what he'd been going to say. 'I saw Kip Sullivan downstairs.'

Patrick, Grace and Jim had assumed that, as in Oxford, they would change tutors each term. Looking forward to working with Kip Sullivan, they'd been brought up short, in their last tutorial, to hear Dr Bastable ask them what they wanted to do for their first essay next term. As Chris and Jackie debated the relative merits of pigeon and rat, three faces gazed at Dr Bastable like cows across a fence. As he wished them all a Merry Christmas, Patrick's voice sliced the first syllable in half.

'Are you saying we're going to have the same tutor all year?'

'That's what we usually do. Unless you'd rather do something else.' Cries of 'No' and 'Shame' from the opposition front bench. Three cow-like faces stared back.

'Maybe we should take a vote,' said Patrick.

'I think we'd just better stick to what we usually do,' said Dr Bastable. 'This is what we usually do. Well, a Merry Christmas to you all.'

'And a happy New Year to you,' said Patrick as they went out.

'Let's talk to Kip Sullivan,' said Jim over lunch. 'See if he can help.'

Kip Sullivan was in the hall with the Director. Patrick, Jim and Grace lined up silently a yard from the pair. The Director looked round and smiled a genial, dismissive smile. They continued to stand. His smile became less genial. He shot them a look that said clearly, 'Buzz off, I'm not playing now.' They stood. 'Ah,' he said. 'The MA students. Come and join us.'

'Have a mince pie,' said Patrick.

'What?'

'I was just saying how much we liked the food.'

'Oh yes, yes.'

'Hyuf hyuf,' said Patrick.

The Director turned back to Kip Sullivan. 'I suppose you know old Kip Sullivan here?'

'Oh yes. Good old Kip.'

'Actually,' said Jim, 'we were hoping to have a word with him when you're finished. We'll be waiting over there.' He walked off, pulling Patrick and Grace after him by magnetic force.

'Spoilsport,' said Patrick as they went.

Kip Sullivan came up in rather a bad temper. 'OK, what do you guys want?'

'Maybe this isn't the best time to talk about it,' said Jim, 'but we're a bit worried about the organization of the course. Perhaps we could come and see you sometime.'

'What's the problem?'

'In a nutshell, we were hoping to have tutorials with you.'

'Oh.' Kip Sullivan's temper marginally improved. 'Have you talked to Jerry Bastable?'

'He says we stay with the same tutor all year.'

'That's right. It's Institute policy. The Director's very keen on it.'

'Why?' said Patrick.

'I don't know. It's a tradition.'

'That's what they always say when they can't think of a good reason,' said Patrick.

Kip Sullivan looked as if he'd like to hear more, but knew he shouldn't.

'We'd really like tutorials with you,' said Jim.

'OK, leave it with me. I'll see what can be done.' He left before Patrick could offer him a mince pie.

The party was now warmed up. The touches of lipstick were beginning to slip, the hairstyles to fray. 'Let's dance,' said Patrick, and Grace followed him upstairs. He danced smoothly, like many of her Oxford friends: nothing extreme or eccentric, just a sort of slow, rhythmic, left-elbow-up, right-elbow-up, peer-to-the-left, peer-to-the-right. Not so much dancing as creating the semblance of dancing; dancing not for the joy of it but because the situation called for it. Much as Grace herself had always danced.

The Institute wasn't culturally homogeneous enough to have evolved

a common style of dancing: the only time all the students met was at the Director's Christmas party. They spoke mutually incomprehensible dance dialects; there were beaglers, foxtrotters, bath-towel wavers, peerers to left and right. People with high intelligence and the ability to ask searching questions. Twitching their limbs like maggots in a jar in the hope of making friends.

The fact that Patrick went along with the ritual made him seem younger, more endearing to Grace. When a slow song came, he didn't reach out for her, but continued to dance his smooth, separate dance.

'Time for another drink,' he said at last; but someone had rifled his hoard. 'Bastards.' He gave her the remaining bottle. 'Here. I'll get some more.'

Grace, abandoned, began to panic. Another failure; another lost soulmate. She leaned against the empty shelf, eyes as dark as dungeon windows. Was he coming back? Should she wait for him? She wouldn't put it one bit past him just to leave her there. Perhaps she was misjudging him: maybe he liked her, was on his way back to her. Maybe he was a friend.

'Hello, all alone,' said the Director. 'Deserted by your friends?'

'That's right.'

'What a shame. You should be upstairs dancing, a fit young person like you.'

Patrick appeared in the archway, festooned with bottles, caught sight of the Director and disappeared.

The Director turned his body this way and that, looking for someone more important to talk to. 'How are you enjoying the course?'

'Very much.'

'Good, good. Er.' His head swung at anchor. 'Who's your tutor?'

Patrick reappeared without the bottles and began to mime his new address. From what Grace could tell, he was on the roof. 'Dr Bastable.'

'Ah. Old Jerry. I wonder if he's about.'

The Director had noticed that something was going on behind his back. He began to increase the scope of his swings, trying to bring it into focus. Patrick would duck behind the archway, and the Director's head would swing slowly back to base. Once, Patrick held up a plate of mince pies, and tried to signal some clearly derogatory message. It was like being tickled in church. Grace's eyes narrowed. She was afraid she was going to snort.

'That reminds me,' said the Director. 'I must have a word with old

Jerry. Well, I've enjoyed talking to you.' You bore me. I'm off. He spun round sharply, but all he caught was a whiff of mince pies.

Grace found Patrick upstairs in the dancing room, with Jim Wotherspoon and Jim's fiancée, Martha. A fiancée. You don't often see one of those. Martha was square-jawed, plain and competent, like Jim. They stood stably together, two horses in harness, sharing life's load. They had nothing to prove. Jim liked a green cardigan with his suit, he wore a green cardigan with his suit. Martha's hair was uncurled; her ears were unadorned. No spark of worry or flirtation sprang between them.

Grace gave Patrick the bottle she'd been guarding, and he added it to his store. 'They're running out of drink,' he said. 'Nature's way of telling us it's time to go.'

By now, the room was dim and the music dimmer. Couples shuffled ear to shoulder, gathering warmth for the journey home. Jim and Martha hitched themselves together and trundled off. Patrick put his arms round Grace and talked directly into her skull. 'Did you have a good chat with the Director, then? Pick up any research tips?'

'He didn't say anything. He was too busy trying to see what was going on behind his back.'

'I should think that's the story of his life.'

They danced mainly in silence, just a few words murmured into the skull. Chris Trent-Horsley came in with Jackie Parker; Patrick whispered what a lovely couple they made. At last he said, 'Let's get out of here.' Filled with the relief of not being abandoned, Grace went to get her coat.

'We'd better say goodbye,' said Patrick, who'd clearly been well brought up. They found the Director swaying at anchor among a group of suits and party dresses.

'We've come to say goodbye,' said Patrick.

The Director looked at them. 'You found your friend, then,' he said to Grace.

'Yes. Thank you for a lovely party.' The Director turned away without saying goodbye.

Mrs Director was talking to Jerry Bastable. 'We've come to say goodbye,' said Patrick.

'Oh, so sorry you have to go. The door's over there.'

'Must rush,' said Patrick. 'We've eaten too many of your delicious mince pies.'

'Hyuf hyuf.'

'Thank you for a lovely party,' said Grace. 'Goodbye.'

'Merry Christmas,' said Dr Bastable. 'See you next term.'

'And may an aeroplane never fall on your head.'

They walked home arm in arm, giggling, and had some more to drink. He stacked some jazz records on the record player, and they sat untidily on his sofa. Then they made love. It was easy for Grace. Patrick had everything she wanted and shouldn't. Also, of course, she was drunk.

She woke in the night feeling thirsty, and fumbled out to the bathroom. She didn't become fully conscious, just enough to think, 'These are funny pyjamas. Oh well, I'll sort it all out in the morning. If I don't have some water, I'll die.'

In the morning she came wide awake. Patrick was slumbering beside her, hair tousled, mouth asprawl. It seemed important to put as great a distance as possible between them. She began to pull herself out of bed.

Patrick turned over and opened his eyes. He noted her as he would note that it was raining; just one of those things that happen in the night. He finished turning over and closed his eyes.

Grace stood up, brain throbbing, body parched. No time for regrets. Coffee, I must have coffee. She wrapped herself in Patrick's dressing gown and went to boil a kettle. Real coffee; nothing less would do.

The flat belonged to Patrick's uncle. It was a grown-up's flat. The front room had a well-cushioned sofa, mahogany bookshelves, an antique desk and a soft green carpet. With stain. Two empty glasses, one overturned; jazz records spread on the floor, sofa cushions awry. Grace drew the curtains, straightened the cushions, put away the records, and removed the glasses and empty bottle. There was nothing to be done about the stain.

Patrick came in, hair still tousled. 'Is there some coffee?' He yawned and went out. She made more coffee. He came back immaculate in his Saturday clothes. 'Still got the pyjamas on, I see.' She smiled. The allusion escaped her. 'Very keen on having some pyjamas you were. "Can't go to bed without pyjamas," you kept saying.' Grace smiled. Dignity and restraint. 'And you got very upset when you spilled the whisky. "I'll pay for it," you kept saying. "I'll pay to have the stain taken out."' He took another gulp of coffee. Grace smiled. It was either that or stab him through the heart. Where was the Isfahan rug, where the understanding too deep for word or touch? Gone, gone, and never called me mother.

'Of course I'd be happy to pay for the stain.' She picked up her scattered clothes and locked herself in the bathroom. When she came out, he was eating toast.

'Have some.'

'I must get home.'

'Oh well. See you, then.' He came to the door with her, chewing.

Such an episode was not entirely new to Grace. She'd made sure no one could accuse her of saving herself for the right man. Rowena, who had grown with Mark from childhood sweetheart to adult love, wanted everyone else to do the same. When Rowena took up gardening, she would want everyone to garden; when she had a baby, she would cause a baby boom among her friends. Her eye fell on Grace and Fergus. Who better for Grace than Fergus? Who better for Fergus than Grace?

Fergus wasn't really a physical person. Though he found Grace exquisite, he felt no more urge to make love to her than he would to a Chinese vase. But Rowena's unspoken assumptions could be very forceful. He began to feel honour bound to make them come true.

Grace had no trouble resisting unspoken assumptions, but Rowena had caught her at a propitious moment, in one of her periodic phases of trying to come to terms with the world. There was no such thing as the ideal man, so why was she waiting around? In an effort to rub her nose in reality, she frog-marched herself into bed. The flirtation with adulthood left as little mark on her as it did on Fergus; they sank back into childhood without a word.

The episode with Patrick was harder to explain. It hadn't been a conscious decision: there didn't seem to be any reasoning behind it; and for an intuitive leap it appeared to have landed badly. Perhaps, Grace thought, the heart has its reasons; perhaps she didn't know it yet but Patrick really was her ideal man. Or perhaps she was getting ready to settle for a quick wit, a handsome face and a well-cut suit. The more she puzzled, the crosser she became. What's the point of a course on human behaviour if it can't explain a simple action like that?

The party was on the last Friday of term. On Saturday evening Andrew phoned. 'How was the party?'

'Fine.'

'I bet you were the belle of the ball.' Pause. 'I missed you.'

'While you were out on the town with Rick and Davy?'

'No, after.' Pause. 'I was hoping you might come round tonight.'

'Oh God. I'm exhausted. I was planning to go to bed early.'

'Shall I come round and tuck you in?'

'Look, it's been a busy term. I've worked quite hard. I went to bed late last night. I want a bit of a rest.'

'Oh.' Pause. 'All right. Sleep well. Maybe I'll give you a ring in the morning.'

The hangover had worn off now, and her brain was working quite well; as well as it normally did, anyway, on bridle and bit. She felt a little guilty for snapping at Andrew, but what's done is done, and can no doubt always be patched up. She felt not guilty but giggly at the thought of his patiently, considerately, all these months, laying siege to a citadel that wasn't there. The slight tenseness when he first took her hand; the gentle evenings in the sandhills of Greece, trying not to frighten her with his demands. See. One wriggle and I slip out of your grasp.

It could have been pointed out here that one swallow doesn't make a meal, nor a few scrambles a jaded sophisticate. But it pleased Grace to comfort herself with these thoughts; at least as long as there was no one around to test them. Also, of course, it would put Andrew in his place. How it was going to do this is unclear, since she would have lied her way from here to Marble Arch to prevent his finding out what she had done. It was really a secret message to herself, which could be taken out and looked at in times of stress. Thousands are called, few are chosen. I never asked you to follow me around.

Next morning Andrew phoned again. 'Did you sleep well?'

'Yes, fine, thanks.'

'Good. Can I come round later? Take you to lunch?'

'All right.'

'I'll be there by one.'

At twelve-thirty there was a knock, and Patrick came in. 'Hello there,' he said. He looked at each chair in turn, chose the most comfortable one, and sat down.

Delight. He did like her after all. They would marry and settle down and raise Isfahan rugs. What a terribly nice man he was. 'How nice,' she said, elated. Unless he was having her on.

'Time for lunch,' he said.

'Oh dear. I'm afraid I've got someone coming.'

'Your boyfriend? Can I come too?'

'Certainly not. I mean, he's not my boyfriend, just a friend.'

'Good. I'll come along then.'

Scrap the Isfahan rugs. 'I'm afraid we've been invited out.'

Just then there was another knock and Andrew came in wearing his

Sunday worst. 'Hello, I'm early,' he said. Patrick settled back in his chair and waited to be introduced.

'Andrew, this is Patrick. Patrick, this is Andrew. Patrick's at the Institute,' she said. Technically, it was Patrick's presence that demanded justification, though perhaps Andrew's clothes also called for a word or two.

'Hello, Andrew,' said Patrick. 'Have a mince pie.'

'I don't imagine Grace has taken up cooking since I last saw her.'

'You'd be surprised what Grace – '

'Patrick,' said Grace. 'We've got to go now.'

'What a shame. I was hoping you'd invite me along. Well, another time, maybe. See you next week.'

'Yes.'

'Goodbye, Andrew.'

He didn't wait for Andrew's reply.

'Who was that prick?'

You said it, not me. 'Someone from the Institute.'

'Where do they dredge them up? If they're all like that, no wonder you're going out of your mind.'

'What do you mean, I'm going out of my mind?'

'Oh, forget it. Let's have something to eat.'

The weather was grey and dingy. The newspaper shops had Christmas frosting around their windows; Santa peered jovially through the panes, wondering what was going on behind his back. Grace and Andrew walked to the pub by the canal. There was an air of bad-will about, with elbows being jogged, dogfights over empty tables, and a general atmosphere of spilled beer. Andrew continued to be grumpy. Grace thought he was behaving like a child. 'How did the evening go on Friday?' she asked, catching some of Patrick's smooth manner.

'All right.'

Grace, having betrayed him, was feeling generous. 'I wish I'd been able to come round yesterday, but I was just feeling too flaked.'

'What on earth had you been doing?'

'Well, the party went on quite late.'

'I wanted to see you,' low. 'I missed you. I was longing to see you.' Pause. 'I rang you at eight in the morning and you didn't answer.'

'Heavens. I must have been still asleep. I got a bit drunk and it always knocks me out. I think it must have been the hangover that made me feel so tired yesterday. Anyway, I feel much better today.'

She smiled, with no warmth. Someone dropped cigarette ash into Andrew's beer.

Andrew wearily chewed his shepherd's pie. At that moment he lost hope of happiness with Grace. He saw her for a silly piece of driftwood, an empty cup. The straight hair would grow grey, the glazed skin would end in sag and jowl, and there would be no warmth or wisdom in her. He looked at her with dislike.

What's done is done. Grace couldn't afford to feel sad. Grumpy grumpy, she thought. Just because I didn't come running when he called.

'What would you like to do this afternoon?' she said.

'Nothing in particular.'

'It's not a very good day for a walk.'

'No.'

'Maybe we could go and see a film.' Full of initiative, Grace picked up a paper that someone had left behind. 'Oh look. *Duck Soup*.' This was a film he wanted to see and had always managed to miss.

'I'm not in the mood.'

'Come with me. I'd like to see it.' She smiled and put her hand on his arm. Under pressure, she had produced a want. She peeped out through her straight hair. If she wasn't careful, he'd lose hope.

'All right,' he said, and they went off side by side. During the film, as he laughed his shoulder brushed against her, and he didn't pull away.

'Let's have tea at your place,' she said when the film was over.

'Anywhere but there. They'll all be round there bickering and squabbling like rats in a cage.'

'Why on earth?'

'We seem to have reached a crisis. I suppose it was bound to come. Until now, we've really just been fooling around: Oxford parties, hunt balls, no one can tell the difference; they don't care what you're playing as long as they can stomp. But Thursday night at the Newt is serious stuff. Agents come, you could get signed up. It's getting a bit close to real life.'

They walked on towards Camden Town, past Christmas lights and Christmas bells, past jovial Santas with sacks of three-by-five-inch file cards, all looking for someone more important to talk to.

'Tell me about the band.'

'You're not interested,' he said. Some of the energy seemed to have gone out of him. He could no longer carry her by himself.

'I am. Please tell me what the disagreement's about.'

'Well, first you have to understand about Rick. You know we went to school together?'

'I didn't know you went to school.'

'Well, they called it a school. It was more a poker academy really. I've known him since I was thirteen.'

'Does he ever speak?'

'About music. He only really cares about music. And poker. Anyway, we started off this group at school: the Leadswingers we called it. It was diabolical. We played at the fifth form dance; rumpled our hair, grew sideburns for a couple of days, and had half a bottle of whisky that we passed round when the teachers weren't looking. We really thought we were the pig's bristles. We came on in the middle of the evening, after the ballroom records and before the old-tyme dancing. No one had a clue what was going on. I mean, this sort of stuff was *really* esoteric then. There we were, tipsy on a few drops of whisky, belting the blues to the girls from the local high school who'd only been let out of ankle socks on condition they were home by ten. On Monday morning our form master said he thought we'd done really well but he hoped we weren't forgetting about our O-levels. At the time, I didn't really see the joke.'

'I'm sure you must have been very sweet.'

'I'm afraid so. Anyway, the point is that Rick hasn't really changed since then. He still doesn't see the joke. He thinks he *is* from Mississippi. "Rick," I say, "how many blues singers went to Croydon Grammar School?" but he doesn't listen.'

'Surely you're just the same? You write surfing songs and you've never been surfing; you sing about the prettiest girl in school though your school can't have had any girls.'

'I like trying out styles; I'll try anything. But I want to do new things, invent new styles. Rick's in love with a style that's already been invented: if he's not careful, it'll strangle him.'

He wasn't really talking to Grace now. His mind was turned inward, reasoning with Rick. They walked on in silence. Grace asked where Bob and Davy fitted in.

'Davy's not fussy: he'll play anything. What he really likes is people looking at him. If you told him he could get to number one by playing "Baa baa black sheep", he'd do it; in fact that's probably what he'd do best. And Bob just wants a good time.'

'You do seem a rather ill-assorted lot.'

'Oxford isn't exactly bursting with rock musicians. You make the best of what there is.'

'So what exactly is the disagreement?'

'Well, take surfing music. I like it, Bob and Davy like it, but Rick doesn't want to play it. Even rock and roll he's not too happy about. He's been hanging around these new blues clubs: that's all he really wants to play. I want to play blues and everything else too.'

'So what'll happen?'

'Maybe it's just a passing storm. Maybe Rick'll find a new group to play with. Maybe we'll get signed up tomorrow and reach number one. It's all dreams, really; it's just a matter of finding one that works.'

'You can't alter dreams.'

'Of course you can. They're there to make life pleasant. If they don't, you find another one that does.'

This seemed immoral to Grace. You can't mess around with dreams.

Andrew was back to normal now. Grace was glad: she didn't like scenes. But when they'd eaten, although now perfectly good-natured, he didn't invite her back to his flat.

On Tuesday, Grace, Patrick and Jim went to see Kip Sullivan. 'I'm afraid it's bad news,' he said. 'I talked to Jerry Bastable and he brought the Director in. It's Institute policy that you remain with the same tutor throughout the first year.'

'Why?' said Patrick.

'The idea is that you get continuity.'

'That's just what we want to avoid.'

'Well, I did my best. I asked my group but none of them want to switch with you. I guess you'll just have to put up with what you have.'

'Let's go and see the Director,' said Patrick.

'A word of warning if you do. I don't know what you guys have been up to, but this may not be the best moment to approach him.'

'What do you mean? We haven't done anything,' said Grace.

'I get the impression he thinks you have. Don't ask me what it's all about, but you seem to be down as some sort of troublemakers. My advice to you is to just cool it for a while.'

'We guys seem to have made a bit of a balls-up,' said Patrick outside.

'What have we *done*?' asked Grace. They ignored her.

'Do you think it's worth going to see the Director?' said Patrick.

'No. Better leave it. Well, I think I'll wander along now,' said Jim, sinking ships not being his line. 'Have a good Christmas. See you next term.'

Grace, having reasoned out from first principles that this ship should not be going down, ignored the flames pouring out of the engine room. 'I've done all my essays,' she said. 'I've been to all the lectures.'

'Never mind. Let's go and have a drink.'

In the refectory, Grace couldn't leave the incident alone. 'It's not fair,' she said. 'It was a perfectly reasonable request.' Radical Grace. Patrick couldn't be bothered to explain.

Grace worked it out eventually. The Director and Jerry Bastable had called Patrick's bluff. They'd seen him covertly insulting them, and sent him back a covert message: we know what you're up to, and it's doing you no good. It had never occurred to Grace that they might be so subtle: Jerry Bastable, whose self-awareness rivalled that of a mollusc; Dr Cadwallader, whose jovial mask, like an ill-fitting toupée, scarcely concealed the snarl within.

'Going away for Christmas?' asked Patrick.

'Yes. Are you?'

'After Christmas,' he said. 'I'm going skiing.' Of course. 'Do you ski?' He could make a polite question sound so rude.

'I hate snow.'

'Not much of an athlete, are you?' She wished he would go away.

'I have to pack,' she said. 'I'm leaving tomorrow.'

'I'll walk home with you.'

Outside her house, 'I'll help you pack.'

'Don't be silly.'

'All right, I'll have some coffee.'

He came upstairs. Grace made coffee. 'Not much of a cook either,' he said. How could she reply? She would have been the first to agree that she wasn't much of a cook. It wasn't logical to find it so insulting to be told.

'Going anywhere nice?' he asked.

'As long as it's away from here it'll be nice enough.'

'Aren't you happy here? Nice tutor, nice boyfriend, what more can you want?'

'I haven't got a boyfriend.'

He was wandering round the room. It would stand up quite well to his inspection. The only jarring element was the pile of Andrew's records on the floor; he looked at one or two of them but didn't

147

comment, a gentleman doesn't comment. Instead, he chose one of Rowena's songs.

Grace was now thoroughly confused. Everything he said was hurtful; surely it had to be deliberate? Perhaps she was being over-sensitive; perhaps his behaviour was perfectly normal; perhaps she'd be cutting her throat to ask for anything more. If he didn't like her, he needn't have come to see her. Therefore he liked her, therefore the insults could be rationally explained; though it wasn't exactly clear how.

'You're not packing,' he said.

'I'll wait.'

'Oh well.' Slowly he put down his cup, stood up, stretched. 'I suppose I'd better be going.' Slowly he walked to the door. 'See you next term.' She heard him go heavily down the stairs.

She took her clothes to the launderette, cleaned the room and packed. She'd arranged to see Andrew that evening; he'd told her to dress up, he was taking her out.

'Come on,' he said. 'You look nice. The taxi's waiting outside.'

'A taxi.'

'Of course.'

Her heart always ached for him when he put himself out for her like this. His skin was smooth and red from vigorous shaving. He would have taken some trouble over choosing that tie: she thought of him hesitating, trying it against him, nodding at himself in the mirror. He had on the same suit he'd worn when he took her out after her exams. So sad when you try so hard, and only manage to make people think, 'He must have tried so hard.'

He'd booked a table at a very expensive restaurant. The waiters flapped them to their seats as if they were sailboats needing a breeze. The menu was the size of a small Ph.D. thesis. Grace turned the pages forwards and back, looking for the Budget Special. The waiter was there, pen in hand, before she'd done more than compute the price of a sauté potato.

'I think we need a little more time,' said Andrew. He would no doubt say the same when he saw the bill.

The restaurant was almost empty. The ratio of waiters to eaters was about three to one. Every bite drew twenty eyes; each dropped pea was tracked to its resting place; after every sip of wine a waiter would leap to refill the glass. With this, and the fact that every dish on the menu was cooked before your eyes with such scraping of juices and scattering of herbs that you felt it would be rude not to watch, there was little

148

scope for sustained conversation. It seemed a shame to come all this way and pay so much when a phone call to British Rail could have revealed the time of her train to Paignton with so much less fuss.

Why had he brought her here? Not, that is, why had he chosen this ghastly place, but why had he wanted to take her out somewhere grand? Because it was Christmas? Was there something to celebrate? When was his birthday? Did he have a marriage proposal written out on his cuff?

'Is it your birthday?' she asked; the waiters turned their heads for his reply.

'No. Do I look older?'

'I just wondered what we were celebrating.'

'Oh, nothing really. It's Christmas, the last time I'll see you this year.' He wasn't going to reveal, with waiters swooping to scoop up every word, that he'd wanted to rise to the level of her smooth Institute friends. He wanted her, over Christmas, to remember him at his best. 'Don't you know when my birthday is? I know yours.'

'Oh yes, you're four months older than me. It must be in July.'

'July the tenth.' She didn't look as if she was memorizing the date.

Grace didn't want any pudding. Andrew, trying to preserve the illusion that his money had been well spent, ordered a zabaglione, which the waiter personally knitted under his nose. Sucking great trailing spoonfuls of it into his mouth, he found it hard to keep his spirits up. He paid and paid, and their coats were ushered from the cloakroom with flamenco stamps.

'I'll just get a taxi,' said Andrew.

'Let's walk,' said Grace. 'It's a lovely evening. I need some exercise after all that food.'

It wasn't actually raining: the drops of moisture were floating in the air rather than falling to the ground. 'Well, let me know as soon as you're tired.'

They walked past the antique shops and lighted restaurants with their potted bay trees and conifers. 'Did you enjoy it?' he asked.

'Oh yes.'

'The food was quite good, wasn't it?'

'Yes. Thank you very much for inviting me.'

'Do you know why I did?'

'You said.'

'I wanted to give you a treat. I'm not always scruffy, you know. I can take you to nice places too.'

149

'Of course you can. You do.'

'Oh, Grace.'

He put his arm round her shoulders and they walked on, not quite in step, so that they would each have to make the occasional jump in an effort to restore harmony. After some distance he adjusted dream to reality and withdrew his arm.

He hadn't really expected Grace to come home with him that night, since it had been established in front of independent waiters that she was to catch a train at twelve twenty next day. 'Do you want to pack?' he asked as they reached the parting of the ways. 'Or would you like to come and have some coffee?'

'Is your place going to be full of people throwing things?'

'It wasn't when I left.'

'Why don't I come back there, then? I've almost finished packing.'

'Great.' Had there been something in the food, or had he just been mistaken when he could have sworn, last weekend, that he was about to lose her? Which was, of course, the real reason for inviting her out.

There was no one there when they got home. Andrew poured some whisky and put a record on. The beat was slow and quiet; occasionally a tiny, distant mouth organ whirred behind the lazy, joyful voice. 'This is Rick's sort of music,' he said as he came and sat beside her on the couch. And it was Rick he was thinking of, not Grace.

'Can Rick sing?' she asked. Not that singing was really the issue. There was a richness here, a variety; it didn't take an expert to appreciate that.

'Not really. Well, not like that. He's a fantastic guitarist, though. He can play anything, any style. I just wish he would.'

'You'd hate to lose him, wouldn't you?'

'It's been a long, long time.'

'Would you sing like that if you could?' She nodded towards the record player.

'That type of singing can't be learned: you've either got it or you haven't. If I had it, maybe I wouldn't be able to do some of the things I can do: the quick, sharp, delicate stuff. If I could choose, I'd have the most versatile voice.'

'So they can't pin you down.'

'No: so I get more fun.'

Andrew began to sing along with the record. 'Do you think I could ever sound like him?'

'Not on half a bottle of whisky.'

'Think of it. There must be hundreds of people all over the world, all trying to sound like that.'

'It's like hundreds of people trying to look good in something only a few people can wear.' The analogy was uppermost in Grace's mind with Andrew close by in his suit.

'I suppose so. I've never thought much about clothes. Is that a fashionable dress?'

'Sort of.' The hours of studying, of trying things on.

'Oh. It's very *plain*, isn't it? I'm not saying you don't look very nice in it. You'd look nice in anything.'

If Patrick had said that, she would have been hurt. From Andrew, it was so clearly not meant to be an insult that she just laughed. 'No cheap imitations here.'

'I can tell you're not a cheap imitation. Imitation, maybe, but after tonight, not cheap. Oh dear. That didn't come out quite right.'

'So *that*'s why you asked me out.'

'Seen through me at last.' The record finished and he switched it off. 'Anyway, thanks for coming. Let's go and get some sleep.'

Grace had been feeling guilty. She couldn't approve of her behaviour with Patrick. When you came right down to it, she couldn't approve of Patrick. How could someone so irresponsible be the ideal man? It was the exams all over again, Grace thought. She'd gone for what the world would admire, gone for a shield against nudges and smirks, a piece of white heather, a rabbit's foot, to keep her safe from the world.

And whichever way you looked at it, she hadn't behaved fairly to Andrew. He was everything that Patrick wasn't: open, honest, thoughtful, friendly. It broke her heart to see him trying, for her sake, to be everything that Patrick was. There was only one thing to do. The problem was how to tell him. The subject was one on which, up to now, she hadn't been known to speak.

It's surprising how much that's highly relevant is passed over in silence. Patrick was a great exploiter of this. He would insult you publicly, but in such a way that you couldn't accuse him. Everyone saw the knife in the ribs; everyone knew who put it there; no one could think of a way to stop him getting off scot free. Patrick was a specialist in creating facts you couldn't acknowledge; Grace had her methods too. She was like the vicar's wife who shows you into the drawing room and goes off to make the tea. Left alone, you can't help noticing a dead body on the rug. The vicar's wife, bringing in the tray, steps calmly

151

over the body. Once you've given in and agreed that it's a nice day, isn't it, your chance of ever raising the matter is gone.

In the matter of bodies, Grace had much in common with the vicar's wife. She refused to acknowledge their existence. She had, as it were, thrown a green baize cloth over the fact that she sometimes spent the night with Andrew: she would pick up his shirt from the chair where it lay, and stroll discreetly off to the bathroom, as one taking a little night air before turning in. Back she would come, stepping over the body, and slip into bed. Once there, whatever enjoyment she received was regarded as purely private; she would go to great lengths to keep her expression blank, her limbs still, so that he never knew if he was giving her pleasure. More tea, Mr Lisle? One lump of sugar or two?

Andrew, from kindness or delicacy, didn't comment. There was clearly a struggle going on inside her; no doubt she would resolve it in her own way. For the moment, he was happy enough to be close to her, even if his presence must remain unacknowledged.

That evening, then, Grace slipped into bed, and slipped into Andrew's arms. It's not clear what thoughts were going through her head. What happened, anyway, was that she hid her face on Andrew's shoulder, on his pillow, against his chest; and at the point where she normally pushed him away, she remained quite still. Puzzled, he awaited further developments. Nothing happened. Was she dead? Should he call the fire brigade? 'Grace,' he whispered at last. 'May I go on?' Her hair moved fractionally on the pillow. She stared politely through closed eyelids as if about to receive a small but useful medal, subject to unavoidable delay. He was speechless with disbelief. It's Christmas morning? Now?

Grace had to leave at crack of dawn. He awoke to find her already out of bed. No time for murmured messages: into the van. She left like a five-year-old late for school. He thrust into her arms the wrapped record he had so carefully chosen, and kissed her harried face as she reached for the door. It was just as frustrating sleeping with her as not.

To Grace, as she riffled through the events of the last few days, one generalization seemed clear: in future, avoid the little black dress.

Chapter 7

Grace was at the station before Joanna, who arrived in full bloom. She looked befurred and bejewelled: you waited for the photographers to appear. 'I thought I'd never make it. So many last-minute things.' Grace was edged back, grimly resisting, into the role of companion to the star.

The train was not too full; it was still some days before Christmas. They found an empty carriage at the front. Joanna sat looking forward; Grace sat looking back.

The impression that Joanna was bejewelled was not entirely unfounded. She had a heavy silver ring on her engagement finger; ivy-leaves chasing each another across a circular stem. Grace instantly knew what it was: the old Coulter family ring. Ivy for parasites.

Joanna was sitting with her left hand posed on her knee, so that the photographers could get a better view. Grace rigorously looked at Joanna's face, midriff, ear, out of the window, at the ashtray fixed between them; Joanna never caught her looking at the ring.

'See?' she eventually said, raising her hand to block Grace's view. 'Do you like it?'

'It's very pretty.' Pause for Grace to ask Joanna where it came from; Grace looked at the ashtray again.

'Stefan gave it to me. It used to belong to his grandmother.'

It's serious, then. A man only has two grandmothers.

'Really.'

'There's the loveliest little verse engraved inside:

I will cling to you,
As the ivy clings to the tree.'

And strangle you.

'It's a shame they couldn't get it to rhyme,' said Grace. 'I suppose "You will cling to me as the ivy clings to the tree" would have sounded a bit presumptuous.'

'I think it's sweet. Like a sort of Victorian haiku, I told Stefan.'

'Where is Stefan?'

'Family gathering: his parents have this old house in Yorkshire. He pretends it's a great bore, but of course I wouldn't stop him going.' Not unless you could. 'And he's coming to us after Christmas. If it's all right with the parents,' she added considerately.

'Have you met his family?'

'Yes, they're gorgeous. I went home with him two weeks ago; we seemed to take to each other right from the start. Marian – she's his stepmother, actually, his parents separated when he was quite little – treated me just like one of the family. She couldn't have been kinder. I feel as if I already belong.'

'Things do seem to be going well for you at the moment.'

'At the moment? I hope it's longer than that. We're getting married in June. It's all happened so suddenly – sometimes I can't believe it's real.'

'Oh, Joanna. I'm glad you're happy.'

'I can't tell you; it's like a dream come true. Still, enough about me. And the best thing is, I won't have to go to boring old work any more. Stefan says he needs me to organize him. It'll be wonderful to feel useful at last.'

'I thought he was a starving artist.'

'He's a very successful artist; but he says with me he'll be even more successful. There's quite a lot of entertaining involved.'

Indeed, where would van Gogh have been without all those dinner parties?

Joanna couldn't help but notice that her announcement had not been received with unqualified joy. It was understandable: anyone could be forgiven for envying her Stefan. 'But there I am, rattling on about myself,' she said, throwing up her hands in droll self-mockery, as well she might. 'Have you done your Christmas shopping yet? What have you bought?'

At Salisbury, their carriage filled up with Thermos flasks and sandwiches, and they were unable to talk any more.

The Ritchies met them at Exeter and drove them to their grandmother's house. Mrs Ritchie had been brought up in Paignton. Her father had been a shopkeeper, a shop owner, a proprietor; creator of Castle's department store, still referred to as Castle's though sold to a chain when Mr Castle retired. He died, and left Mrs Castle living in a largish house on the cliffs, flanked by other Paignton widows watching the weeds multiply in the drive and the windows rot in their frames.

Visits to the house were both frightening and comforting to Grace, like picnicking in a nice spot on a firing range, or being the little girl of the warder on Death Row. You could never quite settle down, in case something terrible was happening out of eyeshot. It was to do with the passing of time.

The house didn't change much, though it was ebbing away. Grace didn't know the slow sweeping and weed-pulling that went on in the weeks before Christmas; how during those weeks time was swept under the carpet and Mrs Castle, going to bed at midnight, thought the house almost looked as good as new. Mr and Mrs Ritchie would have a lovely time over Christmas replacing lightbulbs and mending things, each discovered dilapidation throwing a wrench into Mrs Castle's heart. 'I've cleaned out your bathroom cupboard for you,' Mrs Ritchie would cheerfully say, and Mrs Castle would wait till bedtime and root through the rubbish bin. It was not rubbish; suppose I went through your handbag for you and cleaned it out? Both sides were filled with enormous goodwill.

That evening over dinner, Joanna announced her news. Mrs Ritchie, who had spotted the ivy-covered ring before Joanna was out of the train, couldn't have been more amazed. 'We never *guessed*, did we darling?' as if Joanna had just given birth to a baby boy. 'What a beautiful ring.'

'It's an old family ring. It belonged to Stefan's grandmother.' Mrs Castle put her hands under the table.

'When did it *happen*?'

'I suppose we knew, really, right from the beginning.'

What, that you were going to get married on the nineteenth of June?

'But he only gave me the ring last night. See what it says inside?' She handed the ring to her mother.

'Made in Sheffield,' said Grace.

'Made in *Sheffield*,' started her mother.

'No it doesn't. It says, "I will cling to you, as the ivy clings to the tree." See?'

The ring was passed round for internal examination.

'Actually,' said Grace, ' "thee" would have done it: "I will cling to thee, as the ivy clings to the tree." '

'That makes it sound a bit like a hymn,' said Mrs Ritchie. 'What about finding a tree that rhymes with "you"?' Pause.

'The yew tree,' said Mr Ritchie.

'I will cling to you as the ivy clings to the yew. Well,' said Mrs Ritchie, 'I think they did the best they could.'

'Made in Sheffield,' said Mrs Castle, looking at the inside of the ring. 'Does that mean it's stainless steel?'

Joanna snatched back the ring. 'It's solid silver,' she said. 'It's an old family ring.'

'Very nice,' said Mrs Castle. 'They get them out of Christmas crackers.'

Both Grace and Mrs Ritchie began to feel guilty. 'Is Stefan going home for Christmas?' asked Mrs Ritchie, and tales of the old manor house on the Yorkshire moors came tumbling out, sulkily at first, but with increasing graciousness. Noblesse oblige. Soon the prospect of Stefan's visit was raised, and welcomed on all sides. Another bedroom to clean. Grace could move into the little room at the back, Joanna could move into the one Grace had left, and Stefan could move into the one Joanna had left. Where to take him: what to show (and hide)?

Grace had all her presents neatly parcelled ahead of time. It didn't help: just left more time for remorse and regret. Somewhere the ideal present lay unbought, the present that would quietly reveal the care of the giver for the receiver, the giver's insight into the receiver's heart. What was actually produced, and unwrapped with delight ('How on earth did you think of *this*?') fell humiliatingly short. Everyone else always chose better. How?

Grace thus spent the few days before Christmas wandering through the shops of Paignton despite the wrapped presents at home. The launderette. A year's supply of washing powder. The lumber yard. A spare telegraph pole. Trelliswork for your walls. A do-it-yourself cloister. Nothing seemed quite right, and not easy to carry on to the plane.

On Christmas Day, when the presents had been opened and the Christmas dinner eaten, the children were always sent out for a walk. They always went the same way: Mrs Castle's road was a cul-de-sac which led over a stile on to a cliff path. You could walk to Land's End if you wanted to. If you were lucky, as on that day, you would get the last hour of frosty sunlight and be able to stroll and talk, scarf over ears, issuing mist from the mouth like wan steam trains.

Often, this had been the time of the year when, passions calmed, appetites stilled, Grace and Joanna would talk about the past and the future, how they saw their lives. The previous year it hadn't happened: neither was in an optimistic mood. As they reached the cliff path, it seemed to Grace that those times were gone for ever. As soon as the intention to marry is declared, the relationship becomes subject to the official secrets act, and questions that would before have been accepted and answered become indictable espionage. The partners are transformed into public relations officers; the world is given no idea of how a marriage is going until suddenly trading is suspended and the receivers are called in.

For Joanna, though, the barrier hadn't quite come down. 'Grace,' she said as they walked over the rough grass, 'do you think I'm doing the right thing?'

It wasn't usual for her to ask Grace's advice, seeing more than many of Grace's childish or wilful side.

'You're not having doubts? So soon?'

'No. Of course not. But I'd rather have them too soon than too late.'

'What sort of doubts?'

'I get jealous.' She said it as someone would say, I have two weeks to live.

'Jealous?' You mean other women can stand him too? 'What of?'

'Nothing. You know how attractive he is. People run after him. It's always going to happen. And it makes me quite sick with fright.'

'Have you always felt like this? With other people?'

'Never so badly. I've never loved anyone like this.'

'No accounting for tastes.'

'Don't you *like* him? He's wonderful.'

'I was just trying not to make you jealous.'

Joanna laughed. 'I wouldn't be jealous of you.'

Thanks. 'Have you told him about it?'

'No, of course not. Anyway, it shouldn't be so bad now we're getting married. Don't you think? I mean, once I'm sure of him. He's made such a difference to me; I couldn't bear to lose him now.'

'Is he jealous of you?'

'I haven't looked at another man since I first set eyes on him. I'd wear a yashmak and veil if he asked me to.'

Oh well, thought Grace, that settles that.

She would have wanted to ask as many questions as possible before the barrier came down, but somehow found that, if this was love, she'd lost interest in it; she wasn't going to be the sort of person it ever happened to. They walked on in silence towards Land's End.

Stefan rang later, and was invited for New Year's Eve. Joanna had a few words with the Coulters to say how honoured she was to have the family ring.

'Were they nice?' asked Mrs Ritchie as Joanna came back.

'Couldn't have been nicer. Marian said how glad she was that I was marrying Stefan. I feel almost one of the family already.'

'She's hardly met you,' said Grace. 'Why's she so glad that Stefan's marrying you?'

'Well, she's heard a lot about me; I suppose we just hit it off.'

'What a terribly welcoming family they must be. Do they take in foster children?'

'I know we'll all welcome Stefan just as warmly,' said Mrs Ritchie. 'Do you think I ought to write her a letter?'

'Why don't you invite her down?' said Grace. 'Invite the whole family, the whole street. That would be a really warm welcome. I could move out to the greenhouse.'

'I think you're getting a little over-excited, dear,' said Mr Ritchie.

Between Boxing Day and New Year's Eve, the whole household settled down to mending and rearranging. Mrs Castle had no objection as long as it wasn't for her. Mr Ritchie largely redecorated the bathroom; new towels were bought in Castle's sale, stubborn stains were scrubbed into carpets, curtains hemmed; the pile of bills on the mantelpiece sorted out. If there were no visitors, there would be no tidy houses. In the garden, wood was chopped, hedges were cut, and the greenhouse was cleared out. It was a lovely, cheerful time; people would go about their business, meet over a hasty lunch and get back to work. Once, Grace was in the kitchen cleaning silver while her mother threw together a leftover turkey fricassee. 'Joanna seems terribly happy, don't you think?' said Mrs Ritchie.

'Yes.'

'What do you think of Stefan?'

'I haven't seen much more of him than you have. He's very handsome, I suppose.'

'What are they going to live on? I don't like to ask.'

'Joanna says he's very successful. I know she's giving up her job, so she's not going to be supporting him or anything like that. If he was that sort of person, I'm sure he could do better than her.'

'It's very difficult. I'd hate to think she was making a mistake.'

'There's nothing you can do. It would only remind her of Romeo and Juliet. She's near enough to turning my stomach as it is.'

'Ah,' said Mrs Ritchie. 'Wait till it happens to you.'

'I can't believe you ever went around behaving like that.' But the public relations firm came into operation and the barrier stayed down.

*

Stefan arrived late on the afternoon of New Year's Eve. Joanna put on her film-star looks and drove to Exeter to meet him while Grace set the table and Mrs Castle and Mrs Ritchie cooked. Joanna, when consulted on Stefan's tastes, said, 'Oh, he'll eat anything, he's not fussy.'

'He's a starving artist, after all,' said Grace. 'Just get the leftover turkey out of the fridge.'

'He is a guest,' said Joanna. 'I think we might go to just a little trouble.'

Stefan arrived with a morocco leather suitcase and an enormous box of chocolates. He was excellent; the true hero always is. Servants and dogs adore him, and he can charm any named individual off a tree. Mrs Ritchie was the first to go, beaten by the solicitous smile and the gentle inquiry in the eye. Mrs Castle followed.

'You haven't got a Yorkshire accent,' she said. 'You sound as if you came from just round the corner.'

'Ah,' he said roguishly, 'I'm in disguise. Never trust a Yorkshireman.'

It's not clear why this appealed to her so much; it seemed to her very daring. 'Never trust a Yorkshireman, he says, and he's a Yorkshireman,' she repeated, laughing like a child watching its big brother knock at doors and run away.

Mr Ritchie was won over by gossip. Stefan was painting the boardroom portrait of a slightly scandalous company chairman, and had one or two inside anecdotes. He had a nice way with his eyebrows. The face would stay straight and the voice solemn, so that on a tape recording you would never be sure of the irony; but one eyebrow would go slightly down and the other slightly up to indicate that the explanations he was repeating left something to be desired. Mr Ritchie blossomed with anecdotes of his own.

Why did Grace resist? Suppose this same man had picked her out instead of Joanna; would he have seemed so snake-like to her? Would the little manipulations, the conscious charm, have been smiled over and excused instead of being rooted out with avid snout and unforgiving eye?

Dinner was served with everyone on their best behaviour and the unmended napkin awarded to Stefan. It was a plain, solid, undistinguished room, but Joanna, with her eye for objects, had found a plate or candlestick or two that deserved comment. When Stefan, who knew the value of everything, found something to admire, Joanna would imply, with a pretty shrug, that it was just an old heirloom, lots more where that came from.

'What's this?' he asked, as the rather unusual cheese plate was brought in.

'It's the family plate,' said Grace.

By adjourning for coffee and brandy to the other room, they managed to string things out until almost ten o'clock. Two hours till midnight, as surreptitious calculation established. Could one just wander off to bed on New Year's Eve with a new and important visitor in the house? Could the television be switched on?

Stefan knew exactly what to do. He would pop upstairs and unpack, and then they were going to show him the family photograph album, which Joanna had told him so much about. What better way to see out the old year than learning about the family that you hoped to become part of in the new?

Grace was simply outclassed. She couldn't imagine handling this, or producing anyone who could. Surely it's too much to ask of your ideal man that he have the ideal family too? Would his parents have liked you so much if they met you at a party that they would have invited you to come and spend Christmas with them for the rest of your life? Would you have accepted if they had? No: you and they are in the position of pressed men, who have not only to put up with being captured but to welcome it. And your press-gang has to meet his press-gang and pretend it's just the press-gang that they've always wanted to meet; all this if you're lucky enough to fall in love.

However, the family album worked a treat. Being abroad so much, Mrs Ritchie had used her mother as the repository for all her souvenirs, and her own life and the childhood of Joanna and Grace were fully documented. Grace had been a sullen little thing from the start, a child who didn't adjust her face for the camera and thought the birdie was silly. Often, there was fear and puzzlement in her expression: why has my daddy got that machine stuck to his face? Later, when she understood the function of the camera, a rigidity was added but the fear and puzzlement remained. Joanna, by contrast, loved watching the birdie. Her shining face lit up to order and she was filled with wonder at the stuffed toy being used to deceive her. When she realized what the camera was for, her expression only became more natural and appealing. She was a society child who didn't mind a white lie.

There were stories attached to some of the pictures. This was Joanna with her first sweetheart, a blond soldier-boy who used to follow her everywhere. Here they were with the neighbour's large dog, she peeping trustingly over his shoulder. Grace was standing, eyes slitted, some way apart. 'Do you remember, Grace? David wanted you to stand close to him in case the dog got rough, and you said, "Go away. I can look after myself",' said Mrs Ritchie, laughing. Grace didn't like these anecdotes; they were about her, but she had no control over their content. Who knows what could be revealed? It was like hearing what you had done when you were drunk. Here's Grace crying because she didn't come top in class. Here she is with the wallpaper she scribbled over. Here she is with the precious cup she smashed.

Many of the photos were in the Paignton garden. This was the time it snowed; this was the glorious summer when we lived outdoors. Then there were the sunny bungalows: Cyprus, Singapore; and the tourist shots, when we lived in Brussels, when we visited the Tower before taking the children back to school.

They all had their separate emotions on looking at the photographs, and there would be much private musing as they went to bed. The official emotion, however, is a sort of glad nostalgia: how much we have in common, how happy we have been. When they switched the radio on at midnight for the chimes of Big Ben, they were able to raise their glasses and embrace with genuine warmth. Stefan had seen the inside of the family. He belonged.

He stayed three days, with Joanna playing the role of birthday girl and Grace of skivvy. Whenever Joanna offered to wash a plate or vacuum a room she was told to run along and enjoy herself: there were offstage workers to take care of all that. She played a role as beautifully as he; if you'd never encountered the word 'swansdown', it would rise spontaneously to the lips as she passed by. They took the car and went to fishing villages to watch the catch being brought in; they got into conversation with quaint characters who recited their quaint life histories at the sight of Joanna's smile. They took the cliff path on a clear, almost spring-like day while Grace clanked the dishes in the sink. At home, because Stefan was one of the family, the television could be switched on. The visit really went off surprisingly well.

On the last day they asked Grace to join them on their outing. They were driving to Plympton, where there were some paintings Stefan wanted to see. They asked her publicly, over breakfast, kindly, so that her immediate refusal not only was but sounded rude.

'Oh, Grace,' said Mrs Ritchie, 'do go. I know they really want you to.'

'Yes,' said Stefan with his doctor's smile. 'Skip the work. Just for today.'

It was amazing how sincere he could sound, and how your lips smiled back of their own accord. If this was what Joanna was going to have to contend with all her life, she deserved every sympathy. Grace agreed to skip the work, just for today, but insisted on the back seat of the car, where she sat like an accusation behind Joanna's shoulder.

In the car, Joanna and Stefan gave a word-perfect performance of a couple in love. She drove; he navigated. He didn't question her driving; she didn't question his eyesight. When he missed their turning, their love was unimpaired. 'Er, Joanna,' said Stefan, solemn faced.

'Yes, darling.'

'You know you were wanting to visit my family?'

'Yes, Stefan.'

'Well, I suspect you may be seeing them sooner than you think.' One eyebrow slightly up, one eyebrow slightly down.

'Stefan, are you trying to tell me something?'

'Yes, darling. I think here would be the very place to practise your three-point turn.'

They couldn't do this sort of thing in private, could they? Oh, Stefan. Yes, darling. Just pop along and see if the doctor's available will you, when you've got a moment. You've just sawn off my left leg.

Stefan decided to draw Grace out.

'How's Andrew?'

'As well as can be expected.'

'Has he been ill?'

'Oh sorry, no.'

'What's he doing for Christmas?'

'Going home.' The old family home on the Croydon moors.

He couldn't use his smile on her in case he missed another turning. Joanna stepped in.

'Is he still playing in that place with the funny name? The Lizard.'

'The George and Dragon. Yes. He's doing well.'

'Maybe we should go there sometime, Stefan.'

'I'm not sure it's our kind of scene, darling,' he said jocularly. 'Not our bag.' Vicars speak in that tone in an effort to make their sermons relevant to the young folk of today. 'And all the people passed by on the other side of the road, saying, "It's not my kind of scene. It's not my bag." But it's Jesus's kind of scene, you know; it's Jesus's bag.' And

162

all the old ladies muse to themselves, how did the blind beggar get hold of Jesus's bag?

'Aren't we nearly there?' said Grace. She wasn't going to bring out her stunted romance into the full sunlight of Stefan and Joanna's gaze. There was some tricky navigation for the last few miles, but they weathered it with their love intact.

Plympton Hall, where they were going, had a collection of portraits by Joshua Reynolds, who was born nearby. The house was beautiful, a-dazzle with herringbone brick. Because of the holiday season, it was also full, and they had to join a party of families with children on their conducted tour. Joanna hesitated between the roles of madonna and connoisseur. She picked out one child who was undeniably sweet, and played peekaboo with it for a while, just long enough for the photographers to get their cameras focused. But you can't admire paintings properly while going 'Peekaboo', and the child couldn't see why the game had suddenly stopped. For the first few pictures, Joanna's attempts to listen intelligently to Stefan's words were hampered by increasingly aggressive cries of 'Boo'.

The guide had the usual fund of lying anecdotes about the inhabitants of the house. In the seventeenth century a ten-year-old daughter had disappeared – look, ironically her portrait had just been finished when she was taken. Her room was in the west wing, where ever since, on windy nights, she could be heard crying 'Mama, Mama'. All the ten-year-old girls in the audience shrieked politely, treating the story, quite correctly, as a fairy tale badly told.

The women listened politely too as the guide recited, without a flicker of interest, the number of table-settings that would fit on the dining table at full stretch, the number of curtains you housewives would have to wash if you lived here, and the number of parquet squares in the floor. 'Fascinating,' one would say, catching another's eye. Well, you have to say something, he's probably doing his best.

When he came to the famous Reynolds room, he pointed out that it contained many paintings by the celebrated artist Sir Joshua Reynolds. They had been collected by the then lady of the house, who had also embroidered the cloth for the table in the middle of the room. Everyone except Stefan and Joanna went for the tablecloth, and after the scheduled minute, the guide led them to the door. Stefan and Joanna didn't follow; they were still on the second picture. The guide remained at the door while Stefan and Joanna discussed, with textbook elegance, the merits of the composition. Grace left them and went to join the group, where the child, mistaking her for her sister, cried, 'Boo'.

As Stefan and Joanna moved on to the third picture, the guide said, 'This way, ladies and gentleman, thank you,' and Stefan looked up.

'Please don't let us delay you,' he said with his gentle smile. 'We came specially to see these. We'll catch you up.'

The guide waited for moments like this. Still in his public voice he said, 'I'm afraid I can't allow that, sir, for security reasons. These paintings are very valuable.'

'We promise not to steal them,' said Joanna with her film-star look. 'We won't be a minute. Honestly.'

'By order of the trustees, no member of the public shall have access to any room except in the presence of a guide. I'm afraid I can't allow you to remain here alone.'

'This is ridiculous,' said Stefan. 'If you put paintings of this quality on show, you must allow the public the time to look at them properly.'

'Members of the public wishing to conduct research on the premises must submit a written application a minimum of three weeks in advance. If you have submitted such an application, please identify yourself to the attendant at the admissions office, when appropriate arrangements will be made.'

'Oh really,' said Stefan to Joanna, not lowering his voice. 'This man is *such* a nuisance. I think we'll just leave him to it.'

They looked round for Grace, who was hiding, and turned to go back through the door they had come in by. As they reached it the guide said, 'I'm afraid I can't allow you to leave that way. For security reasons, members of the public must remain with the guide throughout their tour.'

'Look, you're being bloody ridiculous. I want to speak to the person in charge.'

'When the tour is finished, sir, I'll be happy to conduct you to someone in authority. Now you must please accompany me for the remainder of the tour.'

The group moved on, accompanied by explosions of giggling from the children and stiff-necked sideways glances from the parents. Stefan and Joanna were ignored, especially by Grace. There was one whole wing still to do. The guide continued his anecdotes, each ending to gushing laughter as the members of the group got rid of their spare giggles in the only socially acceptable way.

When the tour was over, the guide pointed out the way to the deer park, butterfly house and model railway, and the children bounced out into the cold, the boring bit over. Stefan and Joanna stood waiting for Grace, who didn't want to join them until the group was out of the way. As she looked through her handbag, she heard a woman say how amazed she was at the lack of consideration of some people, and the guide reply that he had his duty to the trustees, he couldn't let the trustees down. At last Joanna said, 'Come on, Grace, we want to leave,' and Grace went to join them, tail between her legs.

On the way to the car-park, Joanna appealed to Grace. 'Have you ever heard of anything so ridiculous? We ought to write to the National Trust, or whoever runs these places. A minute to look at ten masterpieces. They seem to think it's like watching television, march you in at one end and out at the other and that's your dose of culture for the day.'

'I think he was offended because you didn't look at the tablecloth first,' said Grace.

'Oh really,' said Joanna, 'as if one cared about some silly old tablecloth that belonged to someone's grandmother.'

'Quite.'

Stefan was hurt, or embarrassed, or offended: one of the emotions that make you reluctant to smile at anything, however funny, and snappy to any overture, however well meant. Joanna put her arm round him. 'Poor Stefan,' she said lightly. 'I love you anyway.' Stefan went stiff. It was like reaching out to pat a dog with a ridge of hair raised along its neck.

'That's not much use to me at the moment, is it?' he said, bitter and low. Joanna pulled her arm away and looked at the ground.

'I want to see the lake,' said Grace. 'I think it's along here. See you back at the car.' She turned straight down a path without waiting for an answer. Within fifty feet it ended in a compost heap. She stood in the shadow until they must have reached the car, then crept back through the shrubs to see if all was clear. A family coming past to the car-park caught her peering round a tree trunk. Hello, just practising for my Jungle-Tracker's badge. They decided she was probably a lemur and walked on.

By the time she got back to the car. Joanna and Stefan were happy again. 'Was the lake worth seeing?'

'Lovely.'

'Shall we go and have a look?'

'I think we ought to be getting along.'

'OK. Stefan, maps at the ready?'

'Yes, darling.' Back to abnormal.

For lunch, they found a country pub with a roaring fire and a red setter flat out before it. The food was perfect: fresh country food simply cooked by the landlord's wife. The landlord, a retired airforce officer, was glad to welcome people like them. He chatted while they ordered their food, then brought their drinks to the old carved armchairs by the fire. Rusty went over and pushed his face on to Stefan's knee. They were early, and the few other couples didn't disturb the peace. Grace felt desolate, as if her children were buried under the flagstones. Worlds of warmth opened like flowers for Stefan and Joanna; now and again she would catch them in blossom; but they didn't open for her.

They drove back through beautiful Totnes. The town was still in full Christmas dress, but tastefully: it had a reputation to keep up. There was no reference to Christmas itself in the official decorations: just frosted pastel arches looping over the main street and the occasional ring of clear bells in the sunny air. They walked round the big old church, relic of lost glory, then through the second-hand bookstores and antique shops. Joanna saw just the lamp for Stefan's side-table, very good value, and bought it without a second thought. 'Now I'll have to marry you, to get it back.' Such a simple act: you see something, you know it's just the thing for someone, and you give it to them. How? Suppose they hate it; suppose they hate you; suppose their mother just gave them, for Christmas, the very thing for that side-table; suppose they never much liked that side-table anyway, and got rid of it last week?

The days were short, and it was almost dark by the time they left Totnes. Joanna drove slowly, with a few stops for Stefan to look at the map. She would rest her hand on his shoulder while he looked, sometimes turning her face to touch her mouth to his cheek. The buried children stirred beneath their flagstones and cried, 'Mama, Mama.'

At home over drinks they recounted their day: the country pub, the landlord who'd served in Cyprus, the gorgeous Rusty who tried to climb into the car with them when they left. The lamp was brought out and admired. 'Stefan has this little side-table by his sofa, and this will look perfect on it. I told him I'd have to marry him, to get it back, didn't I darling?'

'Oh, I won't let you slip through my fingers now,' he said, and Mrs Ritchie laughed with pride.

'How were the paintings?' asked Mr Ritchie.

'They were the best part,' said Grace.

'It was absolutely hilarious,' said Joanna. 'There was this poor little guide, terribly earnest but he obviously didn't know a thing about the paintings. We got into the Reynolds room and we'd hardly begun to look at them when he said it was time to go. Of course most of them didn't care – they were on an outing from Penge or somewhere – but a few of us were really keen. So there we were pleading with this poor little guide, who kept saying, "Oi've got me orders, Oi've got me orders." ' Joanna produced her symbolic working-class voice. 'The poor chap looked as if he was going to be led off to the dungeons, so eventually we said not to worry, we'd come back another time. You should have seen him. He looked so grateful he almost kissed us.'

'That must have been a bit of a disappointment.'

'Oh, there'll be plenty of other pictures,' said Joanna. 'He was being so brave, guarding the paintings with his life. We wouldn't have hurt his feelings for the world.'

'So you had all that drive for nothing.'

'Oh no,' said Joanna. 'It was a wonderful day. Grace loved it too, didn't you Grace?'

'I don't know how I can bear to go back to London.'

'Oh well, you don't have to go yet. It's only poor old me who has to rush back to work.'

'Are you working on anything at the moment?' said Mrs Ritchie to Stefan. Is there any money coming in?

'I'm always working. Every face I see, I'm thinking how I would paint it. I've already planned how to do yours.'

'Me?' said Mrs Ritchie. 'Good heavens. My face disintegrated long ago.'

'You don't need me to tell you that's not true.'

'What a lovely man you are. And now I think we'll eat.'

She'd spent the afternoon preparing a special meal. 'Not Yorkshire pudding?' said Stefan with a twinkle for Mrs Castle.

'Never trust a Yorkshireman,' said Grace.

'He said that, and he's a Yorkshireman himself,' said Mrs Castle, still working out the consequences of this paradox.

'No, it's meat with a lot of nasty foreign things,' said Mrs Ritchie. 'I expect you'll wish it *was* Yorkshire pudding, Mum.'

'Give me good plain cooking any day,' said Mrs Castle. 'Well, I'll just have a taste.'

They began to discuss the wedding and where it would be. 'I want it to be beautiful,' said Joanna. 'I want to marry Stefan before the world, not rush off to some hole-in-corner registry office.'

'A simple white wedding,' said Stefan. 'In the local church.'

'Have we got a local church?' asked Grace.

'We used to take you to the Methodist Sunday School,' said Mrs Ritchie. 'Down by the station. I expect they'd remember you there.'

'I don't think we can land a wedding party on your mother's doorstep,' said Mr Ritchie to his wife. 'I think it had better be in London. Much more convenient for everyone.'

'But I don't know how you *get* a church in London,' said Joanna.

'I can supply a church,' said Stefan competently. 'That is, if you're all prepared to trek up to Yorkshire. You know how it is in villages: you can't very well not go to church.'

'That's wonderful,' said Mrs Ritchie. 'But won't your mother hate having all this landed on her?'

'Good lord, no. She'll love it. There's not much to do in a village, as you can imagine, except organize things. She'd like nothing better than to have me married up there.'

Mrs Ritchie started planning a letter to Marian Coulter yielding chief organizing rights in the wedding. 'It makes it all seem so much nearer,' she said. 'My little Joanna leaving the nest.'

'Oh, Mummy,' said Joanna. 'I left the nest years ago. Think how much oftener we'll be able to pop over and see you once I've given up my job.'

'You know, of course,' said Mr Ritchie to Stefan, inches above his chair from Mrs Ritchie's kick, 'that Joanna receives no allowance from us?'

'I have a little money of my own,' said Stefan. 'We won't be rich, but with my painting I don't think Joanna will have anything to complain of.'

'Good, good,' said Mr Ritchie, duty done. 'Then I give you my full permission to take her off my hands.'

'Daddy, really,' said Joanna.

'To Joanna and Stefan,' he went on, holding up his glass. 'May you both be very happy.'

'To Joanna and Stefan,' they said.

Stefan and Joanna left next morning. 'What a nice boy he is,' said Mrs Ritchie. 'Let's go and turn out his room.'

Grace helped with the clearing up, then went to her own room to play the record Andrew had given her. He'd chosen well. (How?) She liked it, though she wasn't sure what it said about his attitude to her. The songs were as far from the blues as it was possible to get and still be approved by Andrew, arousing none of the uneasiness Grace sometimes felt on listening to the blues. The voice was sharp, the words were clear, the singer took no liberties: he picked out the melody neat as paint and landed each note on the nose. There was nothing sly about him. When he sang 'Happy Birthday, Sweet Sixteen' there were no hidden meanings. Indeed, far from putting in two meanings, he sometimes seemed to have difficulty inserting even one. Occasionally, he would have to take two runs at a single thought:

> *I'm living right next door to an angel*
> *And she only lives a house away.*

The lyrics were almost wilfully banal. The voice was always at full volume; there was no attempt to put expression into the words. Sad songs sounded just as happy as happy ones: Ho ho Come on baby, let's start anew, For breaking up is hard to do hum hum. The dedoobidoo-dumdums were brisk. It was as if this singer had said, 'You want a high-school song. Well, this is how it should go.'

The record was on the very borderline between rock music and pop. The best definition of a true pop song is a song one likes but shouldn't. A pop song is addictive: it's no sooner finished than you want to hear it again. It's the girl you despise but can't take your eyes off, the boy you hate but can't help hanging round. Andrew's record wasn't true pop. It had the addictive qualities of pop but none of the nasty aftertaste. You came out of it with your self-respect: you didn't feel exploited; but when you said 'I love this song', you didn't mean a lifetime love, but a teenage infatuation.

Grace should really have loved blues. Blues inspire true devotion. Among Andrew's generation of rock musicians, women come and women go, but blues remain a lifetime's passion; they never cheat on the blues.

'That sounds a nice, happy record,' said her mother when she came down to lunch that day.

'Andrew gave it to me for Christmas. It's an old family record that used to belong to his grandmother.'

'I thought I recognized his touch. Does he still play?'

'Ceaselessly. I don't know when he gets any work done.'

'Oh dear. Still, it's probably just a phase.'

'I'm not sure that's the way he sees it. I think he thinks work is just a phase.'

Grace tried to do some work of her own, but ideas were slow in coming. She found she couldn't read for long without running to the music for refuge. She'd practise her dance with thoughts of animals running through her head: as the hours went by, the dance and the animals got increasingly jumbled up. A new song would start and she'd find herself thinking, 'What species of song is this?' She'd turn from a picture of some strange animal wondering, 'What's its rhythm?', 'What's its beat?'

In the last few weeks, her dancing had been making progress. She and Andrew now had a respectable rock and roll routine. She'd watch Bob in the basement whenever she could, not daring to say 'Teach me', then rush away and copy him in the privacy of her room. It didn't look right: there must be some trick. She tried, but it didn't come.

The reading she'd brought was all about instincts. It was no longer enough to know that Kip Sullivan was for them and Jerry Bastable against them: she wanted to decide for herself. At first she'd found them reassuring. They were like the beat in Andrew's records: they laid down a framework, a common structure, that held the members of a species together, made the whole group kin. They also provided useful armour against the whims of animal trainers. It's not true, Grace found, that you can train an animal to do anything at all. The literature abounds with anecdotes of recalcitrant pigeons, self-willed hens, refusing to perform some simple task that goes against their instincts. For example, some species are solitary, others aren't. If you're born a member of a solitary species, friendship isn't even an option: solitary animals won't make friends, however many volts you put through them.

Unfortunately, nothing comes free. Instincts can make you into a puppet, limbs jerking, body twisting, out of control. Take birds, those paragons of selfless parental devotion, winging tirelessly to and fro to feed their darlings worms. It turns out that they're only selfless as long as they hear their darlings cheeping. If the parent goes deaf or the child goes dumb, the parent gobbles up on toast the child it's so lovingly fed.

It's all very well, thought Grace, to have a set of instincts that protect you from external interference; but what's going to protect you from your instincts? From this perspective, the concerns of the animal trainers began to seem less alien to her. If you're worried about oppression from outside, a certain degree of internal rigidity will seem attractive;

if you're worried about oppression from within, a certain degree of malleability will seem important. And if you're anxious, like Grace, to avoid being pushed around, there's no joy in exchanging one form of oppression for another.

Grace had anyway never been much impressed by arguments from nature. I can't help eating so much; it's in my nature to be greedy. I speak my mind: Sagittarians always do. I have to have my own way: I was born to be a leader. It's all right to fight, because look at our friends the wolves. Suppose there were incontrovertible proof, she thought, that humans were selfish, greedy killers. That wouldn't make it all right to kill: it would merely mean that certain instincts have to be resisted.

It occurred to Grace that what she objected to was not so much passion as mindless passion, the belief that you should indulge an instinct just because it's there. Reason is and ought only to be the slave of the passions, but that's not to say its only function is to help the spider get at the fly. The spider might find that, on reflection, it would rather be a vegetarian, or donate its web to the National Gallery. Reflection alone can't create a passion, but it can help you discover hidden passions you never knew you had.

Grace had never thought of the mind as a lofty internal debating chamber, with all the arguments carefully canvassed and decisions made by vote. She saw her mind as a fertile landscape, passions jostling and tumbling over each other to reach the sun. She saw herself as a land-scape gardener, nursing seedlings in a sheltered corner, using reason as a selective weedkiller, shrivelling some plants, allowing others to flourish, new seeds to root themselves in the vacant place. If reason alone can't create a passion, it can stop a garden becoming a jungle. Grace felt no more at home in a jungle than she did in a salon.

Wondering about resistance to instincts, she suddenly thought, 'That's it.' She rushed to the record player and began her dance again. She'd been too polite to the music, she decided, tried too hard to go along with it. Now she tried to go against it, tried to assert her independence. Whatever the music seemed to call for, she'd do something else. Instead of landing right on the beat, she'd land a little bit off; instead of trying to look frenetic, she'd try to stay serene. It worked, of course: well, that's the point. Rock is the music for resisters. It's resistance all the way down.

In the afternoons, she went for long cliff walks, mulling things over: reflecting on her thoughts and feelings, stirring them up, stirring again, reflecting on them again. There were images of Andrew, or of the places she'd been with him. Morning coffee in his room, with the pattern of the window-bars on the floor. Late Sunday afternoons in the basement, with Bob practising his dance steps and Lindsey bickering about where they were going to eat. Ears filled with music in the Newt; being tossed about in the van as they drove home. Grace was surprised at the tenderness these images provoked.

But tenderness isn't love. Grace wanted a love to last a lifetime. She always came back to the same refrain: Andrew was a nice enough man, but he was not the one. If asked, Andrew would no doubt have said he didn't *care* if he was the one. That was really the difference between them. He was prepared to try things out: to have a go and fail. Andrew wasn't bothered by failure: he didn't think it diminished him any. He'd turn it into a source of pleasure: dust himself down and say, 'What's next? I've really learned a lot.'

Andrew was like a beekeeper who strolls through the fields with his sleeves rolled up, who looks on stings as a part of life and doesn't think of every bee as a loaded weapon aimed at him. Grace was like a beekeeper who suspects she's developed an allergic reaction, who stalks the fields in battledress, saying one more sting can kill. She wasn't prepared to try and fail. She'd test every step before she took it: prod the snow for booby traps. She wasn't taking a chance on love, whatever the pop songs say.

Patrick figured prominently in Grace's musings. The night of the Institute party had changed her whole attitude to him. Most men, in Grace's experience, either ranged themselves along the hem of her garment, fluttering to destruction like moths to a candle, or saw nothing in her at all. She'd never been through the teenage phase of wondering about someone's intentions, pulling the petals off a daisy, saying 'He loves me, he loves me not.' Patrick was a new experience: she found herself yearning for him like a schoolgirl in one of Andrew's records. But was he a blues or a pop song? Was it infatuation or love?

Appealing as it was, the thought of Patrick as ideal man encountered serious difficulties. If he was her true love, why wasn't he behaving more like one? Where were the letters, flowers, secret looks? Such difficulties didn't deter Grace for long. Surrounded as she was by earthworks, battlements, moat and drawbridge, the mollusc shell to protect the soft flesh within, she found it easy to think of Patrick as similarly made. The more he stung, changed colour, sprayed ink to make the water cloudy, the more she thought he might have something to protect, some gentle centre where the sunlight played and waves plopped peacefully on the shore.

These musings led to no conclusion. Grace couldn't think what to do about Andrew until she thought what to do about Patrick, and she couldn't think what to do about Patrick. There might be nothing to do: he might walk straight past the next time he saw her, in which case the less thought the better. He might turn out to be her true love, in which case the question of Andrew would take care of itself. Only time would tell, thought Grace optimistically.

Thoughts of love led inevitably to Stefan and Joanna. Grace walked hunched up against the wind, wondering if she was being childish, stamping her foot and throwing bricks because Santa Claus had sent her sister the more enviable toy. Were Stefan and Joanna really ludicrous, or was it only sour grapes speaking? How would their behaviour be different if they were really in love? Could being in love fill an empty head, turn a butterfly into a St Bernard, make a crocodile cuddly? How could Stefan and Joanna be *more* truly in love?

The fact is, Grace couldn't avoid the conviction that Joanna, at least, was cheating. Wanting something impossible, she'd bent reality to fit her dreams. True love indeed, thought Grace. I mean, I ask you, really. What does she think this is, a fairy tale? True love, I ask you, I mean.

On Grace's last evening, over dinner, Stefan and Joanna were the main concern. They were approached obliquely, via the wedding. Shouldn't the Coulters and the Ritchies meet soon? They sounded so nice. But then Yorkshire was a long way away, maybe a few phone calls would do just as well; or maybe the Coulters would like to come out to Frankfurt at Easter. What a relief not to have to think about the arrangements for the wedding; perhaps Grace could bear that in mind when her turn came? 'I want just a simple family wedding in Westminster Abbey,' said Grace.

'Isn't it good to see Joanna looking so happy again?' said Mrs Ritchie. 'I didn't like to say anything, but you can see she hasn't been happy. And Stefan's such a lovely boy. They're obviously crazy about each other.'

'Crazy,' said Grace.

'I'm sure he'll be a great success as a painter. Did you see his hands? He has the hands of an artist. Did you see them, Geoffrey?'

'He has the hands of an unconscionable twit,' said Mr Ritchie.

'What?' simultaneously from Grace and Mrs Ritchie.

'Twit. Unconscionable twit. He has the hands of an unconscionable twit.'

'I thought you liked him,' said Grace.

'What would you expect me to do, attack him with a machete?'

'Good Lord,' said Mrs Ritchie. 'You never said.'

'I was the host,' said Mr Ritchie. 'I was waiting until he'd gone. And I wouldn't have said anything now if you hadn't gone maundering on about the hands of an artist. You provoked me.'

'I had to find something nice to say about him. Lord knows it wasn't easy.'

'You mean you don't like him either?' said Grace.

'Like him? I think he stinks.'

'Well well.'

'Well well, indeed.'

Relief made them slightly mean-spirited. 'Poor Joanna and her ring,' said Mrs Ritchie. 'When Grace said "Made in Sheffield", I nearly let myself down. And Mum didn't help much, did you, Mum?'

'It's not right to make fun of him,' said Mrs Castle. 'I said to her afterwards, "Don't mind them. I'm sure he's saving up for a proper ring." '

They leaned back in their chairs and laughed, catching each other's eyes and starting again.

'You should have seen them at Plympton,' said Grace. 'He kept saying things like, "See the poignancy in that hand," and Joanna would say, "It's enormously poignant, Stefan," while everyone stared at them as if they were Martians. And when the guide wouldn't let them look at any more paintings, he almost stamped.'

Afterwards, perhaps they felt guilty, because Joanna and Stefan were not unkindly mentioned again. If Stefan was coming into the family, they would do their best to make it an easy berth.

Grace left for London a few days later. Her parents dropped her on the way to the airport, hurrying to catch their plane. She'd be glad to get back to London, wouldn't she? Her new room was comfortable? Her new room was fine. So things were working out all right? Oh yes, everything was working out fine.

Chapter 8

The phone went before Grace was inside the room.

'Hello. I've been ringing all day.' It was Andrew.

'Hello, Andrew. I've just walked in.'

'Welcome back, when can I see you?'

'Did you have a good Christmas?'

'I'll tell you when I see you. What are you doing now?'

'Trying to get my key out of the door.'

'Oh. Well, I could come round and help you.'

'All right. Come round.'

As she heard him on the stairs she switched up the record-player. 'Hello,' he said. 'I see your taste in records has improved.'

'I had some help. Isn't it lovely? I know it off by heart.'

He began twitching to the music, stiff-armed, preoccupied, like a clockwork toy. She would have felt silly if he'd rushed up and thrown his arms round her, but she felt slighted when he didn't.

'Did you have a good Christmas?' she asked.

'You must be out of your mind. Of course I didn't have a good Christmas. What a time to go away. And you didn't even leave a phone number.'

'It was only a couple of weeks.'

'As the rescue squad said when they asked what took it so long. I know it wasn't long, really. It just seemed long. Did you have a good time?'

'Great excitement. Joanna and Stefan got engaged.'

'Oh yes?' He didn't seem terribly interested.

'Stefan came to stay.'

'Oh yes?' In fact, he seemed to be trying to make out the words of the song.

'That's the exciting bit. I won't tell you the dull bit in case I wake you up.'

'Sorry. It's the way he pronounces "through". TherERhough. TherAYyough. I just can't get it right.'

He didn't seem to have got his priorities right, either. The return of the loved one should surely prompt some expression of joy. Grace felt like a crusader rushing back to his wife to be told, 'Hang on a minute while I just finish dusting the vases.'

'I'd better not talk, then. I'd hate to think I was interrupting your voice exercises.' She went out to put the kettle on.

In fact, Andrew's priorities were quite in order: it was what to do about them that was puzzling him. By his reckoning, he'd won the Tour de France, cycled up the Champs Elysées in triumph, pedalled his way to flowers and champagne. But who knows how Grace reckoned? Even now she could be asking the judge for a disqualification, demanding a recount, denying that he'd ever been near the Champs Elysées, reserving the flowers and champagne for two quite other guys, declaring that she'd anyway always preferred tennis instead.

Waiting for a lead from Grace, though, was like waiting for a *bon mot* from a glacier. 'Have some coffee,' she said, slit-eyed, coming back into the room. Andrew was now propped against the mantelpiece, joints locked rigid with the effort to appear casual.

'Did you miss me?' he said. Wrong move. What was needed was a declaration of undying passion.

'I didn't have time to miss you.'

'Are you glad to be back?'

'I can't say I'm too thrilled at the prospect of another term like the last.'

'Well, you've always got me.'

A tiny, polite smile.

He removed his arm from the mantelpiece and walked towards her, realizing as he went that he couldn't throw his arms around her without spilling her coffee all over the floor, and took her hands to pull her out of the chair. Wrong move. The arms and shoulders came towards him, but the body didn't follow. He was left stranded, her hands limp in his. He pulled again. Slight stiffening of her arms. It looked like either give in or yank.

'Get up, Grace. I want to kiss you.' A look of faint, polite surprise but she got up. Hurrah for the lion tamer, the circus lives.

She perched quietly in his arms while he stroked her furry back. 'Oh, Grace. I wanted to see you again.' Her ribs tossed gently beneath his hands; he felt at peace.

First come first served, that's what I always say, Grace comforted herself. *Che sera sera*, what will be will be. Just drift with the current and float with the breeze, and we'll see where we end up.

This detached attitude carried Grace through, allowing her to remain suitably distant while re-establishing her relations with Andrew. It left him puzzled and frustrated. I mean, you've either won the Tour de France or you haven't: at some point the race ought to come to an end. Grace, though, kept shifting the winning post. Life with her was one long finishing sprint.

But as one dream flickered, another began to catch fire. Grace's aloofness seemed less important because of a flood of developments on the musical side. At the Newt, the band was a success: they were about to be promoted to the Friday-night spot. When Grace went to hear them after Christmas, she was startled by the change. No empty tables: hardly room to dance. You could feel something being created here; the audience urging the group on with pride and affection, like the home crowd whose local team is unexpectedly up for the cup. The manager of the Newt had powerful friends. There was a seductive whisper that a certain American rock and roll star, due to tour England that summer, was looking for a local act to open his show, and that Andrew's name was on his list.

Grace couldn't believe that such an amateur group could be taken so seriously. Surely you needed qualifications for a career? There must be a Diploma in Rock Music at some polytechnic, an apprenticeship, exam board and licensing body. You couldn't just pick up a guitar and sing? Earn money without getting O-levels? Drift with the current and float with the breeze? Not *really*?

Success drew the band together again. Andrew and Rick shut themselves in with piano and guitar. Squeak, thump, crash from behind closed doors; it was like old days again. They went together to the new blues clubs, where a hundred Ricks and Andrews saw their schoolboy dreams made flesh. They met their heroes, jostled for the chance to stand beside them and play a song or two. They trekked to Ealing, Richmond, Putney, river towns where the water froze that record-breaking winter, where rumours were swapped, amplifiers lent, and drummers found new homes. An army of foxcubs, snapping and frolicking, out for their first night hunt.

There was no room on these outings for girlfriends. Andrew rang Grace most days, and they still met twice a week, but his dreams had flowed into other channels: the tide of his affections was out. Grace worked, and worked, and listened to Andrew's records. A frog in the hand is worth two in the bush. A rat in time saves nine. Manners makyth mouse.

This term Dr Bastable's group were exploring the mammal. To Grace that meant antelope, zebra, tiger; to Jerry Bastable it meant the rat. Grace was dreaming of love and death on the savannah; what she got was the reactions to flashing lights and buzzing tones of starving, shocked, poisoned or irradiated rats. If you took care of the rats, so the argument went, the antelopes would take care of themselves. Everything is basically a rat at heart. Buzz it, bomb it, gas it, starve it, its reactions are essentially the same.

Put more academically, the assumption of these rat-fanciers seemed to be that there were no significant intellectual differences among species. A human is merely a rat that has gone through an extensive period of training. What a human can do, a pigeon can be trained to do too. When training fails – for example, when a suitably conditioned pigeon fails to recite the 'Ode on a Grecian Urn' – this is attributable not to any deficit in ability to learn, but merely to physical limitations, such as deafness or lack of teeth.

Grace had worried that constant reading along these lines might somehow dull her senses; each week she discovered she'd been wrong. What sort of people would claim an essential kinship between rat and human, then subject starving rats to electric shocks; set blinded, deafened, brain-damaged rats adrift in mazes to search for food; take credit for being the first to discover that a rat with most of its sense organs missing could still, with difficulty, run a maze?

Though she rarely said much in his tutorials, Grace did ask Dr Bastable, early that term, what he thought about ethology.

'Ethology?' he said. 'Oh, I see. Um. Ethology?'

'I was reading some over Christmas.'

'It's not on the reading list, is it?'

'No. I read it anyway.'

'Oh. Gosh. Well, the thing is, that though these people are great *fun*, they're not terribly scientific, are they? It's all a bit anecdotal. I mean, what's needed at this stage, really, is some good solid experimental evidence. Then we'll begin to know where we are.'

'It's a bit much,' said Grace to Jim and Patrick over coffee. 'There's all sorts of interesting stuff that he's simply telling us to ignore.'

'Is any of it about rats?' asked Patrick.

'Not that I remember. There's quite a lot about geese.'

'Well, there you are then. Geese aren't scientific. Rats are scientific. Pigeons are scientific. Let in a goose, soon it'll be a goat, and before you know it you'll have elephants all over your laboratory knocking over the beer.'

Over Christmas, the MA group had evolved: Chris Trent-Horsley was now pursuing Jackie Parker. 'Jackie,' he would call across the lecture room, one hand waving, the other patting the seat beside him. He would offer her coffee and chocolate drops; you would have thought she was his dog.

Chris Trent-Horsley had a problem with people. He was an unsuccessful Stefan Coulter, a fake who failed. We all have our postures and pretences: we all hope, at times, to pass for sophisticates, men of the world. The problem with Chris Trent-Horsley was that the gap between pretension and reality was simply too great. He was the sort who snaps his fingers at waiters, then wonders why they spill the wine all down his shirt. However hard he tried, he was instantly recognizable: beneath the top hat, above the white tie, the face of the class sneak still shone.

Jackie Parker had been issued by nature with an unattractive body, an acute awareness of the fact, and a total inability to carry it off. Hardly a crime, but this combination of properties generally carries a life sentence. Most men don't even see you; they're so busy looking at the proper woman over your shoulder that they keep tripping over you in the street. Ask one the time of day and he treats you like a piece of litter. When one of them actually seeks you out, you can't afford to sniff.

Grace watched Jackie hesitate at Chris Trent-Horsley's summons. You didn't need electrodes to know what she was thinking. 'Jackie,' she called one day from her safe seat next to Patrick. 'Come and sit here.' Jackie waved at Chris and sat in the back with Grace.

With Patrick, it was as if the night of the Christmas party had never been. He and Grace had coffee and lunch together; swapped books on Saturday mornings; exchanged jokes about Jerry Bastable and polite nothings about their Christmas vacations. 'Spent it with your boyfriend, did you?' asked Patrick. 'I haven't got a boyfriend,' said Grace.

The Institute had a Human Science club, where visiting speakers came on Wednesday evenings. They were mostly politicians or economists who used the club as a debating society, testing the water, practising new tricks. Grace sometimes went, attracted by the glitter of big names. One week, all the MA students turned up brushed and gleaming: Britain's leading expert on human nature had been invited to speak.

179

Richard Saxon was a man at the height of his powers: say forty-five and definitely distinguished. The Director led him into the auditorium, flanked by the home team of Jerry Bastable and Kip Sullivan, both displaying the red tinge that correlates with the presence in the environment of three or more glasses of free wine. Jerry Bastable, heading for the spare seat saved for him by Chris Trent-Horsley, left behind a succession of stepped-on toes, sharp hisses of pain and backward-tossed mutters of 'Oh, sorry' as the Director tracked his progress with affable smile and steel-plated eye.

'Right,' said the Director as Jerry snapped his seat, arm-rest and left and right-hand neighbours into more comfortable positions. 'As you know, our Wednesday visitors are normally from the business and political worlds, the worlds with which I myself, and many of you, are most familiar. Tonight it gives me great pleasure to welcome a rather different kind of animal. Chuckle. He told me over dinner – and you'll find this hard to believe,' he twinkled tolerantly, 'that he's not very interested in economics or politics. He thinks that once we know what makes people tick, we'll be able to predict how they behave, in the market place, the polling booth, and everywhere else too. And then us economic and political theorists will be out of a job. Well, I doubt if that will happen in my lifetime or yours, but let's give the man a chance. It's my very great pleasure to welcome one of our most distinguished philosophers, Professor Richard Saxon. Richard.'

Richard Saxon, who had sat modestly through this introduction, cheeks unflushed by free wine, stood up with a self-deprecating smile. 'After that introduction,' he said, 'I feel like a gladiator going out to face an extremely large and nasty-looking lion. With all these experts arrayed around, what can a simple student of human nature hope to offer? Well actually, you know, what I most want to offer is a word of caution.'

This was a disarming start. The students, flattered, rearranged their faces into suitable blends of ferocity and caution. The Director chuckled spontaneously and looked at his watch.

'Let me start with a simple question,' said Richard Saxon. 'If we want to understand human behaviour, where should we look? To the abstract realm of thoughts and feelings, hopes and fears, beliefs and desires? Or to the concrete realm of atoms and molecules, nerves and muscles, flesh and blood? To the abstract world described so well by poets, playwrights and novelists, or to the concrete world whose workings scientists are only now beginning to describe? How can the two approaches be reconciled? How can the abstract and concrete interact? The great economic and political movements, the tiny personal acts we perform every day: who can explain them? Who should we believe?

'These are natural questions. They occur to all of us when we are growing up. But you know, not every natural question is a legitimate one. "Which came first, the chicken or the egg?" That's a natural question, but it is not a legitimate one. Only someone ignorant of the facts of evolution could ask it. Now I am a philosopher, and telling legitimate from illegitimate questions is my business. And my word of caution is this. "How can mind affect matter?" "How can thoughts and feelings influence behaviour?" Asking those questions is like asking which came first, the chicken or the egg. Natural questions, yes, but not legitimate. Don't spend your time worrying over them. Better to go out and get drunk.

'I am aware, of course, of this Institute's reputation, and I know that for many of you these words of caution will seem unnecessary. You are scientists, after all: you study material facts and know that ultimately those facts must be materially explained. I know the Director here too well to doubt that you have been properly trained.

'My words of caution are more, as it were, prospective or pre-emptive. There are some fancy new ideas coming out of America' (here the Director spat) 'which have already led a few people astray. These people have fallen into the trap of believing that human actions – concrete physical events – can be scientifically explained in terms of thoughts and feelings. There is no doubting the appeal of this approach. Why did I eat? Because I felt hungry. Why do I speak correctly? Because I know the rules of grammar. Why did the chicken cross the road? Because it wanted to get to the other side. These explanations appeal to the teenager – the poet, the fabulist – in us all. What is wrong, though, what is fundamentally misguided and misleading, is to write poetry and call it science, to offer nursery rhymes as scientific theories. But that, and nothing more, is the latest trend.'

Philosophers, delicate souls, do not name names. You either know what 'a certain philosopher', 'a recent paper', 'a familiar argument' refer to or you don't. Grace only dimly perceived what gang of teenaged fabulists she was being warned against, but Kip Sullivan was sitting back, head tilted, as if he'd had vitriol thrown in his face.

On went the modest, down-to-earth, pipe-smoking voice. 'Plants drink water; they turn towards the light. Why? Of course there's nothing *wrong* with saying that plants drink because they feel thirsty; they turn towards the light because they want to feel the sun on their leaves. It's a way of talking, and quite a natural one. But if you gave these answers in a botany exam, you would quite rightly be failed. Why should it be any different for us?

'Someone might say, "But we have feelings; plants don't." Yes, we have feelings: aches and pains, itches and scratches, twitches and tingles, but so what? We may have them, but they can't make us act. To talk of mind acting on matter is like talking of goblins cooking the meat. It's pretty, maybe; it may sell a few cookers; but alas it is not science.

'A thought, a feeling, is like the froth on a wave. It is a by-product, an accompaniment, tossed up by physical forces. We can experience it, savour it, enjoy it, write poems about it, try and turn it into a work of art. But it will no more get us across a room than the froth on a wave will drive a turbine. To forget this is to end up with a manner of speaking masquerading as science.'

Kip Sullivan put his hand up. Richard Saxon looked courteously at the Director, who had started to snore. 'I think, unless it's a point of clarification, I'd prefer to take questions at the end.'

'Questions at the end,' said the Director, coming wide awake.

'It *is* a point of clarification,' said Kip Sullivan.

'Oh, by all means, go ahead then,' said Richard Saxon.

Kip Sullivan stood up. 'My point of clarification is this. Are you planning to give us any arguments to back up your position, or do you expect us to just accept your unsupported word?' He sat down. All traces of tolerance had left the Director's face. He looked like a headmaster whose least favourite prefect has lobbed a stink-bomb on speech day. Richard Saxon, though, had not got where he was by any failure of social skills. Controversy – or at least the appearance of controversy – was the cherry on his blancmange. If people argued with him, it must mean that he was saying something – or at least appearing to say something. The reaction of the audience bore this out: no more doodling on note pads, everyone listening for his reply.

'Well, Kip,' (all chums together) 'I'll resist the temptation to come down to your level and ask whether you'd recognize an argument if it jumped up and bit you in the neck. It does seem to me, though, that what you have there is a question of substance and not a point of clarification, and I think I'd prefer to present the rest of my paper, and you can come back to me at the end if you're not satisfied. In fact, my remarks so far have been largely introductory, and if you'll allow me I'll go on to the main body of my talk.'

And when he said 'body' he meant 'body'. The rest of his talk was full of leaping frogs, chomping locusts and adventuring rats, all going about their business without a song in their hearts or a thought in their heads; and if they – mere animals – can do it, why can't we?

'In conclusion,' he said, 'I am not a mystic. I believe that humans differ from the lower animals in the size and complexity of their brains, but in little else of significance to us. The study of the human brain is in its infancy. Who can doubt that as it proceeds it will shed new light on the springs of human behaviour? Who can honestly deny that in the fullness of time, our appeals to thoughts and feelings may come to seem as unscientific as appeals to phlogiston now seem to us? And to those who are tempted to disagree, I say, "Keep your hopes and dreams – but keep them out of the laboratory. When you come in to the Institute, leave them at home." Thank you.'

Before he'd finished the word 'thank', Kip Sullivan's hand was up. There were other hands, though, and the Director was able to ignore him. There was a deeply awful discussion of whether animals can think, interspersed with anecdotes designed to show the percipience, ethical commitments and reasoning abilities of various household pets. 'He's right, you know,' Patrick whispered to Grace, 'humans *can't* think.'

There was some support for the view that though it was clearly unscientific to appeal to individual thoughts and feelings in the explanation of behaviour, the thoughts and emotions of social groups were legitimate objects of study, as witness the fact that they could be approached in statistical terms.

There was also some sympathy for the claim that though Professor Saxon clearly had a valid point in *general*, in the case of the questioner's own research topic, voting behaviour on Clydeside 1908–12, interesting and undoubtedly scientific results were being obtained even in the regrettable absence of full neurological profiles of the voters.

Professor Saxon found some of these questions fascinating and the rest important. He discussed, suggested, and occasionally dared to disagree. At each possible break in the discussion, Kip Sullivan's hand went up. Sadly, there was no time to fit his question in.

'Well,' said the Director, 'though I can see that there are still one or two people' (one, actually) 'waiting to ask questions, I'm afraid the clock has beaten us. So all that remains for me to do is to thank our distinguished speaker for a most stimulating and provocative talk, one that I'm sure we'll still be debating for many months to come. Richard, thank you.'

There was polite applause, and members of the audience with unheard pet-anecdotes queued up to talk to the distinguished speaker.

'Let's buy old Kip a drink,' said Patrick. 'He looks as if he needs one. KIP,' his voice bounced off the blackboard, 'come and have a drink.' The Director swivelled his eyes, in mid-congratulation of his guest, to note who had spoken. 'Sure,' said Kip Sullivan, coming up the steps of the auditorium two at a time.

Patrick had his car outside, and drove them back to his flat. The room was ready for visitors: side-lights on, drinks-tray out, open books on armchairs, essay half-done on desk. 'What would you like to drink?'

'Don't ask me,' said Kip Sullivan. 'Just X-ray my head.'

'Whisky, Grace?'

'That's a fascinating and important question, but I think I'd prefer to come back to it at the end.'

'Jesus, what a jerk,' said Kip. 'I don't understand this country. Why is it that over and over again, they put a man like that in a job like that?'

'You heard the answer,' said Patrick. 'The place is run by frogs.'

Grace wanted to know more about the fancy new ideas that were coming out of America, but had not yet had enough whisky to ask. Kip Sullivan needed no prompting. 'What's the *matter* with these guys? Why aren't they *interested*? Give them an exciting hypothesis, compellingly argued, and all they can say is "Pooh".'

So what was the exciting hypothesis, compellingly argued, that Kip Sullivan wanted to defend? Professor Saxon, he said with venom, thought of humans as wind-up toys. Give them food and they'll eat; play them a jig and they'll dance; run up a flag and they'll salute. If you want to modify their behaviour, play on their natures with punishment and reward. From these simple beginnings, the sky's the limit: one day you're training pigeons to play ping-pong, the next you're explaining how the theory of relativity was produced.

Hold on, Kip had been planning to say. How exactly was that last step supposed to go? You haven't given us an account of language learning, and you're proposing to tell us how *Hamlet* got written?

Kip had his speech all worked out. The fact was, he'd been going to add, that not only did Richard Saxon not have an account of language learning, but there was good reason to think that language couldn't in principle be learned in the way he said. And if he'd been wrong about language, mightn't he also be wrong about the mind? Maybe it was a mistake to treat psychology as just an inappropriate name for the study of pigeon behaviour. Mightn't it turn out to be, after all, an appropriate name for the study of mind?

Or something like that; as the bottle passed from hand to hand, the argument became a bit confused. Give them whisky and they'll drink. On the third glass, Kip betrayed himself by revealing his views on the Director, Jerry Bastable, the Institute and England. 'Why *did* you come to England, then?' asked Patrick.

'Oh, the usual story. Oxford, Cambridge, Shakespeare, Dickens, British researchers getting the Nobel prize with two matchsticks and a ball of garden twine. I get here all excited, I try to talk to them in the senior common room, I tell them what I'm working on, and all they do is cough.'

Here Patrick surprised Grace, who would have sworn he was ultimately a cougher, by revealing plans to follow the fancy new ideas to America as soon as he'd finished his MA. Kip was full of advice and recommendations; Grace wished she'd been able to think that far ahead. Still, the bottle was handy. By the time she'd had enough whisky to make her talkative, she was unable to speak for fear of slurring her words. When Kip stood up to leave, she decided it would be safer to remain seated. 'I'd drive you,' said Patrick to Kip, 'but I think I'm too drunk.' And on the whole, Grace found it safer to stay with him than go.

Next morning, she felt as distant from Patrick as ever. Perhaps if he'd made some gesture of tenderness – but gestures of tenderness didn't seem to be in his repertoire. 'Coffee,' he said as he opened his eyes, and went straight off to the kitchen. When she followed him, he didn't speak. When she took her coffee into the front room, he didn't follow. She dressed. 'Must get to the library,' she said. As she went downstairs, she began to feel just the faintest suspicion that Patrick might be a write-off.

In this, she was probably right. Patrick was by temperament a candle, not a moth. Like a candle, he cared not for moths but for matches, fuel to keep him alight, glass shades to shield him from the wind, bearers to carry him where he could see and be seen. He was waiting for some forceful beauty (with nursing qualifications) to shelter him, stir him up, move him around. A relationship between two candles is not on: what can they do but glow at each other, flicker and dance a little, and then go out?

Grace didn't come to these conclusions all at once. Indeed, she never traced Patrick's lack of ardour to its structural source, probing instead for some secret weakness in herself. Of course I'm perfect, she thought, late at night in bed when her resistance was low. Surely he can't have seen through me?

As the weeks went by, her attitude to Andrew was changing; not that that was any business of his. Inch by inch, tiptoe by tiptoe; it seemed to Grace that she had known him for ever. Gestures of tenderness were in his repertoire. Sometimes he would say things that surprised her, that seemed to demonstrate the presence of percipience, ethical commitments and reasoning abilities. It was almost as if he was human, thought Grace.

At the same time, she was beginning to feel something for the music, to appreciate the timbres and rhythms that lifted the face and body, that made you step and smile. While Andrew was out, and the music rippled from the record-player like clear water from a spring, she saw in her head the dancing couple from Oxford, tuned to the same rhythms, weaving their separate patterns, twining their separate dances into a whole.

While Grace was tiptoeing towards him, Andrew was pursuing his dream. What six months ago had been little more than a fantasy was now surprisingly near. At that time, rock and roll's great legendary singers could be enticed to England on a shoestring (Oxford, Cambridge, Shakespeare, Dickens, British researchers getting the Nobel prize with two matchsticks and a ball of garden twine), and had no objection to sharing a stage with any semi-professional group of half-trained musicians the locals could provide. It was all so casual then. The big record companies and promoters, still fixated on the Tennessee Waltz, were only just beginning to feel, uneasily, that there was something of potential commercial value going on behind their backs. The manager of the Newt really could get together with a couple of mates and send their boys off to tour the seaside boarding-houses of England with an all-time great.

Elmo Harper and his pompadour hairdo were going to tour England in June; and it was now as definite as it could be in those unorganized circles that Andrew's group would be going with them. This provoked a serious crisis over names. They'd started at Oxford simply calling themselves the Group; like the Grape, there was only one of them around. No one had been happy with this, but the music had seemed more important than bickering over names. Now the manager of the Newt had said it simply wouldn't do.

Grace was in the basement one Sunday when the question of names came up; was dragged up by Lindsey in fact. 'So what are you going to call yourselves, then?'

Davy wanted something bold and romantic. The Cavaliers, the Bohemians, the Rakehells, the Black Sheep. You could tell what he saw in the mirror: a young lord on the razzle; the one the matrons whisper about while dangling their daughters before him, the one who ends up, having sown his wild oats, pledging title, love and fortune to an irrepressible schoolroom miss.

Lindsey was understandably sharp with these suggestions. 'Who do you think's going to pay to watch you lot poncing about in periwigs and beauty spots? Grow up, for heaven's sake.'

Rick, drowned deep in memories of the southern shack by the railroad track where he'd almost been born and brought up, wanted the Cotton Pickers, the Fireflies, the Dogwood Boys, the Railroad Gang.

'Look,' said Andrew. 'We're not a gang. We're a bunch of hairdressers and polytechnic students. I don't want to play at being something I'm not. We're not the genuine article. Why pretend to be?'

'It's all pretending,' said Lindsey. 'They're all phoney as hell. It's a racket. What do you think they are, a Boy Scout pack?'

'Shut up. You don't know anything about it,' said Rick. It was a pretty long speech for him.

Andrew, however, had been thinking. 'I've got a suggestion,' he said.

'Andrew's got a suggestion,' said Bob.

'All right, I won't tell you; you can work it out for yourselves. I'll give you a clue, though. What's the group for? What do we do?'

'We play music.'

'What else?'

'We play poker.'

'Yes.'

'We sing.'

'And what do you call someone who sings?'

'A singer?'

'A frog.' (From Grace.)

'What's a fancy name for a singer?'

'An opera singer?'

'A songster,' said Rick. 'Oh.'

'A songster. That's right.'

The suggestion had been quite carefully thought out. It appealed to Andrew because it was true: it told no lies, it raised no false expectations, but left room for an element of fantasy none the less. In America, the songsters were the wandering bluesmen who carried the tunes from town to town along the country roads. For Davy, there were added overtones of minstrels and troubadours, Lancelot and Guinevere, the Lady of the Lake.

'The Songsters,' said Davy, trying on his doublet and hose.

'The Songsters,' said Rick, resting his dust-weary feet.

And the Songsters it turned out to be.

To celebrate their new name, the group decided to hold a party. The basement was big enough, and there were few neighbours with enough hearing left to complain. Even here, there were residual ideological bickers. For Rick, a party was something that should just break out spontaneously, like a riot in a jailhouse, or a song and dance in the cotton fields. You don't send out invitations to a riot, or lay on smoked-cheese canapés. Unfortunately, because of his unbroken taciturnity, Rick didn't actually know anyone, and it would have been hard to tell a party organized along his lines from an evening when everyone was out.

Davy had an innate knowledge of the principles of party-giving, at the heart of which lay invitations and smoked-cheese canapés. Not the sort of invitations you buy up ready made, but specially hand-illuminated in next season's colours of terracotta and burnt ochre, and preferably delivered by a hand-dyed pigeon or gun dog. A derelict basement was a fun place for a *comme-il-faut* party (or why would Davy have lived there?). However, a certain amount of interior decorating would strictly speaking have to be done.

Since Davy knew the sort of people who illuminate invitations, hand-dye gun dogs and interior-decorate derelict basements, his ideology prevailed. Sherry offered to deal with the smoked-cheese canapés, not even bothering to look at Grace or Lindsey for help. 'I'll need a few quid for buying things, though,' she said.

'No problem,' said Bob. 'We'll all chip in. And when we get to number one, I'll buy you a mink coat and a diamond ring.'

'White leather,' she said, jotting down her shopping list. 'Straight cut, just above the knee. And a dishwasher for my mum.'

'God give me strength,' said Lindsey, but under her breath.

'All right,' said Andrew, 'who are we going to invite?'

They sent out the invitations for a Friday evening three weeks ahead (to give Davy time to complete the necessary public works programme). Rick invited Heather and the other person he knew. Sherry and Bob invited some of their colleagues from the hairdressing salon. Lindsey invited a journalist she was prepared to speak to. Davy invited some lords and ladies. They all remembered Oxford friends, and new acquaintances from the clubs. And Andrew invited Stefan and Joanna, to pay them back for their dinner party the previous term.

'Anyone else you can think of?' he said to Grace in her upstairs room one night. 'Anyone you knew at Oxford? Or someone from the Institute you like?' But Grace was not having Fergus or Rowena along. She still met them for the odd lunch or drink, but their lives were moving apart; after the Oohs and Hi's and Great to See You's there was nothing much left to say. Never again the day-in, day-out of jokes and gossip and lent sugar and afternoon walks and essay crises. Now it was all phone calls and pencilled appointments in diaries. Grace didn't even have a diary. If they'd ever spoken to each other, she'd have found a lot in common with Rick.

'There's really no one I can think of,' she said.

'What about that chap from the Institute?'

'What chap?'

'The one I met in your room. What was his name?'

'Oh, him,' said Grace, refusing to name him in case the roof fell in. 'No, why should I want to invite him?'

'I don't know,' said Andrew. 'You tell me.'

Goodness knows what he meant by that. Grace pretended to be a Japanese tourist and went to make some coffee.

But Andrew was anxious to provoke something. If he'd been inclined to irony, he would have nodded in recognition that his wish for Susie to stop belabouring him with every passing feeling and fancy had been truly answered in Grace. He was almost sure she *had* feelings (though less sure that any of them were about him). You'd think that in the circumstances he had the right to ask her directly, but he knew without hesitation that to ask her would be asking to be shown the door. On the other hand, he wasn't going to settle for a life of frosty tolerance from Grace. Dammit, he thought. All she needs is to take her foot off the brake. And start the engine. And throw the gear-lever out of reverse.

He followed her into the kitchen. 'Look, Grace, I'm beginning to feel I can't go on like this. I can't live with someone who's always looking over my shoulder for something better. I can't put up with it any more.'

Actually, Grace realized, she was no longer looking for anything better. Despite the constant battering, her feelings for Andrew had grown. They were there and waiting, flower buds forming. It was as if she'd never seen them before and come across them in an abandoned flowerbed, overrun by weeds. Andrew had suddenly come into focus. From now on, a room would look incomplete if he wasn't in it; she'd pick him out in a crowd of hundreds; if twenty people spoke together, he was the one she'd hear.

You'd think this would call for a glass or two in celebration, a glad word to Andrew, a happy sigh, a stroll hand in hand in the sun. Looking at Andrew, though, all Grace felt was dread. Here was a man who liked variety, who always talked in terms of the present, who'd left a string of Susies behind him. He didn't think that love was perennial: he'd treat it as half-hardy annual, devote himself to it for a season, and if it didn't flower just the way he wanted, pull it up by the roots and start again.

Grace simply hadn't been quick enough: she'd known there was something wrong with Andrew, but hadn't been able to put her finger on it; she'd floundered around making stupid objections and missed the crucial fact. The only thing wrong with him, she now saw clearly, was that he'd wake up one morning and abandon her. Leave her like a brain-damaged rat, blind, adrift in a maze.

Andrew wasn't Grace's ideal man. Give him any body you like, dress him in any clothes you like, fill him with any thoughts you like, the essential feature of the ideal man, the one thing you can't take away from him, is that he's permanent. And the people who really care about permanence are not the woolly romantic dreamers but the ones whose basic, bedrock passion is the fear of being abandoned.

We all carry our commitments next to the heart: it's just a question of whether we keep them inside or outside the skin. Outside the skin, you can get rid of them and live to tell the tale. Inside, something organic happens and you have to wait for the post mortem.

Someone was going to have to go against someone's nature if anything was to come of this. 'I am *trying* to change,' said Grace. 'If you haven't noticed how much I'm trying you must be very dense.'

'How? Tell me how you've changed since you knew me.'

'I speak to you. I spend time with you. Can't you see I'm trying to be friends with you?'

'Friends. I don't need friends. I've got plenty of friends. I don't want you to be a friend. I love you, Grace. I want to be part of your life. I want to know what you're thinking when I look into your eyes; I want you to smile with pleasure when I come into the room; I want to share your secrets; I want there to *be* something between us.'

'So do I,' said Grace, moved. 'But maybe these things take time. Why should you expect them to happen all at once?'

'It's not a matter of time: we could go on like this for ever. It's a matter of commitment. You have to make a commitment if it's to be worth our going on.'

'I never heard you make a commitment,' said Grace.

'I made it long ago. Why else do you think I'm still here?'

Aha, silent commitments. Maybe something could be worked out along those lines.

'Well, all I can say is that I'm as anxious as you are to be happy. Why else do you think *I'm* still here? But I'm a bit wary of commitments. It's not easy to undo them once they're made.'

'There you are, you see. You can't stop thinking about how to escape.'

That really wasn't the point, but Grace let it pass. 'Give me time. Just wait a bit longer.'

'Sigh. I'll wait a bit longer.'

As always, under intense Darwinian pressure, Grace evolved to a higher plane. She publicly admitted Andrew's existence by sending an invitation to an Oxford acquaintance, Sadie, with a note attached: 'I'm helping to organize. Do come.'

This was amazing boldness for Grace. For one thing, she was never quite sure if she knew Sadie. They'd been at the same college, in the same year, but moved in different circles, sharing no more than the occasional coffee in the common room late at night. Sadie lived at the intellectual end of the beagling set (reserved for those who not only looked at the pictures in *Horse and Hound* but could also read the captions), and went to balls and country-house weekends. This sat ill, or so Grace felt, with the fey wit she would switch on, sparkling, when there was someone around to charm. She would say outré things with a serious face, and then give a little loony giggle. She played havoc with the beaglers, and was usually trailed by two or three of them, hot on the scent. Grace was puzzled and intrigued. Why was this dainty Christmas-tree fairy wasting her wit on a pack of huntsmen? Surely Sadie could have wisecracked her way into any circle she chose? From beneath that surface looniness, a deeper madness called across the coffee cups to Grace. Like two blonde babies parked in neighbouring

191

prams, they would stare at each other silently, dimly perceiving that they were kin.

Back came a note from Sadie: 'Will come will bring George.' It was now Grace's party too. She joined in the floor-sweeping and wall-scraping. Davy's room was perfect already: a lick of powdered cochineal and a few earth and forest shades had transformed it into the sort of dungeon that a French aristocrat would envy. The main room had a definite feel: it was just a matter of whitewashing the walls, doing something about the floorboards and scattering a few shawls and dried flower arrangements around. The rest of the flat was clearly in need of some gentrification.

Bob showed a surprisingly strong territorial instinct when Davy came to inspect his room. It was only when he realized that by agreeing to decorate he could spend many hours with Sherry behind closed doors that he made even a pretence of falling in with Davy's plans. Sherry moved in with mop and brush, and left her trail all over his lair. She closed off the dank cupboard and bought a gentleman's wardrobe; rearranged the furniture; made curtains, cushions covers and a quilt. She performed her natural female function. She turned a badger set into a home.

When Davy came to visit Andrew, Grace was surprised to feel the stirrings of a territorial instinct in herself. They come in here and modernize our slums. But she resisted. She'd have been horrified if Andrew had tried to make her over to fit his tastes, and couldn't bring herself to stamp her mark on him, dropping soft furnishings and pot plants like imperial flags. She helped with the whitewashing and paint-ing, but made no suggestions for improvement. Andrew looked long-ingly at Sherry sewing. A little hope went out of him every day.

The party was a meeting point between two hostile traditions. In those days, rock stars weren't invited to royal weddings, and if invited, they wouldn't have gone. There was rock music, and there was civiliz-ation, and at the party, it showed. Half the guests were trying to look as if they'd just dropped in from Queen Charlotte's Ball; half were trying to look as if they'd just dropped out of jail. Half of them were really listening to the music; half were waiting for the gaps between the songs. Davy strolled gracefully down the middle, a foot in either camp. In the no man's land between the two extremes, all sorts of exotic hybrids were being born. There were the young lords and ladies who fell in love with the music, who climbed the fence in search of fraternity or freedom; there were the ex-jailbirds who climbed the fence in the other direction, in search of culture, sophistication and invitations to the royal wedding. You could see it happening at the party: a scaling and tunnelling and wire-cutting; great sections of fencing coming down.

Sadie arrived with George. The chief beagle, sad eyed and well trained. He shouldn't have been there; he shouldn't have been anywhere with Sadie, but she was like aniseed to him. Though he rarely spoke, you knew he'd been to a good school and had a loving mother who taught him how to say his prayers. He was tall and fair, and his hair was slightly curly. The word that best fitted him was 'wet'. Yet he too had his dream, programmed deep within him. His face was expressionless and his eyes were dead.

'Grace,' said Sadie, sparkling down an imaginary escalier. From her, even a greeting could sound ironical. 'Do you know George? George, who had never been to King's Cross before, stepped simultaneously forwards and back, afraid of the Apaches outside, afraid of the Apaches within: 'Ah, how do you do.' He took Sadie's cloak and looked round for a butler, then added it and his evening scarf to the pile of coats on the floor.

'What *fun*,' said Sadie, peeping into the ballroom. 'How *are* you, Grace? What are you *doing* with yourself?'

'Oh, this and that, you know how it is. What about you?'

'My dear, don't ask,' with a little loony giggle. 'George,' and she gathered up his leash.

'Come and meet my sister,' said Grace, after a quick scan of the guest list had failed to come up with any dukes. Heading for Davy's room, Sadie passed quite close to Sherry's shimmy, and gave a little hoot. 'Sadie, George. This is my sister, Joanna, and this is Stefan. He's from Yorkshire.' George laughed to show he'd understood the joke: as if anyone from Yorkshire could be called Stefan.

It turned out, actually, that Stefan came from a part of Yorkshire that George didn't even know it was possible for people to come from; but Sadie was soon deep in talk of country weddings in June. Boredom wasn't a problem for Sadie. Whatever she was after in life, stimulating conversation was not high on the list.

'Stefan's a portrait painter,' said Grace to George, hoping to broaden the conversation before she left.

'Ah,' he said, taking two steps forwards and two back; but Sadie had overheard. Learning that one is in the presence of a portrait painter is like learning that one is in the presence of a graphologist or seer. These people can read the secrets of your face: grade the bone-structure, find something . . . interesting in your cheek planes, be challenged by the play of light and shade on your hair. 'She may not have had a conventionally beautiful face,' you can hear them tell each other, 'but by Jove, she had the finest pair of eye sockets it's ever been my privilege to see.' It was obvious that Sadie had overheard by the lift of her chin and the calibration of her smile. There was something she often did when she went into a room, a sort of pause for flashbulbs, when she would just freeze for a moment, choking a giggle, and strong huntsmen would bay at the moon. Stefan was undoubtedly arrested. Soon after, Joanna decided that she wanted to dance.

Now this was a party where there were people who could really dance; but the fact that they were in the presence of masters altered Stefan and Joanna's behaviour not a bit. Out came the bathtowel, rigid grin, furrowed forehead and wagging head. The screaming scorn this provoked in Grace betrayed a secret fear. For her these days, being in the presence of a rock musician was like being in the presence of a graphologist or seer: they can read the secrets of your body; they know whether you can really rock. Once again, the world was divided into two sorts of people; once again, Grace found herself on the outside, looking in.

At midnight, as Andrew was about to change the record, Bob jumped on to a tin trunk and clapped his hands above his head. 'Speech, speech,' and everyone crowded into the main room to see what he would say.

'We're here tonight,' he said. 'Well, you all know why we're here.' Andrew and Davy looked modestly down; Rick and Heather, leaning back boneless on the couch, went on staring straight ahead. 'So we won't bother with that. What I really want to say is, I recently met this young lady. Sherry. Come up here beside me, Sherry, I can't make a speech to save my life.' Sherry hitched up her skirt another six inches and climbed on to the trunk, smiled at the whistles and put both her arms around Bob's waist. 'I just want to tell you that she's wonderful. And we've just got engaged.' His face crumpled. Sherry kissed his cheek and smiled serenely round. There were whistles, stamps, and cries of 'Good old Bob'. The man on permanent watch for a chance to sing 'For he's a jolly good fellow' sang 'For he's a', and there were enough people drunk enough to join in.

Grace was standing behind Davy and Lindsey when the announcement was made. Davy was one of the leaders in the cry of 'Good old Bob'; but as he stamped and whistled, he fractionally widened the gap between him and Lindsey. Lindsey also looked as if she would like to stamp. 'Strewth, what a palaver.' But she didn't look at Davy or try to narrow the gap.

As Bob and Sherry climbed down from the trunk, people gathered round and clapped them on the back. Joanna was drawn to Sherry (another chance to talk about weddings in June), and later Grace saw them in the corridor, away from the noise, no doubt exchanging ideas on place settings and bridal bouquets.

Rick and Heather began to dance. He must have been dancing, because he stopped when the music did. Otherwise, he might have been standing in a bus queue: the distant stare, the shift from foot to foot. Heather was not quite confident enough for this technique: she pointed her face at the floor, swooped towards it and retreated. She would have made an interesting partner for George.

After a while, Rick's stare became fixated on someone else: a black-haired ghost with pale face and lips, whose dancing technique was similar to his own. During the next record, without a word to Heather, he shuffled towards her, cigarette dangling, and took up his dancing posture between her and her partner. The partner, edged out of his territory, wandered off to get a drink.

Heather looked, saw, and went back to the couch. She leaned against the wall, expressionless, as the record ended and Rick did not return. The party was past its height now, tipped over on the downward run to dawn. A series of slow records had begun, and couples were swaying, or staggering, cheek to cheek. Andrew had cupped his hand over Grace's silky hair. Suddenly, screech, squall, chatter, came a racket like squirrels fighting. There was Heather, fur in ridges, tail lofted, teeth bared, chattering at Rick and his ghostly partner from the end of a branch. Couples, still draped, stopped moving and turned their heads. The music, deep and husky, ran on:

Ah my emotion (woo woo)
Is-a deep as the ocean (woo woo)
I'll be true (woo woo)
To-a you.

As the record ended in a wail, Rick looked directly at Heather and said, 'Piss off you silly cow.' He turned his back and re-draped himself over his new partner. Another long speech for him.

Heather rushed into the hallway, tossed coats and scarves into the air until she found her own, and ran up the basement steps, slamming the door. Someone impeccably English put another record on. The ripples subsided; the party flowed on, undisturbed, towards the dawn.

'Andrew,' said Grace in her swallowed voice. 'How awful.'

'All part of the entertainment,' he said, stroking her hair.

'How could you do that to someone who's supposed to be your closest friend?'

'What, scream the place down just because he has a dance with someone else?'

'Abandon her. Just like that.'

'How should he have abandoned her? Things end, you know.'

The music slowed. People were beginning to leave. 'Grace,' said Sadie. 'This has been fun. Let's have lunch soon and talk properly. I'll give you a ring.'

The party thinned to a point where a start could be made on clearing up Andrew's room. Cigarette burns in the quilt, glasses overturned and overflowing: the unthinking vandalism of the party-goer. A couple slumped on the floor took the hint and left. Andrew restored the room to normality by re-hanging the sacking on the window. They sat on the bed, dreamily, backs against the wall, more comfortable together than they'd ever been.

'Fancy old Bob getting gathered in,' said Andrew.

'You didn't know he was getting engaged?'

'I shouldn't think he had much warning himself. I expect all of a sudden he just cracked up.'

'Sherry's very sweet.'

'Yes, but marriage.'

'I know.'

Pause for nightmares. Then all of a sudden, Andrew cracked up. 'I know just how he felt standing there: he felt all blown up, like a balloon. He was so happy he wanted to tell everyone about it, but he couldn't find the right words. I feel like that with you sometimes. You turn and smile at me in the street, I put my arms round you and you lean closer instead of pulling away. You can make me quite speechless with joy.'

'I have this picture,' said Grace. 'Two people who never touch each other in public, who go to parties and separate at the door. And everyone says, "How cold those two are. Thank God I'm not like them." But it's a sort of politeness, you see. They know each other so well, and feel for each other so much, that to let others see would be a sort of boasting.'

196

'And that's what you'd like?'

She smiled.

'Well, we're half-way there. We've mastered the public coldness bit.'

'Yes, the rest seems to be a little harder.'

'I've told you, all it takes is a leap of faith.'

'I'm a rational human being. I'm not taking any leaps of faith. When I jump, I want to know where I'm landing. When I choose someone, I want to know it's the right person.'

'Poor Grace, sitting in your corner counting up people's mistakes. We could make each other so happy. Just a little leap. Try.'

Now maybe Grace had naturally ripened until she was ready to fall off the tree. Maybe her feathers had fledged enough to be capable of sustaining independent flight. As the slow dripping of water wears away a stone, maybe Andrew's pleas had tipped the chemistry of her brain cells from a state of 'off' to 'on'. It seemed to her that she was thinking things out, weighing arguments, coming to a decision, if not a rational one. It seemed to her that she was being brave and generous. In any case, whatever the cause or reason, a few days after the party, Grace closed her eyes and jumped.

Chapter 9

Silently, mind you. You can't just go up to someone and say, 'Hello, I've committed myself to you.' Suppose that since he last saw you he's begun to reconsider, the spark that flamed for no reason has, for no reason, gone out? Suppose he's trying to make out the words of a song and asks you to repeat yourself? Suppose he pulls out his handkerchief and sneezes in your face? Anyway, thought Grace, a commitment doesn't need to be put into words: it's bound to manifest itself in your behaviour.

But how? Generally, the main effect of a commitment is to stop you doing things you weren't officially doing anyway. This is not something that, now committed, it's in your interests to reveal. 'Hello, I'm going to try not to be repelled by the way you eat.' 'Hello, I've stopped sleeping with the man upstairs.' Still, thought Grace, it's bound to show itself, one way or another.

It had a chance to show itself quite soon. Towards the end of term, Davy and Lindsey began to talk of going away. 'Lin needs a break,' said Davy. 'We're going to France. I'm sure I can fix it with Joe.' Joe was the manager of the Newt, the impresario of the Elmo Harper tour. It was in his interests to be nice to them, at least until June. He agreed to let another group fill in for two April Friday nights.

'We could go somewhere,' said Andrew to Grace. 'Get out of London. What do you think?' Grace's new commitment did show itself here. Instead of discovering an unavoidable engagement, she agreed immediately that it would be nice to go away. They decided to take the van and drive to Cornwall. Two weeks alone together among the primroses and seagulls. Two weeks to relax and build up a stock of memories. Two weeks alone together, thought Grace. My God, what will I say?

Here again her new commitment showed itself: that thought was no sooner formulated than pushed away. Away with the interior monologue, away with the reservations. You can't jump without taking both feet off the branch. So when Andrew turned up in Camden Town one spectacular April morning, she did not, for once, go downstairs with dread in her heart. Normally, such a sky on such a day, giving the taste of what a generous cosmos might offer in the weeks to come, would have filled her with despair. If the sun shines on the morning of your holiday, and the hopes creep out like butterflies in the sun – quick, stamp stamp, it'll be kinder in the long run, they'll never have to face a lingering death.

Not that Grace suddenly began to think better of the cosmos. She didn't expect it to put on cap and bells and follow the spectacular April morning with two spectacular April weeks: it was only Andrew, not the cosmos, she'd decided to trust. She merely told herself, quite firmly, that whatever the weather, whatever the problems, with goodwill and intelligence on both sides, every difficulty could be overcome. As they headed south for Salisbury Plain, she leaned over cheerfully and squeezed his arm.

Grace had learned a lot about Andrew from watching him plan the holiday. The very idea of planning a holiday was alien to her: the idea of planning anything that could come crashing about your ears in ruins. But Andrew had spent hours in bookshops reading the guidebooks, and knew exactly what he wanted to see. On his list were follies, viaducts, dams and bridges, fortresses, castles, decaying town walls. What attracted him was construction, building, every sort of imprint left on the landscape by man the engineer.

Stonehenge was the first stop on his list. To Grace, catching sight of Stonehenge wavering in a haze across Salisbury Plain, its most striking feature was its fragility. It was like a fairy ring at the end of your lawn, a dainty, delicate structure that you could crush to nothing on your morning walk. It's monumental, say the guidebooks. We humans built that. Those stones were put up there in the dawn of history with two matchsticks and a ball of garden twine. How can you doubt the human spirit, the mystic attunement to unknown forces, the instinctive reaching out for something greater than ourselves?

Talk of attunement to unknown forces made little impression on Andrew. He knew exactly why Stonehenge was there. For him, humans were born to build, much as birds were born to nest. Stonehenge was no more a monument to the human spirit than a magpie's nest was a monument to the magpie spirit. All those speculations about religious purposes, sun worship and so on were beside the point. Why did they build Stonehenge? Because it wasn't there. To see if it could be done. To pass the time. To have a bit of fun. If religion came in anywhere, it would have been as an excuse: I *have* to spend the morning tinkering with the car, dear – it's my monument to God.

Andrew's mind was at full stretch as they toured the megalithic site: calculating angles, rigging up ropes and pulleys, admiring man and nature at play together. Grace didn't care how Stonehenge got built, but she humoured him by supplying the occasional 'Extraordinary' or 'Fantastic' as he computed the logarithm of the number of man-hours it would take to drag the third rock on the left from Wales.

She walked among the fallen stones and tried to look on the cheerful side. Here was something built to last, and sure enough some bits had lasted: here we can touch them centuries later and wonder what they were for. If you're thinking of immortality, Stonehenge is really the most you can ask; it wasn't enough for Grace. It seemed to her that Stonehenge was, if anything was, a building that thoughts and feelings went into: someone was trying to wave down the centuries, but all that was left were severed fingers: the thoughts had disappeared. However hard she fixed her gaze on objects that were permanent, she kept catching sight, from the corner of her eye, of the fragility of thoughts. As Andrew gambolled back to the van, full of delight at his prehistoric kin, Stonehenge remained for Grace as it had started, a dainty, delicate structure that you could crush to nothing on your morning walk.

They had lunch in a pub in Salisbury and walked round the cathedral afterwards – another monument to the human spirit, or bit of fun, or severed finger, depending on where you see it from. As they drove on towards Old Wardour Castle, the sun shone whitely on pale new leaves, tender enough to eat. Sometimes the van was filled with music, and Andrew's hands would tap on the wheel as a mark of respect.

Old Wardour Castle wasn't really a castle, just a fortified private house with the roof blown off. It was built to last, but the owner destroyed it. The guidebooks tell it like this. Lord Arundell, a Cavalier, went off to fight the Roundheads, leaving his wife, Lady Blanche, behind. 'Trust me,' he said. 'You're quite safe here. You could hold off a hostile army of a thousand and still have change from a five-pound note.' Shortly after his departure, a hostile army of a thousand arrived to prove him wrong. Lady Blanche put up a valiant fight as her house was shot to pieces around her, but was forced to surrender, finally, when they undermined the walls. Lord Arundell came marching back: in trying to recapture the house, he only succeeded in wrecking it; in the end, he laid a mine under it and blasted off the roof. He then picturesquely landscaped the ruin and built a new castle next door.

200

Fragments of a marble fireplace demolished in the fighting were incorporated into a fantastic grotto overlooking the site.

Andrew was impressed by the solidity of the house. 'Listen,' he said, and read out a contemporary comment from a bystander who'd seen it blown up: 'The mortar was so good that one of the little towers reclining on one side did hang together and not fall in peeces.' What a masterpiece of construction. Pity it got knocked down. Still, you can always build another one next door. And when your fireplace gets smashed up, just build the peeces into a grotto and carry on. Grace was more interested in Lady Blanche Arundell and her brave but unsuccessful defence of her home. The guidebooks didn't say what happened to her when led away into captivity, nor report her comment when her husband blew up her house. They did mention, though, that she haunts the mildewed rooms.

They slept in Exeter, in a guesthouse by the river. Andrew had found it in a guidebook, but maybe it had changed hands; or maybe it really was warm, well-organized and friendly for an Exeter guesthouse. Neither Andrew nor Grace was an expert on guesthouses: Grace even thought it was a bit rude to ask to see the room in advance. When they did see it, they had little to judge it by. It was small, but it looked over the river and they could walk to the centre of town. 'We'll take it,' said Andrew, without inspecting the bathroom or testing the bed.

It was the house of someone inhospitable and mean. The walls were picketed with notices: Breakfast 7.30–8.30, no latecomers will be served. Please extinguish light before leaving the room. Rooms must be vacated by 10.00 a.m., any guest remaining after 10.00 will be charged a full day. The room was unheated except for a coin-in-the-slot gas fire. At the end of the corridor, the bathroom was unheated and the water ran slow and cold.

A test of character, this. Grace and Andrew both turned out to be nice people: no stamps, no sulks, no brave sighs and sidelong digs. When they were alone, Andrew threw himself backwards on to the bed, which was like throwing himself backwards into a bog: there was a squelching sound and the mattress rose around him, preparatory to sucking him in. 'My God,' he said, jumping up. 'They haven't invented the mattress down here.'

Grace was preoccupied by the landlady's coldness, the accusing look at a ringless finger, the drawing-in of skirts as Grace passed by. 'You have to adapt to the local customs,' she said.

They surveyed the town with theodolite and guidebook. Guidebooks are always interested in what remains: the severed fingers that survive when thought and feeling have gone. Andrew found such fragments inspiring. When he looked at a building he saw the achievement: this was a clever archway, that was a tricky stair; this one hadn't worked, pull it down and start again. Grace thought mainly of vanished lives, of the people who'd hung their hopes on bricks and mortar, tried to turn them into a home. You paint and potter and mend and dream, store your souvenirs in the attic, your diaries under the stairs; and when you die they shake their heads and bring in the wrecker's ball.

Over dinner they ran out of conversation. Grace found that being committed doesn't make it any easier to talk. Beneath the surface of her consciousness all sorts of flashes and fancies glided; she could feel them dart and slither as she bent her face to her meal. She kept reaching down with her shrimping net, but all she came up with was rusty metal. Andrew was tired and didn't help, or perhaps he was having similar problems. What we're able to fish up and formulate gives so meagre an idea of what goes on in the depths of our minds. How to break down the dam between these rockpools, let their inhabitants flit and frolic together? How to engineer a meeting of souls?

Back at the guesthouse, they fed all their shillings into the meter and watched the flames change from blue to red. Andrew opened the newspaper; Grace sat staring into the fire. Bed had never seemed so uninviting to her. To get into bed, she would have to undress; to undress, she would have to be alone. To undress in front of Andrew would involve a public admission that she had a body, and this she was still not prepared to make. But the thought of undressing in the icy bathroom made her quail. She stared at the flames, wondering if she could perhaps wrap the blanket round her shoulders and undress under it, as people do with towels on a beach. While she was still wondering, Andrew left the room. Leaping up, she ripped off her clothes, grabbed her warm flannel nightie, snatched the newspaper, plunged beneath the bedclothes, and was casually reading, though visibly panting, by the time he came back.

Andrew had still not found the correct response to this behaviour. A man of the world would have freed Grace with a quip; but then a man of the world would have thrown himself backwards into a bog rather than go on holiday with Grace. What was needed was really just a hand held out, a word of reassurance, of admiration. Grace needed to know that Andrew wasn't secretly disappointed, wasn't yearning for another Susie; but all Andrew's fantasies were of willing women who gave themselves gladly to the man they loved. Grace, as we know, had a problem with presents: he mightn't like bodies; he might have one already; what makes you think he's going to like mine? Two separate rockpools, and not a crack where a flash or fancy might crawl through.

The weather next day was almost hot. Good weather in England fills one with a sort of greed: quick, we must do everything before it snows. Grace found a want welling up: not to spend the morning exploring ruins; to be out among the primroses and seagulls, free. They had a picnic lunch on the moors, and were on the north coast of Cornwall by the middle of the afternoon. The idea was to drive right round Cornwall, down the north coast and up the south, settling for a few days whenever they found somewhere that looked nice. At their first try they were lucky: a country pub with a friendly landlord and no notices on the walls.

The sight to see in this part of the country is Tintagel, sometimes thought to be the original Camelot. Tintagel was cleverly constructed with defence in mind, on a promontory joined to the mainland by a narrow isthmus of rock. The guidebook quotes a contemporary comment: 'It is situated on the sea, and is on every side encompassed thereby. Nor none other entrance is there save a narrow rock doth furnish, the which three armed knights could hold against thee, though thou wast standing there with the whole might of Britain beside thee.' 'Look,' the old builders must have said. 'The very place for Camelot.' And the court moved in, and children played in the great halls, and parents gradually lost their fear of attack.

Alas, though cleverly constructed with human enemies in mind, Tintagel was less cleverly sited with respect to the sea, which ate away the cliffs, undermining the foundations of the buildings and the isthmus joining them to land. Crawling along the giddy access path, Grace looked at the crashing waves and looked away. They were not alone. Children were skipping and shouting among the ruins, chasing each other over the fallen stones. As Andrew would have said, you win some, you lose some. At Tintagel, man simply played a hand with nature and lost.

They were really very lucky for the whole two weeks. It wasn't sunny all the time, but sunny enough. They didn't crash, or run out of petrol, or get cross too much. They became good at choosing guesthouses; they saw gardens, tin-mines, viaducts, ferries; they walked on the beach and dipped their fingers into rockpools. Conversation didn't come easily, but Grace was really trying hard. With time, she thought, it would come.

She found it easy to trust Andrew once the decision was made. He was competent, cheerful, energetic, amusing. His mind was like his life. He was full of scattered enthusiasms: in each area of enthusiasm he'd built the foundations of a theory; Grace could see the bricks being added as he talked. All the theories patently had the same architect: you could imagine them gradually joining into a single edifice, where he would live in comfort, adding a room here, an architrave there, the bits and pieces of his life. Grace knew she had a room in it – she'd seen the rocks being dragged overland from Wales – but it was too early to tell what place it would have in the final design.

What sort of edifice would it be? A curious mixture of plain and fancy, granary and bell-tower, gargoyle and glass. Andrew didn't build to a pattern; his house would be his own.

Reaching Plymouth on the morning of their last day, they decided on one more evening together before going back to town. A few miles along the coast, the guidebooks listed a grand hotel, with gardens, stables and Regency drawing room. It was not what they'd become accustomed to. 'Come on,' said Andrew. 'It is our last night.'

Which was how they came to see Hallsands. Hallsands was a fishing village crouched at the foot of the cliffs on the rocky Devon coast. It had survived for generations, protected from the winter storms by a natural bank of shingle which took the force of the waves. When the naval dockyard at Devonport was extended, large quantities of gravel were needed, and the government licensed dredging on the coast just off Hallsands. The villagers protested that their sea defences were being undermined. 'Trust us,' said the government. 'You've nothing to fear. The sea which once built your shingle bank will build it up again.'

The dredgers came and took their haul. The following winter, waves crashed over the depleted banks, broke through the sea wall, and swept away several houses. The villagers painstakingly repaired the damage, built a new sea wall with reinforced foundations, and waited for the sea to restore their bank. In the next great storm, the sea wall collapsed and the village was swept away. Odd rooms with empty fireplaces remain, a testimony to the strength of their construction. The government attributed the disaster to natural causes. A new village has been built on the clifftop above.

That evening, in the hotel bathroom, Grace put on her little black dress. Her hair, newly washed, caught its glossy tips on her shoulders as she turned her head. As he saw her come in, Andrew remembered the party where he'd first spoken to her, and she'd waded straight past him, hair flip-flopping on her back. Now she came up to him and leaned her forehead briefly against his cheek. After all those months of effort, this.

Summer term at the Institute. Sunshine brought thoughts of last year's exams. A summer storm washed over Grace, lashing the foundations of her newly constructed sea defences. In the gardens of the Institute tennis nets went up. Grace thought she would never enjoy the sound of distant ball on racquet again.

When the weather was fine, Jerry Bastable liked to have tutorials outside. It was almost as good as not having them at all. You could waste at least fifteen minutes gathering up your papers, going downstairs, collecting deckchairs, looking for a sunny spot, then moving to the shade; and back inside when, with luck, the sun went in.

They were now investigating higher mental processes in mammals. Rats, it turned out, could not only learn but think. A rat that has learned to run a maze, trundling like clockwork along the same old pathway, will abandon the habits of a lifetime if a new short cut opens up. Learning is a matter of repeating old patterns; thinking can lead to the creation of new ones. It isn't a matter of habit and training: you can think without being connected up to the national grid.

Fantastic, thought Grace: now we're getting somewhere. As it turned out, the only place they were getting to was the end of the book. Having spent two hundred pages on their view of animals as spinning tops, whipped into motion by outside forces, the authors mentioned, almost in passing, as if it had no more significance than a headless mollusc, that animals can think. Thinking, they added, releases the animal from stereotyped behaviour, making possible almost unlimited patterns of response. Grace turned the page, thinking now they're talking. But the authors had folded their scalpels and hopped off.

Kip Sullivan's lectures had kept their sparkle. For Grace, this was due as much to the personality of the lecturer as to the content of the lectures. Kip was a committed man, a crusader against scepticism. He couldn't stand theories that refused to take a leap in the dark. The phrase he hated most was 'nothing but': a human is nothing but a piece of putty; thinking is nothing but electrical impulses; language is nothing but yelps and groans. Grace wasn't always sure where he was heading. What *were* the common properties of language, those mysterious bea-

cons that hold the group together, that make each speaker kin? Most
of Kip's lectures had been devoted to the grammar of English; and
while an auxiliary verb no doubt holds enormous attraction for another
auxiliary verb, if you'd asked her, Grace would have had to confess that
an army of them could have linked hands and sung the Internationale
in front of her without so much as making her raise her head.

But through the gaps between his words, she thought she caught
sight of a comforting vision: of a language with inexhaustible resources,
that you add your own flavour to, so that your utterances would be not
your country's, or your culture's, but your own; of a mind with its own
complex constitution, which no outsider could tamper with, which could
impose its own patterns on a vast array of thoughts, creating new
thoughts, imposing new patterns on them, creating new thoughts again.
To Grace, it was as if a fog were lifting; as if she were reaching an
atmosphere where it was safe to breathe.

As the end of the academic year approached, Kip Sullivan began to
draw the threads together. 'Now you know a bit about language, let's
see why Richard Saxon is wrong.' He asked them to read, before next
time, a book on language by an eminent rat-fancier, and a review of it
by one of the new American thinkers that Richard Saxon had warned
them against. 'Have a look at those and we'll talk about them next
week.'

'I wish we could discuss some of this stuff in tutorials,' said Jim over
coffee that day.

'Why not ask Dr Bastable?' said Jackie, who now joined Patrick, Jim
and Grace for coffee and lunch. They agreed that if a suitable occasion
arose, Jim would raise the topic with Dr Bastable. A suitable occasion
arose half-way through the next tutorial, when Dr Bastable announced
that since they had now covered the syllabus, there would be no more
tutorials that term.

'As we have some time in hand,' said Jim, 'we were wondering if we
could do some reading on language.

'Ah,' said Jerry Bastable, looking at his watch. 'Don't you think you'd
be better off doing that with Kip Sullivan?'

'Yes,' said Patrick, looking at Jerry Bastable's trousers in disbelief.

'As you may remember,' said Jim, 'there was some discussion about
tutorial continuity last term, and it was felt that you should advise us
for the whole of this year.'

'Ah, but next year,' said Jerry Bastable.

'There will, of course, be new lectures and new topics to cover.'

'Oh, OK. I'll put the kettle on,' said Jerry Bastable. He went out, followed by his trousers.

He came back with a new idea. 'Of course, I don't really know what you've been doing in your language lectures. I wouldn't really know what question to ask.'

'Perhaps we could pick something from last year's exam,' said Jim, reaching into his briefcase. 'What about "Discuss any account of verbal behaviour with which you are familiar"? We could work out a reading list among ourselves, and give you our essays, say in ten days' time?'

'And you could give us some tips on where we've gone wrong,' said Patrick.

'I'll see you dead first,' said Jerry Bastable.

They all read the same two things: the book on language and the hostile review of it that Kip Sullivan had recommended. The book, as far as Grace could see, was a celebration of mindlessness. When you speak, you're not really thinking: you're just spewing out words like ping-pong balls, like a frog lunging at a ring of needles, a rat trundling through a maze. The review came along, with wit and venom, and took the book apart. Holes opened up, great gaping chasms. Celebrate mindlessness at your peril: someone's sure to point out gently that your own inability to string two thoughts together may not be a species characteristic but merely a personal tragedy.

The reactions of Dr Bastable's tutorial group scattered over the available space like drops from a flicked paintbrush. Chris Trent-Horsley summarized and endorsed the book and dismissed the hostile review. Jim summarized the book and the review and left it to the reader to decide. Jackie summarized book and review and tried to reconcile them. Patrick used the review to dismiss the book, and then dismissed the review. Grace was entranced by what she could understand of the review, and copied long stretches of it into her essay. So these were the fancy new ideas coming out of America. Maybe next year wouldn't be so bad after all.

Jerry Bastable, it turned out, occupied a still further position in logical space: he hadn't heard of the review. 'Is it recent?' he asked, popping a sugar lump in his mouth and drowning the answer by crunching.

'Only five years old,' said Jim Wotherspoon diplomatically.

'Oh well then.'

'Does that mean,' said Patrick, 'that we don't need to read anything less than five years old?'

'What? Oh, no, no. There's plenty of good recent work. But you've got to be selective, you see. It's best to stick to the established literature, really.'

'Even if it's wrong.'

Especially if it's wrong. 'What? Well, it's not likely to be established if it's wrong, is it?'

'Oh no,' said Patrick. 'I was forgetting that.'

At this time, Joanna was phoning Grace quite often to talk about arrangements for the wedding. All the rooms at the Coulters' local hotel had been booked; the invitations had gone out; the wedding dress had been ordered; the gift list was available on request. The delicate question of bridesmaids had been raised and answered. Joanna wanted everything to be soft and faded and Victorian. Cara, it was agreed, would look absolutely gorgeous with her fair hair hooped in ringlets and a posy of wild flowers in her hand. Then Stefan had these two sweet little blonde nieces who'd look fantastic toddling down the aisle. In this scenario, the only possible role for Grace would be to don black bombazine and stalk like Jane Eyre behind the two little girls.

'It doesn't sound quite me,' she said. 'Why don't I watch from a distance and tell you how it all looks?'

And Joanna said instantly, 'Well, if that's what you really want.'

Joanna was going to move into Stefan's flat, but they were having it redecorated to symbolize their fresh start. It was a gorgeous place, down by the river, very rising young artist, very Stefan. Grace stood there in her black bombazine, going, 'Croak, croak.'

The phone rang first thing one morning. 'Oh, Grace,' said Joanna, faint and slow, as if she was having trouble formulating her words.

'What is it?' asked Grace. 'What's the matter?'

'Oh, Grace,' she said again. 'Can you come round?'

'Yes, shall I get a doctor?'

'No, just come.'

It must be Stefan. He must be dying. Grace snatched up yesterday's clothes and caught a bus.

Joanna was in her dressing gown making coffee. 'Here, I made this for you,' she said. All her lights had gone out.

'What is it?' asked Grace. 'Please tell me. Is it Stefan?'

'It's all over with Stefan,' said Joanna. She put her head on the table and her shoulders shook. Grace, quite against her nature, put her hand out and touched her sister.

'Oh, Joanna. What happened?' she said.

Stefan had been deceiving Joanna. She'd found on his desk a card with a note that read, 'Can't ring Tuesday same place.' When asked about it, he'd stared at her for a while, and then confessed.

'It was that girl we met at your party,' said Joanna. 'Sadie. He's been seeing her.'

'*Sadie*,' said Grace. 'Good God.'

Joanna had picked up her paint samples and walked out of Stefan's life. It wasn't his seeing someone else; it was the deceit. They'd had something special, and he had destroyed it on a whim.

'But at least,' she said, with a brave little lift of the head, 'he was unable to lie to me to my face.'

'How ghastly,' said Grace. Goodness knows what Sadie was up to, though come to think of it, she and Stefan would make quite a well-suited pair. 'Look, Sadie's a bit funny. I wouldn't take this too seriously. She probably just swept him off his feet.'

But no, Stefan had already *been* swept off his feet, by Joanna. Whoever heard of Romeo taking time off for a quick additional romance? They'd had something precious, and he had wantonly smashed it in a moment of weakness which he, and she, would live for ever to regret. Joanna, after a night of misery, was feeling much better now.

Grace felt quite cheerful too. The predicted disaster had come about, but at least there was time to cancel the wedding, and they wouldn't have to put up with Stefan for the rest of their lives.

Joanna didn't want to cancel the wedding just yet. She'd have to talk to Stefan about it; and of course she'd have to give him back his ring.

Two days later, she phoned again. 'It's all right. It's all right. Everything's all right again.'

But it wasn't. Stefan and Joanna were going to be married after all. Joanna had phoned him and he'd asked her round. They had to decide what to tell their parents, what form of words to use in cancelling the invitations, they had to pack up and return the presents that had already arrived. It's even less fun cancelling a wedding than planning one. They grew gloomier and gloomier, and when Joanna pulled the ring off her finger and said, 'Here, this was never truly mine,' Stefan broke down and begged her to keep it.

'At least you'll have one thing to remember me by,' he said sadly, thinking of happiness that might have been.

'I'll never forget you,' she said softly, and they were in each other's arms. Perhaps they could redecorate the flat again, to symbolize their fresh start.

'How wonderful,' croaked Grace, shaking out her black bombazine. 'I'm so glad everything's all right again.'

'It's funny,' said Joanna, 'I feel our relationship will be all the stronger for this. We've found out how much we really mean to each other.' And how much bother it is to cancel a wedding. And how it's as well to read each other's letters just in case.

'Yes, well, goodbye,' said Grace.

Andrew's mind was now fully occupied with plans for the forthcoming tour. The Songsters were to be the opening act, followed by a band called Crocodile, which had made one or two mildly successful records, followed by Elmo Harper himself. Elmo Harper, the great legendary hero, would walk beside Andrew on stage.

Think of the ten best records in the history of rock and roll: three of them were by Elmo Harper. He wrote both words and music, could dazzle an audience on both piano and guitar. There was a time when he seemed inexhaustible, when he'd just sit down at the piano and the frontiers of music would be extended. He didn't even need a spotlight: the energy that poured out of him was enough to light up a stage.

And then, at the height of his glory, he vanished. No more television, no more fan club; it seemed he was in jail. No one would talk about what he'd done. Some said vice, some said gangsters, some said no more than a bit of income-tax fraud. When he came out, in any case, no one would play his records. For a few years, he disappeared.

Rock and roll went up like a rocket, filled the sky with brief, bright spangles, then plunged to earth in flames. The old stars crashed in the desert, to be hauled out every so often and told to get singing, the great rock and roll revival had come. Year in, year out, crawling across the desert, dragging the old songs behind them like a ball and chain.

Elmo Harper had been a tease to start with: the years had made him the cynic of rock and roll. He would come on stage, wearily dragging his guitar. He would look the audience straight in the face, sigh, and play a few dispirited chords. The band would go quietly into his opening number, and he would deliver the first verse into the microphone without moving, without playing, without raising his voice. As the song went on, he would occasionally come alive: a runaway chorus here, a cascading guitar line there, his body breaking into fluid, graceful movement over there. Just enough to show what he could do; but by the end of the song they'd lost him again, and were starving for more. Each song would be delivered with this mixture of apathy and attack. On a good night he would give them more than the occasional glimpse of his abilities; but he never ended his act on a full-blooded satisfying note. Show the customer you've got what he wants, but never, ever, give it to him. His favourite closing number was 'Don't shoot (I'm too cute)' – and unfortunately, he was.

How to open for an act like that? The most sensible answer is: Don't. Andrew actually had a parody of Elmo Harper, but the manager of the Newt had told him on no account to use it. 'He's a bit touchy, Elmo. I don't reckon you'll last too long if you use that. Use your Chuck Berry number. He *hates* Chuck Berry.' So the group simply worked on its ten best songs, some copies of rock and roll classics, some originals of their own. They worked so hard. They really got better during those few weeks.

Grace had assumed that she would be going on tour with Andrew. It turned out, quite soon after their return from Cornwall, that he had not. The tour was to start in Margate, zigzag up the east coast and down the west, and end up in London. 'What's our first stop after Margate?' Grace had said, looking at the map.

'You're not coming, are you?' said Andrew, in a tone that clearly expected the answer 'No.'

'Sorry. I meant your first stop.'

'Because we're going to be pretty busy, and the van's going to be awfully full. Anyway, you've got Joanna's wedding, haven't you?'

That's not going to last three whole weeks.

'I mean, Lindsey and Sherry aren't coming,' he went on.

'Don't worry. It was just a slip of the tongue.'

She was allowed, though, to see the opening night in Margate. They went down by train together after work: Lindsey, Sherry and Grace. None of them had seen Heather since the party, though Sherry had rung and been told that the lot of them could get lost. But as they queued up to hand in their tickets, they saw Heather, quite clearly, in front of them in the line. By the time they got inside, she'd gone.

The theatre was almost full. Waves of young chatter broke over the footlights and lapped against the heavy curtains. Elmo Harper's opening night was worth a trip from London.

The curtains opened, the guitar flickered, and Andrew began to sing, a familiar song. Bye bye to the old life, to the chicken shack and the railroad track, I'm off to be a star. Amplified as Grace had never heard it, slick and clean, it sounded wonderful to her. Each of the group was highly charged, you could feel the energy pouring through them like a heartbeat. The audience loved that opening song, and clapped and hooted for more.

The next song Grace also knew. It was an end-of-summer song: 'When summer ends, will we be left, in the cool of the year, thinking back on things that used to be?' A cheerful, perky inquiry, put forward in much the same spirit as one might say, 'Will the next car to come along be red or blue?' The audience loved that too.

Then one of Andrew's new songs, the first native-born surfing song:

> Sun shines down on the Euston Road
> (London, England, North West One)
> Kids jump along it dressed à la mode
> (Sweaters, baggies, heading for fun).
> What are they holding in their hand?
> (Slipping, sliding, under the sun)
> It's the greatest little surfboard in the land
> And the surf-riding season has just begun.
>
> Surf is up on the Serpentine
> Waves are breaking and the water is fine
> You bring the pretzels and I'll bring the wine
> And we'll party party party till the day is done.

Everything they did made the spirits rise. The audience began to feel as highly charged as the group. The applause came over the footlights like a tidal wave. Lucky Andrew. A dream come true.

Crocodile wasn't built to last. Their three successful records were identical except for their titles, which differed only in order of words: 'Love ya baby', 'Baby baby' and 'Love ya love ya'. What they did was clomp. Clomp clomp on to the stage in steel-tipped boots; clomp clomp on their drums; clomp clomp up in the air and down on the stage, nodding their heads to signify that they knew how awful they were. The audience loved them too; indeed, they loved them more. Clomp clomp went Crocodile. Clomp clomp went the audience's feet. They might as well have been at a hoe-down.

By the time Elmo Harper came on, the audience had been at a peak of excitement for almost an hour, and a let-down seemed sure to come. Now if there was one thing those old rock and roll stars hated, it was to be outdone in applause. They would try any trick to steal the next man's thunder: swallow the drumsticks, pour brandy over the piano and set it alight. Elmo Harper had simply chosen rather more subtle means. His music and manner could not have been further from the clomp clomp of Crocodile. Though travelling without his regular musicians, he'd trained Andrew's group to produce a fair imitation of the precise but gentle rhythms of his records. Where Crocodile clomped, with silences between, there was no silence in an Elmo Harper song: just a steady murmur like a flock of doves on a military fly-past, not a wing out of place. Above this rose Harper's sly, insistent voice and, once or twice, just to show you what you were missing, his dazzling virtuoso guitar. I don't know what effect he had on the audience, but by God, he terrified Andrew's group. He would wait, head laid back, eyes closed, smiling slyly, while Davy played his careful imitation of the solo line on some Elmo Harper record – then fizz, off he and his guitar would dance, for just enough milliseconds to establish that if Davy was thinking of a career in banking, now might be a good time to start. Oh Davy, oh Andrew, thought Grace. But she was carried along with the rest, cast down, raised up, rejected and raised up once more. When Elmo Harper toys with you, you really know you've been toyed with.

Afterwards, Sherry knew how to get backstage (just look like Sherry and show the doorman your engagement ring). The group were still onstage, coiling amplifiers and folding drums, stiff with tension like overwound clockwork toys.

'Hey,' said Bob, spinning round, his arms trailing. 'Woohoo, weren't we great!'

While the audience may feel exhilarated after a show like that, the performers are in the stratosphere, out of reach. Rick floated, Bob clowned, Davy glowed with charm, and Andrew babbled. As they stowed the equipment in the van, as they poured whisky in their communal dressing room, he converted the evening into words: the song that went well, the line that wouldn't come, the time he nearly tripped Davy up, the patheticness of Crocodile, the amazingness of Elmo Harper and being onstage with him – on and on he went, to no one in particular, like a ginger-beer bottle exploding in the dark.

Joe, the manager of the Newt, popped his head into the room. 'Elmo wants a bit of a,' noticing ladies present, 'drink. We're going down the Majestic. See you there.'

In a room at the Majestic, where Joe and Elmo Harper were staying, about thirty people had gathered. There were Elmo Harper and Crocodile, pints of whisky in their hands, surrounded by dressed-up girls who had all got past the doorman by looking like Sherry and flashing their engagement rings. Some of them nudged each other as Andrew's group came in.

Somehow, when the pints of whisky had been handed round, Andrew, Davy, Rick and Bob, with Sherry clamped to his arm, were surrounded, and Lindsey and Grace were on their own, like two empty milk bottles on the doorstep.

'Wanna drink, love?' said a passing assistant stage manager, seeing that all the Sherries were taken. Lindsey was staring after Davy, the skin on her face all tight, as if someone had lifted her up by the ears; and Grace was left to say, 'Yes, please.'

One surprising consequence of Grace's commitment to Andrew had been its effect on her looks. All through Oxford, she'd taken comfort from knowing that, however hostile the environment, her hair, her clothes, her shoes, were perfect: she was fully fortified. But none of that went with Andrew, damp basements and rock music. Gradually, she stopped reading the magazines. She began to wear baggy sweaters, jeans tucked into big suede boots. They altered her walk: that light, liquid movement was gone. She looked, just subtly, incoherent. You see it quite often: the neat, blonde deb who falls for a rake, the socialite at a rugby match, the farm girl at a wedding, fish in slightly the wrong water, swimming slightly against the grain. Grace was well aware of it. Somehow it was linked with her new trust in Andrew, to let her armour down.

'Olivia,' came Davy's voice. 'What on earth are you doing here?'

Many beauties are acquired tastes: it takes time to appreciate the heavy eyebrow, the shaven forehead, the raw-boned look. Unquestionably Grace was one of these. Olivia Hawtrey's beauty had nothing to do with style. Put a garland of flowers in her hair and she would be Titania; fish her out of the water in weeds and she'd be Ophelia to the life. She was whatever you'd always wanted in a woman. There she stood in the doorway, in her plain cotton dress, her brown hair just naturally tumbling over her shoulders, back just naturally straight, head just naturally high, with not a bit of tension in her, and no idea of quite how beautiful she was. It was the look she had of fresh sunny fields, as if she'd just that minute been lightly dusted with pollen, that somehow held your eyes and softened your gaze.

'Hello, Davy,' said Olivia as he came towards her, still emitting well above the permitted dose of charm. She held up her cheek to be kissed, just light and friendly, as easy as shaking hands. 'I'm looking for Joe.'

Joe had turned, like everyone else, to look at Olivia Hawtrey as she came in. She threaded her way towards him like a daisy through a chain: the thick groups parted to let her through. He put his arm round her shoulder. 'Good, good,' he said. 'Elmo.' Elmo was right there beside him, eyes adroop, so relaxed you were surprised he could hold up his glass. 'I want you to meet Olivia.'

Elmo Harper, looking at Olivia, ran his free hand slowly through his hair, reached out and, with the back of two fingers, tapped her lightly on the cheek. 'Hi, toot,' he said.

Olivia didn't draw back insulted, or ask for a towel to wipe the hair-oil off her cheek. If she'd been wired up to a lie-detector, you might have seen a little surge of current; if you'd had your hand on her sinews, you might have felt her stiffen for a millisecond, like a gun dog at point. But all that anyone around her noticed was a smile and a lift of the chin. 'Toot yourself,' she said.

Olivia, according to Davy, was someone one met around. When she left school, she'd been semi-engaged to a nice young minor heir. Everyone loved her. She moved on to someone more dashing, with film and theatrical connections; she applied to drama school. She'd been seen at parties with the lead guitarist of Crocodile, who despite his lack of musical talent had a lovely black cloak and a cascade of black curly hair. And indeed, Olivia gave him her friendly smile, and received his friendly kiss.

Grace and Andrew didn't really speak that night. Towards the end of the party someone pulled a switch and Andrew went, in the space of a syllable, from hyperactivity to semi-consciousness. He had left the party, dropped the others off, parked the van in front of their back-street boarding house and fallen asleep, hardly registering that Grace was by his side. Once, he wouldn't have done it; once, she would have been hurt. But it was all right now: they were a team.

In the morning, Andrew was still abstracted, anxious to get back to the others and on to the road. What had worked well last night? What could be improved? The adrenalin began flowing as soon as he opened his eyes. It's normal, what else can you expect?

'I could come up next weekend,' said Grace. 'Where will you be?'

'Newcastle, I think,' said Andrew. 'You do that. I'll give you a ring.'

He did ring, from a public call-box early one evening before a show. How was it going? Oh fantastic, fine. Who needs sleep, anyway? If

Grace went up on Sunday and watched the show, the band had a free day on Monday and he could take a break.

This time Grace went up on the train alone. Life seemed easier since she'd jumped. Perhaps from the outside nothing much had changed, progress was still no more than inch by inch; but that inch was no longer won by Andrew's gritted teeth against Grace's dragging feet. The obstruction had been removed, the plant could grow into its natural shape. Dreaming out at the landscape, Grace built a picture in her mind. These two seedlings rooted in a field. They grew surrounded by weeds and wild flowers and grasses which obscured the view. Gradually, they emerged through the underbrush, like planes taking off through clouds. Their trunks thickened in the light, their roots spread, their branches put out shoots; two separate trees, neither moving towards the other, each in its separate space. They reached maturity; birds flew between them like messengers of love; they lived together in the same sun and shadow; the same snow bent their branches. When they died, and the men came to cut them down, it was found that their branches had grown into and around each other, so that it was no longer possible to tell them apart.

Grace went backstage before the show: a chaos of thumps and wires and curses and twangs as the fantasy was hoisted into place. Andrew noticed her at once: he left his microphone and piano and came up to take her hands. 'I'll just get this rigged up and we'll go and have a drink.' He was almost whispering, as if he didn't want anyone to know.

'Hello, Grace,' shouted Bob, stamping twice on the boards and turning a pirouette. No sign of tiredness there. Davy looked up and waved, a modest, royal wave: '*I'm* not so far gone up in the world that I'll forget my former friends.' Rick looked over, uncommunicative, and turned away.

More twangs and sudden screeches. 'Come on,' whispered Andrew. 'Let's get out of here.' He took her hand and they pattered on to the street, like children escaping from Sunday school. Grace would have travelled much further than Newcastle for this moment of feeling welcome. 'We're friends,' she thought. 'Fancy, I have a friend.'

The pub was already filling up with people waiting for the show. 'It's good to see you, Grace,' said Andrew when they were settled. 'Just don't ask me any difficult questions, like where we are or what day it is. I feel as if I've been driving round in vans since before they invented the wheel – and that's not an easy thing to do,' he added, wondering if it could be turned into an idea for a song.

'So how's it been going?' said Grace.

'Oh great, great,' said Andrew automatically. 'Well, I haven't a clue, really. We're always gone before the papers come out. But we're having a good time and the audiences seem to like us. It's just a bit disorientating, that's all.'

Grace patted his hand and gulped her drink (that's what friends are for). 'And Elmo Harper?'

'Oh great, great,' said Andrew gulping back. Was there some hesitation there? Grace didn't know him well enough to tell.

If Andrew hadn't said that the tour was going well, Grace could have seen it from the group's performance. The sound of applause can transmute a person into a persona. Rick's impassiveness was becoming part of his act; Bob had discovered that the audience loves a clown; Davy had the letters to prove that he was just as charming as he'd always pretended to be. Only Andrew looked the same; it was the music, not his appearance, that he wanted to change.

They were playing better for Elmo Harper too. Andrew had added some flourishes that weren't on the original records, that occasionally provoked Elmo Harper into a response. For half a minute at a time, you could see the country boy with all his energy and his dreams of being a star, before they signed him up for peanuts and put him on tour with sword swallowers and bicycle artistes. And you wonder why he doesn't write songs much any more.

Afterwards, with a free day coming, there was a little feeling of end of term. In the dressing room, Rick had a silver whisky flask which was thrown from hand to hand. Girls knocked at the door, looking for one or other of the group. 'Hello, we thought you were great. Can we have your autograph?' Bob, with memories of the playground, would write:

'If this book should chance to roam
Box its ears and send it home.'

Davy had evolved a signature that filled a page. Then Andrew would sign in his everyday handwriting, and Rick would add his paw print.

One pair of girls were really pretty, and Davy, handing back the book with one hand, held out the whisky flask with the other. 'Stay and have a drink.' Indeed, he began to build up a collection: boring girls were politely thanked and shown the door, pretty ones were awarded the silver flask.

The lead guitarist of Crocodile wandered in, looked casually around, winked at Davy, said, 'Drinks at Elmo's place,' and wandered out. Grace had thought she and Andrew might slip away, but the music had filled his batteries to overflowing, and he was babbling again. Babbling, indeed, to one of the pretty girls; he just remembered, in the doorway, to look around for Grace.

At Elmo's hotel, the bar was closed and the grille was down, but a stack of bottles and glasses had been laid on. Most of Crocodile were already there, girls at their feet, glasses in their hands. As Andrew's group came in, there was some winking and throat-clearing: who had the prettiest girls? We'll swop you this one for that one. Frankly, it was pretty grim.

Elmo Harper flowed in, his arm flat on Olivia Hawtrey's back, his hand on her hair. 'Party party party,' he said. He never let go of Olivia the whole evening; she stood beside him, his hand pressing her shoulder or fiddling with her hair, as he paid his sly attentions to everyone but her. First he dangled her in front of the lead guitarist of Crocodile. 'Hi, Jeremy, getting yours?' he said politely.

'Hi, Elmo. Yes, plenty to drink, thanks,' said Jeremy, raising his glass. 'Olivia,' and he reached out to kiss her cheek. As they kissed, her head gave a little jerk: Elmo Harper was pulling her hair.

Then he looked round for pretty girls: there was a group of three, crouched on its marks, which sprang towards him at the sight of his smile. They stood before him, nudging and jostling and tossing their heads, like a team of bay horses hitched to harness.

'We think you're great, Elmo,' said the leader, throwing back her mane.

'Well, bowl me over,' said Elmo. 'Aren't you the nicest thing.' He notched his eyelids up a fraction, then let them fall.

'Yeah, we all love you,' said another.

'Hmmh,' he said, his head tilting ever so slightly. 'Have to see what we can do about that.'

Certainly he was conserving his energy for something. He was putting no effort into the pitch of his voice, which ran along on a flat monotone, taking a dive before the end of the sentence was reached. Olivia stood beside him, straight backed, honey drenched, smiling lightly, his hand at the back of her neck. They went through the crowd like gunman and hostage, neither looking at the other, inch by inch, side by side.

'What on earth is she doing with him?' said Grace to Andrew afterwards, as the babble-count dropped and sleep swept over him like nightfall through the tropics. But he was too tired to speak.

The next day all Andrew really wanted to do was sleep. By chance, it was one of those beautiful summer days when the air is clear as new-washed crystal, and the sun is on duty as if it had never been away. Grace, waking in mid-morning and getting no response from Andrew, went out for coffee and smelled the sea. 'Andrew,' she said, dancing back to the room. 'Let's go to the seaside. It's a beautiful day.'

They left Andrew's suitcase in the van and caught a bus to Blyth. Everything went right for them that day. They walked along the clifftops and saw the larks rising straight up from the grass to sing above them. The sea was a deep, deep blue: you would almost have thought it was Greece. 'Remember,' Grace said, filled with affection, proud of the long way they had come. They had taken off through the clouds, could see each other clearly across the intervening space. Of course, Grace told herself, they didn't remotely know each other; they'd done no more than brush against each other's protective carapace. She smiled as she thought of the secret she had waiting, the gentle self beneath the armour plating. In years ahead, when trust had grown, they'd look back fondly at their difficult beginnings. Inch by inch, step by step, it would come.

Andrew couldn't think for the music ringing in his ears. He'd abandoned himself to sensation, feeling. He was swept along on a tide of passions; all his dreams had run together. Grace, Elmo; Elmo, Grace. So much love, so much hurt, so much hope.

They walked hand in hand along the Monday afternoon beach; had supper in a harbourside café; slept in a guesthouse overlooking a garden. 'Not what I've been used to,' said Andrew. 'You should see some of the dumps we've been in.'

Not that it mattered: in bed with the lark, up with the lunchbell and into the van: drive drive, unload, rig up, jangle jangle, scream scream, gulp gulp, and zonk, in bed with the lark again.

He woke nervous, anxious to be on the road. On the bus back to Newcastle, Grace was already receding from his mind. She'd be coming north again at the end of the week, for Joanna's wedding. Perhaps they might meet then? 'Let's see how it goes,' he told her, the notes welling up in his brain. 'I'll give you a ring. Whenever I get the chance.'

Chapter 10

Present-giving time was here again: made easier for some because Stefan and Joanna had a list. Maybe we should all have lists, handing out to new acquaintances our address, telephone number and name of store at which present-list is held. For an only sister getting married, though, you want to do something special; surprise her, find her just the thing she always wanted without realizing it herself. For Grace, there was the added problem of finding something Stefan wouldn't like: something that would quietly exclude him, that would appeal to Joanna over his head, would keep their intimacy alive across marriage walls. Grace thought and shopped and browsed and dreamed, and ended by choosing something from the list.

She delivered it herself to Stefan's flat. 'Oh, gorgeous,' said Joanna. 'The one thing on the list that I really, really wanted. Look, Stefan.' She held it up for his approval. Normally, it's the giver who gets praised or blamed for the choice of present: with a list, it's the receiver's taste which is up for inspection.

'Gorgeous, darling,' he said, and Joanna smiled with pride.

Joanna on her own was elegant and charming; Stefan and Joanna combined were beyond belief. Think of postcard villages: they were a postcard couple, posed for the photographer at just the right angle, a fairy-tale prince and princess. Where's the refuse dump, you wanted to ask? Where's the slaughterhouse? What happens when one of the inhabitants has a heart attack in the middle of the night? Grace drank her coffee and listened to the arrangements for the wedding. 'It'll be gorgeous, won't it, Stefan?' said Joanna.

He put his hand on her shoulder and looked at the camera. 'Absolutely spectac, darling,' he said.

What to wear for the wedding? Clearly, Joanna would expect to be dressed up for; but Grace no longer wanted to be safe and chic. She'd begun to feel solidarity for damaged animals; begun to think of wool and leather, silk and feathers as coming, so to speak, off the hoof, off the bone. With the head removed. Once the thought would have made her avoid them; now it made her want to wear them more. She walked the second-hand clothes stalls like a prospector in a boneyard; each silk dress rescued seemed like an animal saved. Setting off for Joanna's wedding, Grace put on her new-old clothes with love and pride.

Stefan's home village, Caldecott, was near the market town of Louthbridge, which I have to restrain myself from describing as nestling in the dales. It was a town of palest stone, with no visible refuse dump or slaughterhouse, and a lovely market square with a fine country hotel, the Grouse. Here the Ritchies gathered for the pre-wedding wake. Joanna and her parents had dined with the Coulters the previous day, but it's not done for the bride and groom to meet the night before the wedding, in case one of them takes fright and runs.

In fact, the original Coulter marriage had died in childbirth: Dulcie Coulter took one look at Stefan and thought about leaving home. One night when he was three, she set out for a hunt ball and caught the train to Edinburgh, where she married a company director. Two years later, Tom Coulter tried again, and had a daughter, Sarah, now married with her own children, Giles, Eliza and Fay. Stefan called his old mother 'Mum' and his new mother 'Ma'. They called him Stephen, which was his name.

The hotel was full of wedding guests. Joanna promenaded her parents and grandmother round the dining room. Joanna, you look super. See you in church. Lucky Joanna, surrounded by friends, and sunshine forecast for her wedding day. Dinner was spent on mental rehearsal: who would go in which car, with whom, and when. (And why, thought Grace, sticking her nose in her wine.) Grace would drive to church with her mother and grandmother, leaving Mr Ritchie to bring in the bride. After the wedding there would be no need for cars, since the Coulters lived right next to the church.

Over coffee, Mr Ritchie proposed a toast. 'I know,' he said, 'that we'll have toasts coming out of our ears by this time tomorrow, but let's have one before we get too blasé. To Joanna, may you be very happy, may your marriage be all you wish for, and let's hope the groom doesn't forget the ring.'

'And that it'll be a proper one,' said Mrs Castle.

'Thank you, all of you,' said Joanna, with a twinkle for Mrs Castle. 'I know tomorrow will be the happiest day of my life.'

Heavens, what a thing to think: after your wedding it'll be downhill all the way.

'But for now, I just want to enjoy this evening, with all the Ritchies together, and no Coulters to worry about at all. Imagine, this time tomorrow I'll be Joanna Coulter.'

Imagine, they all thought.

Later, Joanna asked Grace to go for a walk. 'Can't go to bed at half past nine on my wedding eve.' They walked along the pale stone streets, washed a deeper yellow as the sun went down. Grace had been hoping for a final handclasp before the barrier came down; but Joanna's hands were full with wedding plans. It wasn't that she didn't want to talk: she would start and then her thoughts would hop away. There were so many details; she was so excited; her mind was racing so fast. 'Hope the flower shop can manage the bouquet: they were given *strict* instructions, but I wouldn't put it past them to "loiven it up" ' – Joanna's working class accent took a bow – 'by adding purple dahlias or something. By the way, I absolutely love your dress.'

'I'll try not to clash with the flowers,' said Grace.

'Who'd have thought it could happen so fast? A year ago, I didn't even know Stefan. Remember when we left for Greece? I'd been feeling quite miserable before then.'

'No second thoughts?'

'Oh, not for a moment. When you meet the right man, you know it straightaway.'

'How?' (How?)

'Oh, I don't know. You imagine yourself at parties with him, taking him home to meet your parents, introducing him to your friends. Somehow, it just feels right.'

I married an accessory, thought Grace.

'What about you?' asked Joanna. 'You haven't met the right man yet? No wedding bells for you and Andrew?'

'I've never felt the urge to introduce him to all my friends.'

'No,' said Joanna, understanding. 'Well, you must come round to dinner when we get back from Corfu. Stefan's got lots of gorgeous friends.'

Oh good, then I can marry a handbag too.

It was too late. Joanna was gone across the water from which no sister returns. Always before, Joanna had led where Grace would have been happy to follow: grown-up girl at the big school, popular prefect, happy undergraduate. Someone to pioneer for Grace through all the stages of life. Now here she was, a pretty young bride, and Grace would as soon have followed her as thrown herself off a cliff. There *must* be real happiness, she thought, surely it can't all be a sham. Inch by inch, step by step, you arrive at something that is not a fake, façade or folly: a place where rules of etiquette aren't needed, where partners aren't hung on the wall like trophies; a place built not to impress the neighbours but to be a home.

Up in the morning, a hasty, jumpy breakfast, then on with the silk and feathers and off to church.

'Look,' said Mrs Ritchie as the taxi drew up. 'You can see Stefan's house from here.'

There, across the churchyard wall, stood Caldecott Manor, pale stone and creeper, windows dark against the sun. As they looked, a peach-blonde bridesmaid skittered through the open door, and back again as someone shouted, 'Fay!'

'No need for a taxi afterwards,' said Grace. 'We can just hitch up our skirts and climb over the wall.'

'I suppose you'd *have* to go to church, living so close,' said Mrs Ritchie, thinking up excuses for the Coulters. 'But I do value my Sundays. Oh,' as a car drew up behind them, 'there's Geoffrey's parents,' and she hurried off to greet her parents-in-law.

They stood in the church porch together: Mrs Ritchie, Mrs Castle, Mr and Mrs Ritchie senior, and Grace. Caldecott must have been important once, because the church was big and beautiful, now spilling flowers out of every crevice and crack. There was Stefan with Cara in the doorway, greeting his future in-laws with outstretched hands. Those saturnine faces look their very best in morning dress. 'I'm early,' he said. 'If the bride can be late, I don't see why the groom can't be early. I'd hate to think I was missing all the fun.'

'What fun?' said Mrs Castle.

'Oh, Mrs Castle, the fun of seeing you.'

But Mrs Castle was far from home, and it had taken her two hours to dress.

Stefan and his best man went off to the front of the church. The choir were frog-marched in, straitjacketed against giggles and pinches by the choirmaster's glare. A car drew up at the churchyard gate, and out of its doors, like blossoms from the bud, came the two baby bridesmaids in peach, followed by a distinguished man in a morning suit holding a posy of wild flowers. 'That's the Coulters,' whispered Mrs Ritchie, as the distinguished man was joined by a charming woman holding another posy.

Cara went forward to take the two baby bridesmaids by the hand,

223

but they, catching sight of strangers ahead, lost all their squeak and skitter, and curled back their hands like slugs recoiling from the prod. 'Cara,' said Mrs Coulter, who'd told Mr Coulter all along that Fay and Eliza were much too young, and had been certain of it as soon as she set eyes on Cara. 'Could you take the flowers for me, darling?' and seized the recoiling bridesmaids as they shrank past. 'Tom.' Tom Coulter, still holding his posy, took Cara's arm and strolled her firmly towards the church door.

If that's how they react to Cara, thought Grace, they'd have had to be handcuffed at the sight of me. What a start to married life, to be followed down the aisle by sobbing cherubs crying, 'Mummy, Mummy, please let me out of here.'

By the time she reached the church door, Cara looked as if she were wishing for her own Mummy, and reacted with surprising friendliness to a greeting from Grace. 'You look lovely,' whispered Grace; but what use were looks if little children, who can see straight to your heart like dogs, decided you were up to no good?

'I think we'd better get to our seats,' said Mrs Ritchie, patting Marian Coulter's arm with a look best transcribed as 'Rather you than me'. They trooped after the usher to their front stall seats, taking the full force of two hundred eyes on the back of the neck.

A huffling in the church door as the bride arrived. Stefan and his best man took up their places, and the organist plunged off the top diving board into the fanfare Stefan and Joanna had chosen as their substitute for the Wedding March.

Joanna came down the aisle on her father's arm, an ivory bride in an ivory veil, a simple spray of peach and ivory in her hand. The child bridesmaids tiptoed after her, peeping shyly into posies held in front of their faces, like too-full glasses they must on no account spill. One stumbled slightly before the end, gasped, righted herself, breathed out loudly, and went on with a tiny frown. Two babies on a tightrope: don't they look sweet?

Cara came forward to take Joanna's flowers, and shooed the children into the waiting seats. Safely gathered, and not a slug in sight.

'Dearly beloved,' said the vicar to this collection of strangers, and the wedding service began. Stefan and Joanna made their vows in firm, clear voices. 'I, Stephen Thomas Coulter,' said the vicar firmly and clearly; 'I, Stefan Thomas Coulter,' Stefan firmly and clearly replied. He and Joanna exchanged looks of love as they said the words 'I do.'

They had a sermon and some hymns, though there are few hymns suitable for marrying a painter, better to marry a military man. They went into the vestry to sign the register. Then the organist plunged from the high board, the choir fell in after him, and Stefan and Joanna walked up the aisle, leaning slightly towards each other, with secret smiles. The bridesmaids toddled after them, posies trailing like teddy bears, blinking shyly from side to side. Cara followed, beside the best man. 'He'll make someone a lovely handbag,' she thought.

The congregation followed the bridal party up the aisle, a troop of wandering pages and bridesmaids, chattering and waving as they went. Outside, Stefan and Joanna waited, Joanna swooping to kiss the children, who galumphed excitedly in the sunshine, while Stefan stood, one eyebrow up, one eyebrow down, to watch. 'Nana,' whispered Fay to Mrs Coulter. 'You see, we did be good.'

A flutter of kisses and handshakes as Stefan and Joanna were congratulated on their performance. As they gathered at the church door for photographs, the bells began to ring. Stefan and Joanna smiled faraway smiles, the children made faces at their posies, and Grace took up the maiden aunt's position at the end of the back row. Then into the wedding car with Stefan and Joanna, smiling and waving at the gathered villagers, while Mr and Mrs Coulter raced through their private gate and across the lawn, to be there ahead of them to welcome them home.

All the world loves a wedding. A congregation of divorced and rickety couples gathers with tears of gladness at the thought of two more young people climbing aboard. Dearly beloved, we are gathered in the sight of God to pretend that these two people have only virtues and know the secret of love. Come back in a year and I'll tell you the true facts.

Grace walked the long way round to the manor house with the other guests. There were John and Tess, Peter and Millicent and Cara's boyfriend, James, and they welcomed each other with the relief that comes from knowing that one will not appear friendless to the world. Hello, isn't this super, don't Stefan and Joanna look gorgeous, aren't the little bridesmaids terribly sweet? And the weather, and the house, etc., etc. Grim. In the circumstances, though, Grace found the mindlessness easy to tolerate. To all intents and purposes, she was having a conversation. For the sake of appearances, she would gladly have spent the next two hours in front of a statue, opening and closing her mouth like a fish.

Luckily, as a member of the family she was in some demand. 'Come and meet Fay and Eliza,' called Joanna. 'Aren't they gorgeous?'

Not on your life: they'd probably curl up and die.

But the boisterous bridesmaids had taken Joanna to their hearts, and pottered after her, trailing their posies, all through the afternoon.

'Joanna, you look really lovely,' said Grace. 'Are you enjoying your wedding day?'

'Oh, it's quite perfect. Sunshine and everything. I was so hoping that the sun would shine. Look, have some food. Dulcie and Marian have spent days organizing it all.'

Indeed, the past and present Mrs Coulters seemed terribly good friends. No doubt they had reason to be grateful to each other: Marian to Dulcie for running off, and Dulcie to Marian for picking up the pieces after she'd gone. If Dulcie had been abandoned for Marian it would have been more of a social challenge. Dearly beloved, we are gathered together in the sight of God to pretend that these three people are not churning inside with guilt and heartache. Come back tomorrow and I'll tell you the true facts.

Why had Dulcie Coulter run away? Grace watched Tom Coulter, who looked so like Stefan and romped so happily with his second family on the lawn. 'Grace, can you go and help Mum with the buffet?' whispered Mrs Ritchie, and the train of thought went dead.

The big french doors had been thrown open, and the guests were wandering in and out in their Ascot hats, or picnicking on the lawn. A table had been provided for the older folk. Grace sat with her grandparents while they picked at their food. 'This is very nice for Yorkshire,' said Mrs Castle. 'Not much fog.' They all agreed enthusiastically that there was not much fog.

'Grace, come and be photographed,' said Stefan. Apart from the formal poses, Stefan and Joanna wanted an informal record of their day; doubling the need to keep up appearances to avoid being preserved for ever as a wallflower in the family album. Here's Grace at Joanna's wedding wondering if her big day will ever come.

Grace joined an informal group posing artificially on the lawn: Stefan and Joanna, Cara and James, Peter and Millicent, little Fay and little Eliza, who had grasped the general theory of being a bridesmaid, but had not quite understood that it was a temporary post: they would toddle after Joanna for life, followed in time by their own bridesmaids, and their bridesmaids' bridesmaids, in a huge geometric progression towards death. And the best man, whose name was Chas.

Chas was an eccentric: they make the best best men. He looked like a rugby player: one of those big squashed faces with a fringe of ruffled fair hair. His walk was a bit of a shamble, his eyes were naturally screwed up against the sun. He was the one on the coach tour who always makes the first joke, the one who jumps in the river to rescue a drowning child and then walks away without giving his name; the one for whom the saying was invented, 'Three times a best man, never a groom.'

He was a nice man, and he thought Grace was great. Well, he thought all women were great, though it was sometimes a little hard to tell them apart. All pretty women, that is; the rest weren't really women to him.

He clowned informally for the camera, perching Fay on his shoulder and crowning her with Grace's feathery hat. Here's Grace looking furious at the theft of her hat. He put his arm round Grace and Cara's shoulders. Here's James looking furious at the theft of his girl. He was the one who always says, 'I don't know what got into her, she just couldn't seem to take a joke.'

Stefan was not a man for close friendships: the tête-à-tête was not his natural habitat. He was a man for dinner parties, yachting parties, country house weekends. Sit him down with a great mind of his generation and he'd reach for the backgammon board. Stefan and Chas, then, were not close friends but childhood comrades. It was what you might call an arranged friendship, not a friendship of love. Until he was six, Stefan was an only child and needed companions; Chas's family were socially suitable and lived not far away. These friendships, when they work at all, tend to stick for life. At ninety you still think of yourself as a friend of the child you knew at nine.

When the time came for the cake to be cut, everyone squeezed into the drawing room or overflowed on to the lawn outside. Joanna and Stefan looked like the icing sugar couple not used, for reasons of good taste, on the cake itself. With a smile and a look of love, they stabbed the cake to the heart and sliced it up for consumption by their friends. 'Speech, speech,' cried tradition, and Chas stepped forward to propose a toast.

He followed accepted best man's procedure, which is to go just too far but no further. 'Steve and I are very old friends. My acquaintance with the lovely Joanna is rather more recent, but I'm looking forward to seeing a lot more of her – though not, of course, as much as Steve will shortly see.'

A touch of frosting was added to Joanna's icing-sugar smile.

'There are one or two things about Steve, though, that I bet Joanna doesn't know.'

The touch of frosting spread to Stefan.

'And one of them someone really ought to tell her. When we were quite small, about five, I found him doing something I'll always remember.'

The frost ran around the guests and overflowed on to the lawn. Was this man entirely sober? If not, if he said something really outrageous, what did etiquette demand?

'He had this doll, a little girl doll. I don't know where he'd got it, but he had it anyway. And do you know what he was doing with it?'

No, and please don't tell us.

'He'd got this bit of lace, from one of his mother's old nightgowns, probably.'

It was Dulcie Coulter's turn to freeze.

'And he'd got it draped all round this doll. "What's that, Steve?" I remember saying. "It's the girl I'm going to marry." "Oh, what's her name?" "She's called Joanna," he said. It's true, I swear it, you remember, don't you Steve?'

Stefan looked modestly round, uncertain whether to claim this imputed clairvoyance, but Joanna knew just what to do. She threw her arms round him and kissed him on the cheek. '*Clever* Stefan. I hope I lived up to expectations.'

'Joanna,' he said, one eyebrow up, one down, 'you lived up to expectations I never even knew I had.'

'Anyway,' said Chas, 'though it's not my place to tell the young couple how to live their lives, I would just like to offer them one or two words of advice. First, never let the sun go down on your anger. In other words, only quarrel on rainy days. Second, remember that in a marriage tolerance is all. When you can no longer tolerate each other, that's the time to get a divorce. And finally, I'd like you to raise your glasses in the traditional toast. To Stefan and Joanna: health and happiness, and may all your troubles be little ones.'

The company sighed and laughed and clapped with relief. 'Stefan and Joanna.' Whoo. Safe home to harbour at last.

When the toast was over, Stefan stood up. 'I'd like to thank Chas for his valuable advice. I'd like to, but I can't.'

'Shame!' shouted Chas, and everyone pressed the laughter button again.

Then Stefan made the bridegroom's speech, whose form is genetically determined: I just want to thank you all for_____; I know we're going to be very_____ ; a special thanks to_____ for_____; now I don't want to go on too long, but before I close I must_____; with an optional slot for an anecdote at the end.

Here is Stefan's anecdote: 'As a portrait painter, the expression "He's no oil painting" has a special significance for me. Take Chas, for instance: now I think you'll all agree that he's no oil painting in the traditional sense' – 'Shame!' shouted Chas – 'but I've found great interest in sketching him over the years: he's a real oil painting to me. Unfortunately, that's how it generally goes. What the world sees as an oil painting I find a terrible bore. On the other hand, though I might find great interest in painting a bucket of dead fish, I wouldn't necessarily want to live with it for very long. What I find so unique and precious about Joanna is that as you can all see, she's an oil painting in the traditional sense; but she's also an oil painting to me. I cannot think of a sounder basis for a happy marriage.'

'Oh, Stefan,' said Joanna, 'that's the nicest thing anyone's ever said to me.'

'Well,' said Mr Ritchie. 'I won't even try to follow that. Every good wish, Joanna, from your mother and me. And the greatest good fortune I can wish you is that your marriage comes close to being as happy as ours.'

While the last toast was drunk, there was a general embracing: Joanna and her parents, Joanna and Grace, Stefan and Mrs Ritchie, who knew that at your daughter's wedding you must take the rough with the smooth; then Stefan and Joanna went upstairs to change.

'Where's my bouquet? I must throw the bouquet,' said Joanna. She dropped it over the banisters, where it was kicked away by Grace and fought over by Cara and Millicent.

'Me, me,' said Fay, running upstairs with her wilting posy, which Chas gallantly caught saying, 'Now you'll have to marry me.' Fuel for more wedding anecdotes in twenty years.

Joanna came down in the coolest of pale green dresses, Stefan bow-legged behind her, a heavy suitcase in each hand. The confetti flew; Eliza threw her posy, Fay threw her piece of wedding cake, Chas grabbed little Giles before he could throw a chair. 'Thank you, thank you, we'll write.' The door slammed, and they were off on married life. Will you, Stefan, take you, Joanna, to be your lawful wedded oil painting? I will; I will.

With Stefan and Joanna gone, the reception began to wind down. A few picnic parties returned to their rugs, but helpers had begun to gather glasses, and out in the lane car doors slammed. The Ritchies and Mrs Castle were driving south, and there was no room for Grace in the car. 'Are you coming back to London?' asked Cara; but Grace couldn't bear to sit in a train for five hours saying 'Super', and said she was staying on.

In fact, she was hoping that Andrew would ring. The Songsters were in Whitby, just across the moors: a train and a bus and she could be with him tonight. He must be busy, because he hadn't rung all week. He had her number, though. There might be a message waiting at the hotel.

'Can I give you a lift anywhere?' said Chas. She asked him to take her back to the hotel.

The good thing about Chas was that he had no tendency to say 'Super'. As he saw it, the past was over, and where's the fun in talking about it? The question was where the fun was coming from next. He and some of the locals were going out that evening for a bit of a knees-up. Grace would be welcome to come along.

'Could you wait a minute? I just want to see if there's a message for me.'

No, there was no message, but it was early: plenty of time before Andrew went on stage. If he rang tonight she could leave first thing tomorrow; they could walk on the cliffs all Sunday afternoon. She arranged to meet Chas later, and went to her room to wait for Andrew's call.

It wasn't far to Whitby. Grace worked out her route, checked the timetables and lay on her bed to read. Her mind was already with Andrew. She saw the van chug along the promenade, around the boarding houses; then off to the theatre, unload the equipment, and join the queue for a phone. An hour went by; hardly a page had turned. A patch of sun climbed up the bedspread and landed on her book. She knelt on her pillow, elbows on the windowsill, like a child sent to bed in daylight. It was beautiful outside; too beautiful to waste.

She couldn't go out. Suppose he rang while she was gone? It seemed to Grace, newly careful of Andrew's feelings, that this might remind him of the old, uncommitted Grace, the Grace whose phone he'd once rung all night, getting only lies for reply. To go out now would be a new betrayal. Grace lay on her bed, filled with a double yearning: to be out in the sun, and to be with Andrew again.

Six o'clock came. It was awful waiting, body in one place, mind elsewhere. Why not just go to Whitby? She could find the theatre, be there when he came off stage. Surprise surprise, look who's come to see you. Oh, hello, Grace, sorry I've made other arrangements for the weekend. It seems so *arrogant* to assume that you'll always be welcome, that your mere presence is a present to your friends.

He didn't ring. She stayed in her room till the very last minute. She left instructions with the receptionist: if someone rings, please take his number and ask him to phone again, however late.

'You're ready. Great,' said Chas. 'Pile in. Beep beep. We're off to Hatton Hall.'

Hatton Hall was a converted country house in the hills beyond Louthbridge. Drinks in the conservatory, whist in the smoking room, umbrellas in the vestibule, croquet on the lawn. In the panelled restaurant couples leant close, celebrating their anniversaries over half a bottle of wine. Voices gentle, atmosphere hushed. Until Chas's party arrived.

Chas's friends were childhood companions. They'd gone to Sunday School together; thrown cakes at each other's weddings. They'd bickered like brothers and sisters; learned to dance in each other's arms. Most of them were now in London, where they'd exchange the secret smiles of kinfolk across a crowded room. Their dinner was a sort of messmates' reunion, a boisterous yearning for the old, free, careless days. Into the room with a hoot and a holler, chairs and voices grating against the hush.

Chas, whose idea Grace had been, felt responsible for her welfare. And what better way to entertain someone than to tell them anecdotes? Where Chas led, the others gladly followed; indeed, the collective diary of anecdotes is fundamental to this sort of group, a source of quotations, jokes, allusions, heroes and villains, an affirmation of a common past and common attitudes. What Chas's friends fondly remembered were practical jokes. The sneezing powder we put in the Bishop's Bible at confirmation classes. The empty gin bottle we left poking out of dotty Miss Whatsit's bag. The sweets we stole from the village shop, distracting old Mrs Thingummy's attention with tales of her lost cat. You know, practical jokes. Gang warfare with a smiling face.

As the wine went round and the voices grew louder, Grace felt forlorn, bereft. These people were baying. The anniversary couples had shrunk like fieldmice in the shadow of a hawk. The anecdotes became harder to follow, as teller and audience were successively felled by great shaking fits of laughter, so that to those who didn't know it already, the story was lost.

'And there he was,' said Chas, who'd been a medical student, 'guts all over the floor, pulling them out by the yard and chucking them over his shoulder,' his eyes creased up, his shoulders shook, and his laughter came out in little snorts and grunts, 'saying, "Where's my bloody box of matches? I can't leave a bloody box of matches in here."'

More snorts and grunts of laughter, a clutching of chests, a hanging of heads, a sagging of jaws. 'Oh don't, Chas. I won't be able to eat if you go on.' Grace grinned until her cheeks ached; she grinned so much she almost cried.

At last the laughter receded, snorting, to its cave, and the party began to look at its watch. Ah well, all good things come to an end. Back to the grindstone on Monday. Lucky Stefan and Joanna, off on their honeymoon in Corfu. Still, it's all been absolutely gorgeous hasn't it? Absolutely spectac.

Chas and Grace exchanged London phone numbers as he dropped her at the hotel. Half past ten; Andrew would just be coming off stage. 'Any messages?' Grace asked as she picked up her key. But no: there had been no call.

Grace went to bed and began to read, that combination of reading and musing where a passing word gives rise to a whole train of thought. The brain's equivalent of digestion after a meal: scenes from the wedding regurgitated as little balls of bone and feather and gristle which the mind had been unable to absorb. Ear poised, hand crouched to spring towards the bedside phone.

Surely he should have rung by now? He knew her number, knew she'd be here today. She'd asked him to ring, said she might come and see him. It doesn't take long to put down a glass, pick up a phone and ring.

Absence makes the heart grow frantic. Grace read and thought and listened and thought. Questions rose and she beat them back. Think of all the times you didn't ring him. But that was different: that was long ago.

At midnight she sort of slept, though her brain was out on night-time sorties of its own: she would catch it when brought to consciousness by a stepped-on floorboard or shutting door. Andrew dancing; Andrew flirting. Look, no Andrew. April fool.

She had breakfast in her room, afraid to leave the phone in case he rang. Breakfast with a book, and the sun pouring through the window, and her mind ranging over the northern resorts, looking for its nest.

At ten the maid knocked on the door. 'Oh, sorry. Will you be leaving today?'

'Yes. I'm just packing. Won't be long.'

Guests were asked to leave their rooms by ten thirty on the morning of departure. At ten twenty-five Grace went downstairs and borrowed a train timetable. There was a fast connection to London at midday and another at half past four. She decided to wait an hour and hope that Andrew would call.

'Can I leave my case here?' she asked the receptionist. 'I'm expecting a phone call. I'll be waiting in the lounge.'

An hour went by and he didn't ring, though Grace could hear the switchboard buzzing, and showed her face to the receptionist each time. Surely he'd be awake by now? Perhaps at this very minute he was outside a phone box, coins in hand, nose pressed up against the window, waiting his turn. Ten more minutes and she could still catch the midday train. There was a prolonged buzzing at the switchboard. Grace rushed into reception, feathers flying, but the receptionist had gone. Teabreak. The switchboard buzzed and buzzed. It must be him. Come on, come on. Her mind leaped over the counter and took the call. The switchboard went on buzzing for a very long time, then stopped.

Look, thought Grace. You're a rational adult human being. Well, an adult human being; well, a human being; well, a being. Are you seriously intending to sit in this hotel from now until Christmas waiting for the phone to ring?

I could wait in London some of the time.

All you had was a passing fancy to see Andrew. You won't be shut out of heaven if the phone doesn't ring. Now: why don't you have a nice quiet lunch with your book, a nice quiet walk around town, and take a nice quiet journey back to London on the afternoon train?

How very adult and rational, thought Grace. That's an excellent idea. And it'll give me another hour to wait for the phone.

A watched phone never rings; or never for the right reasons. Every time the switchboard buzzed, rational, adult Grace would swim towards it, the trout towards the fly, and be left suspended, gills aquiver, by the receptionist's blank look. At last she was shamed into leaving, and set off, ear trained backwards like a radar dish.

At Louthbridge, the river Louth runs wide and tranquil beneath a pale stone bridge, a single span, an albino rainbow, pale gold at either end. Along the quays are tumbling Georgian teashops, white iron tables scattered in the sun. Grace sat on the quays and ate wrinkled Georgian sandwiches, drank coffee made from cloudy river water and read her book, while her mind dipped and paddled in the Louth.

Here was a rowing boat, maneouvred by a man in shirtsleeves, heading downstream. Her mind dog-paddled after it and climbed aboard. Take me to Whitby. Andrew's singing there.

Grace whistled her mind to shore and took it walking along the quays, peering into open doors, sniffing the roast beef, pricking its ears at the clashing cutlery of Sunday lunch. At the edge of town, the houses grew gardens, the gardens grew shrubs, then trees, and the flagstones gave way to a sandy path through fields where calves on delicate hooves raised gentle, puzzled lashes at her approach; proving that Louthbridge did have a slaughterhouse after all. Hello, little cow, don't you look sweet? I've just eaten one of your friends.

Insects buzzed against the sweeping lashes. Buzz buzz, buzz buzz. Hello, this is Andrew, can I speak to Grace? I'm sorry, she's out, no doubt with the young gentleman who brought her home last night. I can explain, thought Grace. I'm innocent. Can't he see I've changed?

Insects flocked above the brown, slow-moving waters where the branches cast their shade. Insects above, molluscs below, all going about their lawful business, pursued by their lawful predators, followed in turn by scientists with nets; who are followed by students with notebooks; who are pursued in turn by professors with theories, and philosophers with theories about theories, in a vast geometric progression towards death.

Here were crickets using their wings as switchboards. Buzz buzz, hello, I'm here on this blade of grass. Here were wood pigeons growling in their necks. Simple thoughts. Fear and food and love and loss. Until someone comes to bag you up and teach you to dance the polka.

Grace walked on past reeds and hedges. Green leaves and water calmed her mind. Not so bad, she thought, to be a creature, living among field creatures. Life on earth need not be grim. Two creatures might meet, from alien species, fearful, shy, noses twitching, ears alert; and perhaps with much coaxing, hearts thumping, blood pounding, put ears, nose and whiskers out of the bushes and dance: not a mindless dance built in by nature, a courtship display of fine pink ears and tabby tail, but a true blend of thought and feeling, mind and body, wit and beauty, grace. Such a dance would be worth the waiting. Walking back through the field of heifers, Grace raised her lashes and smiled.

Going into the hotel to pick up her bag, she didn't even wonder whether Andrew had rung. What matter whether he'd rung or not, whether they met tomorrow or next week? Her fears were gone, her mind was quiet. If you don't trust, you can't dance.

'There was a message for you,' said the receptionist. 'Where is it, now? He rang not long ago.'

Grace's mind put ears, nose and whiskers out of the bushes and zipped off over the moors. Andrew rang. I'll see him tonight. He misses me. He rang.

'Ah, here it is.'

It was Chas, offering a lift to the station.

This time, her mind had flown the coop, and however much Grace whistled, it would not return. As her train drew into York, it came limping back of its own accord, a message tied to its leg: he did not ring; he does not miss you; you will not see him tonight.

Grace woke next morning with a spider dangling over her head: the expected phone call which might drop at any moment into her ear, Silence was a constant reminder: at this very moment he's preferring something else to ringing you. Her mind was perpetually drawn to that jolly party happening elsewhere, the jokes, the van rides, the dingy rooms, which should all have gone into their common diary, thickening the threads that ran between them, of which their friendship was built. Sometimes the phone would ring, the spider would dangle a little closer, and then be jerked away.

'Hello, Patrick. No, I've been away. Oh, it's most kind of you to think of me. How could I bear to miss a tutorial, indeed?'

It was Patrick, letting her know that the time of their next tutorial had been changed: Dr Bastable had caught a cold.

'Are you sure it's a cold? Not psittacosis? Oh well, better luck next time.'

In fact, she'd been planning to skip the tutorial, would have skipped three weeks of tutorials to go on tour, cancelling all those times when she'd abandoned Andrew for work. Here she was, brimful of gestures, all returned unopened marked 'Not known at this address'.

When in doubt, work. After a morning in the library, and lunch with Patrick, Jim and Jackie, the spider was curled up quietly in a corner, the mind at rest in its basket. Patrick was jumpy, though, like a child on the last day of term.

235

'I'm bored,' his slow voice said in her ear as they stacked the trays. 'What shall we do?'

'Well, I was going to work,' said Grace, flustered by friendliness.

'No. You don't want to work. Let's have some fun.'

Fun. What did Grace know of fun? She'd never knocked at doors and run away, put sneezing powder into the Bishop's Bible, distracted Mrs Thingummy's attention while stealing her sweets. No one had ever asked her.

'All right. What shall we do?'

'All the fun of the fair. There's a fun-fair on Totteridge Common. I drove past it last night.'

Grace hadn't been to a fair since she was a child, and she'd never found them much fun: the great rickety wheels, the hoopla cheats, the jerking dodgems which jolt your neck. Maybe it's different when you're grown up and can laugh at it all.

'Heavens, I haven't been to a fair since I was a child.'

'All the more reason. I've got my car outside.'

They drove to Totteridge through the lazy midsummer streets. The fair was empty on a Monday afternoon: the merry-go-rounds had only a teenager or two, a mother and toddler aboard. All that crash and clatter streamed away on the empty air, to mingle with the chestnut flowers and stir the leaves. Over it all rose the great red skeleton on which humans, strapped in and screaming, rode.

'Oh good, a goldfish. Let's win a goldfish,' said Patrick. 'We can give it to Jerry. We can have a presentation at the end of our last tutorial. Dear Jerry, when we saw this fish, we thought of you.'

Grace won a goldfish. She did. The rubber ring, at the sixth try, fell on to the hook above the goldfish jar. The man picking up the fallen rings picked hers off the hook and went back to his shouting: goalfish, goalfish, win a goalfish.

'Hey,' said Grace. 'I won one. Can I have my goldfish?'

He looked straight at her and back at the hook. 'No. It wasn't on properly.'

'It was. Wasn't it, Patrick?'

Patrick, not fancying being lumbered with a goldfish for the rest of the afternoon, just smiled.

'It's not *fair*,' said Grace, wanting to stamp.

'An unfair fun-fair,' said Patrick. 'That's life.'

Grace had some candyfloss to console her, biting neatly into the sugared spider's web, wiping a frosted goat's beard off her chin.

236

'Time for a ride,' said Patrick, looking up at the screaming skeleton.

'Not yet,' said Grace. 'Let's work up to it gradually. How about a nice quiet merry-go-round?'

The dodgems were jerking to a stop, the organ running downhill out of tune, toddlers carried out sucking their thumbs, teenagers, tasting blood, staying on for another go. Grace and Patrick stepped into separate cars, paid their money and away they went. Well, Grace went away and Patrick came after; but then she thought, this is silly, it's only a game. She drove right round in a circle and rammed his side, head jerking, hair flying, and nipped away; and they chased each other like teenagers till the organ ran down.

'My legs are shaking,' said Grace, throwing back her head to laugh as they stepped down. He put his arm round her and they walked on. Well, that's what fun-fairs are for.

It was quite a big fair. Patrick shot pellets at prizes glued to their sockets, which it would have taken a bazooka to knock down. 'We must win *something*,' said Grace.

'Not necessarily,' said Patrick. 'Or perhaps, in this case, necessarily not. Let's have a ride on the Whirligig.'

The Whirligig was a middle-ranking accident spot: more frightening than the bumper cars, but a feather pillow compared with the Big Twister. You strapped yourself into chairs suspended from a sort of horizontal windmill, whose blades rose and fell as you whirligigged round. As the music started, the blades gave a little jerk, then rose sluggishly to a height from which a human hitting the ground would make a bone-crunching splat.

'I'm not sure I like this,' said Grace, looking at the wobbly nuts and bolts that held the thing together. Patrick put his arm round her again.

It's not hard to imagine a nice, smooth fairground ride, which would support you all the way, like a boat on just the right swell, where your seat would not be snatched out from under you, causing whiplash injuries in bones not meant to bend; a gentle ride for lovers on summer evenings. Grace didn't have time to miss it: her limbs were rattling too much. These rides are designed by computing the natural rhythms of the body, then negating them, and syncopating that. The Whirligig was a close kinetic analogue to a song by Crocodile. Played on a parapet.

Why would anyone climb freely on to a ride like that? Well, it takes your mind off things, and when you're finally lowered, lightly puréed, back to earth, you find you're quite glad to be alive; though the world seems more static, duller than before.

'Had a plane ride like that once,' said Patrick. 'Maybe they train the pilots here.'

He didn't seem much affected: no shaking legs and puréed bones, no back-slapping relief to be on earth again. Maybe his eyes were marginally more open. Perhaps he was an addict, needing a ride to keep him functioning at all, loping from fair to fair looking for a fix. They would find her in the morning, drained of blood, two vampire tooth-marks in her neck.

At a fairground, the music is either on or off, with only an out-of-tune modulation in between. Like mechanical dancers who jerk upright and frantically flop, then die. After a time, you need a palate cleanser, a flower, a birdsong, a walk in the woods.

'Have a hamburger,' said Patrick.

'Ugh,' said Grace.

He ate a hamburger (vampire toothmarks in the tomato ketchup). 'Oh look,' he said. 'The Tunnel of Love.'

It's not clear what Grace was expecting from the Tunnel of Love; apart from a blazing fire and an Isfahan rug. What she was offered was more from the designers of Whirligig: wobbly nuts and bolts, a seat for two jerking over bumpy rails, and a mechanical organ playing 'Ride of the Valkyrie' (since the Tunnel of Love was designed for speedy conversion into a Horror Train; a Horror Train being simply a Tunnel of Love with added screams).

It was dark, except for a few blue lights hidden behind plastic rocks and ferns; those same blue lights the butchers hang up to electrocute insects. Water (blood on alternate weeks) dripped down the plastic walls, plop plopping into the gutters. Every so often the tunnel would open up into a grotto, with plastic grass and plastic rabbits acting scenes from the story of love. Beside each scene was a spotlit notice, reminding you how the story went.

They jerked towards the first one. 'What does it say?' asked Grace.

Patrick put his arm round her. ' "Keep off the grass",' he said.

In the first scene, two plastic rabbits, damp and gleaming, faced each other stony eyed: she in headscarf and shopping basket, he in city suit; neither the most appropriate outfit for mushroom gathering in a woodland glade. The notice read: 'Stage one: you meet and fall in love.' At stage two, you get engaged: he fits a snare on your paw while stony-eyed rabbits pop from their holes with glassfuls of champagne. Stage three, the first tiff: two rabbits with boxing gloves staring past each other's ears. Stage four, you make up, propped against each other rubbing frozen cheeks. Stage five, the wedding: the stony-eyed circle is back, dressed in top hats and tails. Stage six, you live happily ever after, followed by stony-eyed plastic offspring in a vast geometric progression towards death.

'What can one say?' asked Patrick as they disengaged themselves. 'That really says it all.'

Patrick was fun. It was fun, the contrast between languid body and nimble, playful mind. What did he think? Simple thoughts? How could one ever tell?

At last, when they'd been internally reconstructed by every ride, cheated at every hoop-la stall and jangled by every fairground tune, they queued up for the Big Twister. You have to go: it looks cowardly otherwise. Perhaps you can get through with your eyes shut; perhaps it's not so bad with someone by your side. Climb on at the bottom, strap yourself in, and there's no escape but death.

At first, the rails went up quite gradually; the seat would stop at ten-yard intervals for another suicidal couple to climb aboard. Then off they would go with a rattle and jerk for another few yards, the rails stretching upwards above the trees and houses, where no human is meant to go.

What goes up must come down, and why not backwards, crashing down the rails? 'This is ghastly,' whispered Grace, holding the bar on the front of their seat as it tilted, jerking, to accommodate the increasing slope.

'It's all right. What goes up must come down,' said Patrick.

'That's what I'm afraid of,' said Grace.

At the last stop, the rails rose in front of their noses; they were already above the trees. 'I don't like this at all,' said Grace; but the fanfare had started, and the throttles were open, before the full stop was out of her mouth. Up, up, up, like a painter's bucket up the side of a house; a pause at the top, the eyes involuntarily carried where the body would shortly plunge. Grace took one hand off the seat bar and seized hold of Patrick's arm. If I go, he goes, she thought.

His arm was relaxed, hand on knee, back unarched, feet unbraced. He was not even holding on. If he goes, I go, thought Grace. She took her hand away and re-clamped it to the seat bar as they toppled over and fell.

After that, no thoughts were possible, only sensations. It was the climbing, not the falling, that was horrible: the jerk and judder up the cliff face, the slow deceleration as the seat ran out of steam and hesitated, slipping a little, whether it mightn't be easier to go back. It didn't get any more tolerable after the first circuit, except that you thought: one step closer to the end.

As last they stood still, stranded high above the houses. Patrick undid his seat belt and stretched, leaning over to see the view. The seat began to rock.

'For God's sake stop it, you revolting moron,' said Grace; only not aloud, it looks cowardly otherwise.

'Well, now we know what it's like to be in a plane crash,' he said, stretching expansively as they were winched to earth. It had certainly cheered him, laced his blood with some energy-giving substance, some secret fix. 'Race you to the car,' he said, and loped off, leaving Grace with trees and houses swirling past.

He pretended to be a racing driver on the way back to town, tilting his body as they went round corners, making vroom vroom noises as they stood at the lights. He drove, without asking, to her flat, switched off the engine and pulled out the key. 'Time for drinkies,' he said. As they went up the stairs, the phone was ringing. By the time she got the door open, it had stopped.

Patrick was in a strange mood. When she went for glasses, he followed her to the kitchen. She diverted him to her writing table with a question about work. They sat in upright chairs, drinks between them on the table, and exchanged Jerry Bastable jokes. Their next tutorial was the last of the year. Months of summer sunshine ahead.

'What are you doing this summer?' Patrick finally asked.

Grace didn't know: Andrew had been fixated mind and body on the tour. 'I haven't really thought yet. What are you?'

'Oh, pottering and pootling around. I might go to France.'

'That sounds nice.'

'Want to come?' he said, picking up a book.

With people like Patrick you never know. Was that an offer or just a request for information? If she said 'Yes', what on earth would it imply?

'I haven't been to France for ages,' she said.

'I thought July, before it gets too crowded.'

'Really. That sounds fun.'

He finished his whisky. He either had or hadn't asked her; she either had or hadn't agreed.

Maybe she had, because he took her hand across the corner of the table, and gently stroked her arm.

A great sigh came out of Grace's bones. A friendly metatarsal from a neighbouring grave. We could clank through life together, side by side; loving each other's haircuts, admiring each other's jokes. We could go to parties together; dogs and children would adore us; I could introduce him to all my friends.

Still, when you've jumped, you've jumped: you can't reconsider direction in mid-flight.

'Heavens, is that the time?' she said, disengaging her arm. 'I've got to go.'

Patrick didn't seem to mind much. 'Oh well,' he said, loping off, 'see you, then.'

'Yes,' said Grace forlornly. 'Thank you. That was fun.'

It would have been Andrew ringing, some deep rapport telling him when she was out. Actually, she'd better go out now, in case Patrick was lurking to see if she had lied. Ring ring went the phone as she reached the bottom stair, here I am on this blade of grass. She leaped upstairs, dropping bag and key. He waited till he could see her, then hung up.

She bought her supper, then returned to the study of the rat. The phone rang. She looked at it, disbelieving. 'Hello?'

'Can I speak to Grace?'

'This is Grace.'

'Oh, hello. It's Lindsey.'

'Lindsey. Is everything all right?'

An accident. A van crash. A message from Andrew.

'Fine. Um. Have you been away?'

'Yes. I've been to a wedding.'

'Oh. Only I wondered if you'd heard anything from Andrew.'

'Not since last week.'

'Do you know where they are?'

'Not really. I'm expecting him to ring.'

'Oh. Oh well. I just wondered.'

'I expect they're awfully busy.'

'Yes. It's just, I've left messages and he hasn't answered; I just wondered if you'd heard anything or knew where they were.'

'No. All I know is they'll be in Kilburn on Saturday. We could go together if you like.'

They agreed to meet at the theatre, and promised to ring if either of them heard.

Grace got on with her essay, turned out her flat, deciding to make it less austere, went on shopping trips for bits of wool and leather, lace and feathers; and waited for the phone to ring.

By the time he rang, on Friday, she was frantic.

'Hello, Grace?'

'Hello, Andrew, how are you?'

'Too tired to think.'

'Poor you. Has it gone well?'

'I expect so. People keep coming, they seem to shout just as loud.' He yawned in her ear.

'Heavens, you do sound tired.'

'I'll survive. Two more shows and then I'll sleep for a week. How are things with you?'

'Fine. Oh. Lindsey rang. Is Davy all right?'

'He'd better be. We're on stage in half an hour.'

'Oh. Well. I'd better not keep you.'

He yawned again. 'OK. See you after the show.'

Grace rang Lindsey to say that all was well. 'They're just very tired, I think.'

'Yeah, from what?'

'Sorry?'

'All those fancy women tarting around.'

Oh. Poor Lindsey. Thinking back to Davy's behaviour, poor Lindsey indeed. 'Oh nonsense, Lindsey. They're much too busy for anything like that.'

Indeed, it had never occurred to Grace, through Andrew's silence, that he might have found someone else. What worried her was that by some coincidence he'd rung and rung and never found her home; had imagined her gadding and gallivanting; and had hardened his heart. Still, he'd rung in the end; he'd probably just been busy; and a heart once melted can always be melted again.

Grace met Lindsey in the ticket queue. Elmo Harper, said the posters, Crocodile, and in little letters, With the Songsters. Lindsey was limp as a sagging sail, her cheeks less plump and shiny, her hair like dying grass. It was her clothes that told you what she must have been through. She'd put on dark eyes, tight skirt and low-necked blouse: conventional lures, poodle clothes that would once have made her spit. Pathetic to be brought so low, thought Grace, who had put her silk and feathers on and off and on.

'Hardly recognized you. So what did he say?' said Lindsey, formalities over.

'Nothing really, he was mainly yawning. He said Davy was OK.'

'That could mean anything, couldn't it?' Lindsey turned with venom to a clattering couple behind, all high heels, stockings and blonde hair.

Look, Lindsey, why worry? If he fell for you, he's not likely to fall for anyone normal, is he? The more Lindsey jittered, the more serene Grace became.

When the curtains opened, you could see how far the Songsters had come. The stage belonged to them. Their movements had a shape, an ease. Their songs had taken on a life, put out unexpected flowers. The Songsters, too, had blossomed. Davy charmed, all nods and winks and pretty cheekbones: I'm famous, but I'm nice. Bob clowned, Rick slunk. They had become an act.

There was something wrong, though. Andrew had lost his fizz. No interplay between him and Davy, no heads together; Bob's clowning passed him by. The energy was there, but it seemed dark, pent up, ferocious; like flood water against a dam. When he made an announcement, the words tumbled from his lips. He was swept from microphone to piano; his fingers dashed themselves against the keys. Something had happened. What was going on?

As the songs went by, Andrew became more tense, like a great wave gathering, sucking the ocean in. At last it broke, tossing him to the front of the stage. 'For me,' he said, 'these last weeks have fulfilled a childhood dream. I grew up idolizing Elmo Harper, and now I've actually been on tour with him. You get to know a lot about someone on tour, and I can't end without trying to give you some idea what I've learned. So here it is, in some words of my own I've put to one of Elmo's songs: "Hello Darling". Thank you.'

'Hello Darling' was a typical Elmo Harper song. Hello darling, look at me, I'm great, why don't you climb into my car, let's cruise, and I'll show you how to have some fun. Innocent enough when sung to a sweet little rock and roller by the teenage rebel next door; though in Elmo's treatment the gleam of a switchblade shone through. Grace hadn't heard the Songsters perform it; indeed, it seemed to come as a surprise to Davy and Bob, who looked ready to claim they'd never heard of the song. But Andrew hit the keys, Rick hit the strings, and nothing short of a wildcat strike could keep Bob and Davy out.

The first verse sounded pretty much like the record: those precise notes and creeping rhythms, that sly, slippery voice. Hello darling, let's have some fun, why don't you climb into my car? The rest of the song, as far as Grace could tell through the blurry amplifiers, gave excellent reasons for refusing to enter even the same superhighway system as the former teenage star. Why don't you climb into my car? I'll drink you up like a bottle of pop, then I'll throw the bottle away; I'll eat you up like a candy bar, then I'll drop the wrapper for trash; I'll smoke you up like a cigarette till all that's left is ash; I'll take your smile and I'll squeeze it out, then I'll be on my way.

The song had a powerful effect on Davy. No nods and winks and cheerful cheekbones: he was playing as if he wasn't really there, his body squeezed into the smallest possible space, as if expecting a bullet in the neck; all his attention centred on the strings of his guitar. Bob, after a moment of surprise, just shrugged his shoulders and got on with it; Rick was, as always, unmoving and stony eyed.

Not that anyone noticed. Andrew had swallowed up the audience's attention. His body seemed a battleground of forces beyond his control. The fury which had hurled him into action could not withstand the beauty of the song: the gentle rhythms, the hush-hush murmur of the dove's wings calmed him; then you could feel, like dawn creeping over stormy waters, joy break out. The music had him. Each move, each smile, belied the bitter words. He loves me, he loves me not; he loves me, he loves me not. Watching him sing was like watching a whole sad passionate affair.

'What was all that about?' said Lindsey as the curtains swung to and the audience, fresh off the Whirligig with Crocodile, went out to bathe its ears. 'Andrew's gone round the twist.'

'I don't think anyone noticed,' said Grace. 'You'd have to have been listening pretty hard to get any of the words.'

'You'd've had to have been dead not to notice,' said Lindsey. 'What with Andrew foaming at the mouth and Davy crawling under the floorboards. What's going to happen when they have to get up on stage with Elmo, that's what I want to know.'

When the curtains opened after the interval, the Songsters were already on stage. The audience clapped, then clapped more loudly as Elmo Harper came on. There was something wrong here too. This was not the Elmo Harper Grace had seen before. Indifference was gone. He was playing as you always knew he could. That sly voice now pounced and threatened; those pussy feet had changed to panther paws. Grace had watched him stand politely, guitar silent, while Davy played his laboured solo line. Now he swooped and danced round Davy, notes cascading from his guitar; bit through the neck of Davy's sickly lambling and carried it off to peaks and eyries where he tore the flesh from its bones. Davy, already rattled, soon lost his nerve and lowered his guitar. Before the first song was over, you could have crumpled him up and put him in your pocket.

Rick, though a far better guitarist than Davy, had refused to play lead guitar for a rock and roller who wasn't also a blues singer, whose act included no element of the blues. Now, inspired, he began to answer Elmo with wails and screams from his own guitar. Together, they seized the song and shook it till it bled. It was wonderful to watch. Your shoulders tensed and twitched like wavelets on the surface of a deeper tide. After a while, Elmo stopped playing and began to dance. He leaped and prowled; he crouched and sprang. It was as if he'd been plunged in joy. Oh, he could dance. He was with the music heart and body. He made you want to float, to soar.

Andrew, who had at first looked subdued, abstracted, came wide awake at the sound of Elmo's guitar. He was an honest and honourable man, who recognized the rarity of what was happening, and could do nothing but respond with his best; even if his best wasn't good enough: he played his best and let comparisons go hang.

On his early records, Elmo had played both piano and guitar. More recently, he'd bent with the fashion, and you rarely heard him play the piano now. As the songs went by, though, his head began to turn in Andrew's direction; then he approached the piano on delicate feet. He stood at Andrew's shoulder as Andrew played his heart out; then he began to dance again. The change in his mood was immediately apparent. Grace thought, he's going in for the kill. As the song ended and Andrew stepped back to bow, Elmo sprang towards the piano and kicked the stool away. He leaned forward and said into the microphone, 'Now let's see who can really play.'

As Andrew had earlier, he launched into the introduction to 'Hello Darling' without waiting to see if anyone would follow. In fact it didn't matter who was following: he had a whole orchestra in his hands. On the left, the cannons; on the right, the twinkling piccolos. He hit the keys so hard the piano came alive. It looked as if they were wrestling, but all the time he wrung from it a true Niagara of notes. While he played, he sang, and Rick responded, frolicking like a dolphin among the waves; and Andrew stood by, knowing he would never leap to the crags with Elmo Harper; holding his head up and tapping his foot.

At the end, the audience leaped to its feet and stamped and clapped and shouted 'Elmo, Elmo' till the roof came off. He was breathless, glittering with sweat. Only he bowed. The others didn't move, and he didn't stand aside to acknowledge them, just flicked his hair back and bowed once more. Turning to walk off, he looked straight at Andrew, and Andrew looked, unflinching, back.

An illicit recording of that evening is the only Elmo Harper record anyone should buy. That was Andrew Lisle's contribution to cultural history.

At Kilburn, the stage door system was well organized: you couldn't get past by looking like Sherry and flashing your engagement ring. Well, maybe Sherry could. The stage doorkeeper had a list. Grace was on it; Lindsey wasn't. Lindsey began to jitter. 'She's with me,' said Grace, inspired by the music. He stood aside and let them by.

The dressing-room door was open. Inside, it was like the ruins of Pompeii. The inhabitants, frozen in everyday postures, were covered head and body in volcano ash. Here was a hand still holding a guitar; here a beer glass, here a face in the mirror; but no one spoke, or looked around, or breathed. You could tell Davy: he was the shrivelled one holding a guitar, in an attitude that future archaeologists would have to describe as 'sulky'.

'Well, that was a bit of a disaster,' said Lindsey, puffing her cheeks and walking straight in.

'Lindsey,' said Davy, crumpling still further.

'God knows what that was all in aid of,' she said to Andrew. 'Made a right twit of yourself, anyway.' She picked up a beer can, took a gulp and handed it to Davy. 'Here, get your gear together and let's go.'

He drank the beer, sulkily, and some of the wind came back into his sails. She took his guitar and he stood up, picked up a sweater, shook off the volcano ash, ignoring the others, and they left the room. As Lindsey passed Grace in the doorway, her cheeks were fat and shiny; she looked up at the ceiling with an expression that any mother any-where would recognize as saying 'Kids!'

Well, time to go home, thought Grace, since no one came forward to claim her. Then Sherry arrived to show how these things are done. She didn't lurk. 'Bob,' she said, all smiles, hands outstretched; and they ran into each other's arms. Yes, well. 'Andrew, Rick,' she added, glad to see them, never doubting they would be glad to see her too. And they were, of course.

I'll go out and come in again, thought Grace. Maybe someone will notice the second time around.

'Hello, Grace. Were you out front?' said Sherry. 'I never saw you. I could have done with a bit of company.'

'You don't need company,' said Bob. 'You've got me.'

The manager of the Newt came in. 'If it wasn't the last night I'd sack you,' he said to Andrew.

'If it wasn't the last night I'd resign.'

'You can't do that. I've got you under contract.'

'Sue me,' said Andrew, turning away.

'Who needs you anyway?' said the manager of the Newt. 'We can replace you tomorrow, can't we, boys? With someone who can sing.'

It seemed there would be no celebration party tonight. Andrew threw Rick the keys. 'Can you get my stuff in the van? See you,' and walked out.

Grace followed him in silence. Should she cough? Had he recognized her? Had he noticed she was there? At the stage door Davy, charm reviving by the minute, was signing autographs while Lindsey stood protectively by – he's drained, it just drains him, you know.

Andrew went past without a sideways look, Grace after him like an imprinted goose. Drop me off at the underground, she thought. I'll get a train from there.

At last he stopped and turned to her. 'Do you want something to eat?'

'Do you?'

'I suppose so.' He put up a hand as a taxi came by.

'Do you want me to come with you?'

'I suppose so,' and they got in.

In the taxi, neither seemed prepared to break the silence. All that passed between them were those grudging words that have to be said when you're not speaking but still have to do the chores. Where are my car-keys? In the dustbin. That sort of thing.

They walked through Soho, past restaurants warm with theatre crowds. He stopped at an Italian place they'd been to before. 'Will this do?' he asked, not stopping to wait for an answer. They stared at the menu in silence while the waiter lit a candle. Am I a silent support or a silent burden? thought Grace.

They ordered wine, often a solution. It made her talkative before him. He was buried deep in thought. She reached out and touched his hand. 'Andrew,' she said. 'I thought you were wonderful tonight.' Puke.

Here you are, a BA Hons from Oxford, using the language of the Valentine cards. OK, if you're so clever, you tell me what to say.

He looked up from the debris of his dreams. 'Oh, fantastic. One of the world's great musicians.'

'It wasn't the music. It was you, being you.'

'I didn't *want* to be me.'

She waited for him to go on, but he tapered out. She filled her glass, and his.

At last she said to him, 'Andrew. Talk to me.'

He'd stopped eating, and was turning his dessert fork over, front, back, and propping it on its side.

'I just don't want any more of it,' he said.

She waited. 'Of what?' (The veal pizzaiola?)

'He was never one of my favourites, but who's to say they're not all like that?'

'Like what?'

'Like that bastard. I'm not wasting my time on something a man like that can do so well. I've lived and dreamed this music. I thought it was an art, a way of looking into people's souls. I thought, it doesn't matter what he says or does, when I hear that music, I *know*. I don't care if he stole cars or abandoned his wife. Here's someone who's rich in qualities. Here's someone who could be a friend. I was so happy at the thought of meeting him. I didn't care if he never spoke to me: I just wanted to be on stage with him.'

'I know. So what happened?'

'At first I kept making excuses. All right, he's behaving badly. Yes, he's loud, arrogant, demanding and rude; but that's a protective shell. He's just a small-town boy who dropped out of school, who's been cheated by managers, exploited by record companies, humiliated by disc jockeys, insulted by journalists. How else would you expect him to behave? It doesn't matter: I know what he's really like. I've heard his music; I *know*.'

He tapered off again.

'He was fantastic tonight,' said Grace, as the waiter came to remove their plates.

'Yes, he's fantastic. But after a while you run out of excuses. He may be rich in qualities, but he never seems to have used them outside his music. All that wit and warmth and subtlety, but you name it, he hates it: niggers, broads, fags, commies. Except for his Aunty Rena; he loves

248

his Aunty Rena. And then he says the devil's in the music and he's going to give it up and dedicate his life to God.'

'Oh.'

'You see?'

He began turning his fork over again.

What can a bystander do? Because that is what Grace was in this affair. Hold the victim's hand while the blood runs out, lean over and look into his drowning eyes, like a dryad looking down a well.

'Have some pudding,' said Grace.

They drank their coffee and paid.

'I'll take you home,' he said.

They took a taxi to Camden Town. She was putting her key in the front door when he stopped her. 'I'm very tired. I think I'll just go on home.'

'Stay here,' she said. 'You can sleep just as well here.'

'I think it's better if I go home.'

Better than what? Go on, ask him.

She looked round. 'I'd like you to stay.'

The delicate laying down of cards. A high heart, this.

He yawned; not a loud, expansive yawn, a yawn considerately suppressed: the eyes crinkle, the jaws lock; but a yawn. Trumped by a yawn.

She took her key out of the door. The taxi had gone, up the lamplit street with the branches nodding. She looked at him. His feet were already pointed the way he wanted to go. This was a chore to him.

'There's no point, really, is there?' he said.

He must have said it: the words hovered like smoke rings in the air.

He was going to go, like that: kick, bang, crumble, build the peeces into a grotto and start again. Dynamite the slate clean and build a highway through.

Grace didn't fight. She didn't summon the gestures that once had charmed him, or pull on the rope that once had held him. If she'd known the levers that worked his brain she wouldn't have used them. You can't feed humans love potions. If they want to go, you can't stop them; any more than you can dress them up to please you or tell them how to wear their hair. They're not dolls. No point in pushing or pleading. As his train slid out of the station, Grace did have one last try. She reached into a swept and polished alcove of her memory where she kept the image of their first meeting; when he'd asked her what she thought and she, against all the odds, had told him the truth. She turned to look at him. 'Andrew. Tell me what you think.'

He yawned, overtly now. MOOOOOOO. A cow in a cave. 'I think it's time to go to bed.'

'Look,' he said; he was an honest and honourable man, he could see something was called for, he wouldn't let her down. 'There *is* no point, you know.' He said it gently.

'Why not?' Why not, doctor, what do the tests reveal?

'Well, it hasn't really worked out, has it?'

Bloody hell, we haven't even left the starting blocks, we don't know each other, we've never even met. You can't do that. I'm not a liver: I don't regenerate. I *told* you. You promised. You did.

'Oh. I thought things were getting better.'

'They are, but it's too late. Given what's already happened.'

'Oh. I see.' She nodded. She didn't know what he was talking about. 'Well, goodnight.'

'Goodnight, Grace.' Not even a handshake to carry into the dark.

There was her room, her nice new room that Andrew would never see. It was very late, if she wasn't careful she'd moo. She looked at herself in the mirror. She took off her silk and feathers. Back to earth, like a dead pelican, beak first.

An affair like this is normally regarded as a learning experience. In my view it's about as much of a learning experience as having your legs shot away. It's not a bar to running a maze, but it doesn't make it any easier to get around.

Grace was sure he would ring. For years, when the phone rang she thought to herself, 'At last.' Her ears nearly wore out listening; but he didn't ring.

The theories she made about what exactly had gone wrong. Lost letters, misdialled numbers, misconstructions, malice. You know the sort of thing. She prowled the wreckage like an air-crash investigator, playing and replaying the last words from the flight deck, sifting the charred remnants for evidence of design faults, pilot error, parts failure, freak circumstances, navigational defects. It seemed to her in her calmer moments a simple question of aeronautics. The crisis had come when they'd taken off but were still at stalling speed. A few months before, he'd have needed her more, his love might have been enough on its own to carry them; a few months after, the fragile craft might have reached its cruising height. The engine had failed at that vulnerable point between earth and sky when loss of power can be disastrous. They joined the accident statistics; the sad mathematics of love.

Andrew didn't think much about Grace. He'd loved her all right, the feelings were genuine. She was like a record that had got into his head. For a whole year she'd filled his senses, he'd played and replayed her, he'd woken to the sound of her, hummed snatches of her walking down the street. But she was only a footnote to a longer story, an incident in a longer dream. Nothing in Andrew's life ever matched his passion for the music. When his lifelong love came tumbling down, he hardly noticed, amidst the shambles, that Grace had been swept away. That's the thing about rock music. It arouses just the feelings one has for humans: the same sensual pleasures, the same romantic yearnings, the same dashed hopes and reawakenings; the whole roller-coaster ride.

Luckily, a love so strong doesn't die so easily. Andrew went home to Croydon and slept for two days, then set off to hitchhike round France. In Le Lavandou he heard some blues and felt a fluttering in his fingers. On the hills above St Raphael he had an idea for a song. Back in King's Cross, his piano stood idle, but the music filtered through the keyhole and his foot began to tap. One day there was a knock on his door. 'Listen?' said Rick. 'I've written a song.' Within fifteen minutes, Andrew was playing again.

It's life, you know, *c'est la vie*. No point crying over spilt wolves. It's a long worm that has no turning. Can't blame people, they're only human.

Yes, well.

Angela Carter

NIGHTS AT THE CIRCUS

£4.99

'Angela Carter has influenced a whole generation of fellow writers towards dream worlds of baroque splendour, fairy-tale horror, and visions of the alienated wreckage of a future world. In *Nights at the Circus*, she has invented a new, raunchy, raucous Cockney voice for her heroine Fevvers, taking us back into a rich, turn of the nineteenth-century world, which reeks of human and animal vitality ... *Nights at the Circus* is a book with many stories but Angela Carter has not softened her demands upon the reader. It remains the language that holds the power source: rudely colloquial perhaps but none the less dense, and detailed with delight'
The Times

'*Nights at the Circus* is a glorious enchantment. But an enchantment which is rooted in an earthy, rich and powerful language. Life is ever present as images ricochet around the reader picking out this and that, then discarding it with infinite resonance. It is a spell-binding achievement'
The Literary Review

'A glorious piece of work, a set-piece studded with set-pieces. The narrative has a splendid ripe momentum, and each descriptive touch contributes a pang of vividness. By doing possible things impossibly well, the book achieves a major enchantment'
ADAM MARS-JONES, *Times Literary Supplement*

'Angela Carter's fiction has always been written with a fallen angel's touch for the freaky and sinister, alleviated just a bit by a soiled fairy's relish for black but also puckish comic turns. Ms Carter's novel is a mistress-piece of sustained and weirdly wonderful Gothic that's both amusing and also provocatively serious. This is a big, superlatively imagined novel'
Observer

Angela Carter

LOVE

£3.99

Love is Angela Carter's fifth novel and was first published in 1971. With surgical precision it charts the destructive emotional war between a young woman, her husband and his disruptive brother as they move through a labyrinth of betrayal, alienation and lost connections.

This revised edition has lost none of Angela Carter's haunting power to evoke the ebb of the 1960s, and includes an Afterword which describes the progress of the survivors into the anguish of middle age.

'The novel and its afterword form a fascinating study, an erstwhile aesthetic object unravelled into realism and commitment'
The Guardian

'Now we can see how acutely Carter caught the dying throes of the love generation'
New Society

'Angela Carter is one of the most intelligent novelists writing in English today'
Quarterly Review